MISSING, PRESUMED

Susie Steiner began her writing career as a news reporter first on on local papers, then on the *Evening Standard*, the *Daily Telegraph* and *The Times*. In 2001 she joined the *Guardian*, where she worked as a commissioning editor for eleven years. Her first novel, *Homecoming* – described as 'truly exceptional' by the *Observer* – was published by Faber & Faber in 2013. She lives in London with her husband and two children.

Also by Susie Steiner

Homecoming

MISSING, PRESUMED

SUSIE STEINER

THE BOROUGH PRESS

The Borough Press
An imprint of HarperCollins*Publishers*
1 London Bridge Street
London SE1 9GF

www.harpercollins.co.uk

Published by HarperCollins*Publishers* 2016
1

A catalogue record for this book
is available from the British Library

ISBN: 978-0-00-812329-1

Set in Minion by Palimpsest Book Production Limited,
Falkirk, Stirlingshire

Printed and bound in Great Britain by
Clays Ltd, St Ives plc

MIX
Paper from
responsible sources
FSC
www.fsc.org
FSC™ C007454

For John & Deb

'The end of all our exploring
will be to arrive where we started'

Little Gidding, T. S. Eliot

17 December 2010
Saturday

Manon

She can feel hope ebbing, like the Christmas lights on fade in Pound Saver. Manon tells herself to focus on the man sitting opposite, whose name might be Brian but could equally be Keith, who is crossing his legs and his foot bangs her shin just where the bone is nearest the surface. She reaches down to rub it but he's oblivious.

'Sensitive', his profile had said, along with an interest in military aircraft. She wonders now what on earth she was thinking when she arranged it, but then compatibility seemed no marker for anything. The last date with a town planner scored 78 per cent – she'd harboured such hopes; he even liked Thomas Hardy – yet Manon spent the evening flinching each time his spittle landed on her face, which was remark-ably often.

Two years of Internet dating. It's fair to say they haven't flown by.

He's turned his face so the light hits the thumb prints on his glasses: petroleum purple eggs, the kind of oval spiral they dream of finding at a crime scene. He's talking about his job with the

1

Rivers Authority while she looks up gratefully to the waiter who is filling their wine glasses – well, her glass, because her companion isn't drinking.

She's endured far worse than this, of course, like the one she travelled all the way to London for. 'Keep an open mind,' Bri had urged. 'You don't know where the man of your dreams might pop up.' He was tall and very thin and he stooped like an undertaker going up the escalator at Tate Modern – giving it his best Uriah Heep. Manon thought that escalator ride was never going to end and when she finally got to the top, she turned without a word and came straight back down, leaving him standing at the summit, staring at her. She got on the first train out of King's Cross, back to Huntingdon, as if fleeing the scent of decomposing flesh. Every officer on the Major Incident Team knew that smell, the way it stuck to your clothes.

This one – she's looking at him now, whatever his name is, Darren or Barry – isn't so much morbid as effacing. He is talking about newts, she's vaguely aware of this. Now he's raising his eyebrows – 'Shopping trolleys!' – and she supposes he's making a wry comment about how often they're dumped in streams. She really must engage.

'So, one week till Christmas,' she says. 'How are you spending it?'

He looks annoyed that she's diverted him from the flow of his rivers. 'I've a brother in Norwich,' he says. 'I go to him. He's got kids.' He seems momentarily disappointed and she likes him the more for it.

'Not an easy time, Christmas. When you're on your own, I mean.'

'We have a pretty good time, me and Col, once we crack open the beers. We're a right double act.'

Perhaps his name's Terry, she thinks, sadly. Too late to

ask now. 'Shall we get the bill?' He hasn't even asked about her name – and most men do ('Manon, that's a funny name. Is it Welsh?') – but in a sense it's a relief, the way he just ploughs on.

The waiter brings the bill and it lies lightly curled on a white saucer with two mint imperials.

'Shall we split it?' says Manon, throwing a card onto the saucer. He is sucking on a mint, looking at the bill.

'To be fair,' he says, 'I didn't have any wine. Here.' He shows her the items on the bill that were hers – carafe of red and a side salad.

'Yes, right, OK,' she says, while he gets out his phone and begins totting up. The windows are fogged and Manon peers at the misty halos of Huntingdon's festive lights. It'll be a cold walk home past the shuttered-up shops on the high street, the sad, beery air emanating from Cromwell's, and out towards the river, its refreshing green scent and its movement a slithering in the darkness, to her flat where she has left all the lights burning.

'Yours comes to £23.85. Mine's only £11,' he says. 'D'you want to check?'

Midnight and Manon sits with her knees up on the window seat, looking down at the snowy street lit by orange street lamps. Flakes float down on their leisurely journey, buffeting, tissue-light. The freezing draught coming in through the sash frame makes her hug her knees to her chest as she watches him – Alan? Bernard? – round the corner of her street and disappear.

When she's sure he's gone, she walks a circuit of the lounge, turning off the lamps. To give him credit, he was stopped short by her flat – 'Whoa, this is where you *live*?' – but his interest was short-lived and he soon recommenced his monologue. Perhaps, now she comes to think of it, she slept with him to shut him up.

3

The walls of the lounge are Prussian blue. The shelving on which the television stands is Fifties G-Plan in walnut. Her sofa is a circular design in brown corduroy. Two olive-green velvet wing chairs sit to each side of it and beside one is a yellow domed Seventies floor lamp, which she has just switched off at the plug because the switch is bust. The décor is a homage to mid-century modern, like a film set, with every detail of a piece. The scene for a post-ironic East German comedy perhaps, or *Abigail's Party*; a place absolutely bursting with taste of a charismatic kind, all of it chosen by the flat's previous owners. Manon bought the lot – furniture, lamps, and all – together with the property itself, from a couple who were going abroad to 'start afresh'. At least, that's what the man had said. 'We just want to shed, you know?' To which Manon replied, 'Shed away. I'll take the lot.' And his girlfriend looked around her, swallowing down her tears. She told Manon how she'd collected all of it, lovingly, on eBay. 'Still, fresh start,' she said.

Manon makes her way to the bedroom, which at the point of sale was even more starkly dramatic: dark navy walls with white-painted floorboards and shutters; a whole bank of white wardrobes, handle-less and disappearing into themselves. You had to do a Marcel Marceau impression to discover the pressure points at which to open them.

The previous owners had a minimalist mattress on the floor and a dishevelled white duvet. Under Manon's tenure, however, this room has lost much of its allure: books stacked by the bed, covered with a film of dust; a cloudy glass of water; wires trailing the floor from her police radio to the plug, and among them grey fluff and human hair, coiling like DNA. Her motley collection of shoes makes opening the cupboards additionally tricky. She kicks at a discarded pair of pants on the floor, rolled about themselves like a croissant, throws off her dressing gown (100 per cent polyester, keep away from fire and flame) and retrieves, from under the bed-clothes in which he has incongruously lain, her flannelette nightie.

Up close he smelt musty. And vaguely sweet. But above all, foreign. Was this her experiment – bringing him close, out of the world of strangers? Was she trying him out? Or smelling him out, as if intimacy might transform him into something less ordinary? People who know her – well, Bryony mainly – disapprove of her emotional 'immaturity', but the fact is human beings are different up close. You find out more through smell and touch than any chat about newts or shopping trollies. She becomes her mammalian self, using her senses to choose a mate. She's read somewhere that smell is the most efficient way of selecting from the gene pool to ensure the best immune system in offspring. *So she puts out on the first date!* She's a scientist at the mating frontline.

In her darker moments – and she can feel their approach even now – she wonders if she is simply filling an awkward gap in the conversation. Instead of a ghastly shuffling of feet and 'well, that was nice, but we should probably leave it there', she forces the moment to its crisis. It's like running yourself over to avoid shaking hands.

In the bathroom, she picks up her toothbrush and lays along it a slug of toothpaste, watching herself in the mirror as she brushes. Here is the flaw in her argument: the sex was pretty much a reflection of the night's conversation: all newts and shopping trollies and a definite lack of tumultuous waterfalls or even babbling brooks, if you wanted to pursue the waterways analogy.

She looks at the springy coils of her hair, bobbing ringlets, brown mostly but with the odd blonde one poking out like a rogue pasta twirl – *spit* – unruly and energetic, as if she is some

5

child in a playground, and discordant now – *spit* – that she is on the cusp of her forties. She can feel herself gliding into that invisible – *gargle* – phase of womanhood, alongside those pushing prams or pulling shopping wheelies. She is drawn to the wider fittings in Clarks, has begun to have knee trouble and is disturbed to find that clipping her toenails leaves her vaguely out of puff. She wonders what other indignities ageing will throw at her and how soon. A few centuries ago she'd be dead, having had eight children by the age of twenty-five. Nature doesn't know what to do with a childless woman of thirty-nine, except throw her that fertility curve ball – aches and pains combined with extra time, like some terrifying end to a high-stakes football match.

She wipes a blob of foam off her chin with a towel. Eventually, he asked about her name (her moment in the sun!) and she told him it meant 'bitter' in Hebrew, and she lay back on the pillow, remembering how her mother had squeezed her secondary-school shoulders and told her how much she'd loved it; how 'Manon' was her folly, much as her father objected. A Marmite name, you either loved it or loathed it, and her mother loved it, she said, because it was 'all held down', those Ns like tent pegs in the ground.

There was silence, in which she supposed he wanted her to ask about his name, which she couldn't really, because she wasn't sure what it was. She could have said, 'What about yours?' as a means of finding out, but by that point it seemed unnecessary. She had smelt him out and found him wanting. Her mind was set on how to get him out of her flat, which she did by saying, 'Right then, early start tomorrow,' and holding open her bedroom door.

She smoothes out the pillow and duvet where he's been and pushes her feet down under the covers, reaching out an arm

6

from the bed to switch on the radio, with its sticker reminding her it remains 'Property of Cambridgeshire Police'. A cumbersome bit of kit, and no one at detective sergeant rank is supposed to have one at home, but it is not a plaything. It is the method by which she overcomes insomnia. Some rely on the shipping forecast; Manon prefers low murmurings about road traffic accidents or drunken altercations outside Level 2 Nightclub on All Saints Passage, all of which she can safely ignore because they are far too lowly for the Major Incident Team.

'VB, VB, mobile unit to Northern Bypass, please; that's the A141, junction with Main Street. UDAA.'

Unlawfully Driving Away an Automobile. Someone's nicked some wheels. Off you pop, Plod. The voice begins to sound very far away as Manon's eyelids grow heavy, the burbling of the radio merging into a pebbly blur behind her eyes. The clicks, switches, whirring, receivers picked up and put down, colleagues conferred with, buttons pressed to receive. To Manon, it is the sound of vigilance, this rapid response to hurt and misdeed. It is human kindness in action, protecting the good against the bad. She sleeps.

SUNDAY

MIRIAM

Miriam is washing up, looking out over the bleak winter garden – the lawn smooth as Christmas icing. She'd have liked a bigger garden, but this is about as good as it gets in Hampstead.

She's thinking about Edith, her hands inside rubber gloves in the sink, washing up the Le Creuset after lunch's monkfish stew. The pancetta has stuck around the edges and she is going at it with a scourer. She's so lucky, she thinks, to have a girl, because girls look after you when you get old. Boys just leave home, eventually going to live cheek by jowl with their mothers-in-law.

And then she curses herself, because it goes against all her feminist principles – requiring her daughter, her clever, Cambridge-educated daughter, to wipe her wrinkly old bottom and bring her meals and audio books, probably while juggling toddlers and some pathetic attempt at a career. Her own career hadn't recovered from having the children, those three days a week at the GP surgery feeling like time-filling in between bouts of household management.

Feminism, she thinks, has a long way to go before men take on the detritus of family life – not the spectacular bread and butter pudding, brought out to 'oohs and aahs' (which always has the whiff of 'Man makes pudding! Round of applause!'), but ordering bin liners and making sure there are enough light bulbs. When the children were little, Miriam felt as if she were being buried under sand drifts from the Sahara: music lessons, homework folders, kids' parties, thank-you notes, fresh fruit and meter readings. It silted up the corners of her mind until there was no space for anything else. Ian sidestepped it with strategic incompetence so that his mind remained free to focus on Important Things (such as work, or reading an interesting book). It was one of the biggest shocks of adult life – the injustice – and no one had warned her about it, certainly not her mother, who felt it was only right and proper that Miriam take on the more organisational tasks in life because she was 'so *good* at them'. She'd better not think about it now, or she'll get too angry.

She lifts the Le Creuset onto the white ceramic draining board, wondering why people rave about the things when they are almost un-lift-able and scratch everything they touch. Ian hasn't made it home for lunch so she's eaten the stew by herself, then struggling to lift the damn heavy pot in order to pour the remains into a Tupperware box and struggling also not to feel hard done by. She's alone so much these days, in part because when the sand drifts receded, along with the departure of the children, they left an excess of time, while Ian's existence maintained its steady course, which was essentially Rushing About Being Important. She has to fight, very often, not to take umbrage at the separations and also its converse, to retain some sense of herself in their togetherness. Wasn't every marriage a negotiation about proximity?

9

The temptation she feels during periods when he's very busy and she's left alone a lot is to become defiantly independent, but then it's hard to let him back in. She has to make herself de-frost in order to come back together. She wonders how far Edith has travelled on this rather arduous journey or whether she has even embarked on it with Will Carter. When you are in your twenties, the problem of dependence and independence can be swiftly resolved by ditching your boyfriend, and she has a feeling Edith might be on that brink.

She squeezes out a cloth and wipes the kitchen surface in slow, pensive swirls. It is a slog, marriage. How could she tell her daughter that without making it sound worse than it is? Built on hard work and tolerance, not some idea of perfection as Edith might have it. Miriam has had the thought in the past that Will Carter's handsomeness is an emblem of Edith's belief in perfection – or at least her belief in appearance. She hasn't realised yet that looks count for nothing, that how things appear are nothing next to how they *feel*.

If she were here now, Edith would no doubt spout forth – rather self-righteously – on all the shortcomings that she, herself, would *never* put up with in a marriage, as if there were some gold standard from which she could not fall. She gets that from Ian, of course. Well, life isn't like that. It is full of compromises you never thought you'd make when you were young. Marriage is good – that's what she should say to Edith: that you get to an age when your attachments are so solidly stacked around you, like the bookshelves that reach to the ceiling in the lounge, and they are so built into the fabric of your life that compromise seems nothing next to their dismantling. Yes, she thinks, running the cloth under the tap and enjoying the warmth of the water through the rubber gloves, with age comes the recognition that one is grateful for love.

Looking out again to the garden and squeezing the cloth, she thinks back to their evening at the theatre last night; all their clever friends who loved to talk about books and philosophy. She'd wondered if they had more money and more sex (they couldn't possibly have *less* sex) and better second homes or whether they were, perhaps, (well, one shouldn't hope for these things) secretly miserable and having affairs.

'Are we all here?' Ian said, on the snowy pavement outside the Almeida theatre. 'Ready to set off?' Miriam looked at him, her handsome husband with his impeccable scarf in a cashmere double-loop. He was commanding – well, that's Ian of course – but also vaguely distracted. Work, probably – it so often took over his mind. That was the cost of being married to The Great Surgeon and she noticed, then and there, a swell of pride.

They set off towards Le Palmier restaurant, talking and laughing, arms looped in arms. Miriam walked by herself, though she was at the centre of the group. She'd been crying – *Lear* always made her cry – and her body had a rather pleasurable spent feeling of release, while her stomach growled in hot anticipation of dinner. Someone took her arm – it was Patty, pressing her body close to Miriam's. She got a blast of Patty's perfume – Diorissima – even over the cold.

'I thought that was just wonderful, didn't you?' said Patty.

'Completely wonderful. I feel wrung out, in a good way,' said Miriam. Thought Gloucester was a bit shouty though.'

'Yes, quite. Why can't they just *say* their lines? There's a sort of Shakespearean delivery, which is so irritating. Ah, here we are. I'm starving.'

They handed their coats to the maître d', who bowed slightly while draping them over his arm and then hung them in a wardrobe. Their table was broad and round and the spotlights twinkled off the glasses and highlighted bright circles on the starchy white tablecloth. Miriam felt happy with her very cold glass of something dry and Argentinian (Ian being the wine expert). She watched him across the table, feeling in his breast pocket and taking out a pair of reading glasses with leopard-print frames – a pair she'd bought for £4.99 at Ritz Pharmacy on Heath Street. He put them on the end of his nose in order to read the menu, while Roger talked away at him and Ian laughed at something Rog was saying. The glasses were small and feminine on his patrician face.

'Darling,' she said to him, reaching an arm across the table, but with her head turned to Patty, who was talking about the play.

'Oh yes, sorry,' he said and took off the glasses to pass them to her so she could read her menu. 'Come on, everyone, are we ready to order? Nothing will come of nothing, after all.'

And everyone laughed.

Xanthie told the table she'd been re-reading Boccaccio's *Decameron*. 'It's so witty! I mean, really, I've been laughing out loud on the bus.' And the way she said 'bus' was like some glorious egalitarian experiment. Their laughter around the table had the tinkle of money in it.

Now Miriam is peeling off her rubber gloves as her thoughts return to her daughter, as if to a favourite refrain – her beloved topic. Yes, she hopes for more for her daughter than the things she anticipates for her. Now she frowns. It doesn't make any sense. She wants Edith to fulfil her daughterly duties (thoughtful Christmas presents, regular phone calls, eventually home-cooked meals when Miriam's in her dotage) yet at the same time she wants to liberate her; she wants for her total professional freedom and a truly feminist husband who empties the dishwasher without being asked. And mingled in, she wants her daughter to share in her suffering, the same sacrifices, and she doesn't know why. Is it a hunger for fellow feeling or a fear that Edith might succeed where she failed? That Edith might actually throw off the shackles when Miriam . . . well, she's spent thirty years effectively wiping the kitchen surfaces and doling out antibiotics for cystitis. It's so *complicated.*

She reaches into the cupboard under the sink for a dishwasher tablet, thinking about her beautiful daughter who is still young, who has a flat belly and tight little arms, who can still carry off a bikini, who has yet to fall in love, and she feels pricked with envy. Oh, Will Carter is all right, but he's a bit up himself and she suspects he isn't The One. Edith still has that ahead of her – all the pleasure and pain of it. Lucky thing. The older you get, the less choppy life becomes. But Miriam misses it too – the lurching outer edges of feeling that accompany youth. Nothing is exciting any more, though to listen to Xanthie, you'd think reading Boccaccio's *Decameron* on the bus was euphoric. Perhaps it is only Miriam for whom life has become duller and sadder, like the silver hair on her head.

'Where've you been? I woke up and you weren't here,' she says, smiling at Ian who is coming through the kitchen doorway carrying an orange Sainsbury's bag and bringing the cold in with him. He is wearing his polo-neck sweater and tracksuit bottoms. He has that curious inability that the upper classes have to wear casual clothes convincingly. She wonders if he emerged from his mother's vagina in a sports jacket.

He comes over to her at the kitchen counter, kisses her cheek and she smells the winter on him. 'Got up early and went to the office – I've got a ton of paperwork hanging over me.'

'Poor you,' she says. 'Shall I warm you up some stew?'

'No, no. I'm fine.'

'I can microwave it; it's no trouble.'

'No, I had a sandwich. Edie call yet?'

13

'Not yet, no.'

'Tell you what, let's light a fire. It's freezing outside.'

'Good idea, that'd be lovely,' she says, and the house feels complete again with him in it. His smell, his bigness, his company. Married love has been a revelation to Miriam – not the lurching outer edges of feeling, no, but the sheer depth and texture of it. All her memories – thirty years of them, especially the really vital ones, like having the children – involve him. And loving the children. He is the only person on earth who can talk about the children with the same exhaustive gusto that she does, as if they are both examining Rollo and Edith at 360 degrees. And she is wrong to be quite so consumed by feminist rage. It's not as if he does *nothing*: the cup of tea, for example, he brings her in bed each morning; his final checks on the house at night (doors locked, lights off); the way he'll run upstairs to find her slippers when she sighs exhaustedly and says, 'Darling, would you . . . ?' These are small, repetitive acts of love.

They spend the afternoon in a Sunday-ish homely fug, the log fire spitting and then dying down in the lounge. It brings back the smoked, countrified scent of Deeping, where they will spend New Year. (Must buy light bulbs for Deeping, she makes a mental note to herself.) Miriam could watch those flames for hours until her face is cooked and her eyes dried out. Ian is in and out of his study, some Mozart piano concertos drifting through the house from his iPod dock. She potters about too, tidying up mostly, putting some washing on or reading the 'Review' section of the newspaper.

In the evening the doorbell goes and Miriam opens it to the florist delivering 300 stems of scented narcissi and the fresh holly wreath for her front door. This and her mulled wine spice, and the clove oranges she makes will fill the house with festive perfume. Just as she is closing the door against the night, the phone rings and she answers it, still holding the narcissi like an opera singer at her curtain call.

'Calm down, Will . . . No, she's not here . . . Since when?' she says, as Ian joins her in the hallway, slightly stooped and craning to hear. 'So you've just got home?'

'What's he—' says Ian but Miriam frowns at him to shush.

'Well, she's probably out at a friend's or gone to Deeping,' she says into the phone while looking into Ian's eyes.

Miriam listens, placing the flowers onto the hallway table, then she cups her hand over the phone's mouthpiece. 'He says he found the door open and the lights on. She's left everything in the house – her keys, her phone, her shoes. Her car's outside. Even her coat's there.'

Ian nudges her aside to take the phone off her. 'Will? It's Ian. When did you last speak to her? Have you called Helena?'

She watches him frowning at the hall table, listening. Then he says, 'Right, call the police. Straight away, Will. Tell them what you've told us. Then call us straight back.' He puts the receiver down.

'No,' says Miriam, looking into Ian's eyes and shaking her head, her hand clamped over her mouth. 'No, no, no, no.'

Manon

Manon cries some more. It is the way Bryony listens, as if she has an arm around her, that makes Manon's barriers dissolve.

'Was he awful, then?' asks Bryony. 'As bad as the last one?'

'No, that's the thing, Bri, he was all right, but that's the worst feeling, that it was just all right, nothing special. Just nothingy, like I can't ever rise to the occasion.'

'Maybe you need to give it more of a go. Nothing's perfect, you know.'

'He wanted me to pay more for the meal because I had wine.'

Bryony is silent.

'He didn't ask me anything about myself.'

'Yeah, well, that's just men, I'd say.'

Manon presses her fingers into her eyes. This is what she *doesn't* want Bryony to say. People in couples, they always want you to settle for anything, as if you are a second-class citizen. Just because you're lonely, you have to make do with the scrap ends.

'You want me to make do with the scrap ends.'

'We're *all* making do with the scrap ends, Manon,' says Bryony. 'This is something you fail to grasp.'

'The sex was quite good, unexpectedly,' says Manon.

'You what?'

'Well, I thought it'd be rude not to.'

'Don't make a joke of it.'

Manon doesn't reply.

'You don't need to do that, y'know,' says Bryony, her voice full of disappointment.

'No, I know.'

'When's the next one?'

'Next week. Not sure I can stand it.'

'Treat it like a job. It's a game of numbers. Your lucky one will come up eventually. Only don't shag them. Not all of them, anyway.'

Manon can't stand to talk about it any more. 'How are the kids?' she says. 'How was your Sunday?'

'Freezing playground, 8 a.m. Started to sleet but we stayed there anyway. Me and Peter had a row. Lunch at 11 a.m. Bobby threw a cup of milk down me, then shat in his pants. The usual.'

'Relaxing.'

'I can't wait to go to work tomorrow, just to have a sit-down. Canteen lunch? Whaddya say? I'll buy you a watery soup to cheer you up. Or are you frontline officers too important?'

A familiar prod, beneath which is Bryony's peevishness over all the excitement she thinks she's missing out on. She's an officer at Cambridgeshire too, but mostly desk-bound since the children – filing court papers or on disclosure.

'My diary is remarkably free at the moment,' Manon says. 'Never know what the day'll throw at me though. So yes, great. In theory. One-ish?'

'Don't know if I can hold out that long. I'm on toddler time. And Manon?'

'Yes?'

'You'll be all right, you know. You'll find him – the right man. I just know you will.'

Manon puts the phone down and shuffles under the duvet. She turns the dial on the radio, hears the reassuring murmuring which blends into the fuzz before sleep, when all her darkest ideas bubble up. 'Victor Bravo, one-two, VB quite concerned by what we've got here. Can I have a supervisor please and can you notify on-call SIO.'

Manon opens her eyes and sits up. She knows what the gaps mean, what Oscar One in the control room is getting at, without being able to state it over the airwaves. Something serious. The balloon's gone up. Senior Investigating Officer? That's jumpy. Others will be hearing it too and start heading that way, but George Street is around the corner from her – five minutes if she jogs it. She hears DI Harriet Harper's voice over the radio, saying she's on her way.

Manon can get this, it's hers. She flings back the duvet, listening intently to the radio while she pulls on trousers with one hand, reaching for her phone with the other.

'Missing female,' says Harriet on the phone. 'Signs of a struggle. Meet me there.'

The cold cuts into the short gap between Manon's scarf and her hat, but the place it hurts most is her toes. Bloody Chelsea boots. She might as well have worn flip-flops, and she'll likely be out in the cold all night, at best in a stationary car with a phone pressed to her ear. She digs her hands deeper into her pockets and hunches her shoulders up to her ears, hearing the clean squeak of her boots in the fresh powder. The trees hold lines of snow like sleeves on every branch. The snow has made a rather unprepossessing urban street (one of the routes out

18

of town and close to the railway line) prettier than it is. As she turns up the garden path to number 20 – a neat little worker's cottage, identical to its neighbours – she uses a gloved hand to free her mouth of scarf, but Davy speaks first.

'High-risk misper; looks like it, anyway,' he says, stamping in the snow. He claps his hands. The tip of his nose is glowing red.

'Any sign of forced entry?' says Manon.

'Door was open, but not forced. There's some blood, hallway and kitchen, not that much of it, to be fair, and the coats on the floor,' says Davy. 'Where's your paper suit?'

'Where's your scene log?' she says, looking past him into the house.

'Shit, you got me,' he says, smiling, and she is reminded how good it is to be around DC Davy Walker. His simple affable kindliness. If all men were like Davy, there would be no wars.

'Can I get a suit from your car?'

'Here you go,' he says, holding up his keys. 'I'll start a log now. Don't tell Harriet.'

She returns, rustling in white paper, her egg-shaped hood encasing her face, and holds Davy's arm as she pulls on some blue outer shoes.

'Very fetching,' he says.

'I think so,' says Manon, at his knees. 'Who's in there?'

'Harriet and the missing girl's boyfriend. She's keen to shut the place down. I'd wait out here if I were you.'

Manon straightens. 'Bollocks, I won't touch anything. Why've we not got a DCI on this?'

Davy shrugs. 'Christmas rota. Draper's on an aggravated burglary in Peterborough. Stanton's in the Maldives. Staffing's back to the bone.'

She steps into the hallway where the coats have dropped from their hooks like fallen soldiers. They scatter the floor.

Some of the hoods retain the pointed imprint of the hook on which they hung. Light anoraks (one navy, one red), a fleece (grey), two thick winter coats of the padded kind, one an olive parka with fur trim, the other navy. Leaning against the wall is a rucksack with the handle of a tennis racket poking out; some trainers line the skirting; a Hessian shopper with the words 'Huntingdon Estates' written on it. In front of her, on the laminate floor leading to the kitchen, are a couple of drips of blood – not a copious spattering or pooling of the kind they saw in killings, but the type of blood that might come from an injury such as a cut.

Harriet appears in the kitchen doorway.

'Manon, can you come through? Watch the floor, there,' she says as Manon tiptoes towards the threshold. 'Don't step in the evidence. Manon, this is Will Carter. Mr Carter, this is Detective Sergeant Bradshaw. Mr Carter has reported his girl-friend Edith Hind missing. He returned home at 9 p.m. this evening to find the front door ajar, the coats in disarray and blood over there.' She points to a larger spatter on the kitchen floor, and some on the cupboard door just above it.

'Miss Hind's phone, keys, shoes, and coat were all in the house,' Harriet says.

Will Carter is pacing, running a hand through his hair. He is preposterously handsome, wearing tracksuit bottoms and a cable-knit jumper, as if he has just stepped out of a razor advertisement. Manon glances at Harriet, who gives her a look which says: *Yes, you can shut your gob now.*

'Is there anyone she might be with – a friend or relative?' asks Manon.

'I've called everyone I can think of,' says Carter. 'I've called her parents; they're in London. They haven't heard from her. And her friend Helena, she was with Edith last night at a party.

20

She says she dropped Edith back here at around midnight. Hasn't seen or heard from her today.'

'When did you last speak to Edith?' says Harriet.

'Saturday early evening, just before she went out with Helena.'

'Did she sound her normal self?'

'Yes, I mean, it was a very quick call.'

'And I'm sorry, Mr Carter,' says Manon, 'you were where?'

'I've been away for the weekend in Stoke. Visiting my mum.'

'Is there anywhere she might have gone?' asks Manon. 'A favourite place? Might she have just wanted time alone?'

'I don't see where she could have gone without her keys or her phone or her car.'

'Car's outside,' explains Harriet.

'I've gone through the contacts on her phone, called people who were at the party on Saturday night, our friends at college. Everyone I could think of. No one's heard from her. I started to panic. Her parents told me to call the police. I mean, not that I wouldn't have called, but you never know if you're over-reacting, d'you know what I mean? Can you get officers out there looking for her? It just doesn't feel right. Something's not right.'

'What about her passport?' asks Manon. 'Is it here?'

'I don't know,' Carter says. He goes to one of the kitchen drawers. 'She keeps it in here,' he says, pulling it out. He turns, holding up a small burgundy book. 'It's here. There's a second home, Deeping – it's her parents' place, about half an hour's drive away, near March. Edith's got keys, but they're on her key ring, there.' He points to a bundle of keys on the kitchen table amid bits of paper with numbers written on them, an open diary, and mobile phones. 'And anyway, you can't get there without a car.'

21

'Someone else might have driven her, perhaps?' says Manon.

He shrugs. 'But who? The phone, her keys – she never leaves that stuff. I mean, who does?'

'Is there any reason she might have wanted to frighten you? Were you on good terms?' asks Harriet.

Carter is shaking his head before she has even stopped talking. 'No, no, she wouldn't. We were on the best of terms. Everything's good. Better than good. When will you start searching? It's freezing outside and she hasn't got her coat.'

'How do you know, sir?' says Harriet. 'The coats appear to have fallen all over the place.'

'I checked,' says Carter. 'I looked through them. I don't know if I should have, but I wanted to know if she had it or not.'

'It doesn't look like you've gone through them. They appear to be as they fell.'

'It only took a cursory look to see that her coat is there – the green one. The parka with the fur trim.'

'Might she have taken another one?'

'She hasn't, I know she hasn't, and anyway, why would they be all over the floor like that?'

'A word, Manon, please,' says Harriet, gesturing outside the kitchen. They step around the blood drips in the hallway and into the lounge next door, which is under-furnished and struggling to emerge from the miasma of an energy-saving light bulb. They speak in low murmurs.

'Blimey,' whispers Manon. 'He's . . .' She blows out through her cheeks.

'Very agitated, yes. What do you think? Enough to qualify as a high-risk misper? Davy and I have done a search of the house. We need to scope this country place, Deeping, soon as.'

'Anything upstairs? Any signs of struggle?'

22

'Not that I can make out. I want to shut the place down so we don't lose anything, get SOCO looking at that blood.'

'She might have disappeared in the early hours this morning,' says Manon, looking at her watch.

Harriet nods. 'That's twenty hours.'

They are silent. They both know the first seventy-two hours are critical for a high-risk missing person. You find them or you look for a body.

'If that blood's hers, which is pretty likely, then she could be out there bleeding in some garden or lay-by. We need dogs and we need a helicopter. I want you to set parameters for the early search. I want you to get as many bodies up here as you can to begin house to house and we'll need to start scoping for CCTV.'

Manon nods. 'Can I have Davy?'

'Yep.'

'Shame Stanton's missing out.'

'That's what happens when you fuck off to the Maldives.'

Manon sends officers straight to Deeping, but there is no sign of the girl there. The helicopter takes two hours to get to them from the Midlands. It hovers loudly, searching back gardens, alleys, and motorway verges for a woman in her twenties clutching an injury, or a slumped figure. The helicopter's underside is like a black insect against the navy sky, the beat of its blades rhythmic and relentless. It covers swathes of ground in a way officers on foot or in cars cannot hope to do. If its throbbing drone hasn't woken the neighbours then the dogs will, panting and snuffling under hedges and straining up paths, the scent of Edith Hind still on their snouts from her nightdress. Or the door knocks, neighbours emerging with bed hair in the brash light of their hallways. It's clod-footed, this type of early

23

search – urgent and messy. Manon coordinates it all on the phone in Davy's unmarked car, calling in officers from across the county, hearing them report back from house to house, keeping Harriet up to date back at the station, where she is re-interviewing Will Carter.

At 6 a.m. there is a hiatus when there are no more calls she can make, so Manon returns home for a shower and to change her clothes. She pulls at her eyes in the mirror and sees the undernourishment of the night on her skin but also the adrenalin, which has made her pupils dilate. This is why she entered the police – cases like this. Whoppers, the ones you wait weeks or months for, a whole career, even.

Harriet is the same. She'd been made DI after her work on the Soham murders, the case which shaped Cambridgeshire policing more than any other because it was so high profile and because it came to define the battle lines between police and press. The disappearance of two pretty girls in the shimmering, lazy news lull of August. The press had been on their side for one or two days, driving the appeals for witnesses, and then it grew ferocious, like a dog unmuzzled, with resources that outstripped the Major Incident Team's. Officers suspected hacking, enraged that they themselves had to wait days for authorisation to trace phones; they found themselves showing up to interview potential witnesses, only to find reporters had been there an hour earlier. Some of the more brazen Sunday tabloids hired private detectives and they were all over it, corrupting with their money, turning over evidence, leaving their mark.

Manon holds in her hand a photograph of Edith Hind, auburn-haired and smiling – a face almost confident, the gorgeous bloom of childhood still radiating from her skin. She is wearing a mortar board and gown, with a scroll in her hand.

Graduation day at Cambridge. Just like the photo Manon's father has on the shelf.

Yes, she thinks. This will be big.

She learned as much as anyone from Soham but remained a DS because if you were smart, you realised things didn't get better when you climbed the ranks. She wanted to stay on the ground, interviewing suspects, running her team of DCs and civilian investigators, not holed up in an office attending management courses and filling in Main-Lines-of-Enquiry forms. It certainly wasn't, as Bryony maintained, that she was too busy humping her way around the Internet to focus on the exams.

She's left Davy at the scene in George Street, letting in SOCO – the Scenes of Crime Officer, as it is currently known, or CSI or FSI. She has never known an organisation to love an acronym as much as the police, nor to change them so often. She longs for the day some sleepy mandarin comes up with the Crime Unit National Taskforce.

She picks up the keys to her car and goes to collect Davy, to take him to Cambridgeshire HQ for the morning briefing.

MONDAY

DAVY

He stands at Edith Hind's front door and looks down the path to the men in pressed suits with puffa jackets over the top, loitering at the gate and stamping the snow off their boots. The frozen morning air emerges from their mouths in white clouds. You can tell they're the locals because of the suits and the polished shoes – national press are scruffy. Chinos with round-neck jumpers in jaunty colours if they're broadsheet; rumpled suits that fall at the shoulder and concertina into creases at the base of the jacket if they're tabloid. Local reporters, on the other hand, have to live among their subjects: attend their council meetings, Christmas fairs and sports days. A pressed suit's the least they can do.

Davy sees DS Bradshaw's preposterous car pull up just beyond the men, on the opposite kerb. A Seventies Citroën – long nose, sagging leather seats, spindly steering wheel with gear stick to the side. She's convinced it makes her look like Audrey Hepburn, but behind her back, the DCs at the station make reference to Inspector Clouseau, putting on exaggerated French accents and saying, 'In the neme of the leur' while watching from the window as she parks. Davy doesn't care about impressions. He hates travelling in her car because it's always cold, often doesn't start and smells vaguely of wet dog. Thank God it's usually him driving, her on the phone, in a warm and anonymous unmarked police vehicle.

'C'mon, tell us something,' says one of the reporters at the gate, but Davy pushes past him.

'How long's she been missing?' asks another. 'Any signs of a struggle? Has she been kidnapped?'

'I'm sure there'll be a briefing soon,' says Davy, careful not to meet their eye.

He ducks into Manon's car and looks at her, but she's counting up the men at the gate through the smears on the windscreen.

Yes, she's grumpy, but a skinny latte soon takes the edge off her, most days, anyhow – like throwing a steak into the lion enclosure. He wishes he had one to offer her now but instead he has to watch, unarmed, as she squints into the shards of broken sun. He rubs his hands together and blows into them.

Perhaps it's her age that's making her bad-tempered and he can understand that. She must be at least thirty-nine, the loneliness rising off her like a mist. He'd be the same if he didn't have Chloe. He's seen Manon, more than once, red-eyed coming out of the second floor toilets and his heart goes out to her on those occasions, watching her hurriedly wipe the snot away and try to act normal. Well, pissed off, which is normal. Him and Manon, though – somehow it works, he doesn't know how, and this seems to rankle Chloe. Even now, pulling down on his seatbelt, Davy's face falls as he remembers the time he described Manon as 'good in a crisis'.

'Good how?' Chloe asked, trying to seem casual about it

27

but he knew all about 'casual' and its parameters. Chloe's questioning could put CID to shame. 'You share a joke, do you? Manon make you laugh much, does she? D'you think she blow-dries her hair, then, before coming in?' Whenever Davy makes a positive comment about her – and Davy works hard at being positive about pretty much everything – Chloe's face can darken as fast as the April sky.

'She sometimes sees things that others don't,' he'd said on this particular occasion, shovel in hand, cheerfully digging himself deeper into the pit. 'Makes connections. Bit left-field sometimes.'

'Well, I don't see how that's any more than most women have got – intuition. I mean, I can make connections between things if I want to,' Chloe said, then barely talked to him the rest of the day.

Manon puts the car in gear, her eyes still on the men, saying, 'Four. Just the locals.'

'Course it's the locals. Still early doors.'

'Won't be long before they ring the tabs. This time of year, missing girl. Nothing like a festive stiff to warm the cockles of your front page.'

'She's probably just got a new boyfriend – done a runner,' says Davy.

'Leaving her phone and keys and the door wide open? I don't even go to the toilet without my phone. And what about the blood? No, I'd say she's definitely come to harm.'

She's put her aviator shades down, pulling out from the kerb. Davy looks at her and shakes his head.

It's only a ten-minute drive to the station from George Street. They jog up the steps of Cambridgeshire HQ, a festival of sick-yellow brick squatting in an acreage of car park. For Davy,

28

climbing these steps with an important job to do makes him inflate with pride and elation. He wishes someone could see him, Detective Constable Walker of *Cambridgeshire Constabulary: supporting law-abiding citizens and pursuing criminals relentlessly since 1974.* This mission statement is actually on the Cambridgeshire police website, but it could have been something Davy came up with.

When he brought Chloe for a tour of HQ, he was smiling to himself the whole time and even though she described it as 'a cross between a Travelodge and a conference centre', it hadn't dented the dignity of his calling. She said the reception, with its curved wooden desk, spider plants, and smell of brewing coffee, reminded her of an STD clinic, but what he saw – what he was so proud of – was the electronic notice board announcing the life and death work going on here (*2–4 p.m., conf. room 3: crime data integrity working group; protocol briefings: ambulance teams, Hinchingbrooke; UK cross border agency; 4–6 p.m., Commissioner*). So much sexier than the jobs he could have had: regional manager for Vodafone or selling fridges in Currys, like his school friends. Which would you rather? Flogging some twenty-four-month contract with 3,000 free minutes or wondering whether the Dutch woman got on a train to Brighton to kill herself there, or whether she was murdered? Human stories, base and sexual. The police operated in the seedy low light: drug runs, burglars in botched stick-ups, murderers who said they were nowhere near the scene but whose smart phones provided a handy GPS map of their movements. Boyfriends controlling girlfriends, friends paying off debts, love triangles, honour killings. That, or: 'Would you like to extend your warranty on this microwave for an extra two years, sir?'

'Look at you, Davy,' Chloe had said, as he showed her the

forensics lab and the phone-tracing department. 'You've really drunk the Kool-Aid, haven't you?'

Davy and Manon enter the MIT department just as Harriet is gathering team four for her briefing: DC Kim Delaney, DC Nigel Williams, Colin Brierley – a retired DI, now civilian investigator who runs the tech side – and a couple of other DCs.

They fall in behind their desks, shaking off their coats.

'You're going to have to hit the ground running, Stuart, I'm afraid,' Harriet is saying as Manon shakes hands with the new recruit – an extra civilian investigator to type interviews into the HOLMES computer system and listen to Colin's un-politically correct diatribes, lucky chap. 'Baptism of fire. These guys will show you the ropes.'

Davy nods his most welcoming nod at Stuart. Sometimes CIs were retired officers, like Colin, sometimes young, like this one, fresh from a three-day induction course. They were cheap and they didn't leave the office.

'Right, everyone,' Harriet continues. 'Edith Hind, twenty-four, Cambridge postgrad student, missing from the house she shares with Will Carter in George Street. Parents have driven up and are waiting downstairs, so let's get a family liaison officer with them asap. Main lines are as follows. One: scene and examination. SOCO are in. I've just had a call from them: two wine glasses – one clean on the kitchen worktop, the other broken in the bin with traces of blood at its edges.'

'She could have been waiting for someone,' says Manon.

'That was my thought,' says Harriet. 'Two wine glasses out ready for a rendezvous, one of them becomes a weapon. We'll see what forensics tell us on that score.

'Two: search ongoing, including dogs. Polsa should be on board by midday today. That's Police Search Adviser,' she says to the new chap. 'The search teams, in other words. Three:

house to house. Four: FLO and victimology. Five: media. We'll get a photo of Edith out this morning. I'm meeting with Fergus in an hour to discuss Press strategy. Six: intel work. Colin, you've got her phone and her laptop. Let's trace her car reg on ANPR – that's Automated Number Plate Recognition, for our new recruit here. And Will Carter's too, while we're at it. I want all of the council's CCTV looked at. Seven: persons of interest. That's Will Carter, obviously, and Helena Reed, the friend she was with on Saturday night. Is that enough to be getting on with?'

'Hypothesis, boss?' asks Nigel. Manon says he's needy, always looking to senior officers for answers. Davy would never express something so judgemental, though it's fair to say Nigel is permanently exhausted since having the twins.

'I would say she's opened the door to someone she knows or at least to someone she wasn't immediately afraid of. The blood indicates an injury, possibly when someone tried to remove her from the house. The amount of blood doesn't suggest a murder on site; it's more likely it's come from a cut of some kind. A sexual encounter of some sort? He makes advances, she's not keen, and there's a blow from the wine glass in the tussle. All supposition at this point. We are within the golden hour, so let's press on.'

MANON

She pulls out a swivel chair and wheels herself next to Colin, who smells of bonfires – the obscure brand of cigarettes he smokes.

'What's her phone telling us then?' she asks.

'In terms of the victim's usage, nothing past 8 p.m. on Saturday night, when she texts the friend, Helena Reed,' says Colin.

'What does she say in that last text?'

'"There in five. E."'

'Anything else?'

'Before the party she does some texting. Someone called Jason F.'

Manon reads Colin's screen.

What time u getting there? E

Later, somewhere to be first.

Don't be long, will you?

Why not?

Wouldn't like you to miss anything . . .

'There are others, too,' Colin says. 'She texts her tutor, Graham Garfield, to say, "Hope to c u tonite." He replies, "What's going down?" Trying to pretend he's not fifty-seven, if you ask me.'

'And she says?'

'"Karaoke, tequila, and bad behaviour." To which he replies, "On my way!"' says Colin.

'What about Facebook?'

Colin clicks on his screen and up pops a collage of Edith – her neck, her arms, brown legs crossed, laughing, her head thrown back. Edith cuddling a cat. Edith in cut-off shorts. Edith wearing a Stetson. Black and white, some with colours blown out by Instagram, which gives them a smoky, Seventies sheen. Beneath these are comments to the tune of 'Gorgeous!' and 'Beautiful, beautiful girl' and 'Stunning'. Each photo is 'liked' by Will Carter. In a few she's in a living room, stretched out on the sofa with her feet in Will Carter's lap as he nurses a goblet of red. In many of the images, another girl is somewhere off-centre or in the background, curled in an armchair reading; just a half of her face, a lick of her hair.

Over four hundred photographs.

'They're all of herself, pretty much,' says Colin.

Edith's posts are random music lyrics, Bruce Springsteen mostly. The odd literary article about Seamus Heaney or Toni Morrison. Bo Diddley is my new jam. Nick Cave is my new jam.

'She has four hundred and eighty-two "friends",' Colin adds, drawing quote marks in the air.

'D'you know how many I've got?' says Manon, a yawn

33

stretching her face, while Colin scrolls down. 'Four. One's my dad. One's the electrician. I'm not even sure I know the other two.'

'She's a member of these groups,' says Colin, clicking again. 'Guerrilla Gardeners.'

'What do they do?'

'They grow food on communal ground. Recipes . . . Here's a photo of a hot pot they made using free veg picked from a community wasteland garden. She's a member of Cycle Power – a lobbying group which aims to ban cars.'

'Scroll up a minute. What's that?' says Manon, pointing at the screen.

Colin clicks on the image and Manon reads Edith Hind's caption:

Bunting made from recycled copies of the FT. Happy Christmas, planet!

She and Colin look at each other.

'It's a wonder she wasn't murdered sooner,' says Colin.

'Those are exactly the sorts of thoughts I want you to keep to yourself,' Manon says, rising. 'Keep at it, Colin. Her hard drive, Google searches, matches on all her phone records.' And then she marches across MIT to Harriet's office.

'So what was the interview with Carter like?'

'Seems genuinely worried,' says Harriet, hitching at her bra strap. 'Keeps crying, pacing, asking for an update on the search. We need to be all over his weekend in Stoke. We can ask the Hind parents a bit more about their relationship, and the friend, Helena, whether there was anyone else in the background, boyfriend-wise. Tabs are already ringing the press office, Fergus said.'

'It won't be like Soham,' says Manon. 'Not in this climate, not after phone hacking. Things have changed.'

'Don't bet on it, not with her parents being who they are.'

'Who are her parents?'

'Sir Ian and Lady Hind. He's an ear, nose, and throat surgeon. Fits the Royal grommets or something.'

'Oh God.'

'Yup. We have to tread carefully; the type who'll complain over anything.'

'Is it a ransom job then? He must be worth a bit.'

'We'd have heard from them by now. Anyway, I'm not handing this to any centralised fucking crime unit, no way.'

She gets up, pacing behind the desk, as if the speed of her thoughts is physical. The wings of her jacket are pinned back by her hands on her hips. She's full of fire, unbridled. If Manon ever went missing, she'd want Harriet to head up the search.

'Once Polsa's on board, the pressure will ease off a bit,' Harriet says, as much to herself as to Manon.

The police search adviser and his specialist teams knew how to find people, or at least where to look. They would take the search further and wider than that clumsy first night: across meadows, along railway tracks, into woods, behind the doors of lock-up garages, in attics and cellars, and soon enough down below the opaque surface of rivers.

Harriet looks at her watch. 'Eight thirty. If she went missing shortly after midnight on Saturday, then we're talking thirty-two hours. It's sub-zero out there.'

'I'll send someone to bring in the friend, Helena Reed, shall I?'

'Yup. I'll go and talk to the parents. Urgh, this is the bit I hate – they'll be frantic. Then I'm meeting Fergus in the press office. We'll probably do a short briefing at 11 a.m., just me

35

and the agencies and locals. Got to get those photos of the girl out and an initial appeal. We need to look at her bank activity. Can you start someone on that?'

Manon and Davy slip into interview room one, where Sir Ian is pacing in a navy wool coat.

'So, hang on a minute, you're saying there isn't a DCI on duty to run the search for my daughter?' He has an imperious face, straight nose, pale eyes and thin lips. Charles Dance without the ginger colouring.

'DC Walker and DS Bradshaw enter the room,' says Harriet to the recording device. 'It's quite normal, Sir Ian, for a DI to run a case such as this. If you'd like to sit down, there are a number of things we'd like to ask you.'

'What I want to know first is who is conducting the search. Who is *actually* out there in the snow, searching for her, because if she's injured—'

Lady Hind, who sits at the table opposite Harriet, takes his hand and holds it to her cheek, then kisses the back of it and this seems to give him pause. Her hair is grey, in a straight bob, with a beautiful streak of white framing her face. Her coat hangs expensively, her fingers glinting with diamonds.

'Sit down, darling,' she says, her voice quavering with suppressed tears. 'We must help them in any way we can.'

Sir Ian takes up a chair next to his wife.

'Thank you,' says Harriet. 'Edith's phone shows a few missed calls from you over the course of the weekend, Sir Ian. Were you having trouble reaching her?'

'We always have trouble reaching her, don't we?' he says to Lady Hind. 'She's terrible at calling back. So we call, and we call.' At this he gives Harriet a strained smile. 'We were anxious to know her plans for Christmas, weren't we, darling?'

'She hadn't told you her plans for Christmas?' Manon asks, directing the question at Lady Hind.

'Edith's fond of prevaricating. She can be . . . non-committal, would you say, Ian? With us, anyway. We'd agreed she and Will would spend Christmas with us in London and then she'd said, "You never know", or something to that effect.'

'You never know what?' asks Manon.

'I took it to mean she couldn't be certain Will would join us.'

'So there was trouble between them?' Harriet says.

'No, not trouble,' says Lady Hind. 'Ambivalence, I'd say. They're only twenty-four, after all. They're not married.'

'And this ambivalence,' says Harriet, 'would you say it was more on her part than his?'

'Yes,' says Lady Hind.

'Has there been any violence between them – heated rows, say? Would Edith have reason to be fearful of Mr Carter?'

'No, no, no,' says Sir Ian. 'It's not like that. It's ordinary stuff. Will is a marvellous fellow, devoted to Edie.'

'But if he sensed her feelings were cooling, perhaps—'

'Detective, we are not that sort of family. I'm sure you deal all the time with people whose lives are chaotic, who drink and brawl and abuse one another. But none of us – these things are not part of our lives, our experience. I'd be very surprised if Will is involved in this.'

'Right,' says Harriet. 'Can you think of anyone who would want to harm Edith?'

The Hinds look at each other, their expressions bewildered. 'No, we really can't,' says Lady Hind. 'Can you tell me, how do you . . . Please, you have to find her, I can't . . . The thought of her lost, you see . . .' Her eyes brim as she looks at the officers, one to the other.

'I'll explain how we go forward from here,' says Manon.

'Search teams will work in concentric circles out from the house and, at the same time, we'll be building a picture of Edith, working outwards from her most intimate circle – yourselves, Will Carter, Helena Reed. We'll look at all aspects of her life, based on what you tell us, her phone, computer, bank cards. So it's important you leave nothing out.'

'She doesn't have any bank cards,' says Sir Ian. 'She feels the whole banking industry is corrupt. According to Edie, if none of us used banks, then the whole global economic collapse wouldn't have happened. It's not a view I share, but she holds these beliefs very strongly. If she could pay everyone in muddy vegetables and repaired bicycle tyres, she would, but her landlord wouldn't have it.'

'OK, so how does she live? Where does her income come from?' asks Harriet.

'Me,' he says. 'I give her a MoneyGram transfer via the Post Office every month – £1,500 on the first. She pays the rent on the cottage in cash to the landlord – that's £750, I think. He lives next door. I pay the utilities directly from London. The rest she lives off.'

'So there would've been quite a lot of cash in the house,' says Harriet. 'She would have been seen collecting wads of it at the Post Office . . .'

'Look, I feel it's risky,' says Sir Ian. 'And I've argued with her about it. I've said I'd rather she has a bank account into which I can transfer the funds. But she just won't have it. She says someone has to break with the status quo. I think she'd prefer not to receive any money from me, to do everything her own way, on her own terms. Twenty-four-year-olds are like that. So I don't argue with her because I want her to have my help.'

'Also,' says Lady Hind, 'and we discussed this, oh God,

endlessly, because it worried us, but we reason that £750 goes more-or-less straight to the landlord, so it's not as if it's all under the bed.'

'You get to a point,' Sir Ian adds, and it's as if he and his wife's sentences are a continuation, 'where you don't want to fall out with your children because you don't want to lose them. The balance of power shifts, you see. I want her to have my money and these are the terms on which she'll have it.'

'How many people know about this cash arrangement?'

'Well, Will, of course. We have sort of been supporting Will by default because he lives in the house and we pay for the house,' says Lady Hind. 'As to others, Edith doesn't keep quiet about her views. She's quite vocal.'

'So this weekend,' Harriet says, 'there should have been how much in the cottage, at a guess?'

Sir Ian glances at his phone. 'It's the nineteenth, so she's halfway through the month,' he says. 'Christmas is a bit more expensive, so I'd imagine no more than £300. Surely not enough for someone to . . .'

'You'd be surprised,' says Harriet. 'Why not pay her rent directly? Why not transfer that, like the utilities?'

'The landlord gives her a slight reduction in return for cash-in-hand. I assume he's fiddling his taxes somewhat.'

'Fifteen hundred pounds is a generous allowance,' says Manon. 'Is she extravagant?'

'Quite the opposite. Edith believes in treading lightly on the earth.'

'But she has a car.'

'An electric car,' says Lady Hind. She swallows, and Manon sees she's keeping down a swell of desperation. 'A very old electric car. A G-Wiz. It used to be my run-around. Edith needed it when she moved to Huntingdon – to get to lectures

39

and supervisions at Corpus and to Deeping, which is only half an hour from here.'

'We'll need to take a closer look at Deeping, I hope you don't mind – get our forensic teams out there,' says Harriet.

'It's almost impossible to get to without a car. Middle of the Fens, about three acres,' says Sir Ian. 'Quite a rough place, really. Edith loves it there but, like I say, without the G-Wiz . . .'

'She might have gone with someone else,' says Harriet.

He nods. 'Would you like my keys?'

'No, it's all right, I've got Edith's set. Can I ask, is there any way she could gain access without her keys? A spare set at the property, perhaps?'

'Yes, in the porch, high up. If you feel along the architrave, there's a key resting there for emergencies,' says Sir Ian. 'The house is in the middle of nowhere. Hardly anyone even knows it's there, so we're quite lax on security.'

Harriet is writing in her notebook. She looks up and says, 'Now, we just need to get an account of your movements over the weekend so we can eliminate you both from the enquiry.'

'Yes, of course,' says Lady Hind. 'We were at the theatre on Saturday night with friends. *King Lear* at the Almeida. After the theatre, we went for supper at Le Palmier – six of us. We left there about midnight. Yesterday, we were at home mostly with the fire on – it was so *cold*. Ian went to the office briefly in the morning, didn't you? I made a monkfish stew for lunch. In the afternoon, we pottered about at home, reading, I watched bits of a film – one of those World War Two black and white ones. Ian was in and out of his study. In the evening, I took a delivery from my florist – she was getting all her Christmas orders out, hence why she was delivering so late on a Sunday. Then – this was about nine – Will rang, worried sick about Edith.'

'And your friends at the theatre,' Harriet says. 'Could we have a list?'

'Rog and Patty,' says Sir Ian, looking at Harriet's notebook. 'That's Roger Galloway and his wife Patricia. I'm sure their security detail will confirm everything for you.'

Manon, Davy, and Harriet shoot a glance at each other and Harriet says, 'A word outside, you two.'

'Don't say anything,' hisses Harriet, like an angry swan. 'Don't fucking say anything until we're in my fucking office.' Manon is right behind her as she pelts up the staircase. Those, she thinks, are some mightily clenched buttocks.

Once in her office, Harriet turns, breathless. 'Fuckety, fuckety fucking fuck,' she says. 'Right, I've thought of a name for this case. We're calling it Operation Career Fucking Suicide.'

'Let's just calm down,' says Manon. 'So he was at the theatre with the Home Secretary. All that means is that his alibi probably stacks up.'

'Ye *think*?' says Harriet.

'It probably is quite tight, to be fair,' says Davy.

Manon and Harriet look at each other, Harriet turning up her palms.

'Right,' she says, 'so if we thought the press were all over it before, we should see what happens when they get hold of this. Not just the Royal Family, but "did the Home Secretary interfere with the investigation in any way?" Well, that'll be the *Guardian*. Before I know it, I'll be in front of some sodding select committee at the House of Commons having my career buried under a steaming pile of procedure. I predict a call from Galloway to the Commissioner in—' she looks at her watch – 'oooh, the next couple of hours?'

This was the nightmare of being the SIO: pressure from every quarter, having to make decisions about which lines to investigate in what order of priority, trying to work out which information is important and which can be discarded, and all those decisions being scrutinised from above and often from outside.

'Let's not get bamboozled by Ian Hind,' says Manon. 'We still need to confirm their movements.'

This appears to have a calming effect on Harriet, who takes a deep breath and allows her shoulders to drop.

'Yes, right. You're right. Let's put a call in to Galloway's security detail. I want you two to drive out and scope this country pile, Deeping. See if that key's been disturbed. And I want CCTV from the Post Office on the first of December – see who was looking over Edith's shoulder when she picked up all that cash. Get Kim to check whether the landlord was paid his rent. I'm assuming he was interviewed during house to house. This is looking more like aggravated burglary by the minute.'

Manon and Davy make for the door.

'And from now on,' Harriet calls after them, 'we treat Sir Bufton Tufton downstairs with the utterly slavish deference he so richly deserves.'

On one of the rare occasions Harriet had come to Cromwell's and got drunk, she'd told Manon she had two consolations in life: swearing and Elsie.

Elsie was ninety-three with Parkinson's. She lived in a care home, which had been raided by Harriet during an investigation into abuse of the elderly. Elsie had been in better shape then, standing with the help of a frame in the pink, over-heated hallway. She'd regarded Harriet with beady, critical eyes – they all saw it. It was as if the team stood still, as Harriet and the old girl locked on to each other. *Some enchanted evening.*

Elsie shuffled into the room to be interviewed, her shins thick, the colour of pine in tan tights, chenille slippers on her rigid, calcified feet. Harriet asked Elsie if she had been mistreated by any of the staff at the home. 'Don't be *silly*,' Elsie barked, and Harriet had been momentarily chastened. The balance of power was all with Elsie, who snapped and criticised ('Ever done this before, dearie?'), but Harriet persisted. Nightgowns removed how? What if the soup was unfinished? And if you wet the bed?

Gradually it emerged that Elsie believed her forgetfulness merited the odd slap. Her shaking hands drove them mad, you see. She couldn't dress any more – well, that's bound to get their backs up. Who'd want to dress a scrawny old bird like me?

Harriet said to leave it there just for now, and she fled the room. When Manon next saw her, she was leaning against a panda car, smoking a cigarette, looking furious and tearful at the same time. This is what Manon likes most about Harriet – no, not likes, understands: she isn't on an even keel. She feels the work in every fibre and it hurts her.

'I'm going to shut that fucking place down,' she said, the cigarette tight between her fingers. 'And that manager's going to prison.'

Harriet got Elsie out of there by nightfall, much as she protested. The care home was taken over by new owners and the manager received a year's sentence for wilful neglect, which was suspended 'for previous good character', so she walked free, confirming all Harriet's suspicions that the courts are 'a fucking joke'.

Manon knows that Harriet, and most of their colleagues, cleave to the view that criminals either get off or get off lightly; that the system is stacked against the police. She's aware that if police officers were allowed to draw up the legislation, it would probably contain the words *'and throw away the key'*. What worries Manon is she's joining their ranks. It can often feel as if they're fighting a tide of filth and losing; you only needed to do a week in child protection to lose any liberal tendencies you ever had.

Harriet became Elsie's visiting daughter, because Elsie had no children of her own – she was twenty-five when the war took the boy she loved at Arras in 1940. His name was Teddy and she kept a photo of him by her bed, but Manon thought he was more an emblem of what had gone wrong. Elsie had had an abruption in her life. Grief had held her up, during which time she worked in a munitions factory and discovered how much she liked to work, when it had never really been an option before. When she emerged from mourning after the war, she found herself looking at a timer where the sand was running low.

'There were no men left,' she told Harriet, laughing. 'None who wanted an old spinster in her thirties like me, at any rate. It just never happened for me, the family thing.'

Harriet called on Elsie every week and Manon occasionally went with her, witnessing between them a conspiratorial warmth. Elsie looked at Harriet with mischievous eyes, saying, 'Thrash you this time.' They played cribbage, or bridge when they could make a four with other stooped residents in the care home, though death often intervened ('Wilf not here?' 'Not any more, no.'). Blackjack, beggar-my-neighbour, sudoku, and crosswords. Then, as Elsie became more vague – the shaking and the vagueness accompanying one another as if staying fixed in thought and deed was ungraspable – the games became more infantile: Guess Who?, Connect Four, puzzles, and pairs.

Elsie humanised Harriet, who had a tendency to be hard. She was the obligation that made her feel stretched and needed.

44

Her joyful complaint. That drunken night when Harriet had confided in Manon (her kindred spirit in singleness and childlessness), she said, 'When you don't have kids, everyone assumes you're some fucking ball-breaking career freak, but it's not like that. It's more, y'know, a cock-up. It's something that happened *to* me. Elsie gets that. Plus, I really fucking hope someone will visit me when I'm pissing my pants in a care home.'

Davy and Manon drive out of HQ car park in an unmarked car that wears its snow like a jaunty hat, but as soon as they turn out of the gates, they slow to a halt. The traffic is always terrible on Brampton Road, a permanent feature of their forays out on jobs, but this queue has been made worse by the diversions set up around Edith Hind's house on George Street, combined with considerable rubbernecking from the fine folk of Huntingdon. Davy taps on the steering wheel with his gloved hand, a marker to Manon that he is unperturbed.

'This'll take hours,' says Manon, slumping down into the passenger seat and wedging her feet onto the dashboard, her knees up. She has her phone in her lap, texting Bryony.

Can't do lunch. High-risk misper just blew up in my face. M

'Sarge,' says Davy.

'Hmmm?' she says, and she looks up to see Davy casting anxious glances at her feet and at the spotless fascia of his glove box.

'You couldn't—'

Her phone bleeps.

No worries. Am loving my court papers. Nothing cd tear me away. Not even pepper-flavoured water. B

45

'Sorry, what?' she says to Davy.

'Your feet,' he says, with another furtive glance at the offending boots, as if they might detonate.

'It's not even your car,' she says, her fingers working on her phone. But she takes her feet down.

Tomoz maybe. M

Is Harriet losing the plot?

Yep. Crapping herself. Victim's family mates with Galloway.

Holy Shit.

Yup.

At least your career isn't in cul-de-sac. May chew arm off if have to do more filing.

Go away, please, am in middle of Very Important Investigation.

All right, Mrs Big Tits. Laters. PS. It's always the uncle. Or the stepfather. Or the boyfriend. Or possibly a complete stranger.

'How was the date, by the way?' Davy asks.

They are moving now – *at last* – having turned off onto the A14 towards the Fenland village of March.

'Don't ask.'

'Can't have been that bad.'

'Can't it?'

'Well then, there'll be others – other responses to your ad.'

'It's not an ad, Davy. I'm not selling roller blinds. It's a profile.'

And what a work of fiction that 'about me' section is.

Genuine, easy-going. I love life and laughter, a bottle of wine with friends, cinema and walks in the countryside.
Passionate about what I do. Looking for someone to share all this amazing world has to offer.
Age: *35*
Looking for: *fun/a long-term relationship/let's see what happens*
Likes: *sunshine, the smell of fresh coffee, walks on the beach*
Dislikes: *unexpected items in bagging area*

Manon cut-and-pasted most of it from someone else's profile – a woman called Liz Temple from Berkhamsted, who claimed life was not about 'sheltering from the thunderstorms' but 'learning to dance in the rain'. Except the bagging area joke – that was Manon's and she was pretty pleased with it, feeling it made amusing reference to emotional baggage, of which there was a surfeit on the Internet.

Were she to tell the truth, her profile would go something like:

Misanthrope, staring down the barrel of childlessness.
Yawning ability to find fault. Can give off WoD (Whiff of Desperation). A vast, bottomless galaxy of loneliness. Educated: to an intimidating degree. Willing to hide this. Prone to tears. Can be needy. Often found Googling 'having a baby at 40'.
Age: *39*
Looking for: *book-reading philanthropist with psychotherapy*

47

training who can put up shelves. Can wear glasses (relaxed about this).
Dislikes: *most of the fucktards I meet on the Internet.*

'Mustn't give up, Sarge,' says Davy.

'Like I'd take relationship advice from you. Still treating you mean, is she?'

'She keeps me on my toes.'

'That's one way of putting it.'

Davy is twenty-six but seems still a boy; has been in the force since eighteen, and something about him is irresistible to Manon. He has this naive intensity – like an only child, neither at home with the adults nor one of the children – and those enormous ears always on the alert. His affable demeanour and positive outlook have earned him the nickname 'Silver' among the DCs. Silver Lining, the boy who's always looking on the bright side. He thinks the world might still come right if he just tries hard enough – which he does, all the time, mentoring at youth centres and looking out for every troubled child who crosses his path. But every silver lining has a cloud, and that cloud is Chloe.

Manon has seen them together more than once, though she and Davy never socialise outside the safety of office dos, Davy being of a different generation and this gulf becoming canyon-like outside the familiar hierarchies of work. One evening, however, they found themselves in the same pub, The Lord Protector on Mayfield Road. Manon was in a group from the station – a rowdy bunch, all pissed and telling terrible jokes ('Invisible man's at the door. Tell 'im I can't see 'im. Hahahahahaha.'); Davy sat in a quiet corner with Chloe. Table for two.

Manon had watched them as the hubbub went on around

her: Davy all animation, eyes on Chloe as if she were lit by some celestial cone, describing something to her. Chloe was looking over his shoulder, her face unmoving. She was a woman in a perpetual sulk and Davy was forever chivvying her out of it.

'Face like a slapped arse,' said Kim Delaney, looking across the room with Manon. 'Dunno what he sees in her.'

But to Manon it makes perfect sense. Davy's at his best when rectifying. He often comes into the office with a carrier bag destined for the youth centre where he volunteers – 'Choccy Weetos for Ryan', 'Rex needs socks' – and the brightness in his eyes tells her how much satisfaction this tenderness gives him. Warming up a frozen, miserable girlfriend is his destiny. If Davy got together with someone indomitably cheerful . . . well, Manon doesn't know what he'd do with himself. End it all, probably.

'I believe this leads to the abode,' he says, as they turn down a wooded track. Bare tree branches bend over the car and verges rise up on either side. The sky seems to darken as the countryside burgeons around them.

'Drop the Shotley guff, will you?' says Manon, irritably. Davy loves the jargon they inculcate at police school. He's forever saying the suspect 'has made good his escape' with his 'ill-gotten gains'.

'Bit peckish?' says Davy, reaching into his pocket for a rich tea biscuit, which he hands to her.

'This place is a bit Hansel and Gretel, isn't it?' says Manon, eating the biscuit and peering up at the menacing tree fingers that reach for each other above the windscreen. The car is rocking over stones.

'Shouldn't be far down this track,' says Davy.

The track is bordered by logs, sawn ends forming a honeycomb

49

grid. Their tyres plough through mud, which splinters with ice in places. The light lowers a notch, soaked up by the seaweed-gloss leaves on a row of bushes – rhododendrons, Davy says – ribboned with snow.

He is hunched towards the windscreen as they emerge in front of an ivy-clad house, broader than it is tall, with a pitch-roofed porch and a carport to the side. The house is ensconced in countryside, the woodland growing denser and darker to the sides and behind them.

With their arrival, a sensor light has clicked on above the front door – a rectangle of fire in Manon's eyes. The ivy running up the walls of the house is straining in at the windows, whose wooden frames are painted greyish green.

'Glad I'm not Polsa having to search this place,' she says.

Davy turns off the engine so that all they can hear is its ticking and a blackbird, its lonely cry seeming to tell them the place is deserted.

Manon pats along the high shelf of architrave in the porch, and there it is, among dust and dead insects – the key. She puts it in an evidence bag, then uses Edith's set in the lock. The brass knob, green-gold, is icy even through her latex gloves, and its round skirt-plate rattles loosely. They step into a black-and-white tiled hall with slate-blue walls. The house smells of wood smoke and the outdoors – an oxygenated, muddy smell that is not quite damp. An umbrella stand is filled with brollies and walking sticks, and to their left – Manon peers around the door, painted mustard yellow – is a boot room, wallpapered with Victorian images of birds as if in a shooting lodge. She squats next to a line of wellingtons – one black pair and three green – and touches the mud that cakes them.

'Davy?' she calls, and he appears by her side. 'Does this look fresh to you?'

50

She swaps places with him and follows the hallway out to a baronial-scale lounge. The ceiling is double height, the walls blotchy with blood-red lime wash. There is a grand open fire-place with white stone surround – the sort you could rest an elbow on when you came in from fishing in the Fenland rivers. A charred black scar runs up the back of the brickwork in the hearth. Manon squats beside the grate but it contains only the cold, crocodile husks of burnt-through logs.

The fire is surrounded on three sides by red sofas patterned with fleur-de-lys and collapsing with age and gentility. She can imagine the Hinds reading their Dickens hardbacks or their subscriptions to the *New York Review of Books*, fire roaring and some string music playing in the background.

From the lounge is a staircase leading up to a minstrels' gallery and off it, the bedrooms. Manon is feeling her way, the house cast in painterly shadows. Swathes of muddy colours curling up the staircase or viewed through an open bedroom door: mustard, rose, slate blues and grey, one leading on to the next. She pushes open a door to a vast bedroom – Ian and Miriam's, she assumes, because it is furnished with a grand French bed, its headboard framed in ornate gold and uphol-stered with grey linen. There is an imposingly dark French armoire, too, its bottom drawer slightly open. Manon walks to the window – a long cushion in the same grey linen has created a window seat with two Liberty-print pink blossom pillows at either end. From here she can see the front drive and their car, and she has an urge to go towards it, to drive away.

She jumps at the sound of a door slamming and her heart thuds in the shadows of the mansard window.

'Boss?' calls Davy, entering the room.

'Have you checked all the downstairs rooms?'

'I have.'

'Right, well, let's check the rest of the rooms up here and the outbuildings. Then Polsa can take it from there.'

'Not a bad little bolt-hole,' says Davy.

Manon shivers. 'Gives me the creeps.'

HELENA

They've left her waiting in interview room two and in the waiting, she can't help but rehearse what she'll say, though she fears the rehearsal will make her appear guilty, like trying to make your face seem natural when going through passport control in Moscow or Tehran – the more you think about it, the more rictus your expression becomes. Not that she's ever been to those places, but even in the queue at Brittany Ferries she has made a point of catching the immigration officer's eye and smiling, so as to say, 'You won't find any contraband in *my* backpack.'

The strip light above Helena's head fizzes then plinks, as if there's an insect dying inside it. She's always rehearsing, having imaginary conversations in her head which pre-empt real encounters – like she's rehearsed her return to Dr Young's couch after the Christmas break and how she'll tell him all that has happened with Edith. She used to rehearse her sessions so much that when she first started with Dr Young, it had taken quite a long time to get her to diverge from the script and 'allow things to emerge', as he put it.

53

Helena hears a door slam somewhere in the corridor, brisk footsteps, and her heart quickens at the prospect of someone coming in. She sits upright, brushes at her skirt, but the footsteps clack past the door and drift away. She slouches again. They are keeping her waiting deliberately in this empty room with only a Formica table with metal legs and blue plastic chairs – two on the other side of the desk to where she is sitting, so presumably there will be two of them. Outnumbered by detectives. She's never met a detective before.

'Hello,' she mouths, picturing herself half rising and putting out a hand. 'I've never met a detective before.' Then she catches her reflection in a pane of brown-coloured mirror set in the wall, her lips moving soundlessly (or like a psychiatric patient, depending on who's watching). *Is anyone watching?*

'I wanted to get Edith home safely,' she murmurs, her eyes flicking to the mirrored wall. 'I never imagined that home wouldn't be safe, that something could happen to Edith *after* I had dropped her home to George Street.' No, saying that seems to implicate Will. She must phrase it some other way. Just go back to the beginning. Keep the narrative simple.

Edith had shouted, 'Geronimo!' and tipped back another tequila shot, one of many she drank at The Crown that night. Then the barman rang last orders.

Helena told Edith they should go, it was 11.30 p.m., they'd miss the bus back to Huntingdon otherwise. And anyway, she was tired – hot, tired, and fed up. The Crown was heaving; she was jostled by the crowd – townies, rowers, Corpus post-grads like herself and Edith.

'What are you studying, Miss Reed?' she imagines being asked.

'Psychology. I'm a psychology fellow. My PhD is on gratification and its links to obesity.'

The door opens and a woman walks in – dishevelled, with a mass of curls. Behind her is a young man, about Helena's age, with an open face and friendly, sticky-out ears.

'Sorry to keep you waiting,' says the woman, holding out her hand. 'I'm Detective Sergeant Manon Bradshaw; this is Detective Constable Davy Walker. We just need to ask you a few questions.'

'No, I mean, yes, of course.' Her heart beats so hard she fears it might be audible. While they set down notepads and fiddle about with a recording device, Helena puts a hand to her cheek, hoping the heat she can feel there is not visible. 'I don't know anything,' she blurts.

'If you just wait a moment,' says DS Bradshaw. 'We can begin once I get this machine set.'

A long beep is emitted from the recording device.

'Most postgrads live in Cambridge, don't they?' asks DS Bradshaw.

'Yes. Most, but not all. There are apartments for married couples and single rooms provided by the college, but we – Edith and Will, and later myself – moved out towards the end of our undergraduate degrees. To Huntingdon.'

Edith and Will, and later myself. It would be foolish to mention how they teased her about her own move to Huntingdon. Edith was always teasing.

'It's cheaper,' Helena remembers saying to them, rather defensively. 'And I like the quiet, y'know? Being in halls can be so . . . claustrophobic. I'll definitely get more work done here and the commute's easy-peasy.'

'It's all right, Hels,' Edith had said, not even looking up from chopping vegetables. 'We know you're our stalker.'

55

'Wouldn't your Christmas do normally be in the college? In Corpus Christi?' the detective asks.

'Well, yes and no. The graduate bar can be a bit damp. Jason – Jason Farrer, he's an English PhD like Edith – wanted something a bit livelier. They can be a bit socks-and-sandals, the postgrad lot.'

'Socks and sandals?'

'Yes, you know, drilling down into the minutiae – sex life of chives, that kind of thing. All very nerdy. They're not the best at letting their hair down. Jason arranged the Christmas do – he chose The Crown.'

'And Edith, how did she seem?'

'Well, drunk, to be honest. She wanted to do karaoke. She was doing tequila shots. I told her we should go – this was about 11.30 p.m., last orders.' Helena stops.

DS Bradshaw waits. 'How did Edith react? Did she want to leave?'

Helena thinks back to Edith sticking out her tongue in Helena's direction, then swivelling on the balls of her feet to the makeshift dance-floor-cum-karaoke stage.

'Miss Reed?'

'Yeah, no, she was fine. She gave us a terrible rendition of "Use Somebody" by the Kings of Leon.' Helena stops again. She must be careful where this ventures.

DS Bradshaw is looking intently at her, waiting. 'Something you're remembering? About the evening?'

'I'll tell you who was sniffing around that night,' says Helena. 'Graham Garfield, Edith's Director of Studies. Asked me where Will was. Bit predatory.'

'Predatory how?' asks DS Bradshaw.

'Well, he's always hanging around the students, y'know? Even though they're half his age. He was watching Edith, watching

56

her singing, and he just had this look. He saw how out of it she was.'

'And what did you tell him?'

'I told him Will was away for the weekend, but that things were – are – solid between them. Edith and Will, I mean.'

MANON

'And you say you got the guided bus home?' Manon says.

Helena Reed is shifting about, straightening, crossing and uncrossing her legs. 'That's right,' she says. 'You know, the one that runs along railway tracks part of the way, between Cambridge and Huntingdon.'

She wears a coral scarf looped tightly about her neck and a camel cardigan buttoned up – a rather Parisian, precise attire. Manon has an irrational mistrust of very tidy-looking people. They work too hard at concealment, and besides, she doesn't understand how they pull it off. Manon seems to emerge from her flat, even at the start of the day, with a rogue bulging shirt button showing a flash of bra, or a smear unnoticed in the half-light of the bedroom (she often finds herself wetting a bit of toilet roll in the second floor toilets and going at a stain, only to lace it with beads of wet tissue).

Helena's knees are pinned together and her pencil skirt is smoothed tight (Manon covets the idea of the pencil skirt, much as she covets the idea of being a tidy person, but hasn't the knees for it). Helena Reed is held in, Manon decides, and rather concerned with what others see, though as soon as Manon passes this judgement, she wonders if it isn't genetic – the whole personal tidiness thing. One is destined to become one's mother, after all. This thought makes her smile to herself – there are worse things.

'I led Edith off the bus and walked her back to George Street,' Helena is saying. 'It was snowing and a bit slippy – she was tipsy and rather giggly, so I had to hold on to her. And when we got to the cottage, I got her keys out of her bag to let her in.'

'And you closed the door behind you?'

'Yes, it self-locks when you close it – a Chubb, you know what I mean. I led her to the kitchen, helped her to take off her coat—'

'This was the green parka, with the fur trim?'

'Yes.'

'What did you talk about?'

'The night at the pub, the people who were there. She was flirting with Jason Farrer, the guy I mentioned? Bit of a letch, in my view. I s'pose I told her off a bit.'

'Did you have an argument?'

'Not an argument, no. She shrugged it off, really; told me I was being an old prude.'

'Did you or Edith get out two wine glasses while you were there, to have another drink?'

'No, God, no. She'd had more than enough and I was tired. I didn't even take my coat off.'

'Did she seem anxious, frightened of anything, or anyone?'

'No, she was happy – drunk and silly. If anything, it was me who was grouchy.'

'Did she talk about Will Carter at all?'

'Not really. At one point she said I was "as bad as Will", meaning boring, I s'pose.'

59

'Edith's mother mentioned a certain cooling between Edith and Will. Do you think Edith wanted to end the relationship?'

'Not to my knowledge. She complained about him sometimes, but that's normal, isn't it? If you're suggesting that Will had something to do with Edith disappearing, that's mad. He'd never—'

'Just answer the question, Miss Reed.'

'No, she didn't mention breaking up with him, not to me.'

'Did they fight – physically?'

'No, God, no. Look, it wasn't like that. Will wouldn't say boo to a goose. His worse crime is that he can be a bit dull.'

'Were you aware that Edith kept a lot of cash in the house?'

'The MoneyGram transfers? Yes. We all thought it was a bad idea, but Edith's a bit of a warrior in that way. She won't be budged.'

'Did you notice any cash lying around in the house on Saturday night?'

'No. It's not like she leaves wads of twenties by the kettle. She isn't stupid. She hides it in various different places. Will will know better than me. You know, a tin in the kitchen cupboard, another in the bathroom. That sort of thing.'

'Who else knows about the money?'

'Only her friends. Not anyone who would rob her, I don't think.'

'Going back to Jason – you say Edith was flirting with him. Flirting how?'

Helena frowns. 'You know, giggling with him. I . . . I don't want to . . . I don't want to land her in it.'

'I think we've gone beyond that, Miss Reed. Edith has been missing for thirty-five hours now. Time is very much of the essence.'

'So, OK, Edith and Jason went outside the pub. I don't know what they were doing, maybe just having a cigarette.'

'How long were they outside together?'

'Oh, not long. Five minutes. I know because I was casting about for her. I wanted to leave. She came back in, I had her coat ready, and we left pretty much straight away.'

'Thank you, Miss Reed. If you wouldn't mind waiting here for a bit longer, we may have some further questions for you shortly.'

'Thank you for coming in, Mr Farrer,' says Manon, setting her clipboard down on the table in interview room three while Davy fiddles with the recording device, saying the date and time and names of everyone in the room.

Jason Farrer leans back in his chair, legs wide apart, one elbow bent behind him on the chair's backrest. He wears a yellow knitted waistcoat with leather buttons, brown baggy corduroys, and a checked shirt. His hair hangs in a foppish wave across one side of his face. He straightens as she takes up her seat opposite him.

'Look, I want to help in any way I can.' His aristocratic accent comes as a shock – surprising to hear and awkward to deliver. He is barely moving his mouth, the words escaping out the sides.

'Bit unusual, isn't it, for postgrads like Edith and Will to live outside the town – as far as Huntingdon, I mean?' says Manon.

'Not just unusual, practically unheard of. Everyone lives in Leckhampton, where the dining room is and the bar. But they're like that, Edith and Will. Superior. Like being out on a limb.'

She's wrong-footed by his candour. Charmers like him normally fight hard to mask themselves with affable decency towards absolutely everyone. Then he leans forward towards her across the desk, his hands clasped, and she realises he's drunk. Rolling drunk. The ethanol rises off him in an energetic dance with the air.

'They have a project,' he says.

'I'm sorry?'

'To live truthfully. Grow food, cook wholesomely, cycle, or chug along in that trumped-up lawnmower of hers. I think they thought student digs would corrupt them. Course, her father pays for everything – the house, the *evil* gas and electricity. She is Will's flexible friend in so many ways.'

'Who's driving this project then – Edith or Will?'

'Oh, they're both really into it. The aim is to live a simple but, I s'pose, pure life. They called it living truthfully, which made me want to self-harm. I thought it was vanity. You have to understand – Edith and Will are the most beautiful specimens Cambridge will ever produce. When they got together in our final year, it was like Kate-Middleton-Barbie had found Ken.'

'Sorry, I don't get it. How is growing fresh food vanity?'

'Life's a competition,' says Farrer. 'Their superior lifestyle was their quickest route to looking down on people. I mean, that's why people do it, isn't it? Grow loads of chard? It isn't because they *want* chard. I mean, no one *buys* chard. It's so they can tell someone else they grow chard. And that someone will go away worrying about the fact they don't grow chard.'

'Except you.'

'I've never wanted to grow chard.'

They look at each other. Farrer is slumped, lolling with the drink. He lets out a little girlish giggle, like gas bubbles escaping – then puts a hand in front of his mouth to stifle them.

'You do realise you're being questioned in relation to the disappearance and possible abduction of a young woman,' says Manon.

'Sorry,' says Farrer, another little giggle escaping involuntarily. 'I find it hard to take anything seriously. Look, they used to bang on about it endlessly.' His words are not quite slurring but rolling up against each other, like waves swelling out at sea. 'You know, "Here's some organic muffins I made." "Will is at home, fashioning us a table out of reclaimed crutches." It was tiresome.'

Manon nods.

'Still, it's not enough to murder someone, is it?' says Farrer. 'I mean, you don't think Edith was abducted because she had a curly kale glut, do you?'

'You don't seem very concerned,' says Manon.

'That's me all over.'

'Can we go back to Saturday night at The Crown? You were with Edith at the bar.'

'Yes.'

'And what made the two of you go outside?'

'She put her mouth next to my ear and whispered, "Let's go outside, Farrer." Very sexy it was, too.'

'Had she been flirting with you in the run-up to that night?'

'God, no. Edith always treated me with the utter contempt I deserve. That's what made it so exciting when she came on to me.'

'So you went outside. Then what happened?'

'Well, lots of heavy breathing. She was up against me, against the wall of the pub. It was freezing and dark. She was whispering sweet nothings in my ear. Then we had . . . Well, I'll protect her honour, if you don't mind. Then she suddenly stopped and went back inside.'

'I'm sorry, we're going to need some detail. Did you kiss?'

'I'll say.'

'Did it go further than that?'

Farrer smiles at Manon but she has done too many of these interviews to be squeamish.

'Digital penetration?' she asks.

'You make it sound so romantic,' he says.

'Answer the question, please.'

'Yes.'

'Consensual?'

'I had given my consent, yes,' he says, giggling again.

'How did Edith call a halt?'

'She pulled my hand out from her knickers, straightened her clothes, and went back inside the pub.'

'Did you follow her?'

'No, I didn't.'

'You didn't want to pursue her, to finish what she started?'

'Yes, I can see how you'd think that,' he says thoughtfully. 'But I'm not really the type to pursue anything. I don't really have it in me.'

'You're doing an English PhD at Cambridge,' says Manon. 'You must be able to pursue things rather vigorously.'

'Gosh. Vigorous. What a terrific word, Sergeant. It's certainly never been used to describe me. But you're right, of course. Poetry is my secret weapon. Give me a spot of Gerard Manley Hopkins and I soar. In all other areas of my life, I'm a total fuck-up. No one believes I'll finish my PhD, least of all me.'

'How did you get home from the pub?'

'I walked – well, fell, really – down Grange Road to my rooms in Leckhampton House. Porter'll confirm it, and no doubt some of your evil big brother cameras have me weaving about the streets. And then I spent the night with the lovely Ros or Rosie – at least, I think that's her name – who happened to be in the kitchen when I got back. Your chaps are checking with her now, I believe.'

'And Edith went back in to find Helena Reed.'

'The Limpet. Whenever Edith turns around, the Limpet's sure to be there.'

'How d'you mean?'

'Ask yourself why Helena lives in Huntingdon. I mean, Edith and Will, they're cocks with a project. But Helena? What's she doing there? Bit suffocating, wouldn't you say?'

'Go on.'

'Ask the Limpet what Edith gave her as an early Christmas present.'

'Why don't you stop beating around the bush, Mr Farrer, and tell me what you mean.'

He stops, looks down to the floor by his side, his arms dangling, and Manon wonders if he's going to be sick. He has the soaked-in drunkenness of someone who's been marinating in it for some time – days, probably.

'They were at it. Edith told me – when we went outside the pub together. Of course, it could be she was just trying to turn me on.'

'What did she say exactly?'

'She said she'd been having it off with Helena and now she couldn't get rid of her.' He lets out another high-pitched giggle.

'Did you expect this type of behaviour from Edith?' asks Manon.

'Well, no, it wasn't typical. But Cambridge is full of people toeing the line, swotting in libraries to please Daddy, and then rebelling and taking up crack or throwing themselves out of a tower. You know we actually have a *day* called Suicide Sunday. It's a fucked-up place, once you get under the skin of it. I figured Edith had just freaked out like the rest of us.'

The adrenalin has swept away Manon's tiredness as she and Harriet pummel down the stairs towards interview room two, back to Helena Reed.

'Is he reliable?' Harriet asks, pushing through the double doors.

'No, not at all. He's drunk and feckless. But I don't think he's got any reason to lie about this.'

'Unless he's covering his own tracks.'

'Let's just see what she has to say.'

Helena looks up at them as they enter the room. Kim is standing by the wall with her hands clasped behind her back.

'I told you, we're friends,' says Helena. She unloops her coral scarf and places it on her knees. The colour is high in her cheeks. 'I've known her since our first day at Corpus. Sorry, may I have a drink of water?'

'Just friends?' asks Harriet, leaning both elbows on the table and scrutinising Helena.

'I don't know what you mean,' she says. She looks up as Kim places a plastic cup in front of her. 'Thank you.'

'Jason Farrer says you and Edith were lovers,' says Harriet.

'Well, Jason Farrer's lying,' she says. 'He's not exactly trustworthy.'

'He says Edith told him, when they went outside the pub together.'

She is looking wildly now at the two of them sitting opposite her, and Manon senses she cannot see them. Her skin has taken on a sweaty sheen.

'Oh God,' she whispers, covering her entire face with her hands.

'Were you jealous when Edith went outside with Jason Farrer?' asks Harriet.

Helena keeps her face covered.

'Did you confront Edith about it when you got home to George Street? Things get a bit heated?'

'No, no, no,' she says, still with a hand shielding her eyes, her face directed at the door, away from their gaze. 'It wasn't

66

like that . . . It was . . . I don't know how to explain it to you because I don't understand it myself.'

'Helena, do you know what has happened to Edith?' asks Harriet.

'No, I don't. I swear I don't.'

'Do you think Will Carter found out about your affair?'

'I don't think so, no.'

'How long have you been lovers?' asks Manon gently.

'Lovers?' says Helena with a soft laugh. 'You make it sound so enchanting. It was one night – well, a night and a day – it happened twice, that's all. A mistake, a terrible mistake. The first time she seemed affectionate, at least. She said, "It's always been you." But then, last Wednesday, she was out of it. I couldn't even tell if she loved or hated me. Please, I don't want anyone to know.' She starts to cry. 'My parents . . .'

'It's all right,' says Manon. 'We're asking you solely for the purposes of this investigation. There is no reason for your parents or anyone else to find out. Did Edith instigate it, the relationship?'

Helena nods, the back of her hand to her mouth, her chin trembling.

'And when was this?'

'A week ago. I mean, the Saturday before this one.'

'So that would be the tenth?'

'I s'pose. She came to my flat late – about 2 a.m. – she was drunk and she, well, she kissed me.'

'And did things progress?'

'Yes, but I've never been with a woman before,' Helena says in a rush.

'And after that Saturday?' says Harriet.

'She came again on Wednesday in the day. She was much more distracted, much more . . . not herself at all.'

67

'Not herself how?'

'Sort of reckless. Kamikaze. I felt as if she was using me, as if she hated me. She wouldn't look me in the eye. She'd brought a bottle of wine and we ended up in bed. When I said, "What about Will?" she snapped, "It doesn't fucking matter." Then she left very suddenly, as if she'd changed her mind.

'Did you want things to continue? Is that why you went home with her on Saturday after the pub?'

'I don't know what I wanted. I felt, feel, confused. Chewed up and spat out, if I'm honest. I feel . . . mortified. I never thought anyone would find out. I swear to you, I left her in her kitchen. We didn't even talk about it. I didn't even have the guts to mention it. I wish I'd left her in Cambridge now. I wish I'd come back to Huntingdon by myself.'

HELENA

Standing on the station steps, she blinks into the low sun, which flashes off the car roofs like knives. She can see slices of Will Carter striding towards her – his hair, his chin, a black donkey coat and scarf, but not his eyes.

Will bedded down in her lounge in the early hours of this morning, after his police interviews were done, and when she'd gone in to draw the curtains around 7 a.m., while he was in the shower, the room smelled thickly of unfamiliar male. She folded his sleeping bag and laid the pillow neatly on top, and when he came in to get dressed, she retreated to the kitchen to brew them a pot of strong coffee. They sat at the breakfast bar, hollow-eyed, going over the night's events.

He won't want to stay with her after this. She can't make out his expression – is there mistrust already? – because of the distorting shards of sun. She can hardly breathe at the thought of what he is about to find out. He jogs up the station steps.

'Are you all right?' he asks, taking her elbow. 'You look awful.'

'It's just,' she says, 'a bit rough in there. Scary. What's happening.'

'I know. They want to re-interview me for some reason, God knows why. I've told them everything about five times already.'

'I guess new stuff keeps cropping up,' she says. She is grateful to the flash and glare for obscuring his face.

'Well,' he says, 'I'll see you back at the flat. Is it OK if I stay another night with you? Our house is cordoned off.'

'If you want to – why don't you see how you feel?' She puts both hands over her forehead to create a visor. 'Listen, Will, the police – they're saying all sorts, trying to poke about and stuff. Don't listen to them – I mean, not all of it can be true.'

'What sort of things?'

'I'm just saying, some of it is just trying to get a rise out of you, y'know? See how you'll react.'

'I don't understand,' he says.

'Doesn't matter, forget it.'

'Look, I better go in. I'll catch up with you after.'

Helena strides headlong into the light, taking wide steps because the tarmac is flat and predictable, and with some steps the sun recedes and she can see, only for it to flash off a wing mirror or window – like peering through the slats of a blind. He'll be going into an interview room, greeting the officers who will tell him what she and Edith have done together behind his back. He might look back towards the station steps, to where they have only just spoken, run a hand through his hair in shock.

A tree provides welcome shade and she can see gridlock on the road into Huntingdon. She reaches the concrete underpass, the sun slanting against its elephant grey-green hulk, almost painterly. The cars are bumper to bumper into town, and as she reaches the top of George Street, she can sense a frisson in the air. Perhaps it is the drivers craning to see what the hold-up is; the hooting of horns, as they grow tired of the delay; the slowing pedestrians on the pavement. Helena has to weave through a throng as she nears the house itself and then she is in front of the familiar gate, which she has pushed open without thinking so many times, now cordoned with police tape and guarded by a WPC in a fluorescent windcheater and regulation black trousers, her radio crackling with blurred voices.

Ten feet further down the road is a group of men – they appear from this distance to be a black huddle, like a murder of crows landed on crumbs, but as she gets nearer, Helena sees there are one or two women among them. She sees the cameras slung over their shoulders like handbags and the note-pads. They are laughing, at ease. One of them smiles at Helena as she edges past them on the pavement and she increases her pace, pushing her chin down into her scarf. She edges around the next group – two women with toddlers playing about their legs, and a pensioner with a square wheelie shopper. 'Was at the university, apparently,' is all she catches, to which one of the women says, 'Terrible.'

Helena stops herself from breaking in to a run. Her heart pounds at the thought of the women turning to look at her in horror, their faces ghoulish with opprobrium, the cameras pointed at her with sudden piercing focus.

Her breathing returns to a more normal rhythm once she is safely inside her flat, until she becomes aware of the beeps coming from the answering machine in the lounge. She unwinds her scarf. Perhaps it is Dr Young. Perhaps he has heard about Edith's disappearance on the news and has rung to check she is all right. *Beep.* She holds the scarf against her chest. Or her father. If it's her father, she can call him back, tell him what's happened and ask to come home for the weekend to Bromley, get away from all the intrusion and the questions. *Beep.*

71

What if it's Edith herself, explaining away all the confusion in that breezy way she has – 'Lighten up, Hels' – like the time she'd rung on the intercom at 2 a.m. Helena answered the door irritably in her tartan pyjamas, and when she saw Edith swaying there, said, 'Is anything wrong?'

Edith, breathing tannin from some Shiraz or Merlot, her gums stained black, giggling and pushing her way through to the lounge. Edith's tiny lace bra was lilac with a diamante stud at its centre and so pretty against her skin. Her bones were delicate, breakable, her breasts neat and perfectly round, her arms beautifully thin. Helena found she could circle her thumb and middle finger perfectly around Edith's wrist like a bracelet. And Edith held out to her in those lovely hands the promise of excitement and discovery, as if the only thing holding them both back was the smallness of Helena's horizons.

'Let's loosen you up a bit, Hel,' Edith murmured, biting at the corner of Helena's mouth while her hands worked down the buttons on her pyjamas.

Helena walks slowly to the lounge, placing her scarf on the end of the sofa, unbuttoning her coat. She presses play on the answering machine.

'Hi, this is a message for Helena Reed. It's Bethan Jones from the *Mail on Sunday*. We're doing a special piece on Edith Hind and I wondered if you wanted to tell us, you know, what she's really like – as her best friend. It'd really bring the piece to life. I'm sure you're worried about Edith and obviously coverage like this raises her profile, so if you wanted to talk, you know, to help the police appeal, then you can get in touch with me on—. I really look forward to hearing from you, Helena. Thanks, then. It's Bethan Jones, by the way.'

DAVY

He lowers his head to the left, feeling the long stretch down the side of his neck, then to the other side. His body is beginning to take umbrage at having been in a broadly vertical position for more than twenty hours. Evening now – a full night and day on shift – and they're waiting for the 6 p.m. briefing. Only last week he'd heard a radio programme about research showing the toll night shifts take on the body, tearing through its natural rhythms, giving you cancer.

He increases the stretch by placing a hand on the top of his head and pulling gently. Even while doing this he wants to go to sleep. One side, then the other. He sees the department tilted on its side: Kim pouring herself some stewed coffee, Stuart sitting next to Colin, Harriet and Manon up front by the whiteboard, all of them gathering lugubriously, waiting for Fergus. Things are heating up in the press office.

Thirty-six hours missing. You'd expect a body or a firm sighting by now, or an injured girl, limping away from whatever trauma has befallen her. But this? Murkier and murkier it's getting, and Davy doesn't like the look of it.

73

He's just come from interview room three, where Will Carter kept running a confused hand through his hair and saying, 'Edith? And Helena?' As if he and Manon had totally lost their marbles. 'No,' Carter mumbled. 'No, I don't think that can be right.'

'Helena confirmed it to us,' Manon said, without nearly as much sympathy as Davy would have liked.

He's seen it all before, of course, but that doesn't make it any less depressing – watching people reassess their entire surroundings as if buildings have been moved or reconfigured, roads diverted. The people they think they know have hidden lives: other women, other men, money stolen, debts hidden, a previous life in a cartel or on the game, children fathered in secret. It exhausts as well as fascinates him, churning it all up with their big stubby stick. Can't you all just keep it simple, he wants to sigh. Can't you keep it buttoned, keep your fists out of it, stop drinking, stop *shagging*? Isn't life complicated enough?

And here was Will Carter, bewildered. He wasn't standing up all of a sudden, like most of them did, trying to turn the table over and shouting, 'You're having a fucking laugh!' or kicking a chair. No, he was rather genteelly running a hand through his hair, saying, 'Edith and Helena? Seriously?' And just looking mildly shocked.

'Looking back,' Manon said to Carter, and Davy thought, go easy, now, the man's had a shock, 'can you see evidence of that relationship?'

'We were always together, always close, the three of us. I never questioned it. Shows what a fool I am.' And Carter laughed in a self-deprecating way, which once again made Davy think, you poor chap.

Manon didn't seem to share his sensitivity. 'Perhaps you

74

did know, Mr Carter,' she said. 'And became incensed by it. Jealous. Perhaps you came back early to confront Edith about it.'

'No. I honestly didn't know. And it makes me look like a total chump. And I know there are people who think you should know – you know, the inner workings of your nearest and dearest. But the fact is, if they don't tell you . . .'

'Did you have the feeling that Edith was going to leave you?'

Christ, Davy thought, give the man a sodding break.

Carter blew out through his cheeks. 'No, no I didn't. Are you going to tell me I'm wrong about that too? Listen, I can live with infidelity. A fling with Helena – it wouldn't change how I feel.' And his eyes brimmed with tears, fat droplets swelling to their bursting point but remaining just there, on the brink, beneath his slate eyes with their brown flecks. 'But please don't tell me she didn't – doesn't – love me any more. Please don't do that, not with her missing.'

Davy had put a hand on Manon's arm.

'No, of course not,' said Manon softly.

And Davy exhaled, feeling reassured she would not go in and sock him with the Jason Farrer fumble. One infidelity at a time, eh.

'Money,' Harriet says, bending her middle finger down in her new list of priorities. 'Edith didn't use banks. There was no cash in the house when we searched it. Now that either means Edith spent it all, or it was on her when she was abducted, or it was stolen and that her disappearance is the consequence of an aggravated burglary. Nigel, where are we with CCTV from the Post Office on the first of December?'

'Owner doesn't know how to burn it onto a DVD,' says Nigel.

'Well, go down there and do it for him,' says Manon. She and Harriet exchange irritable glances.

Nigel shrugs. He's been destroyed by life with newborn twins, thinks Davy, and now he's too tired even to take umbrage. Have a dig, his dead eyes seem to say, I don't care, as long as I can lie down.

'Manon, can you take us through Will's journey to Stoke and back, please?' says Harriet.

'We've got him travelling to Stoke, as he described, on Friday evening. He's picked up by ANPR at three points on his outward journey and obviously his mother confirms his stay.'

'Well, she would, wouldn't she?' mutters Harriet. 'Sorry, carry on.'

'She says he left her house in Stoke at 5.30 p.m. on Sunday evening. He says he took a longer route home because of Sunday roadworks, which means his journey took closer to three hours, getting him back to George Street at 8.30 p.m. He then spent half an hour searching the house for Edith, calling various people such as Helena Reed, before phoning her parents, and then us at 9 p.m. Now, we haven't got that return journey on camera. Might be that the cameras are out on this route, we're checking that, or that he was tailgated by a lorry or something, or that mud splashed on his plates, which prevented a reading—'

'Or that he was at home murdering his girlfriend,' snorts Stuart, with rather more confidence than is merited for a first day in the office, if you ask Davy, which no one ever does.

'Ah, Fergus,' says Harriet. 'The floor's all yours.'

Fergus Kelly, a neat man in spectacles, never a speck on his suit. He has worked in the press office for ten years, including through the mayhem of Soham, which shook him more than the rest of them because it laid waste to half his contacts and all the unsaid niceties that had previously governed the flow of information.

'So, the tabloids are well and truly on to this now,' Fergus says, pushing his glasses up his nose. He has a fresh outbreak of acne on his chin, incongruous for a man in his forties, but understandable when you combined stress with the heavily refined carbohydrates stocked in the canteen. One of his daughters has cerebral palsy. Davy doesn't know what's made him think of this, but something about Fergus being under pressure doesn't seem fair. 'Obviously we can use the press interest to flush out information, but we need to control it – all enquiries must go through the press office. The Hinds have agreed to do a press conference at 11 a.m. tomorrow and we may wheel Will Carter out to see how much he sweats. Obviously, in the first days, the press tend to be very helpful in promoting the police line. It's after a couple of days,' he rubs the sweat at his brow, 'when there's nothing new to report, they can become quite . . .' He coughs into his fist. 'It's important there are no leaks,' he adds, making eye contact with every member of the team, especially the new recruit, in a way that is pleading rather than authoritative. 'And that we stay in control, as I say, of the flow of information.'

MANON

Manon runs her tray along the counter, looking into rectangular metal pans of beans, sausages, watery mushrooms, tomatoes from a tin and scrambled eggs that have congealed into a solid square. A permanent breakfast offering in a lightless room, at 8 p.m. on a Monday evening, for people who have ceased to observe normal day and night patterns.

'Hello, missy,' says Larry from behind the counter. He is from Gabon. His name can't be Larry, but he allows it, this lazy Anglicising of his name. 'You look tired, dahling. Is long shift?'

Larry is smiling at her. He is always smiling, even though he works punishing hours on minimum wage, serving cheap food to an almost entirely white Cambridgeshire police force. Occasionally she hears him speak a beautiful African French to a female colleague behind that divisive counter. Manon often resolves to ask him about Gabon and how he came to Huntingdon, but there never seems to be a right time.

'Big case, Larry. No rest for the wicked. Beans and sausages, please.'

She takes her tray to an empty table and looks up at the television, which is bracketed near the ceiling. Sky News is rolling out a stream on Edith Hind's disappearance. The red ticker along the base of the screen reads: *Huntingdon latest: 24-year-old Cambridge student Edith Hind missing. Father is Sir Ian Hind, physician to the Royal Family.*

She goes to get the remote control from another table. Around the room are a smattering of officers on the case or supplying auxiliary support, including Stuart, who has a habit of catching Manon's eye in a way she finds faintly inappropriate. Davy is a couple of tables away. He picks up his tray and moves over to Manon's table, looking expectantly at the telly as she flicks over to Channel 4+1 for the news.

'Officers say they are very concerned about a twenty-four-year-old woman who went missing from her home in Huntingdon on Saturday night,' says the presenter, 'very concerned' being code for 'we think she's dead'. 'As Cambridgeshire Police launch a manhunt, we have this report.'

Their home affairs correspondent is stood in the grey slush outside Edith's house. The blackness of the winter night is lit around him, white puffs emerging on his breath and flurries of sleet blowing about behind his head.

'Police are investigating what happened to Edith Hind after she got home from a party in Cambridge on Saturday night.' Manon saws into a processed sausage, its meat sickening-pale. Purest eyelid and spine, she thinks. 'The postgraduate student was shown on CCTV laughing and singing at The Crown pub in Cambridge with friends. She and her friend Helena Reed then made their way back to Edith's house, here in George Street, and said goodnight. What happened next is a mystery.

'DI Harriet Harper, of Cambridgeshire's Major Incident Team, is urging anyone with information about Edith to

79

contact the dedicated enquiry line. Edith's parents and her boyfriend, fellow Cambridge graduate Will Carter, will be issuing an appeal for information tomorrow morning.'

The food is filling up Manon's belly with warmth, which spreads up to her temples and fills her with an intense desire to sleep. She wants to eat more – as she always does when she works a punishing shift – as if she can replace a soft bed with carbohydrates. She spoons in some beans.

'She put up with me,' Will Carter told them when they re-interviewed him in the light of the Helena Reed revelation. Manon found herself staring at him with her mouth ajar and when she looked over at Harriet, who had joined herself and Davy halfway through the interview, she had the same expression on her face: *You cannot be real. You are a pretend boyfriend, created by DreamWorks.*

But it wore off, his handsomeness and its presence in the room, which initially made Manon wind one of her curls about a finger and Harriet hold her stomach in. The two of them questioned him about every aspect of his life with Edith, and though his barriers were down, and they were in the midst of the biggest case either of them had seen in years, nevertheless his answers had a curiously narcoleptic effect on them both. Manon rubbed her eye, which felt as if a bit of grit was caught in it, and cast a look at Harriet, who was stifling a yawn.

'Shall we break for coffee?' Harriet had said at one point, and they convened in whispers next to the coffee machine in MIT.

'Every time he speaks, I want it to be over,' said Manon, her eyes locked on the middle distance.

'Yes,' said Harriet. 'It's not boring, but it's like you just can't keep your mind on him at all. I found myself thinking about some shopping I have to pick up. Fascinating, isn't it?'

Carter described how he and Edith had met – the May ball, the velvet dress she wore with a sweetheart neckline, and her reciting Yeats to him across a lawn with her stilettos in one hand and a bottle of Becks in the other.

Manon takes another bite of sausage and looks at Davy – or through him, more accurately. He is saying something about phone numbers, a phone number that was found on Edith Hind's phone.

Soon there would be flowers – either at the site where a body was found, or outside the house – from members of the public who wrote cards saying 'you're safe now' or 'rest in peace' or 'looking down from heaven'. They scare her, these tragedy tourists, as if they are hungry for catastrophe, a line from the inside of them to the inside of suffering – like a hook inside the cheek of a fish. Manon knows death and she knows it is no rest or journey. *Do not go gentle into that good night.*

She thinks of Lady Hind's terrified face and realises the pain for relatives of the missing is that there is no clear face to stare into – neither the abyss of death, nor hope, but a ghastly oscillation between the two. If ever there was real purgatory, it's this.

'This number, unknown-515,' Davy is saying, mouth full of egg, 'it's on her phone twice. Edith called it on the Monday – the twelfth, I think it was – before she disappeared, that was a twenty-minute call. Then she called it again on Friday the sixteenth. That's got to be significant.'

'Who's it registered to?'

'Pay-as-you-go, no records attached, purchased in cash in Cambridge. I'm trying to get more on it. Why would Edith be calling a dirty phone?'

Manon shovels in a final mouthful of baked beans. Her eye is irritable – gritty, the shards of sleep deprivation or the beginning of a stye – and she predicts that when she wakes tomorrow it will have inflated like a blister. That'll look excellent when there are scores of TV cameras about. She stops herself rubbing it, even though the urge is overpowering, and knows in about three seconds she will claw at it rapaciously.

TUESDAY

MIRIAM

Two in the morning, our second night awake, thinks Miriam, noticing that she'd thought – told herself – Edith would be back with them by now. She should have been found. And she is aware that the passage of time – forty-eight hours now by police reckoning – is like a growing tumour for a missing person, as if time itself drains the life from their bodies. She cries every hour or so about the things Edith might have experienced. Or be experiencing still. Her own daughter and she can't make it stop, can't protect her. And then her mind can't bear it and it clicks into a numb state.

The hotel room at the George is overheated in the way hotel rooms often are. Airless, the windows impossible to open, the curtains like lead. They'd pushed dinner around their plates out of a vague respect for life's little routines, but eventually left the dining room when their awareness of the television and newspaper reporters sitting at adjacent tables became too much: constant furtive glances, the way conversation dropped when they walked by, and the lowered gazes when she accidentally met their eye. It was dirtying.

When she's not crying, she feels disconnected, as if the hubbub is happening to someone else: the news reports, the cameras outside Edith's house, the sheer drama of it. She is discombobulated when they are in the public eye, walking in and out of the police station or up the hotel steps, white lights shining in her face, camera flashes exploding. She allows herself to be carried along by Ian's hand on her arm. Propelled by him. She doesn't know what she'd do without him commanding everything.

After dinner she had a bath and, lying there, had thought about what she should wear for the television appeal. Is it wrong, that she cares about what to wear to appear on national television? She found herself wondering which outfit was more slimming – the navy jacket or mustard waterfall cardigan? How could she think about any of this (even idly wondering which seemed more grief-stricken)? Yet the mind must chew on something, else it will chew on itself.

Lying in the bath, she heard Ian on the phone to various people – to Rollo, about how soon he could fly back from Argentina ('I'll pay for a first-class ticket, if that's all that's available. Yes, yes, OK. So you'll be home by Wednesday evening? Yes, I wish it were sooner.'). She got out of the bath at this point, wrapped a towel around herself, and took the phone from her husband.

'Is that really the earliest you can come, darling?' she said to Rollo. 'I'll feel so much better when you're home. Did she say anything to you? No, well, OK, till Wednesday then. And Rollo? I love you, darling boy.' Just the sound of his voice was a bolster to her tremulous heart.

Then Ian spoke to DI Harper and to Rosemary from the practice, telling her he wouldn't be working for the foreseeable future and not to talk to the press.

Ridiculous trains of thought, wondering if she has somehow caused this. Was this her *fault*? Had she been remote as a mother? Because Edith was always over-dramatising her feelings, as if to make herself heard over a din. And this . . . event seems to Miriam somehow typical. Her eldest had never realised that a simple statement of fact was enough; it had to be 'the worst time ever' or '*literally* a nightmare'. Edith was always poorer, ill-er, more unhappy than the next person. It had made Miriam all the more aware of Rollo's understatement; when he rather queasily said as a child that he didn't feel quite right, she would rush to feel his fevered brow. When Edith wailed that she was *dying*, Miriam rolled her eyes and packed her off to school. And so are our children formed and yes, it was always going to be Edith at the centre of a drama – *a police hunt, for Christ's sake.*

She screws her eyes tight, her head tipped back, and tears squeeze from their corners, because she loves the bones of Edith and is critical only as if she is a part of herself. This separation is like a rending of her flesh.

She sits up. We have to *do* something. She hears a sound and looks across the bed, sees Ian's back through the charcoal dark. He is sitting on the side of the bed in his vest. He has his elbows on his knees, his head in his hands, and he is crying. Quietly, so as not to wake her.

She climbs over the bed to him and rubs his back.

'I thought she'd be at Deeping,' he says. 'Lying on her bed with headphones in her ears, reading a book. That she'd look up and wonder what all the fuss was about.'

'Let's go there now, see if she's turned up,' says Miriam. 'I can't stand doing nothing. I've just got this feeling – that house, she loves it there. It would draw her, if she were in trouble, I mean.'

'The police don't want us there. Forensics are all over it.'

'What if she's been run over, what if she's injured somewhere? And we don't know. Ian, we *don't know.*'

'That's why they've used sniffer dogs, to locate her by the scent of blood.'

'You know an awful lot all of a sudden,' she says, and it comes out more harshly than she intends.

'We've got to *think.* Where could she have gone?' They are both prone to this, thinking their way out of their predicaments, as if sheer force of intellect could control the random world.

'France? I mean, I know we haven't been for years and years, but she does speak the language.'

He shakes his head. 'Border control – she hasn't got her passport, remember? You should ring Christy and Jonti.'

'Yes. They won't know anything, but yes. She hasn't seen Jonti in years. Does Rollo have any ideas?'

'No, he says not, but he says he's setting up a Find Edith Facebook page or something. I wish it didn't take so long for him to get here. Miri,' he says with a sudden gasp.

'I know,' she says.

They are in this together; they love Edith together with lion-like force. Whatever rows there had ever been between them evaporated when Edith tottered towards them on chubby legs or made a funny face or delighted them in the myriad ways she did, and they would find themselves looking in the same direction, grinning stupidly at their girl. Together. Thank God they are together. The only person in the world who feels as much terror as she does is here, by her side.

She starts to cry. 'If she's not all right then I will never be all right.'

'Darling Miri, come here,' says Ian, taking her in his arms. 'We'll find her. We'll keep on looking until we find her.'

MANON

Engine's off and the wind squalls about the car. She should get out, look lively, jog up the steps ready for a new day, but instead she rests her forehead on the steering wheel.

'Morning,' says a muffled voice beyond her driver's side window. Davy, of course, smiling in at her, coffee in hand, the light glowing behind those marvellous ears, like red quotation marks. She winds down the window and a tinny hail of cold rain buffets in.

'How does my eye look?' she says, trying hard to open it fully.

'Looks normal to me. I've got you this. Warm you up. Haven't we got a briefing at eight?'

'Gimme a minute,' says Manon.

She winds up the window, using both hands and all the force of her shoulder. Davy has stepped back and is standing beside the car, holding her coffee like a royal attendant. She flips down the sun visor to look in its cloudy mirror. Her left eye is half-closed, red, and sloping downwards as if she's been punched. She opens the car door. It is perishing cold, the chill cutting into her ankles and toes and about her wrists and neck, making her hunch and tighten. She locks her car, takes her coffee from Davy and they walk up the steps of the station.

'Come in, both of you,' says Harriet, from the doorway of her office. She is pulling at her bra straps. It's as if she's never comfortable, the upholstery springing a tack.

'What's happened to you?' she says, peering at Manon's eye.

'Oh, nothing. Bit sore, that's all.'

'Looks like you've been beaten up.'

Harriet's jumpy. The girl has been missing for fifty-four hours now without a single firm lead but about six possible avenues for investigation. There is mercifully still no sign of their boss, Detective Chief Superintendent Gary Stanton, yet interference is palpably not far away: in the air space above them, the vague suspicion that calls might be passing between the Home Office and Cambridgeshire Commissioner Sir Brian Peabody, the odd mention perhaps at Annabelle's or in the Pugin Room at the House, perhaps some quiet pressure filtering down to the Chief Constable, who will certainly be taking a keen interest. 'Best brains on this Hind girl, old chap. Wouldn't want a cock-up on something this big.'

Manon and Davy take up seats in Harriet's office, Manon nursing her coffee with two hands.

'What's happened to her?' says Harriet, pacing. 'It's like she's evaporated. There's no CCTV, no sightings . . .'

'Where are we with the search?' asks Davy.

'Polsa's widened it beyond Portholme Meadow – more than a hundred officers in all – and sometime today Spartan Rescue are going to start on the River Ouse.'

'Take a week or two for a body to float up,' says Manon.

'What about that Graham Garfield chap, the Director of

Studies?' asks Harriet. 'He was sniffing about on Saturday night.'

'His wife says he was home with her after the pub,' says Manon.

'Think we have to be a bit circumspect about alibis given by wives and mothers.'

There is silence for a moment.

'Right, the press conference with the Hinds. We're going to watch Will Carter, see how he fares. Kim Delaney is trawling River Island for clothes similar to the ones Edith was wearing on Saturday night – jeans and a blue sweatshirt.'

'Boss?' says Colin, at the door. 'We've got something.'

They all look at him.

'Carter had another phone. Phone mast in Huntingdon picked up activity from a T-Mobile number registered to him on Saturday night.'

They all look at each other.

'What sort of activity?' asks Harriet.

'Two calls, one at 5 p.m., another at midnight. That's all we can tell before the full traces come in, but it puts him in Huntingdon on the night we think Edith disappeared.'

'Where's the phone now?'

'Dunno, it's switched off.'

'Have we tracked his car out of Stoke yet?' asks Manon.

'No, we haven't,' says Harriet. 'Nigel's doing some work on the smaller routes, checking alternative cameras. We need to question him on this – no more tea and sympathy.'

'Hang on,' says Manon. 'Let's let him do the presser, see how he holds up. Then we'll ask him about what his phone was doing in Huntingdon when he says he was in Stoke.'

'I want officers on the door,' says Harriet. 'And I want us all over his alibi. House to house in Stoke around his mother's address, see if anyone saw him leaving earlier than they both say. And CCTV.'

Manon perches one buttock on the edge of Colin's desk and looks up at the monitor, which shows an empty table with four chairs behind it and microphones along the front, pointing at the chairs.

The rest of the team gathers around her: Colin in his swivelly chair; Kim back from River Island; Davy, of course; and the new recruit, Stuart Leach. Manon eyes him in her periphery, her eyes flicking from his shaven head to the monitor, then back to his broad shoulders in a billowing shirt (she loves a billowing shirt on a man, especially with sharp creases), his square jaw and dark eyes, which have a certain amused mischief in them. He catches her eye and smiles.

'So, it was the boyfriend, was it?' he says, and she can feel all his charm being launched at her like a hand grenade – mischief slash disrespect.

'Looks like it. We don't know for sure,' she says, looking upwards at the monitor and simultaneously tightening her body under his gaze. She's going to have to cut back on the Marmite toast. 'Here they are.'

They watch as Harriet sits in the chair to the right of the screen. The Hinds then inch into view from the left, shuffling into their seats on half-bended legs and holding hands, their gaze downward. Will Carter enters last, wearing a mid-blue shirt that brings out the slate colour of his eyes. Manon can almost hear the female reporters in the room sitting up straighter. Flashes going, the electronic burr blending into the shuffling and murmuring of the crowd settling: TV news, locals, nationals, agencies, digital channels, web reporters. Manon sees the grey hollows beneath Sir Ian's eyes. Lady

Hind's are red-rimmed. They are silvery in their ageing, as if covered by a hoar frost. Carter runs a hand through his hair and the cameras seem to flurry in response.

Harriet introduces the pertinent facts about the investigation, the timeline of Edith's disappearance, details of the police hotline. Her glance repeatedly flicks to Will, whose gaze is directed at the cameras.

Somewhere in the room behind Manon, a phone starts ringing.

'Crikey, already,' says Colin. 'Here come the tank-top-wearing schizophrenics.'

'Shut it, Colin,' says Manon.

'It'll be the ladies offering to comfort Mr Carter,' says Kim. 'Even if he's killed her, he'll get a few marriage proposals.'

They watch Harriet introduce Sir Ian. There is a pause before he speaks.

'We are desperately worried about Edith,' he says, lifting his gaze to the phalanx of reporters and cameras, and for a split second, utter distaste is visible on his face. Lady Hind strokes his hand. 'She is a resourceful, clever, and talented girl, but the circumstances of her disappearance are obviously giving cause for mounting alarm. Edith, if you are watching this, please contact us to let us know you are safe. And if anyone out there has seen our daughter, do please contact the police.'

'Mr Carter,' says a female voice. 'Keeley Davis, *Hunts Post*. You must be devastated.'

'I am. I'm . . . I'm . . .' Will Carter looks about the room. 'I haven't slept. This is torture, a nightmare. We just want to know where Edie is.'

Manon thinks she can see Lady Hind close her eyes in a tiny grimace, but perhaps she's imagining it.

'Sorry, one more question,' says pushy Keeley Davis, who will no doubt be off to *The Mail* any day now, with her tight suit and that retro Nissan she drives, the automotive equivalent of a Prada handbag. 'Was there anything about her behaviour in the days before she disappeared that gave you cause for concern?'

'No, not at all,' says Will. He is giving Keeley maximum eye contact, furrowed and serious and frankly adorable. 'This is totally out of character. We were happy, *are* happy. We're incredibly close. She is my world. Y'know, she was working hard on her PhD, looking forward to Christmas. Normal stuff.'

Harriet points to another member of the audience. 'Yes, Terry.'

'Terry Harcourt, *The Mirror*. Sir Ian, can you tell us more about Edith – what sort of girl is she?'

Sir Ian looks vaguely lost. 'Well,' he says, halting for a moment as if he hasn't understood the question, 'as I say, she is clever. She has a double first from Cambridge and is studying for her PhD. She is quite sporty, dedicated to the environment.' Manon watches his bewildered face as the shutters click and the flashes blind him. He knows what they want – incontinent emoting. They want him and Miriam Hind to break down over 'their angel'.

Harriet moves it along. 'Yes, Andy, from *The Herald*.'

'Sir Ian, you are physician to the Royal Family. Has the Queen sent you any messages of support?'

'I don't think that's relevant to the purpose of this press conference,' says Sir Ian.

'Right, yes. Nick, ITN,' says Harriet, pointing to the back of the room.

'Sir Ian, you are personal friends with the Home Secretary. Is he putting extra resources behind this investigation?'

'I can answer that one,' says Harriet. 'All the resources of the police force are at our disposal in the search for Edith. This would be the case for any high-risk missing person.'

'Is it true you're looking for a body?' shouts a voice into the room.

Manon sees Lady Hind flinch. The room buzzes with enlarged murmurings.

'What's your name?' asks Harriet.

'Tony Thackeray, *Eastern Daily Press*. Missing person, more than forty-eight hours, sub-zero temperatures. This must surely become a murder investigation at some point. And isn't it also true that Cambridgeshire MIT has been criticised in the past for not upscaling a missing person to suspected homicide early enough? The case of Lacey Pilkington . . .'

'*Shit*,' whispers Manon.

Sir Ian and Miriam frown at one another and then at Harriet, who says, 'Our priority is to find Edith.'

'Aye aye,' says Colin, nodding at the screen. 'Here's Officer Dibble back from 'is holidays.'

They all notice Detective Chief Superintendent Gary Stanton, who has come to stand at the edge of the room, his body leaning against the wall. The buttons on his white shirt are straining; his civilian suit sharp and navy. He has the look of a man who has just stepped off a plane: his face and bald pate basted brown like a cooked turkey and shiny with good living. His gaze is on Harriet and she bristles with it.

'We are going to have to wrap things up, I'm afraid,' she says, shifting in her seat. She's eager to collar Will Carter, Manon can see it in Harriet's agitation – that's why she's closed it down so quick. 'Thank you all for coming.'

93

DAVY

'It was stolen,' says Will Carter, pacing with a hand in his hair, the other on his hip. 'Look, I know it looks bad but it honestly didn't occur to me to mention it. I've been taken up with . . . just, you know, my whole mind is on Edie.'

Davy is stood with his back to the wall, behind Harriet and Manon, who are sitting at the table facing Carter. Davy has the sense that Harriet is using him as a 'heavy' though he doesn't really have the face for it. He's been told he always looks faintly embarrassed or surprised, so he's trying to lean sardonically against the wall, as if he's a mass of thick-set scepticism. Harriet is leaning, too – back in her chair, twirling a pencil about her fingers. The disbelieving detective. Manon, however, is sat forward, her position saying: *I want to try to understand.*

'Go on,' says Manon.

'It didn't seem important. I forgot about it.'

'When and where was it stolen, Mr Carter?' says Manon.

'From my car. On Friday as I was preparing to leave. I left it on the seat, slammed the car door and ran in to get my bag.

94

I was only going to be a minute, maybe it was more like five, but when I came out, it had gone.'

'Did you see anyone – running away or near the car?'

'No. I glanced in either direction but the street was empty. Maybe they were hiding behind a hedge or something, I dunno. I wouldn't have gone after them anyway. I'm a coward when it comes to things like that – I don't want to get punched. I think they must've been watching me and seized their chance when I went inside.'

'And you didn't think to report it?' says Harriet.

'I wanted to get on the road – my mum was expecting me. I'll be honest, I didn't think there was much the police could do. I thought it was my own stupid fault and I just had to suck it up. Anyway, I stopped at the Tesco phone shop in Kettering – it's open late – and got a pay-as-you-go, just so I could give Edie a number, y'know, so she could call me in an emergency.'

'Sorry, Mr Carter, but how did you not think this was relevant to our investigation?' asks Harriet.

'I don't know. I just wanted you to find Edie. I was so worried, it didn't occur to me.'

'So you phoned Edith from Kettering?'

'No, I texted.'

'You didn't want to talk to her about the fact you'd just been a victim of a crime?'

'I tried to call her.'

'You tried to call her,' says Harriet, her voice dripping with exhausted frustration.

'I did call but she was busy and she didn't pick up. I knew she wouldn't recognise the number so I explained in a text and she texted back saying "OK".'

He has stopped in front of them.

Davy can't see Harriet's expression, but she is probably

frowning. 'Forgive me, Mr Carter, but perhaps you can see why we're confused. You say everything's perfect between you and Miss Hind, you say everything was normal in the run-up to her disappearance—'

'OK, not normal.'

Harriet is gesturing at the chair in front of them, the patient mother. Carter sits at last.

'One minute everything was normal,' he says, 'and then it wasn't. One minute we were making dinner, watching *Sherlock* on iPlayer, and then – about a week ago, I guess – I dunno, she cooled off, like she was cross with me. Froze when I touched her. Kept saying she had loads of work on, as if she was avoiding me. I suppose that fits with what you said about her and Helena.'

'Can you give specific examples?' asks Manon.

'Well, the Saturday before . . . a week before . . .' He colours up, doesn't know how to refer to the 'event' of Edith's disappearance, which might or might not be her death. 'She went out, I don't even know who with, got really drunk, and on the Sunday she spent the whole day in bed with her laptop on her knees. And then in the afternoon, about three, she put a track-suit on and her boots and took her car keys. When I asked where she was going, she said, "Out." It went on like that, passing each other in the house like strangers. Then on Friday, the Friday I was going to Stoke, she was suddenly really full-on, emotional. We made love – this was in the afternoon – and I thought, oh, it's all right again, it was just a passing thing. But she started crying immediately after – after the sex, I mean – and she said, "I'm sorry." I suppose now she was talking about Helena, I dunno. I said, "What for?" And she said, "For being a bitch to you." I said, "You haven't been, not so I've noticed." Which was bollocks, of course, I had noticed, but I was just glad she was back with me, I wanted to be close again, and I didn't want to argue. Anyway, it seemed to make it worse. She snapped at me, "That's right, Will, let's tell each other lies." I'll be honest – I didn't know what was going on.'

Poor chap, Davy thinks. He wouldn't be the first man whose girlfriend was a mystery to him. What law is it that says you can't be a hapless good-looking bloke – well, a model, pretty much, actually – in the wrong place at the wrong time?

'It has taken you an awfully long time to tell us all this,' says Harriet. She wants to nail him, wants his alibi broken and an arrest before Stanton can go clod-hopping all over her investigation. She'll be thinking he set up the phone theft – stopped at Kettering to buy a PAYG as part of his alibi – then slipped back early to Huntingdon to murder Edith because he was furious that she was leaving him, or being unfaithful, or both. It was often both.

'It was private, all right?' says Carter, not quite shouting, but defensive. 'My relationship with Edie is private and I didn't want to tell you lot about it.'

Davy looks at the ringlets springing from the back of Manon's head and wonders what she makes of Carter. He hazards a guess: Manon would say go easy, trace the phone, track his plates, follow up on the Tesco phone shop in Kettering and the petrol stations on his return journey. Because cases, as she was forever telling him, aren't solved on hunches. They're solved with dogged, stoic donkey work.

MANON

Harriet takes a circular tin of Vaseline, green and white, from the depths of her handbag. Without looking at it, she twists off the lid and dabs some onto her middle finger, stroking it across her lips so they glisten. Her gaze is on the middle distance. These shifts are ageing us, Manon thinks. She keeps glazing over too, and when she does, her mind returns again and again to Deeping – its painterly swathes, colours murky and creative – perhaps because it's the polar opposite of police HQ, all pale laminate and strip lighting. The exposure of dark corners.

People are preparing to go home. 'We can't keep you all here indefinitely,' Harriet said. 'Get some sleep. See you back here at seven tomorrow morning.' Coats being threaded onto leaden arms, bags gathered, families phoned. ('Yes, Dawn, I know it's late. Well, I'm sorry, but there wasn't anything I could— Shall I pick up something for us to eat?')

'Don't walk home tonight,' Harriet says, and Manon blinks into focus, sees her flicking her hair out from under her coat collar.

'No, I've got the car. Hang on, I thought Carter was our suspect.'

'Yeah, well, you heard Stanton.'

She'd been in on the meeting, Stanton hitching up the back of his belt, his belly its counterweight, while he told Harriet she didn't have the evidence against Carter: 'No body, no forensics, no witnesses, nothing.'

'We need to shake him up,' Harriet said, but she was already on the back foot.

Stanton doesn't want the headlines, the pay-out in compensation if they're wrong and the press going to town. His manner had said: You've both got a bit over-excited, but now my steadying hand is back on the tiller. 'We wait,' he told them. 'We investigate all avenues. Trace. Interview. Eliminate.'

'Just . . . don't walk,' Harriet is saying, covering a yawn with her fist. 'You don't know – we don't know – who's out there.'

'Anything on unknown-515, that mystery number on Edith's call register, Davy?' says Manon, as he walks towards them.

'Nothing,' he says.

'Fancy a lift?' Manon says.

He seems to falter, then says, 'OK, yes, thanks very much.'

Manon's wipers push doggedly at the rain but do little to dissipate the fog on her windscreen, so she winds down a window, letting in sprays of wet. Rough winds buffet the car as she pulls on to the A14 to avoid the cordon which has closed George Street and created gridlock in central Huntingdon. She'll follow the ring road around to suburban Sapley, where Davy lives. The roads roar with wetness and the damp mingles with the musty interior of her car. On the banks of the motorway, just visible in the dark, are the last sketches of snow being pummelled by the rain.

'Have you got any hobbies, Davy?' she asks, peering into the dark.

'I do, yes,' says Davy. 'I do my mentoring at the youth centre, kids in care. I like a spot of gardening, though I haven't got a garden at the moment. I do help look after my mum's.'

'See? You've got plenty of hobbies. I haven't got one.'

'Why d'you ask?'

'I had to fill in a hobbies section – for the dating site – and I drew a complete blank. I literally don't have any. So I've decided to get hobbied up.'

'And how is that going?' asks Davy, with a hopefulness that would imply he'd never met Manon.

'Awful. I hate it. I mean, what's the point of doing something just for the sake of it, when it isn't your job?'

'Well, to relax.'

'I even went to a pottery class so I'd have something to type in. But I just couldn't get past the pointlessness of it. I mean, it's not like I'm ever going to have a pottery wheel in my lounge, to relax with.'

'You don't know that. Demi Moore had one in *Ghost*,' says Davy.

She looks at him, but he maintains his cheerful gaze straight ahead.

'So I'm going to try Zumba instead,' says Manon. 'Thought I'd go tonight, actually. Help me wind down. It's been quite full-on. Do you find that – difficulty falling asleep?'

'Nope, not me. My head touches the pillow and bosh, I'm off. Did Harriet suggest that – the Zumba, I mean?'

Manon shoots him a sharp look. 'No, she did not. Why? What's she said to you?'

'Nothing, no, nothing. It's just good if we all keep fit, that's all,' says Davy. 'For catching villains. Ah, here we are,' he says, patting his knees. Manon slows the car and Davy gets out, then leans in through the open door. 'Right, well, cheerio,' he says.

He waits, but she doesn't respond, so he closes the car door.

WEDNESDAY

DAVY

He's in bright and early, and as he stands beside his desk taking off his coat, he surveys the MIT department. The support and admin staff who dominate the building have subsided into a loose, festive spirit – this being the last working week for many – and this is mulling its way into the investigations team. Kim is standing on a chair, hanging some Christmas cards on a loop of string, a row of flapping birds. One of the administrators has made an attempt to stretch some accordion gold chains between the strip lights, one of which pings off its Blu Tack, fluttering down against the wall.

Four days to Christmas, seventy-seven hours missing, the golden hour having ebbed away. He looks up at the television screen which is bracketed to the wall and sees the aerial shots of the search teams, muted on the twenty-four-hour-news channel – tiny people in navy vests with 'Police' on the back, or in florescent yellow windcheaters, combing squares of gardens, beating bushes with sticks; white vans on street corners; and huddles of officers bent over maps or talking to residents. All of it silent while the red ticker along the bottom of the screen says: *Missing student Edith Hind, latest: frogmen search the Ouse.* The image flicks to a navy dinghy skirting the brown soupy surface of the river. Must be the worst job, he thinks; you could only ever come up with something nasty or nothing at all. Then there's a shot of the members of the public who have joined the search, forming a long line to inch their way across Portholme Meadow. Most appear to be chatting to one another, without so much as a glance around them.

He drapes his coat over the back of his chair and is about to get a coffee from the filter machine where it stews and burns, when Manon enters the room. He lifts his empty mug at her and she nods back, a thumbs-up. She seems to be walking gingerly, and having trouble taking off her coat. As Davy gets her a coffee, he sees Stuart, the new recruit, approach and lift the coat from her shoulders while she winces, and they both laugh at something.

Davy doesn't know how he does it, but every time Stuart looks up from under his Disney Princess eyelashes, every woman in the room titters as if she's at a sixth-form disco. He's got so much confidence, like when Harriet had been talking to him about some quirk of the HOLMES database, and he'd picked a bit of fluff off the shoulder of her jacket and, momentarily, she hadn't known what on earth to do with herself. Davy would never have the guts to be like that with senior police officers. Marvelling, he carries two coffees back to his desk, puts down his own and hands the second to Manon, who takes it while looking at her screen.

Christmas is weighing on Davy's mind, especially what to buy his mother. Bed socks, perhaps – cashmere – or would that be too strong a reference to her bedridden years? All those weeks and months when Davy cast himself as the light bulb to her dark recess. He wants to get her something nice, because Christmas is hard on her, the way it dredged up painful memories of when his father left, seventeen years ago. She asks Davy endless questions about his father, who continues to live happily with Sharon the lollipop lady in Kent. He couldn't, of course, go and spend Christmas with them – even though their Christmases sound rather raucous, with Sharon's extended family gathering for one long knees-up and walks along the Whitstable seafront. No, that would be a disloyalty too far.

'There's a briefing,' he says to Manon. 'This afternoon. Child protection teams, multi-agency. It was on the board.'

'Can't go to that,' says Manon, sipping her coffee. 'Too much to do.'

'Boss says we have to. Three-line whip.'

'What time?'

'Three o'clock. Short one, but we can't get out of it.'

Davy is glad it's compulsory. They should know, his colleagues, what's really happening – what he sees at the youth centre. He's been mentoring a lad called Ryan, twelve years old, who was taken into care at ten after being admitted to hospital a second time with broken forearms. There were boot prints on his skin. Every time Ryan walked through his front door at home, he got a pummelling, if not from whichever lowlife his mum was seeing, then from his mum. She liked to put her cigarettes out on him.

Davy bought Ryan a fart gun for his eleventh birthday, which Ryan looked at with contempt, saying it was for babies and he wanted a Nintendo DS or a Wii, but Davy had ignored him, letting off the gun under the table at McDonald's so that diners at the next table began to whisper and grimace. Back at the centre, Ryan started to play with the gun, parping and trumping at his friends as they texted irritably on the red foam sofas. Ryan laughed and laughed, ticklish, tearful giggling, and it was as if he was four years old, and six years old, and eleven – all the ages he hadn't been allowed to be. He loved to laugh, Ryan did, once he granted himself the freedom of it, which was hard to come by, and when the laughing overtook him, as it had with the fart gun, his face radiated like sparkling sunshine on water.

'They're sending me back,' Ryan told Davy on his last visit.

'Back?' said Davy, stunned. 'Where? Back to your mum?'

Ryan nodded, swallowing. 'No room for me at Aldridge House no more. They cut back two of the staff – Evangeline and Rob, the only nice ones. Now there's not enough adults for all the kids – the ratio, they call it – so I have to go.'

'What does your mum say?'

'Dunno, they haven't got hold of her yet. All she cares about is the money.' He put on a screeching voice. '"How am I supposed to feed 'im when I got naaa money?" C'mon, let's play.'

Then, when they were standing around the green baize table taking turns, Ryan returned to the subject. He had the snooker cue across his shoulders, his arms draped over it like a coat hanger, and he said, 'Least I'm not Jayden.'

'What's happened to him?' asked Davy, leaning his whole body on the table to pot the red.

'He's been kicked out of Aldridge an' all. Been placed in a house with two paedos. Everyone knows they're nonces but social services say it's all they've got. I'd rather be on the street.'

'How old is Jayden?' asks Davy, rubbing chalk on the end of his cue while Ryan walks around the table, looking for angles.

'Ten.'

If Davy could do what he actually wanted this Christmas, he'd spend it with Ryan at the youth centre. Serving watery turkey with packet stuffing. Playing pool in his snowman tank top with a paper hat on and letting off the fart gun when Ryan least expects it.

MANON

She gazes into the middle distance, yawning while the room settles. They're waiting for a morning briefing with Harriet, who is ensconced in her office with Stanton and the search adviser.

Colin is bowing his head low over the desk and muttering in Italian.

'*Posso avere quella senza aglio?*' he says to his iPhone.

'What are you doing, Colin?' says Manon, rubbing at the grit in her eye again. She pulls out her eyelid and blinks downward.

'My Learn Italian app,' Colin says. 'Translation – can I have that without garlic? Can't stand the stuff, nor can Gwyneth.'

'P'raps Puglia isn't your ideal holiday destination then,' says Manon, the blinking not having made any difference.

'Don't see why they can't cater to our tastes,' says Colin, 'seeing as we're paying.' He rocks back with his glasses pushed up onto his bald pate. Manon wonders: did Gwyneth look into Colin's small, bloodshot eyes and say, 'You are the UKIP-voting misogynist for me'? She must have done – they'd been married for thirty-odd years. And there was luck in that; you were lucky if you could be happy with what life threw your way (even if it was Colin) instead of generally dissatisfied, as Manon is. Colin's Google searches were testament to the richness of their life together – boutique hotels in Margate, painting courses in Giverny, walking tours of the Tyrol.

'Look, here's one of the pensioni we're staying in,' Colin is saying, scrolling through some images of wafting muslin curtains framing a view of the sea.

This is one of the many things Manon hates about the open-plan office, apart from the way it favours crazed extroverts – it throws up so much envy. She's regularly stabbed by it: envy of Colin and Gwyneth's tour of Puglia; envy of Nigel and Dawn's gurgling newborn twins; even of Davy and Chloe's Friday night takeaway in front of the telly.

Stuart is leaning against the wall, his gaze intense into the room so that every time Manon looks up, she seems to catch his eye. Only his third day in the job, yet he has a strangely dominating effect on the department. His hands had brushed her neck as he helped her off with her coat, sending a charge through her, and she made a self-deprecating reference to over-doing the exercise last night. 'Won't be trying that again,' she said. 'From now on my fat arse stays on the chair.'

Her legs and arms have seized up completely, so that she can barely put on or take off a coat, and her attempts to zip up her boots this morning resulted in her rolling across the floor in a ball like some petrified hedgehog. She takes a sip of coffee. The tiredness has hit her forcefully – a wall she must scale. It's always worse for a night's sleep which, instead of giving the mind and body nimble new energy, seems to trans-mogrify exhaustion into cement.

Edith Hind is all over the morning papers, every front page

106

carrying pictures of Sir Ian and Miriam. Most of it is straight reporting, but Manon noticed a couple of columnists in the mid-market titles commenting on the couple's demeanour. 'When all a parent can say of the child they love is that they were "very academic", we need to look again at our value system,' wrote one mop-headed moralist.

She looks down at the sheet prepared for her by Davy, detailing Edith's known movements in the week before she disappeared. ANPR cameras have picked up one trip to Deeping in the G-Wiz on Sunday, 11 December, a week before she disappeared and the day after her affair with Helena began.

'Looking forward to Christmas telly?' says Davy, to no one in particular, as if trying to cheer up the room in general. 'I'm going to be watching *Polar Express*.'

Manon has clasped her two hands around her mug. 'Did you notice,' she says, 'Edith Hind and Will Carter didn't have a telly?'

'It's not a human right,' says Davy.

'Bloody is,' says Colin, without looking round.

'I can't stand people who don't own tellies,' says Manon.

'How very reasonable of you,' says Stuart, his eyes meeting hers, his arms crossed over his chest.

'Shall I tell you why?' says Manon, looking back at him.

'Think you're going to,' mutters Davy.

'Because they just watch loads on iPlayer and then go on and on about not having a telly to people who do have tellies.'

'D'you want to know my theory?' says Colin.

'Oh God,' says Manon, 'close the windows, someone might hear.'

'I think Edith Hind fancied a meat feast pizza, a movie, and a good ol' shag without having to boil any mung beans or discuss the metaphysical poets.'

'Right, yes, thank you again, Colin.'

Harriet and Stanton have entered the department and Harriet is clapping her hands for silence and saying loudly, 'Right everybody,' at which point Stanton says, 'Harriet will be taking this briefing. I've got a press conference downstairs at nine. I think you should know, however, that my line will be that it is now more than seventy-two hours since she went missing and that, in our view, it is highly likely Edith Hind has come to harm.'

He's reacted, Manon thinks, to Thackeray in that press conference and the criticism surrounding their last high-risk misper. Twelve-year-old Lacey Pilkington disappeared three years ago on a Peterborough estate. Stanton was SIO, then as a DCI. In a standard review, his investigation was criticised: officers had been blinded by the belief the girl was alive, which delayed appropriate action. It should have been upscaled to a suspected homicide sooner, and as a result, time and evidence were lost. Stanton, they said, had become hidebound by the emotions of the victim's family. Who, incidentally, Manon recalls bitterly, were the ones who'd killed her.

'I shall also be making clear,' Stanton is saying, 'that the main focus of our investigation is her complex love life.' He turns, nods, and says, 'Thanks, Harriet,' then walks out of the department.

'Ian Hind is going to *love* us,' says Manon.

MIRIAM

'Not long now,' says Miriam, sitting in the moulded plastic chair of interview room one. 'To see Rollo, I mean.' She can smell vending-machine instant coffee, dispensed in those squat brown cups that crackle in the hand.

Ian doesn't answer her. He is pacing still. She doesn't know how he keeps going; he seems to expend so much energy every minute of the day and isn't resting at night either. He has been out there, standing next to the parish priest who joined the community in prayer, doing his best to hide his distaste for the members of the public joining the search (and failing, in Miriam's opinion: she's never seen a thank-you speech so faltering and pinched), paying to print posters, T-shirts and balloons emblazoned with Edith's smiling face and the date 17.12.2010.

He was pleased, at first, that Detective Chief Superintendent Gary Stanton was overseeing, as if someone at his own level was finally in charge – *a chap* – someone who could actually make something happen. Then he watched this morning's press conference on Sky. It caused him to puff, then stand up and walk around the room, then tut again, the tension fizzing off him and transferring itself to Miriam.

More than seventy-two hours. Edith has been gone more than seventy-two hours and there is a palpable cooling in the atmosphere surrounding the investigation. It has slowed. Officers have returned to normal shift patterns. The search is ongoing, dogged, hundreds of police inching forward with sticks or torches or in diving suits, but Miriam has sensed it no longer contains the urgency of searching for someone alive.

She takes a deep breath, leans her head back, and closes her eyes. She's not sure she can take another night in this town – another night sweating and dry-mouthed in that airless hotel room; another meal in the bar, at a slippery table, her clothes infused with the smell of deep-fat frying. She can't wait to see the back of Huntingdon, its dirty snow, pound shops and grey, hunkered streets. She realises she harbours a fantasy that when she leaves this place, she'll leave behind this nasty business – the terrible feelings, the sleeplessness, the way her mind oscillates wildly between terror and blankness. Back in Hampstead, she might return to the woman she was only four days ago, preparing for Christmas, snipping stems of eucalyptus, steeping dried figs in brandy, untangling strings of white pin lights. She feels a growing anger with Edith for putting her through this, as if she were some limitlessly absorbent sponge for her daughter's mess. And then her anger makes her cry again because she wants nothing except to have Edith back.

'Sir Ian, Lady Hind,' says a male voice, and Miriam wipes her eyes and sees DCS Gary Stanton, DI Harriet Harper and DS Manon Bradshaw, all three re-introducing themselves.

Oh no, oh no, they must have found a body. Why all three

like this? Like some ghastly triumvirate. Miriam looks up at them, a hand clasped over her mouth, her eyes flicking from one to the next.

'There's nothing new to report,' says DS Bradshaw, acknowledging her terror.

'What the hell was all that this morning?' Ian is saying.

'I felt I had to say what I thought,' says Stanton, calmly. 'I'm sorry if it was upsetting for you.'

'Do you have any idea what the tabloids are going to be like after this?' says Ian, though Miriam knows that it is the 'come to harm' line which has upset him more than any of the salacious things they said about Edith's love life. He cannot, will not, bear it.

'We need information. The press is the best way to flush that out.'

'You effectively told the press she's dead.'

'We have to be realistic . . .' says Stanton.

'You have to find her, that's what you have to do. Find her. Stop posturing and just bloody well find her—' says Ian, stopped by tears which seem to ambush him.

Miriam's gaze has settled on DS Bradshaw, who is leaning against the closed door, her hands behind her back. Beautiful curls, unruly. She's always observing, and she now returns Miriam's gaze, though neither woman smiles.

'We feel,' says DI Harper, 'that you would be more comfortable back at home, rather than holed up in a hotel in Huntingdon surrounded by the press.'

'What you're saying is, you're giving up,' says Ian. 'You're closing down the search and you don't want me breathing down your neck.'

'Absolutely not,' says Stanton. 'This is not, in any way, a scaling down of the case. The search for Edith will continue at full tilt and you will be kept fully informed by your liaison officer.'

'Great, you're sending us away with a depressed shadow,' says Ian. 'Do we get to keep her for Christmas?'

'Ian,' says Miriam, almost in a whisper.

'Your liaison officer is there to support you. We simply don't feel it's sensible to keep you in Huntingdon,' says Stanton. 'But please be reassured this is not a scaling down of the case.'

Of course it bloody is, thinks Miriam.

'I won't allow this to go cold,' says Ian. 'I won't allow you to stop searching for our child. If I have to call Roger . . .'

He is standing beside her chair, and Miriam takes hold of his hand and squeezes it, then presses it against her lips and closes her eyes tight to stop the tears from coming, because the smell of him, and the soft feeling of the hairs on the back of his hand against her cheek, and the way he is fighting so hard for them both, for all of them, is making her well up.

'I know it's hard,' says DS Bradshaw, much softer than either of her bosses. 'Leaving this place – it must feel like leaving Edith. But you can't stay in Huntingdon indefinitely. And your home is less than two hours away so . . .'

'They're right, darling,' says Miriam, looking up at Ian, still holding his hand against her cheek. 'We're not doing any good here. We might as well go home and sleep in our own bed. But please God don't make us take that basset hound of a woman with us.'

'It's for the best,' says DI Harper, 'and I can assure you there will be no diminution of effort or dedication.'

MANON

'There will be no diminution of effort?' says Manon, as she and Harriet climb the echoey staircase to MIT, without Stanton, who has gone off to stoke his belly with another large lunch. 'Bit of a mouthful, wasn't it?'

'Oh look, he gets right on my tits. I can't think straight with him looking at me, thinking—' Harriet puts on an upper-crust Sir Ian accent – 'What manner of fuckwit are you?'

'Yes, he's a bit . . . austere.'

'A bit?'

'Well, he's worried. I'd want my dad to do the same.'

'S'pose. She's a bloody cold fish, too.'

Manon stops, a hand on Harriet's arm so that she turns on the stairs. 'No, she isn't,' says Manon. 'She isn't at all. She just doesn't put it all out there.'

'We really need to get on and identify the people in the Post Office queue,' says Harriet. 'Nigel's got the footage but some of them are shielded by hoods or they're just standing at the wrong angle.'

'We can get the staff to corroborate with their paperwork. Where's Will Carter staying?'

'Not with Helena Reed, that's for sure. We've let him go home to Stoke but asked him to stay put so we can keep him informed. The Hind brother's due in this afternoon. I want you and Davy to interview him as soon as he arrives, OK? What are you up to tonight, anything nice?'

'Another date,' says Manon. 'To be honest, I'd rather look at a thousand hours of local authority CCTV.'

They sit in a row in conference room one, waiting for the child protection briefing, everyone on their smart phones. Manon has just received the latest demand for a dating update from Bryony. She's next to Nigel, who has turned his back to the room and is hissing into his phone, a hand cupped over the mouthpiece. Dawn, obviously. Colin is downloading confirmation of his Ryanair flights. Kim is yawning, her feet up on the chair in front. The room is an oasis of police-blue – blue foam chairs, blue curtains, blue carpet – and smells of brewing coffee. It is filling up, people shuffling along the rows, slight bend at the knee: ambulance crews from Hinchingbrooke, passport control, CID. People nodding, saying hello. A few uniforms, rustling fluorescent jackets with zips and toggles and crackling radios, which make them seem larger than the rest. Amazing she can't find a date among this lot.

Davy, to the other side of Manon, is sat bolt upright, his neck straining upwards so he can look at the woman at the podium, who is shuffling papers before she begins.

'You should listen,' he says to Manon. 'This stuff's important. You wouldn't believe what's happening out there.'

But Manon is texting Bryony.

This one's a poet. Therefore not simply fucktard, but fucktard who cannot pay mortgage.

'Hello everyone, and thanks for coming,' says the mousey voice at the podium. 'I am Sheila Berridge, head of child protection services.'

Manon's phone vibrates.

You don't know that. He might be laureate-in-waiting. Anyway, I admire you for being dating daredevil. B

Manon yawns, hears the words 'cross-sector involvement' and 'joined-up thinking' waft across the room towards her.

'We all need to be aware of the crisis in our children's homes and how this spills out into all our sectors.' Sheila Berridge warns of unprecedented numbers of children entering the care system as more and more families bump and skid below the poverty line. There are currently sixty-seven thousand children in care in England, she says.

Davy leans in to Manon, whispers urgently, 'Sixty-seven thousand. That's a city three times the size of Huntingdon.'

'A city of children,' says the woman at the podium, as if she and Davy are telecommunicating, 'children with their attachments broken, the majority – seventy per cent – having experienced abuse or neglect. Once in care,' she continues, trying to get above the shuffling and bleeping and restlessness of the room, 'many children experience the instability of multiple short-term placements. They are more likely to go missing, making them vulnerable to harmful situations such as sexual exploitation.'

'I see this all the time,' Davy whispers to Manon, 'at the youth group. I mean, they're *children*.'

115

'The pattern of neglect,' says Sheila Berridge's harried voice, 'is getting worse. We know of gangs of men who prey on girls in care, getting them addicted to alcohol and drugs, then grooming them for sex. Paedophiles are operating in many care homes. This affects all of us, every agency in this room.'

Manon looks to the other side of her, away from Davy's keen expression, and sees Nigel yawning. He casts her a look as if to say, 'Boring, huh?'

'We must be aware of how difficult these children are to help,' says Sheila Berridge, her voice now raised and powerful, 'and to be mindful that they *must* be listened to, however much they change their stories, however dangerous and unpredictable they seem. We must listen to what they tell us. We must take them very seriously indeed.'

DAVY

He smiles at Davy, proffering his hand warmly. About my age, Davy thinks, bit younger maybe, so why do I feel inferior in front of Rollo Hind, whose face is friendly and open – unlike his father's.

Inferior's too strong, Davy thinks, sitting behind the table while Manon fiddles with the recording machine. There's been quite a bit of preamble, along the lines of: 'Good flight?' and 'Thanks for coming all this way, sir, we really appreciate it', and 'How was Buenos Aires?'

Suburban, he thinks, putting his finger on it. He feels suburban next to this tall, tanned chap. Perhaps it's the hair. Davy's just sort of sits there, on his head – it'd be pushing it to call it a 'style' – whereas Rollo Hind has a natty quiff, up from the parting, a bit rockabilly, a bit mod; dead sharp. Or the bright blue eyes, sparkling out from his face, a golden shimmer at the temples. Rollo Hind seems all Hollywood, while he and Manon, their complexions the colour of canteen mash, are rocking the fifteen-hour-shift look.

'You had a text conversation with Edith on Tuesday, thirteenth

117

of December, which was quite self-questioning, wasn't it?' Manon says.

Davy has read the texts, extracted by Colin from Edith's phone, which had been conducted over WhatsApp, the free texting application.

E: Do u think of yourself as good person, Rol? I mean, do u think your goodness innate?

R: I'm definitely good, yes.

E: But don't u think everyone thinks they r good, even if they r bad? A bad person wd prob say, 'I'm essentially good, but there are these extenuating circumstances.'

R: Don't know what u r on about. Btw, have you seen Natalie Portman in *Black Swan* yet? She's HOT.

E: But do u think your goodness innate, or are u good because u hv been told to be good, because u r conforming to societal norms?

R: FFS, Smelly, what's brought this on?

E: Wondering: what's core, as in part of self, or what's there because society demands it. Or is goodness genetic?

R: Not in our family. Praps skipped generation?

E: Don't joke.

R: What's up with u?

118

E: U r lucky, Dad never expected much from u.

R: Thanks! Low expectations = freedom. Listen, am knackered, sis. Can u have yr existential personality crisis some other time?

E: No worries. Love you, Rol.

'I feel terrible about that now,' Rollo says, 'that I didn't take it more seriously, but it wasn't that out-of-character, not for Edith. I mean, she's prone to this sort of thing. She's a serious person, y'know? Gets fed up with me, says I'm glib about everything. When we travelled around Italy together interrailing, she was always wanting to talk about E. M. Forster and personal freedom versus duty. She likes to . . . intellectualise things.'

'So she would text you existential questions like this, without preamble?'

'Well, OK, this was slightly out of the blue. I mean, it came from nowhere, but it wasn't enough to make me think . . . It didn't make me *worry*, is what I'm saying. And maybe it should've done, with hindsight. She's a student at Cambridge – they're all at it, sitting around till 2 a.m. pondering Kierkegaard and the essence of being. I thought it was just part of that.'

'And now?'

He shrugs. 'After what Mum and Dad told me, about Helena and all that, I wonder if she's talking about being unfaithful – about goodness in terms of what she was doing to Will. She would've felt really guilty about that.'

MANON

She's laced them too tight, the boots. The strings dig into her ankles and the cold rises up off the ice, radiating towards her face. Her fingers are cold. Her cheeks are cold. Why have we come inside to get *cold*? Her shins are painful with the tensing of her muscles. She inches forward, one foot then the other, gripping hard on to the handrail.

'Really fucking hate skating,' she mutters, shuffling forward towards the poet, who is ahead of her.

He smiles. He has a meek face under a head of curls, but while her own emanate from her head at wild angles, his hang limp and wet-looking. She nods back at him, her body bent forward from the waist, her legs like scissoring crutches.

He doubles back to her, fast on his skates, and stops with a spray of ice dust, his skates a balletic 'V'.

'Are you all right?' he says, his hand on her arm.

'Fine, yes, all fine.'

'Try to straighten up a bit. Here, take my arm.'

She holds on to him, his old suede jacket rough under her hand – she catches a whiff of mustiness from it – and tries to

120

push her tummy out to straighten her body but her feet immediately slide forward and out from under her. She hits the ice hard – right on her coccyx. She hisses as the cold follows on from the pain, tries to get up, holding him, but her feet are scissoring wildly and she's grasping at his smelly jacket while he tries to keep his balance, and then her arms are actually around his body, clambering up him until they are face to face.

'OK?' he says, smiling.

'Take me to the rail.'

At the rail, she says, 'That's enough for me,' and walks through a gap onto the rubber mat, relieved – so very *relieved* – that her feet can grip something. 'You carry on. I'm going to get a hot chocolate.'

Two years of sifting through the detritus of the Internet, the sexually incontinent to the intellectually subnormal. Prior to this, she'd spent five deluded years gambling on meeting someone 'naturally', though there was nothing natural about turning up to every random gathering wearing too much slap and a desperate gurn, disappointed evenings in the pub, then clip-clopping home on uncomfortable heels. Christ, she'd even gone for drinks with the *neighbours*, at which everyone was coupled up and about fifty-seven. With this particular outing, she thinks, unlacing and pulling off the skates, she has plumbed a new low.

Her feet, however, are in a state of bliss. She can walk, she can un-tense, she is light as air. It is almost worth ice skating for the feeling of buoyancy of having functional feet back. Why do people do this – create for themselves physical uncertainty when there is so much of it to be had in daily life for free?

Her mind goes back to the child protection woman and the 67,000 children, as it has intermittently since she came out of the briefing, which must be Davy's doing or perhaps the niggling feeling that there is something she cannot see through the half-closed smear of her sore eye – an irritation she forgets about for long enough to stop her visiting a chemist. She resolves to sort it tomorrow.

The hangar housing the rink is noisy and smells of hot dogs and rubber with the odd whiff of socks. She waits for him at a Formica table which is riveted to the floor, occasionally spots him whizzing round, pushing his body forward, confident and free. She is tempted to do a runner but alas, here he is, edging in front of her, between the plastic stool and table, both immovable.

He smiles but doesn't say anything. She has noticed he's a man of few words and when he does speak, it is so softly that she has to crane forward, cup her ear like a pensioner and say, 'What was that?'

'You're a good skater,' she says.

He nods.

'When did you learn?'

'When I was young.'

They look out at the rink – at the laughing skaters on faster dates.

'So you're a poet,' she says.

He nods.

'Where do you write?'

'Anywhere.'

'Is it lonely?'

'Not really.'

'Least you don't have to do the office Secret Santa. Thank God for Huntingdon's pound stores, is all I can say!'

He nods again. The relaxedness of his nodding says, 'This silence is your failing. You should fill it.' She notices she wants to dig her heels in: I won't put you at your ease, she thinks.

122

He looks out at the rink as if he's alone.

'Do they rhyme?'

'I'm sorry?'

'Your poems – do they rhyme?'

'Do you like poetry that rhymes?' he asks.

A full sentence. There is a God.

'I'm not a big poetry fan,' she says, which is an out-and-out lie. She has inhaled everyone from T. S. Eliot to Wendy Cope.

You take up yoga, walk and swim.
And nothing works. The outlook's grim.

'Really?' he says, his interest only vaguely pricked. Even jabbing him with a stick doesn't work. 'What do you read?' he asks.

'Thrillers. Love them. The bigger the gold lettering, the better. So how do you make a living? I mean, poetry doesn't pay, does it? Are you a poet who also serves pizza?'

'I couldn't do that. I prefer to keep my living costs down. I don't pay any rent . . . and I sign on.' He takes a sip of hot chocolate. 'I live with my ex-girlfriend – at least, I sleep on her sofa. She doesn't mind. We stopped sleeping together and, well, I never moved out.'

'Christ, isn't that a bit awkward?'

'We're really good friends. We were always really good friends. More friends than . . .' The rest is a mumble.

Manon cups her ear. 'Sorry, can you say that last bit again?'

'I said it's a bit more awkward now she's got a boyfriend.'

'I can imagine.'

'She likes it if I stay out – you know, in the evenings, give them some space.'

Manon looks at him. Smiles. Wonders if she can make him want her. 'You could always come back to mine,' she says.

He looks into his hot chocolate, making her wait.

'We could,' he says, as if she should do more to persuade him. Another silence which she feels the pressure to fill.

'I've got wine – a nice bottle of red,' she says.

Her hand feels warm around the paper cup containing her hot chocolate but her heart is darkening. She pictures herself writhing above him, the sex just like the skating – stilted and awkward. He will expect her to put him at his ease, then lay the failure of the exercise firmly at her door. Her life seems as if it's on a loop, round and round, nothing ever changing.

'Actually,' she says, surprising herself, 'forget that. It's probably not a good idea.'

'But you just said—'

'Yes, I know. I don't know why I said that.'

'We could just talk,' he says. He has reddened.

'Talk?' she says. 'I think there'd be only one person talking and it wouldn't be you.'

He swallows, watches as she shuffles out between the nailed-down table and the nailed-down stool.

'To be honest,' he says, 'I like petite women.'

'Right, of course. I should have expected that,' says Manon.

The night air drips with moisture, dank and lonely. Up the broad pedestrian thoroughfare, yellow-smeared from the street lamps, deserted now, past the soldier on the war memorial, deep black stone receding into the night, only the shine on his elbows and knees and helmet are points of light. Aimed at him on all sides, and now shuttered up behind locked grilles, are the pound shops, one after another, which in the day give out a tinny cacophony of jangling and kerchinging, *tink tonk, rat-a-tat-tat*, dancing Santas, and teddies with drums.

Huntingdon. Beset with mobility scooters. Once described

124

by a Shakespearean drunk in the cells as 'a pimple on the protruding buttock of England'. Scene of dogged animal rights protests outside the Life Sciences lab. Never short on fog.

She passes the white frontage of the *Hunts Post*, which signals the end of the high street, and into the darker residential streets, pavements glistening with rain and the last of the melted snows, the houses either blackly empty or glowing with their curtains drawn. She hears her own footsteps slapping on the slush and another's behind her. A man or woman's? She can't be sure, though it doesn't have the timbre of feminine shoes. Wide steps. A man. Seeming to keep pace with her. She quickens, her heartbeat thudding like a bee against glass, clenching her fists inside her pockets. She puts a hand to her handbag strap, which crosses her body, pulls the bag itself to the front. Purse, keys, phone, badge. Should she put a hand on her badge? He is still behind her and she can hear him breathing. He has taken up a threatening proximity at her back. The street is entirely empty and in front of them, the black river. She steps to the side to allow him to pass – perhaps a businessman in a hurry. He is forced to go beyond her, a hunched figure in a hoodie, his head in total shadow, his movements edgy, she notices, as he turns.

'Hello, love, all right?'

She delivers a wan, business-like smile. He is blocking her path now.

'What you doing out so late?'

'Leave me alone,' she says, high-pitched and breathy. She has reached a hand surreptitiously into her bag.

'C'mon,' he says. 'Just bein' friendly.'

Drunk? He is more quivering and energised. Drugs. Still with his face in shadow. She couldn't pick him out in a line-up.

'Can you let me pass, please?' she says, and she wishes her fear wasn't so audible.

125

'Where you going? Wanna go somewhere together, you an' me?'

She stops trying to edge around him, looks him in the eye, thinking: this could be it, the moment he punches my lights out or pulls a knife. She feels for her badge and holds it up to his face.

'Fancy being arrested, mate?' she says. 'Police. Major Incident Team. I'm wondering what you know abut the disappearance of Edith Hind, seeing as how you like to threaten women.'

He is taking wide steps backwards, his palms up. 'Woa, woa, *woah*,' he says. 'I wasn't doing nothing. I wasn't . . .' Suddenly he turns and runs to the end of the street and onto the towpath.

It might be relief. Probably tiredness. Or hating ice skating and the limp attacks of the poet, or having been frightened, or the flickering question of who would report her missing if she disappeared, but she shoulders into a hedge in tears.

THURSDAY

MANON

They've made her fingertips sooty, the filth rubbing off on her. 'Missing Edith had complex love life' (*Daily Mail*). 'String of lovers led her into danger, say Edith cops' (*The Mirror*). Her father would say it's fair game, a big story, and why shouldn't they be all over it? Sex and death – there was no better combination for shifting copies. Being a local paper editor, he had a sneaking admiration for the tabloids, and part of Manon's problem with the press is she can see both sides.

She looks up from the pile of tabloids on her knees, peering through the car window to see a muddy sky pressing down on the flat roofs of the Arbury estate in Cambridge, built like Lego. The great thumb smudge of cloud begins to release fat droplets as she and Nigel slam their car doors and head for the block.

Day four of the investigation: interview known offenders – burglars, rapists, sociopaths and addicts – with an MO that plausibly fits the bill.

Both of them now out of puff, they have reached the uppermost open walkway and they stop outside Tony Wright's blue gloss front door. Tony *Wrong*, as he's known in MIT. 'To be fair, he hasn't put a foot wrong since he's been out,' his probation officer said.

'No one's answering,' says Nigel, stamping his feet next to her. He leans over the balcony and shouts, 'Oi! Hop it!' to a group of kids surrounding their car, and they scatter like birds.

Manon bangs again with her fist.

'All right, all right,' says a woman's voice behind the door. It opens and Manon has her badge ready, mid-air.

'Cambridgeshire Police, DS Manon Bradshaw and DC Nigel Williams. Tony in?'

The woman, mid-thirties, in a pink velour tracksuit, has skin the colour of tapioca and oversized hoop earrings. She turns, without saying anything, to reveal the word *Juicy* written across her back in sequins. She schlumps to the lounge where the television is on.

There is Tony, ravaged king: his face a collapsed cliff face, white hair in a loose ponytail at the nape of his neck, matching the goatee like a long drip of milk from his chin. Rounded spectacles, which make him seem curiously intellectual, or like a folk-singing hippy. His tattoo sleeves are visible, creeping all the way up to his neck.

'Hiya, Tony,' says Manon. They've known each other of old.

'Come in, Manon. Cup o' tea? How about you, Nigel?'

'I'm all right, thanks, Tony,' says Nigel, standing with his hands cupping his testicles.

'How're the twins doin', Nigel?' Tony asks. 'That's a lot o' work, twins.' His Scottish brogue adds to the affable air, the gentle grandpappy. Hard to believe he'd broken into a young woman's flat in the dead of night, took a knife from her kitchen, which he then held to her throat, forcing her to strip. He robbed

128

her that night, not simply of her peace of mind for all perpetuity, but every other valuable thing in her flat too. Wright was sent to Whitemoor, the maximum security prison just outside the village of March – a fifteen-year sentence – where he was a model prisoner, running the library. He's been out on licence for eight months.

'They are a lot of work, Tony. They're wearing us out,' says Nigel, smiling.

'Tae what do I owe this honour?' Tony asks. 'Is there, perchance, a crime for which youse two would like tae finger me? Shopliftin', is it? Arson? Murder?'

'We want to ask you a few questions, Tony, that's all,' says Manon.

'And if it isnae all right? What if now isnae a convenient time? Because frankly, ah'm watchin' *Loose Women* right now and this Coleen Nolan, she's got many interestin' things tae say.'

'Do you know anything about the disappearance of a young woman from Huntingdon, called Edith Hind?'

'Now why would ye think that?'

'Where were you on the night of seventeenth of December, Tony – Saturday night?'

'Och, that's easy, we had a lock-in an' a singsong at The Coach. You ask anyone on the estate, everyone was there. Great night, wisn't it, Lyn?'

Lyn nods, smoking.

'What time did you leave The Coach, Tony?' asks Manon.

'Aboot 2 a.m., wis it?' he says, looking affectionately at Lyn.

Really, butter wouldn't melt, Manon thinks, marvelling. Dangerous people seldom broadcast their peccadilloes – you learned that in child protection. It's not the creepy bloke in a stained mac; it's the jolly fellow who chats to you in the queue in John Lewis.

'And Sunday morning, Tony?'

'Well, I got up, no' too early after the night before,' he laughs, the phlegm bubbling in the bottom of his throat before it turns into a cough. 'Sorry,' he says, his hand over his mouth. 'Then I went tae meet Paddy at ten, as usual.'

'Paddy your probation officer?' says Manon.

'That's it. We went for a fry-up, it being Sunday mornin'. Mug o' tea, eggs and bacon, a whole stack o' bread an' butter, steamed up windaes against the cold December morn. Lovely.'

God, he's so *likeable*. Must stop warming to him, immediately.

'We'll be checking all this, you know that, Tony,' she says.

'Oh aye, you fill yer boots, Manon. I know you'll do yer job. Come an' arrest me when youse are ready.'

'We'll see ourselves out,' she says.

Manon strides up Huntingdon high street towards Cromwell's, dread churning at the prospect of the office Christmas 'knees-up', as Davy liked to call it – already an overstatement. Just a few of them having drinks, with their mobiles on in case the duty team needs to update them. Besides, they're all exhausted. Colin will bore everyone rigid about the latest iPad upgrade; Nigel will ask if she's still single and then go on about the comfortable pleasures of being 'an old married man', though he'll appear to be in no hurry to get back to 'the lovely Dawn' and the twins.

She stops outside the bar, its silver lettering attempting to give it an air of modernity. It is the kind of place twenty-two-year-old boys come for stag dos when they haven't the money or imagination to reach for Bratislava. Manon scans the room as her eyes adjust to the darkness. Fruit machines glow in one

130

corner. In another, she spots her colleagues and Bryony at the centre of the group, waving to her, then making two fingers into a gun and shooting herself in the mouth.

Manon has come later than the rest. She's been gathering in CCTV of Tony Wright's weekend; getting nowhere tracing 'unknown-515' – the number Edith rang twice in the week before she vanished; and working out which computers she worked on in the college library. 'Get all the data off that one,' she told Nigel.

And she was still trawling through Edith's personal hard drive, reading her PhD research, her emails, her postings on the Internet, the latest one being: *'Our deepest fear is not that we are inadequate. Our deepest fear is that we are powerful beyond measure.'* Beneath it she wrote: 'Not said by Nelson Mandela, but amazing anyway.'

Manon was reminded of her own youthful diaries; how much she too had been in love with a notion of herself at that age, energetically self-analysing. Edith had typed out a long passage from George Eliot's novel, *Daniel Deronda*, into a Word document titled: 'Just as I see it'.

. . . her horizon was that of the genteel romance where the heroine's soul poured out in her journal is full of vague power, originality, and general rebellion, while her life moves strictly in the sphere of fashion; and if she wanders into a swamp, the pathos lies partly, so to speak, in her having on her satin shoes. Here is a restraint which nature and society have provided on the pursuit of striking adventure; so that a soul burning with a sense of what the universe is not, and ready to take all existence as fuel, is nevertheless held captive by the ordinary wirework of social forms and does nothing particular.

Edith's screensaver is a picture of a bare-breasted woman running towards the camera with her arms thrown up and the words *Still Not Asking For It* written across her chest. She is a member of No Means No – an anti-rape group. Her PhD is on the fight against the patriarchy in Victorian literature, with reference to John Stuart Mill (*The Subjection of Women*) and *The Tenant of Wildfell Hall* ('the first radical feminist novel'). Her writing is impassioned, the beat of it like a fist punching the air.

'Hello, chicken,' says Bryony, handing Manon a vodka tonic as they survey the group together.

Colin is talking at full tilt to Davy, who sits forward with his elbows on his knees, nodding and listening intently. Stuart, wearing a black leather jacket and black jeans, which are arousingly tight, is chatting to Nigel. Kim is knocking back a pint.

'I'm already having a bad time,' says Manon.

'Oh, come on, what's not to like? It's dark, there's a faint whiff of vomit, Colin's talking technology.'

'You've got yoghurt down the back of your top,' says Manon, picking at some dried white crust on Bryony's cardigan. 'At least, I hope it's yoghurt.' She smells her fingers and frowns.

'Hang on,' Bryony says, craning over her shoulder. 'Hold this,' and she hands Manon her drink. She rummages in her bag and fishes out a toy car, then a box of raisins and finally a wet wipe. 'Go at it with this, will you?'

'I put my book in the bin on the way home,' says Manon, rubbing at Bryony's shoulder.

'Good for you. Is it coming off?'

They both detest MIT's yearly Secret Santa charade, organised before the Hind case kicked off, which had played itself out in the office at leaving time – everyone with their coats on. It was about as festive as a queue for the bus. Manon had

132

received a book on dating – *Grab Your Man Before Someone Else Does* – from the cut-price bookstore in the precinct. It was still in the pink and white striped paper bag, sealed with Sellotape, and the lack of wrapping put it firmly at Colin's door. Colin, whose response to every crime was to shake his head saying, 'Takes all sorts', had received a bag of Liquorice Allsorts, with 'Liquorice' replaced with the word 'Takes'. ('Good one,' Manon said to Bryony.) Harriet had, inappropriately enough, been given a pair of sheer stockings ('Not Stuart, surely,' Bryony whispered, horrified). Davy got a nodding dog for the car. Bryony a baby's bib that said: *What happens at Grandma's, stays at Grandma's.*

'Shame she's in a home,' Bryony whispered sadly. 'What happens at Grandma's is a lot of peeing in her pants and the odd ill-timed sexual outburst.'

'That probably should stay at Grandma's,' Manon said.

The whole thing was like being handed a placard saying: *This is what everyone in the office thinks of you.* Stuart got a seduction kit in a tiny tin (perhaps it wasn't off-target after all). Manon had been forced to buy for Kim, the office enigma. She literally knew nothing about Kim. Even her age was a mystery. So she'd bought her a bag of old-fashioned sweets and some socks. Kim seemed practical that way and when she'd opened it, she'd nodded and said, 'Fair dos.'

'Another drink?' says Kim now, having weaved her way over to Manon and Bryony.

'Why the fuck not?' says Manon. 'We're on vodka tonics, thanks, Kim.'

'Righto,' says Kim, her broad back disappearing towards the bar.

'She's an enigma wrapped in a riddle, that woman.'

'How did it go with the poet?' asks Bryony.

'He took me skating.'

'Oh my God, you hate skating.'

'Then he told me he was still living with his ex.'

'This one's sounding like a keeper. Please tell me you made your excuses and left.'

'D'you know what? I actually did, for like the first time ever.'

'Good on you, kiddo. How did he take it?'

'Told me he preferred his women petite.'

'Jeez, narrow escape then,' says Bryony, chinking her glass against Manon's. 'You did the right thing.'

They stand looking out at the bar. Manon feels her shoes pinching at the sides of her toes and at the heel. Kim returns and hands them their vodkas, venturing past them to her seat with her pint. You've got to like that about Kim – she doesn't impose 'the chat'. Manon takes a sip from the glass and realises it's a double. She's already beginning to feel anaesthetised in her lower legs and light in her head, as if her blood were heading south. She shifts on her feet.

'Christ, look at Davy,' Bryony says, 'listening away to Colin like he doesn't want to chew off his own arm.'

'He's a lesson to us all, that boy.'

They drain their glasses and new ones appear – always doubles, some with Red Bull, some with tonic. The bar seems to get darker, more blurry, the music swimming in and out of Manon's consciousness with snippets of conversation as she sways on her painful shoes, at times her eyes half closed.

She sits on the arm of Davy's chair while he fiddles about with his phone, looking up at her by way of explanation, saying, 'Chloe. She likes to check up on me. Make sure I'm not getting up to mischief.'

'Make sure you're not having any fun, more like,' says Manon, realising too late that she's said it out loud.

She looks to the banquette close by, where Kim is frowning and nodding, and Bryony is leaning in too close, a smudge of mascara down her face, shouting above the music in a slurry voice: 'I moan about them, right, Kim. I mean, I'm never knowingly under-moaned. But fuck me, Kim – I don't mean that literally, Kim,' and she burps into her fist, 'but fuck me, the kids, they're everything.'

Stuart is to Manon's right, seeming malevolently sober. He asks her where Harriet is.

'Got a dinner with the brass – retired plods get-together or something.'

Stuart nods.

Then Davy is asking Stuart about where he's from and what he did before joining the force.

'Teaching assistant at a school in Peterborough, but it was crap.'

Davy nods, his curiosity laid gently to rest like a dead cat, and the two men sit in silence, both leaning forward, elbows on knees.

'Why was it crap?' Manon shouts eventually, casting an irritable glance at Davy.

'Headmistress thought she was God's gift, lording it about.'

Stuart addresses this to Davy, who nods placidly, ever the piercing observer of human interplay.

'Isn't a headmistress sort of supposed to lord it about – in her own school?' shouts Manon again, scraping a chair in to join them.

'She'd never listen to anyone's opinion 'cept her own,' he says, and she sees bitterness, the charm having fallen at one corner, like a faulty curtain.

'Your opinion, you mean?'

'Yeah, my opinion. Why not my opinion?'

'Er, because you were a teaching assistant and she was the head?'

He frowns at her and then seems to remember himself, fashioning his face into an ironic smile. 'What will you be up to over Christmas then, Sarge?'

'Oh,' she says, looking away. 'I'm on the rota over Christmas.'

Manon lies in bed. She has mascara down her cheeks and the radio burbles beside her, at too low a volume for her to make out the words. She has been lying there thinking she must turn it up so she can listen, but the thought fails somehow to translate itself into action. Her limbs are heavy, sunk into the mattress, and the room is all broken apart, the ceiling rotating at a different rate and in a different direction to the walls and floor. Her clothes lie in a hastily discarded pile next to the bed. She closes her eyes but this increases the spinning, so she opens them again. If she could just turn up the volume on the radio so she could hear Control, she might get to sleep.

Her mind is a slur, a fluid, sliding mess of thoughts taking her back through time, the door to her mother's bedroom ajar, her fourteen-year-old self, leaning on the door frame, seeing the coroner standing over the body in the bed. Ellie was behind her, and she had pushed her sister back, wanting to shield her, knowing if she saw, she would never get it out of her head.

Forward and back, a mudslide of dark association, her mind turns to Tony Wright. Deeping and Whitemoor Prison, both in the village of March. Did Wright find his way to Deeping one night, rising out of the Fenland marsh like some twisted Magwitch?

Back again, loose and morbid. *Do not go gentle into that good night.*

The image she had shielded from Ellie: their mother's eyes

open, her head on the pillow, her skin purple and mottled where the blood had stopped moving – it had gathered along the base of her like red wine in a tilted glass. Lividity. She knows the word for it now, but she didn't then. 'The black and blue discoloration of the skin of a cadaver, resulting from an accumulation of deoxygenated blood in subcutaneous vessels.'

FRIDAY

MANON

'Is it just me?' says Harriet as she and Manon gaze at the CCTV footage of Tony Wright's various movements on the weekend of 17–18 December.

'It isn't just you,' says Manon.

'What the fuck's he up to?' asks Harriet.

'Guys, Kim, Davy, come and look at this.'

They amble over, their faces in various states of disarray after the night before: Kim's looks like a doughnut with eyes; Davy is sporting bed hair ('Been to the Vidal Sassoon night salon, I see, Davy,' says Manon). Nigel is permanently ravaged by sleep-deprivation, so he looks the same as always.

They look at the screen, amid yawns and eye-rubbing.

Tony Wright traversing the Arbury's open walkways, various angles, jaunty. Coy glances at the camera. Tony Wright entering The Coach pub on the estate, a knowing smile on his perfectly captured visage. Tony Wright playing his ukulele to a packed crowd in The Coach. Tony Wright leaving The Coach at 2 a.m. after a lock-in (little wave). Sunday, 9.46 a.m., Tony on his way to meet his probation officer, hunched, hands in the pockets of his denim jacket. Tony and his probation officer entering the local greasy spoon.

'Talk about cast iron,' says Davy.

'When was the last time The Coach had functioning CCTV, I mean with film in it?' asks Harriet.

'Never. Every nefarious deal on the estate is done in there,' says Kim. 'If they used CCTV, they'd have no customers.'

'He wants us to know he's there,' says Harriet.

'Which means?' says Manon.

'That a crime is going on elsewhere,' says Harriet. They look at each other.

'Wait, this crime or another crime? Someone's kidnapping Edith Hind for him while he plays the ukulele?' says Manon, frowning.

'Rrrrrargh,' says Harriet, pulling at her hair roots. 'Why is he messing with my head? I don't like it. I don't like it at all. Bring him in.'

'You showing us you've got a face for radio, Tony?' asks Harriet, standing over him in interview room two, her knuckles on the table. 'All that smouldering eye contact for the camera?'

'Now, I'm feelin' a lot o' negative energy coming off of you, DI Harper. I'm sensing you're really pissed off because my alibi stacks up,' says Tony, smiling at her like an indulgent parent. 'Did I just ruin yer Friday, did I?'

'What's going on, Tony?'

'Look, you people arrest me every time I chuff,' says Tony, reasonably enough. 'So these days, I walk where the cameras can see me, that way there's no confusion. I got fucked off w' havin' ma arse hauled in here and bein' shouted at fir stuff I did nae do. This is how I stop it – smile for the camera! Say cheese, Tony! S'no biggie.'

139

'Do you know what happened to Edith Hind?' Harriet demands.

Tony leans forward, his forearms on the desk. He is looking at them over the top of his glasses. Manon avoids his gaze, focusing on his dagger tattoo, the point of its blade ending at his wrist, and for some reason she wishes Davy was in the room with them.

Tony says, very low, 'Youse two want tae watch yourselves, ye ken? 'Cos youse know, an' I know, you dinnae have grounds tae arrest me. So unless youse want a whole lot o' trouble – an' I'm sayin' this for yer own good – youse need tae back the fuck off.' He leans back again, friendlier now. 'Now, is there anythin' else youse lovely lassies want tae talk about?'

A WEEK LATER
FRIDAY

MIRIAM

'Muuum?'

The call drifts up the stairs to where she lies fully-clothed on the bed, followed by stomping.

'Mum?' more gingerly at the door, and there is Rollo's darling face. Reminding her she is still a mother.

'Mum,' he says, coming to sit on the side of the bed. She smiles at him, that preposterous haircut he's brought back with him from Buenos Aires – a slant upwards from the parting like a wedge of cheese. 'Side quiff,' he'd told her, smoothing it upwards with a palm.

'Can I get you anything?' he says now. 'Cup of tea?' He has a hand on her shoulder. What would she do without Rollo?

'What are you wearing?' she says to him fondly, her voice tired – woolly like the thick shadows in the room. She hasn't slept more than two hours at a stretch in the twelve days since Edith went missing.

He looks down. 'This?' Purple cardigan with shocking pink trim, buttoned up over a white shirt and beige jeans which taper tightly to the ankle. Winkle-pickers. 'I told you, Mum, I've got a look.'

The good humour radiates from her youngest. He has been a revelation to her since the day he was born. He cracked his first joke on the breast at two months – had come off, milky-mouthed, to smile up at her, all gums, then blew a raspberry and laughed. He was his sunshine self, right from the off.

When they'd spotted Rollo down the corridor at the police station in Huntingdon, both she and Ian felt the weak gratitude of the elderly. They ran towards him and flung their arms around him, in need of holding him close. Here were reinforcements. And even though Rollo's relationship with Ian had always been strained – he was aware Edith was Ian's favourite, his academic acolyte – even Ian seemed to exhale. Later, they discussed poster campaigns and fundraisers, Rollo's Facebook and Twitter appeals forging connections and sprawling outwards like blood vessels, keeping Edith in people's minds.

'Thank you, son,' Ian said, rather formally, and Miriam caught him looking at their boy with a needy gaze that she shared, as if Rollo were honey and they were the bears.

They brought him back with them to Hampstead, and with his bag slumped by the kitchen counter and the glittering sheen of the beach still at his temples, the three of them sat shell-shocked around the table, nursing tea. Tea had featured heavily in the past fortnight. Miriam sometimes felt her belly sloshing with it, like a waterbed, yet still she took tea when it was proffered, for the symbolism, she supposed – solicitude, comfort, warmth. It is the English way, after all. Since 18 December, she has taken it with two sugars.

'I reckon she wants time alone,' Rollo said on that first night back, getting up to boil the kettle yet again, then leaning against the kitchen worktop, and she marvelled at how big he was, her little one. 'Time away from Will. He's enough to do anyone's head in.'

'He's a decent person,' said Ian.

'He's a coma-inducing bore,' said Rollo.

'There are worse crimes,' said Miriam.

'I'm not so sure.'

'He was always very good to Edith,' Ian said.

'We don't know that, do we?' Rollo said.

'The police don't think he had anything to do with it.'

'Stop talking about her as if . . .' Miriam had blurted and Rollo came over to her, cupping her head to his chest.

'This is typical Edie,' he muttered over her head. 'Always hogging the attention.'

The light in the bedroom has an evening feel, though it's mid-afternoon. They hear a group of youths shout in the street.

'New Year's Eve tomorrow,' says Rollo, looking towards the window.

'That's all we need,' she says.

Fireworks will no doubt sputter and fizz half the night, like some war on her feelings. She'd never before noticed the forced jollity of this time of year and what injury it adds to those who are bereft: all those television adverts demanding everyone be happy.

'Are they still outside?' she asks, referring to the photographers, and he shakes his head.

'There were only two and they've sloped off,' he says.

They are relieved, also, to be shot of Will, who arrived late on Christmas Eve and departed on Boxing Day, and even that was outstaying his welcome. Ian made them a cold collation – a 'smorgasbord', he called it – for Christmas lunch because it seemed wrong, somehow, to feast on turkey. Instead they sawed little rectangles of cheese onto sesame Ryvitas, which shed their crumbs across the table like builders' grit (Miriam kept sweeping them into her palm, then, realising she couldn't be bothered to get up, shook them onto the floor by her side). Pâté, which had developed a liver-red crust at its edges because Ian hadn't covered it in the fridge, pickled gherkins, and celeriac slaw, like some incongruous French picnic.

At night – endless and sleepless, all of them padding about at some point downstairs or to the bathroom – she could hear Will snivelling in the guest bedroom.

'She was in my care,' Will said at breakfast. 'It was on my watch.'

She and Rollo had shared a wearied glance, Rollo waiting for his toast to pop up.

The phone starts ringing, distantly.

'I'll go,' says Rollo, standing.

Miriam lifts herself from the pillow. 'No, I'll get it. I'm hoping it's Christy.'

MANON

Her canteen lunch of shepherd's pie and boiled carrots has collapsed into the four corners of its yellow polystyrene box. Brown gravy, Bisto-infused, the mince pebble-dashing her throat as it goes down. Piped mash – has it *ever* been potato? Not bad. Not bad at all.

She has pushed her keyboard to one side to make way for the rectangular box and the *Daily Mirror,* and she scans the News in Brief column, seeing *Search for Edith* relegated there. One paragraph on the planned television reconstruction, which will go out in the next episode of *Crimewatch.* Twelve days missing and Edith's a NiB – a reflection of the investigation's stalemate. Forensics from the scene showed only Edith's, Will Carter's, and Helena Reed's DNA at George Street, as you'd expect. The blood was Edith's but no rogue DNA on the glass shards in the kitchen bin.

'Gloves,' Harriet said, 'or it was someone whose DNA is already there.'

Meaning Carter. They are still tracing his return journey along minor roads back from Stoke; still watching that mobile

145

number 'unknown-515'; still waiting for data off the Corpus college computer – everything taking an age because of Christmas rotas, skeletal staffing. Every email met with an 'out of office'.

'Good Christmas?' asks Marie from Accounts as she passes Manon's desk, the question she dreads and tries to shrug off.

'Yeah, good thanks,' she says, barely looking up from her newspaper and some story she's not reading about a muscled pop star on his third marriage, though *This time it's for keeps'*.

She was pulled off the Hind case Christmas Eve, onto a suspicious death. It was bound to happen sooner or later. Elderly man burnt to a charcoal slump just inside the front door of his bungalow on the outskirts of Peterborough. Cover-up for a burglary, or obtaining money with menaces, or perhaps he'd done it to himself. She picked over the charred interior of the man's home and found a selection of wigs, cheap and matted – platinum blonde, mostly; a rail of polyester women's dresses in a wardrobe untouched by fire; and below a jumble of dusty high heels with slits cut in the sides and back to make room for his man-sized feet. He had worked the bins for Peterborough City Council all his life.

Manon spent Christmas Eve and Christmas Day tracing his family and yet there were none; at least, none that said they knew him. She tried to capture CCTV, which took double the time when no one but the dimmest or most desperate was on duty, and she included herself in that. Never go in for an operation or become a victim of violent crime on a major national holiday, that would be her advice.

Still, the death of old Mr Cross-Dresser did away with the day. She picked up a takeaway from The Spice Inn on Christmas night, stepping into the darkness of her flat and heading straight to her kitchen. She set her phone on the kitchen counter, its

146

screen illuminated then darkening, like some sleeper rousing then turning over again in the bed, and she remembered the calls from her father she'd ignored.

Her kitchen was the one area of the flat overlooked by the mid-century modernisers: gloomy with brown floral tiles; the grouting cracked and orange behind the taps; the cupboards dark and over-twiddled with vaguely medieval handles. Bryony said she should paint the cupboards. 'Cornforth White. Brighten it up no end.' But Manon never got around to it. Shifts blurred into shifts, overtime into more overtime. They filled her bank account but not her fridge, so that when the tide rolled away, only empty wastes remained. A deserted life. Celery that hadn't been opened but had gone rubbery. Pants and tights spilling from the top of the basket. Apples that were woolly to the bite, so that she spat them into the bin. Manon would determinedly fill the fridge, resolve to paint the cupboards Cornforth White while the washing machine churned; resolve, too, to eat beetroot more and take up Zumba, only to have it all disappear in the suck and tow of the next tide.

Bloated with korma, she listened to her father's message. 'Hi, lovey. Just wanted to wish you a Merry Christmas. Um, we've had a good day up here. Una cooked a terrific salmon terrine to ring the changes. So that was good. Yes. Well, don't work too hard. Call when you can, Manon, OK? Righto then. Bye.'

She had hoped for one from Ellie – even double-checked her missed calls, but nothing. So she told herself it was Ellie's fault, this silence. She called her father back, reluctantly, because he would inevitably ask for a festive-jollity meter reading and hers was set at zero, so to head him off, she told him about the cross-dressing corpse, which left him satisfyingly at a loss. She could hear Una getting restive in the

147

background, whispering as loudly as possible, 'We really must go, Robert.' So Manon had said, 'Go on, then. Obey her.'

She wished she could call Ellie, if only to slag off Una, but the climb-down was too hard to face.

A phone rings somewhere across the room and Manon raises her head to see Davy walking back from his canteen lunch with Stuart and Nigel. Colin is Internet shopping as usual – a TV sound bar, he says. ('You can get some real bargains in the Christmas sales.')

Manon ignores the ringing, which is shrill in the strip-lit yellow room, bouncing off the birch laminate desks as broad as mortuary slabs.

'Sarge?' says Kim.

Manon turns. Kim is looking directly at her, the phone held away from her body, in a way that makes the department stop.

'Spartan Rescue,' says Kim. They continue to look at each other, Manon's heart quickening. 'A body. In the Ouse. Just shy of Ely. Dog walker found it this morning.'

No one moves.

'Sarge?' says Kim.

'Tell them we're on our way.'

'I honestly thought . . .' Davy begins.

'Poor Miriam,' says Kim.

'Poor both of them,' says Colin, and Manon looks at him. Even Colin's face has gone slack.

She and Davy jog down the municipal stairs in silence, out to an unmarked car. Everything will be new territory for the Hinds now, a life before and a life after, and very soon that first life, the one untouched, will recede, like some blithe foreign land-scape. That first life was when Manon used to read books with

148

a torch under the duvet, the illicit thrill as her mother passed her door on her way to bed. That first life was one of lurching passions and furies, all played out against her mother's solid breast. Not happy, exactly – she could never understand people who described their childhoods as happy. She looks across at Davy driving and thinks it's probably how he'd describe his. Childhood seems to Manon (at least what she can remember of it), a time of frustration and effort, things that were frightening and new, and the retreat back into familiar comforts before the next foray.

Davy has pulled out onto the A14. The sky is a fragile blue, very far away, and the sunlight harsh and breakable and thin, sending its glassy shards through the windscreen so they both have to pull their visors down. They begin to leave the conurbation behind and the snow, which has all but melted in town, gains confidence the further they drive out into the Fens.

And then it happened. 'Sudden Death Syndrome', the coroner had said, and everything after it was another life, a new territory, one about to be discovered by the Hinds now that Edith was floating face down in the Ouse. And all the events of Manon's life were played out in its wreckage.

Much of daily life for her fourteen-year-old self and twelve-year-old Ellie remained the same. Their father had been advised to keep the routines stable for the girls' sake. School. Their bedrooms and the childish circus-print curtains their mother had chosen. Weekend swimming lessons. Crisps eaten on the back seat afterwards, the chlorine rising off their wet hair, their tights twisted wrongly about their sticky legs. Their father glancing back at them in the rear-view mirror, the seat empty beside him. They wandered helplessly through it, their rucksacks on their backs, gazed at by the more fortunate, their father never quite pre-empting their needs so that the shopping ran out and there was nothing to make a packed lunch with. Uniforms fished out of the dirty laundry basket and sniffed to see if they passed muster. They appeared to be functioning, did well in exams. Manon was top in her class because work, in comparison with living, was so easy. Reading was an escape. But she and Ellie were not – and she knew this even as a fourteen-year-old – *intact*, in the way other children were. There was a surface and then there was this gulf between it and their inner lives, shattered like a broken cup.

It was as if her mother had taken with her any strategy Manon ever had for living. When she got into Cambridge to read English, it was taken as a sign of success, as if no one could see it was a refuge. She hasn't spoken to Ellie for three years now – a rift which has grown outwards in layers of resentment like rings in a tree. It began when Ellie broke with their sibling protocol: the wilfully immature hating of Una.

'You went and *stayed* with them?' Manon asked her, incredulous. 'You didn't tell me.'

'Didn't think I had to,' Ellie said. 'Una's all right, once you get used to her.'

'Una's *all right*?'

'Yeah, she is. You know, you have to fold the toilet paper to a point after you've pulled off a sheet, but apart from that—'

'Judas.'

Davy pulls up the handbrake and they sit, listening to the car ticking. In the distance, she can see frogmen from Spartan Rescue milling about on the riverbank, and an ambulance, its back doors flung wide, a red blanket smoothed flat on a waiting stretcher. She sees the pathologist from Hitchingbrooke, Derry Mackeith, talking to a uniform.

'I hate the smell of these,' she says to Davy as they get out of the car.

'MIT,' says Mackeith, striding towards her from the riverbank. 'To what do we owe this honour?' The purple thread veins on his nose are livid in the cold and his breaths emerge as white puffs.

'Is she out of the water?' says Manon, trying to look past him, but the frogmen and Spartan Rescue officials are blocking her view.

'She?' says Mackeith. 'It's not a she.'

Manon looks at him. 'What do you mean? Are you saying it's not Edith Hind?'

'Not unless Edith Hind was a young male of mixed race,' says Mackeith.

'I thought—'

'Ah, yes, sorry about that. Spartan Rescue seem a bit jumpy about not having found the Hind girl. False alarm. Pretty obvious the minute we hooked him out. We did try and call you. You're welcome to have a look but I'd say you guys are not needed. He's a jumper, if you ask me. We'll get an ID from fingerprints, I should imagine. Coroner can take it from there.'

Manon looks past Mackeith, and the throng of frogmen and uniformed officers has parted to reveal the body: muddied, discoloured, and vastly distended. A blue, marbled Buddha.

'How long ago – any idea?' she asks.

'This time of year, water's quite cold. There's only moderate decomposition. Two to three weeks, I'd say.'

'Did you find a wallet, phone?' she says to the representative of Spartan Rescue, who has rustled towards them in his expensive windcheater. Navy, with pink fleecy trim.

'No, ma'am, nothing. Just the clothes he was wearing – jeans and a hoodie and some rather expensive trainers, which would've helped him sink to the bottom. If you've nothing further, we'll get him to the mortuary.'

*   *   *

151

They stand on the doorstep of a sawdust-coloured barn, brash new timbers bordered by prissy hedges. But when Manon and Davy walk inside, to interview the dog walker who found the body, they both look up in silent awe at the double-height atrium, thick oak beams criss-crossing the vaulted roof and cathedral-size windows.

'We'll try not to take up too much of your time,' says Manon.

'No, please. Come and sit down. Can I make you coffee?' His voice is deep and slow. He walks with a slight stoop in his voluminous corduroys. His bowed head is gentle and apologetic.

'Coffee would be lovely, thanks,' says Manon. 'It's freezing out there.'

'This place is amazing,' says Davy, who has approached the window. The sky has turned pink, striated yellow; a radioactive lozenge at its centre, reflected in the river. Along its banks, leafless trees are silhouetted. The pink of the sunset – so fleshy and garish – has stretched its arm into the room, giving them all a Californian tan.

In front of the wall of windows is a refectory table with two benches, its surface strewn with newspapers. On the other side of the room, a wood-burning stove and russet-coloured dog in front of it in a basket. It raised its head when they entered but lowers it again now, un-fussed.

'She's very elderly,' explains Alan Prenderghast (Davy has whispered his name in Manon's ear), who is now at the open-plan kitchen area, turning levers on a complex silver coffee machine. The kitchen is a dark U-shape with slate-grey cupboards and black worktop.

'Lovely view,' Manon says, joining Davy at the windows and watching the sun squat on the horizon, peppered with birds. She looks to her right and sees a frayed armchair and a pair of binoculars on a table beside it. Silence for a while, which Davy would normally try to fill, but they are both hypnotised by the stillness and scale of the house and its view.

At last, Mr Prenderghast comes to stand next to her and is handing her a cup of coffee, froth covering its surface.

'It's my favourite thing about this house,' he says, looking out with her.

Her cup's roasted smell drifts up like smoke.

'You see that field opposite – on the other bank of the river? Every winter it's allowed to flood and it fills up with literally thousands of birds. Ducks, geese, swans. Teeming with life. Great skeins of them fly in from Scandinavia. I could watch it all day, the landing and the flying off. It's a very sad view, somehow.'

His voice is calm. It is as if he is selecting every word. The ruffled sleeve of care – his voice could un-ruffle it. She looks at the view, the sunset colours like a bruise, and the bare trees. He's right – it is the saddest view she has ever seen. She wants to stay in this kitchen, which is so warm and yet so quietly morbid – silent and slow and away from the town – even though she has never been one of those people for whom the countryside is an idyll.

'It must've been a shock, finding the body,' she says.

'It wasn't what I was expecting, no,' he says. 'I've never seen one before and it was much worse than I imagined, actually. Who was it?'

'We don't know yet. A young man. We'll have an ID by close of play today.'

'Not the girl, then,' he says. 'The one who went missing before Christmas.'

'No. Not the girl.'

He nods, stooping to sip his coffee while his free hand digs into his trouser pocket.

153

Davy is sitting at the refectory table with his notepad out. 'Can I ask what you do for a living?' he says.

Manon has strolled over to the bookshelves, which are to one side of the stove. They are tall and crammed, with a library ladder propped against one section. *Tender is the Night. American Pastoral. Far from the Madding Crowd. Birthday Letters. Jane Austen and the War of Ideas.*

'Yes, of course,' Mr Prenderghast says to Davy. 'I'm a systems analyst at Cambs Biotech.'

Freud. John le Carré. A history of Labour foreign policy in the post-war years.

'What's a systems analyst, if you don't mind me asking?' says Davy.

'Oh, it's terribly boring. I basically make the computer system work for a large pharmaceutical company – the sort of global conglomerate that *Guardian* readers hate.'

'Where's it based?' asks Manon.

'Outskirts of Cambridge, towards Newmarket. One of those charmless industrial estates. But I've been working from home this week – the office is deserted this time of year.'

'Did you study English at university?' asks Manon, glancing back at the bookshelves.

'No, quite a few of those are for a course I'm doing. Open University. The others are for pleasure. I wasn't . . . I didn't go. To college, I mean.'

'And you were walking your dog this morning?' says Davy, pen poised.

'Yes. My usual walk, to give Nana her run-around. Well, more of a hobble these days. We took the path along the river. Nana,' he says, nodding at the dog, and her eyebrows move independently at this, like two caterpillars, though her head remains lowered in her basket, 'started to scratch at some tree

154

roots close to the bank. I kept calling her but she wouldn't come away, so eventually I went to fetch her and that's when I saw it. Just the back. It was face down in the water.' He coughs. 'I shouldn't say "it" – I mean *him*.'

They are all silent for a moment, in reverence for the body.

'Thanks, Mr Prenderghast,' says Manon. 'I don't think we need to detain you any longer.'

Davy and Manon begin to gather their coats. It takes them a few moments to re-bury themselves in scarves and gloves.

'Going out celebrating tomorrow night?' asks Davy.

'Ah yes, it's New Year's Eve, isn't it?' he says, smiling. 'I'd forgotten. No, I'm afraid it's not my thing. I'm not good with crowds.'

'I love a New Year's knees-up, myself,' says Davy.

'I'm with you, Mr Prenderghast,' says Manon. 'I can't stand it.'

'Call me Alan, please. I'll be staying put. Watch a film maybe.'

'What, by yourself?' says Davy, appalled.

Manon casts Alan a conspiratorial look, as if they are Davy's weary parents.

He laughs. 'I do think there's the most terrible fear of solitude these days – as if it's some kind of disease. People can't tolerate it. They want to be seen in a constant social whirl.'

'I didn't mean . . .' says Davy.

'No, no, I was only making a general point,' he says, with one hand on the open door. 'I can go on a bit, sorry. I'm probably defensive. Perhaps my unconscious wishes I'd go to a party, DC Walker. Well, thank you, officers. If I can help with anything else, then do call.'

SATURDAY

DAVY

The cycle path – marvellously flat and open – takes him across the marshy flatlands of the Fens and though it's bracing (he'd had to make himself brave the winter weather this morning), now he's out in the air and going at an exhilarating speed, there's nothing better. Davy has always kept himself active, though shift patterns sometimes intervene (especially during a whopper like the Hind case). Most mornings he runs at 6 a.m. or takes the bike out. He would never let himself slide, not after his mum and all that staying in bed or staring at the telly, shoving in chocolate bourbons like she was daring him to try and stop her.

This morning, Chloe had gone off to her job in Next on the high street – today being not just a Saturday, but New Year's Eve, so a busy one – and he drove the car an hour out of Huntingdon, to Wisbech, so he could cycle some of the many excellent Fenland routes. He's been yearning for time to think about how to have The Conversation with Chloe, and he's been yearning also for a feeling of movement. There's really nothing else like it, your body and your bike going at speed and the fresh scent of the countryside blowing into your lungs; big skies, in an enormous dome over the flatlands, and the river like a cool, grey road beside him.

He pedals harder, away from the images the river conjures, of the body from yesterday – the inflammation of his flesh, his blue-purple colour inhuman. Just a boy. And Davy can't help but think about Ryan – what might happen to him without the protection of Aldridge House. He resolves to put in more calls, see if the social worker can do anything. Davy must try his best to stop Ryan ending up like that boy in the river, because before you know it, it can be too late, and he finds himself in a silent argument with Chloe, because she was always saying, 'You love those kids more than me,' and going into a sulk.

He wheels around a bend in the towpath, following the curve of the river, loving the way the bike tilts with him on it, against the laws of gravity, almost – they should topple but speed keeps his wheels turning, and the wind roars into his face and through the bare winter trees. No, he tells himself, this thinking time is not for Ryan or the Hind case, it's for Chloe. Tonight could be the night to broach the subject of The Future, yet every time they're together and the moment seems appropriate, something puts him off: music coming on a bit loud in the restaurant; bumping into someone they know in the pub; the urgent need for a poo (his, not hers – she'd never discuss something so vulgar).

He slows his bike and looks up at a blue sign pointing left, which says *March*. He could duck down there, have a nosey around Deeping. The case is bothering him more and more: Harriet still nagging away at the Tony Wright alibi; Will Carter far from in the clear, his return journey from Stoke still not verified. Manon reckons they should be looking more closely

157

at the Director of Studies – this Graham Garfield chap – because when Davy and Manon asked about Garfield during one of their many interviews with the Hinds, they'd expressed 'doubts'.

'Doubts?' Manon had said.

'Well, Edith called us up very excited during the first term she had him. Said he'd told her she was exceptional – the brightest student he'd had in years,' Sir Ian replied.

'Why would that raise doubts?' asked Davy, genuinely nonplussed.

'Perhaps it shouldn't have, DC Walker. But when a middle-aged man is that effusive about an attractive twenty-year-old—'

'Come on, Ian, that's not fair,' Lady Hind said. 'Maybe Edith was just working at full tilt.'

'Yes, maybe, but there were other reasons. When she'd been out with her peers – this was when she was an undergrad – she mentioned he was often around, in the college bar and such like. Just seemed a bit . . . creepy, that's all.'

'And there's that girl he had a fling with,' Lady Hind said, touching her husband's arm.

'Yes, what was her name?'

'Oh God, I can't remember. Edith told us they were sleeping together. She actually said something along the lines of "Ew, gross."'

'None of it, of course, was threatening,' Sir Ian said. 'I think he's a bit of a, well, pest is the word Edith used, to be honest.'

Dirty shagger, Davy thinks, wheeling away from the sign and the left-hand turn he hasn't taken to March. That's what Graham Garfield was, same thing his mum called his dad when his dad went off with Sharon – 'dirty shagger' and 'selfish bastard with no thought for anyone but himself'.

Davy suggested they go easy on the Garfield chap, there being no law against being a dirty shagger, and it was not as

158

if there was anything directly linking him to Edith on the Saturday night, his wife having confirmed that Garfield came home to her after The Crown.

'Remember what Harriet told us, about alibis given by wives and mothers,' said Manon. 'You think because Garfield reads Tennyson, he couldn't rape someone? You're a snob, Davy Walker.'

'Not that, he just seems too . . . gentlemanly, like he's never had it rough.'

'Posh people do fucked up just as well as everyone else,' she said, 'sometimes better.'

And he supposes she'd know, being half-posh herself, or on the way to it after going to Cambridge. So he's trying to view Garfield in the light of Manon's mistrust – the way, for example, Garfield wore the uniform of the academic (corduroys and elbow patches) and had the books he'd written facing forward on the shelf. Manon said this showed intellectual insecurity, though Davy thought it just made him look clever. Shaved heads and tattoos, that sent a different message altogether, and he thinks of Ryan again and the rough estate he used to live on (though God alone knows where he's living now) and the unsavoury men who circle his mother.

Davy's thoughts go round and round like the wheels on his bike, when he's come out here to think about Chloe, because New Year's Eve can take a romantic turn, although if he's honest, he'd rather be going out on the razz with his friends. Chloe doesn't meld with them too well, and whenever he's tried to mix the two – his girlfriend and the gang from school – he's ended up in the corner of the bar asking her over and over what the matter is. Perhaps he'll skip The Conversation, after all, there being no hurry . . .

He's forced to squeeze hard and sudden on the brakes,

and he turns the front wheel sharply, the gravel spraying. A duck proceeds on its stately waddle across his path, one eye blinking at him with faint disdain, until it plops into the river to Davy's right.

Manon

Swedish season at the Cambridge Arts Picturehouse, all red velvet and the smell of brewing coffee. Women wearing big beads. She relishes the prospect of a Swedish film – it doesn't even have to be *noir*. The Swedes are a nation who appreciate morbidity, unlike the British, who are just as depressed as everyone else but who like to project their darker feelings, saying to people in the street, 'Cheer up, it might never happen!' Cat calls like that make her want to take out her Taser.

She parks on a single yellow, less than a yard from the cinema's broad steps. The cold is bitter and thin and she realises how fed up she is of it, how long it has been going on, tensing her body against it. Her left eye has become re-infected, the grit scratching her eyeball. It had recovered somewhat over Christmas and then, following the use of a particularly unappetising mascara, the soreness returned worse than before, her lashes gummed with a secretion which peeled away in clumps. It's less painful if she keeps it shut. With the other eye, she sees various trouser legs and shoes on the cinema's white step as she joins the queue, willing it to be quick so she can get out of the cold.

'DS Bradshaw?' says a male voice.

She looks up, still with one eye shut, and sees Alan Prenderghast stooping to search out her face.

'Hello there,' she says, her neck cricked – the reluctant mole. She smiles thinly, making a show of trying (but barely trying at all) to hide her disappointment at the prospect of him occupying her mind and preventing her losing herself in the film. And regret that she looks like she's been punched in the eye.

'So,' he says. 'We've had the same idea.'

'Yes. The only way to spend New Year's Eve, if you ask me.' She looks away from him across the street. He strains his neck upwards to look over the heads in front and see how near they are to the kiosk. They shuffle forward slightly.

'I found that, after yesterday, I didn't want to be by myself after all. I felt the need to be in the town. Among people. Alive people,' he says, with a damp sort of laugh.

'Yes.'

'We don't have to sit together,' he adds. 'I rather love going to the cinema on my own, so I do understand.'

'Oh, OK,' says Manon, relieved and rejected. They shuffle forward and then to the snacks counter where she orders a real lemonade and organic popcorn, and he takes a coffee, which makes her feel like a child for ordering the sweet stuff. Then he asks for a family-sized box of Maltesers.

They walk into the dark plush of the screening room, velvet seats fraying on the arms. He nods, saying, 'See you later, then,' and moves down the aisle. They are watching *Together* by Lukas Moodysson, about a hippy commune in the 1970s and the waifs and strays who come together there.

Alan Prenderghast sits four rows ahead and to her left, so the side of his head is visible, though not his expression. Despite her obscured view, she thinks she can see him laughing when she glances across at him during the film, which she does often, the daylight scenes illuminating his head in flickering blues. She thinks she can see enjoyment written all over his shoulders. He seems to be hugging his family-sized box of Maltesers in delight and hugging his aloneness too, and taking pleasure in a good film with chocolate and a worn, comfortable seat, though who is to say whether it is his enjoyment or her own hopes for it, streaming forward like dancing rays from the projector.

She is ahead of him in the slow shuffling of people exiting the cinema. At the doorway, she smiles.

'I'm going for a drink upstairs if you fancy joining me,' he says.

'Oh yes, that's a good idea.'

The upstairs bar is art deco with wooden tables and ferny plants in pots. She watches him bring two coffees, squat white cups balanced on saucers, back from the bar to their table and she notices how high-waisted his trousers are. His trainers are terrible too – great white ships, the kind you're supposed to play tennis in, not wear for leisure. He looks like Fungus the Bogeyman, she thinks, and she, with her half-swollen eye, like Quasimodo.

Sitting in a tree.

K.I.S.S.I.N.G.

'So, what did you think?' he says, unlooping a maroon scarf and draping it over the back of his chair.

'I thought it was fabulous. Funny, moving, great knitwear.'

He laughs. 'It's a very touching idea, isn't it, these misfits coming together and keeping each other company. That it's better to be together.'

'Yes,' she says. 'But they weren't idealised. They were a genuinely motley bunch.'

'It's not so easy, in real life. To make contact with people.'

'No, it isn't. I sometimes think I don't actually like anyone that much. That all I ever want is to be on my own. And then I can't cope with it – with myself, just myself all the time, and it's like *I* become the worst company of all – and there's this awful realisation that I need people and it's almost humiliating,' she says.

He looks at her and smiles.

'I don't know where that came from.'

He shakes his head. 'I totally get it. I live in that great barn and sometimes on a Sunday morning it's like heaven, sitting in front of that massive window with my coffee, with the sun coming in, reading. And then by 11 a.m. I'm desperate for someone to call round, but of course they don't, because I live in the arse end of nowhere.'

She laughs. 'Except the police, occasionally.'

'Or a corpse. Well, he didn't come knocking.'

'No. Have you recovered?'

'I don't think there was anything to recover from, really. I mean, it was shocking and I spent a day thinking about death more than usual – and I'm someone who thinks about death *a lot*. But it's not like I knew him or cared for him. It was the fact he was young that bothered me.'

'Yes.'

'I suppose you can't talk about the case.'

'No.'

She rubs her eye, hard, feeling the crystals work into her eyeball.

'That eye looks sore,' he says.

'Yes, I don't know what it is. Feels like I've got something stuck in it which I can't get out. Been like this on and off for a fortnight.' And she feels the moment race towards her, unannounced, an awful parody of *Brief Encounter*, where he will feel invited to come close to her face and look deep into her eyes to see what's there. She hadn't intended that at all.

'Looks like conjunctivitis to me,' he says.

'Really?' she says, disappointed.

'Yes. You can get antibiotics for it over the counter.'

Out in the street they find their cars are nose to tail. His is an anonymous silver Ford, just the kind she'd expect from a systems analyst wearing tennis shoes. The seats look as if they've been recently vacuumed.

'This is me,' she says, waiting for him to comment on her Seventies mustard Citroën with the black leather seats. Waiting for him to take in *the package*.

'This is your car, is it?' he says mildly.

'Yup.' She pats the roof.

'Right, then,' he says. He is digging one hand in his trouser pocket. He brings out a handkerchief and holds it to his nose. It blooms white and big across his face, and he pushes it side to side, bending his nose. She has never seen anyone under seventy use a handkerchief.

'Do you fancy . . .' she begins. 'We could . . . go on somewhere?'

He looks at his watch. 'I think everywhere will be packed with awful drunkards right about now. Sorry,' he says, stifling a yawn, 'I'm going to have to call it a night. This is burning the candle for an old fart like me.'

'Right, yes, of course. I suppose we're in opposite directions.'

'I suppose,' he says. 'Well, Happy New Year.'

165

She wonders if he is going to bend to plant a kiss on her cheek but he shifts slightly. He places a hand on her upper arm and she lifts her cheek but he turns away.

She watches him duck into his warm, practical car.

SUNDAY

MANON

Bryony's husband Peter opens the oven door with padded hands like paddles and lifts out an angrily spitting pan. He holds it before him, the furious beast, the God of their lunch, and the room fills with the atavistic smell of meat fat. The trail of it curls across the room to Manon in the corner armchair – the salty maple smell of the meat – and together with the dry white wine she is sipping, it works on her stomach juices to produce the sweet anticipation of being fed.

The windows of the kitchen are fogged, as if the world Bryony and Peter have created – the roast lunch, the baby she is putting down for a nap, the toddler playing Lego in the next room – has erased the outside because it is not needed. This world, their world, is inside.

'Looking good, elephant woman. Shouldn't you get that seen to?' says Bryony as she enters the room.

Manon puts a hand to her left eye. 'Yeah, probably.'

Bryony and Peter move around each other at the counter, a nonchalant ballet of putting forks in the dishwasher, getting out bowls, broccoli steam hitting their faces, carving the meat.

167

And Manon watches them. Isn't this what she should have? Isn't it what she should want? She knows she comes here, like the third child, to inhale some of it, to slouch in the soft cushioning of the corner armchair where passivity is king. Sometimes she is pricked by jealousy – or at least she wants to possess it. Not wanting to leave or not having the energy to pick herself up and send herself out into the cold world alone. She rubs the infected eye and it re-opens slowly, the picture watery, as if she is looking through smeared glass. Those vicious shards of loneliness cannot seem to prick them in here, in this inner world, where someone has taken an eraser to the view. But its innerness is also airless.

'D'you know what drives me nuts?' Bryony once said. 'I can't even take a shower without some kind of family summit on the logistics of being out of the room for ten minutes. Never mind pop to the shops.'

It's not these notional practicalities that bother Manon. It is the loss of separateness, the dependence which might cause her to meld formlessly into someone else until she no longer knows where she begins and ends, until she is no longer capable of saying, 'You might like that, but I don't like it, because I am different from you, separate from you.' Or 'I will not eat now. I will eat later.'

'We changed the clocks,' Bryony is saying from across the room, sliding some cauliflower cheese from a foil tray into a serving bowl, 'so it said midnight. Then we said, "Cheers, Happy New Year!" and went to bed. About nine thirty, wasn't it?'

'About that,' says Peter. 'Just think of all the poor bastards out there getting drunk and snogging strangers.'

'I know, I pity them,' says Bryony. 'I mean, who would want that kind of sleazy, low-rent thrill?'

Manon takes another slug of wine. 'I went to the cinema.'

'See? She's one of us,' says Bryony.

Their three-year-old son Bobby comes gambolling into the room on fat little legs. He is all cheeks and brilliant eyes. Manon notices Bryony's involuntary smile.

'Hello, little chap,' says Manon, setting down her glass and lifting him onto her knee. She has the urge to shower him in affection, not because she loves him – she feels, in fact, an angular separateness from other people's children – but because she loves Bryony and she can make a display of it this way. 'Shall we do "This is the Way the Lady Rides"?'

'Lady wides,' says Bobby.

'Cuddle first,' says Manon, and she folds the boy's solid body in her arms and luxuriates in the cashmere of his cheek against hers. She kisses him and when he begins to struggle, squeezes him tighter. 'One more kiss,' she says and then blows a raspberry into his neck, which smells of warm bread, but he is shouting, 'Lady wides!'

The lunch is devoured in twenty minutes. Their lips glisten with the meat fat as they suck on bones. Bobby begins to fidget in his booster seat and knocks over his cup of Ribena.

'Come on, sausage,' Peter says to him. 'Let's go and watch *Top Gear*.'

When they have gone, she and Bryony pour themselves more wine and sit together at the kitchen table, strewn with cloudy glasses and smeared plates. Manon is wiping hers with a finger and licking the gravy off while she tells Bryony about the cinema and Alan Prenderghast, and it's as if she can't wait to, as if she's been waiting for Peter to take Bobby off, so she can launch into it.

'He's nice, but he's not boyfriend material,' she says. 'He's forty-two.' She is picking at charred roast carrots, wiping the little chunks in gravy and popping them in her mouth.

169

'I hate to break it to you, kiddo, but you're not in the first flush of youth yourself. Forty-two is the perfect age for you.'

'No, but . . . just, no. He's not, I dunno. He's really uncool. Like massive trainers, bad flappy trousers.'

'So take him shopping.'

'He's got big ears.'

'You've got no neck.'

'He didn't go to university.'

'Jesus, Manon, who fucking cares?'

'He *has* got a nice barn.'

'There you go then.'

'He's just kind of . . . odd.'

'Odd is good. You're really odd. It's one of my favourite things about you. Stop doing that,' and she removes Manon's plate. 'Ice cream?'

Manon shakes her head. Bryony yawns and stretches her arms up and forward, until her muscles judder.

'Anyway, how's disclosure?' asks Manon. 'Is the filing getting to you?'

'No, the exciting news is I've been seconded – HOLMES support on a trafficking ring. Massive case, joint ops between border control and public protection. Really good.'

'You mean girls trafficked into prostitution?'

'Yeah – some girls in a brothel in Luton are talking. But also just ferrying illegals in across the border. Lorries of Afghans, Syrians, wherever there's a war, basically, coming in through the ports. P&O Ferries, that kind of thing. You would not believe how leaky our borders are right now.'

'Think I would.'

'Anyway, it's really interesting. Nice change from *Fireman Sam*.'

'They charging anyone?' asks Manon.

170

'Not yet. Looking at a chap – an Afghan called Abdul-Ghani Khalil.' Bryony has got up, taking their plates over to the sink. 'Couple of the prostitutes mentioned him, and a neighbour said he thought Khalil was making a fortune bringing people in, but not enough to charge him yet.'

Manon's mobile phone has begun to vibrate across the table. 'Hang on,' she says to Bryony. Manon stands and her insides swim with the wine. She is loose, but she must hold it together because Harriet is on the phone.

'Harriet,' she says brightly, a finger pressing her other ear shut against the tinny sounds of *Top Gear* from the next room and the clatter of Bryony stacking the dishwasher.

'The body from yesterday, the jumper,' says Harriet. 'We don't think it is a jumper.'

'Why not?'

'He's from Cricklewood, name's Taylor Dent.'

'*Cricklewood?* How's he ended up in Ely?'

'Exactly. Can you come in? Stanton wants a briefing.'

Harriet hangs up. She has no time for pleasantries at the beginning and end of phone calls.

'Can you drive me in, Bri?' she says as her phone thunks to the bottom of her handbag. 'I've had too much to drink.'

'Yes, sure thing. Just let me put my shoes on. Don't want anyone at the nick to see me in these,' says Bryony, slipping off her bright fur slippers with bunny ears – pre-teen pink, the colour of the sunset through Alan Prenderghast's double-height windows.

'Sit down, Manon,' says Stanton, his back to them.

Harriet is already seated on Manon's side of the desk, her crossed upper leg bouncing outwards. She is reading a brown file, which drips downwards at its corners.

Stanton is standing by the window, wearing a navy shirt with an ebullient floral pattern on it. Boden, from the looks of it – a Mrs Stanton purchase, Manon guesses, fresh from the packet for a New Year's Day family lunch or knees-up with the neighbours. She imagines him dad-dancing, his teenage children rolling their eyes.

Manon has always liked Gary Stanton. He's straight, in that suburban, slightly overweight, Kia-driving, golf-playing way. He can rub along with the boss class without taking umbrage. As a result, he has slid noiselessly up the ranks. No flashes of brilliance. No feuds, either.

Harriet hands Manon the file as Stanton turns, reaching back to scratch his shoulder blade.

'Taylor Dent,' he says. 'What's he doing in one of our rivers?'

'He killed Edith Hind, then killed himself?' says Harriet. 'He was Edith's bit of rough, her dealer? She owed him money?'

'What if he's the link between Tony Wright and Edith?' asks Manon. 'Tony's gofer.'

'We need to look at all of it. I want George Street and Deeping swept for his DNA. Annoying there are no cameras around Deeping. I want you two liaising with the Met on Dent's background, links to Wright. I want interviews with the Dent family. Did he know Edith? Was there any connection through friends – a dealer, the Hind brother? Every avenue. Let's look at routes from London to here, CCTV at King's Cross around the time he disappeared, roads, ANPR any vehicles he might have had access to.'

Stanton looks depressed. Last thing he needs is a fresh murder enquiry clogging up officers' time, slowing up the Hind investigation; more forensics and an expensive postmortem draining his budget.

'Phone work,' he says. 'We need to check this Dent boy's number against Edith's phone and against Carter's and Reed's. Let's see if he's unknown-515.'

'Will Carter's alibi holds up,' Harriet says to Stanton. 'His return journey from Stoke was verified by the cashier at the Texaco garage in Corby. We showed her a picture and she said, "Oh yeah, he was *lush.*" ' Harriet reaches for her bra strap but her arm stops mid-air and she lays it back in her lap, like a dead thing. Has someone – Elsie? – told her she's a fidget? Still, her foot is going. Kick, kick, kick, as if the energy must escape from somewhere.

Manon has opened Taylor Dent's file and is reading. Seventeen years old from Cricklewood, North London. Mixed race. Nigerian father, whereabouts unknown. Irish mother, Maureen Dent, known alcohol and substance abuser. Taylor Dent made his money the way lots did: bit of this, bit of that. Knock-off gear, cigarettes off booze cruises sold in markets or to nefarious newsagents. If he dabbled in drugs, he didn't appear to partake in them.

'Says here he was arrested for indecency in 2008 but let off with a caution,' she says, frowning.

'Had some high-profile customers,' says Stanton, 'who didn't wish a prosecution to come to court.'

Stanton has a look of distaste. He is a man who likes to avoid confrontation, like a loyal dog tied to a railing – he does not wish to bark or snap, certainly not at the wrong heels.

'Interesting,' says Manon, still reading. 'Says here Dent was clean.'

'Well, to our *knowledge,*' starts Harriet. 'A forensic post-mortem will tell us more.'

'Not necessarily,' says Stanton, turning away from them back to the window where the sky has darkened to a slate blue, smeared with the yellow street lamps over the car park. 'Toxicology will have washed away. PMs on river deaths are pretty inconclusive, in my experience. He'll have been beaten about by tree roots, got at by animals. Cause of death unascertained, I'll put money on it. To think that's what we pay them three grand for.' He shakes his head.

Manon guesses he's marvelling at the riches of forensic pathologists in their BMWs with cream leather seats.

'Speaking of money, the cost of the Hind investigation is getting to the point where the Home Office is going to have to bail us out. I've had a note from Sir Brian Peabody about it.' He waves a bit of paper at them. 'Polsa teams, SOCO, television appeals. Now this forensic PM and more officers on Dent. The profile of it, well, it's making our good Commissioner jumpy.'

'What're we supposed to do?' asks Harriet. 'Stop looking for her? Not look as hard?'

'Just look more cheaply,' says Manon.

'They're not pulling the plug,' says Stanton. 'But we're under scrutiny, that's all. If we had a body, then we'd have an unlimited murder budget, but Edith Hind – it's moot whether she's a high-risk misper, a suspected homicide, or even just a misper in Peabody's view.'

'Is there anyone who seriously thinks she's alive?' asks Harriet.

'Look, Peabody's just looking ahead,' says Stanton. 'Enquiry gets to this size, and there's always an enquiry into the enquiry, questions in Parliament about how much we spent, what result we got and why we didn't know it was "so-and-so" three weeks before we caught him. Everyone throwing in their wisdom with the benefit of hindsight. Doesn't help that Hind is mates with Galloway. I can see how itchy Peabody is about that. There are already mutterings about a review of our investigation by another force.'

'Bound to happen, sooner or later,' says Harriet.

'Manon, I want you to go to Cricklewood first thing tomorrow. Liaise with Kilburn CID. Visit the Dent family, get what you can out of the mother and the brother. Then you can pop up to Hampstead and update the Hinds.'

'Perhaps she should inform Sir Ian that his dear friend's austerity budget means there aren't enough resources to find his daughter,' says Harriet. 'Let's see him bring *that* up at their next Hampstead dinner party.'

'I'll pretend I didn't hear that,' says Stanton, with a smile at Harriet that says: *we're on the same side.*

'Least I don't have to tell them we've hooked their daughter out of the Ouse,' says Manon.

Stanton closes the door to his office. They watch him turn the spindle on his Venetian blind and disappear.

'D'you need a lift anywhere?' asks Harriet, as she and Manon put their coats on.

'No. Getting the train to Bedford to pick the car up. Shouldn't take long. I forgot to ask – how was Buckaroo with Elsie? Did she throw in a custard cream?'

'Long,' says Harriet, picking her bag up off the floor. 'Very, very long. It's not a game I'd recommend for someone with advanced-stage Parkinson's.'

'No, no, I can see hooking those little plastic . . .'

They both shake their heads at the thought of it.

'I just didn't think it through,' Harriet says sadly. 'I'm a complete fucking idiot sometimes. She wouldn't give up, though, I'll give her that.'

'S'pose you should steer clear of Operation as well.'

'Anyway, how was yours? Wild partying, I bet.'

'I went to the movies instead. Swedish season at the arts cinema. Bumped into that dog walker, actually – chap who found Taylor Dent.'

'Oh yeah? Davy mentioned his amazing barn. Said he fancied the pants off you.'

'Oh,' says Manon, flushing like a marzipan fruit. 'I don't think he did.' And her inner world shudders as if a host of celestial doves were fluttering up inside her ribcage.

Her lonely bench, police blue, on a deserted Sunday platform; wondering what's left in the fridge for tea. The problem of food for one: it symbolises everything. She wants delicious morsels yet cooking for herself is so defeating: a surplus of ingredients, the washing-up unshared, and the sense that it doesn't matter – the production of it or whether it's nice. The daily slog of being alone washes over her on the cold latticed bench, the sense of being unassisted in the minutiae: broadband down; washing machine stuck on spin cycle. Oh yes, people spoke of the freedoms – no one to answer to! – but there was such a thing as a surfeit of freedom, a sort of weightless free fall through nothing. She wonders what Alan Prenderghast is like at fixing things, or renewing roadside breakdown assistance. Masterful, if his Ford Focus is anything to go by.

There is a solitary fellow passenger two benches down, and as he turns to look at her, Manon is careful to turn her head away. Never catch their eye.

A songbird trills, curiously rural amid track and all the metal clutter overhead. The man gets up from his bench and starts towards her, carrying a holdall that looks as if it could be laden with half a torso or firearms but probably contains a mildewed towel and some unpleasantly brief Speedos. He reaches the bench next to hers just as the headlamps of their First Capital Connect train hoves in to view, screeching and puffing and crawling up the platform like an elderly sex symbol keeping the fans waiting. The brakes squeal, a gush of air from somewhere.

Manon waits for the man to choose his carriage so she can choose a different one. Never board first, otherwise they can follow you in.

The familiar blue tartan seats, the smell of warm air pumped through metal floor vents, and someone's fast food.

In Bedford she stops at her car and looks at the orange glow through the drawn curtains of Bryony's windows, imagining Bryony and Peter cuddled up on the sofa in front of the TV.

MONDAY

MIRIAM

A new year and it feels so old, worn out and tin-rusted. 2011, fifteen days missing. Time pants away from her disappearance like a locomotive and the rawness of it dissipates, as if this might be an acceptable new status quo.

'Right,' she says to Rollo, gathering her keys from the kitchen table. 'I'm off to see Jonti.'

Rollo is eating more toast. It's Herculean, the loaves he can get through. 'Say hi from me,' he says through a full mouth.

Miriam's journey to Jonti's shop in Kensal Rise is typically vigilant. She searches every face these days, examines every doorway bed, sees Edith everywhere – the spun gold of her hair; her long slender neck; the back of her head, beloved oval, unaware and vulnerable.

Only yesterday, Miriam had hastened across the scratched grass of the Heath to the bench overlooking the ponds, stumbling happily, she was so sure it was Edith, thinking, Ian *will* be relieved. Edith in an unfamiliar coat, staring at the tall Parliament Hill houses across the water.

'Oh,' Miriam said, as the stranger's face turned up to hers

178

questioningly. She felt furious and frowned at the woman as if it were her fault.

She looks rough sleepers in the eye, where before she scuttled guiltily past them; she seeks out faces in the hot metallic air of the tube as commuters avoid her eye. She has visited soup kitchens in King's Cross, the other volunteers mistaking her interest for just another dose of middle-class guilt – it being the time of year for it. She has joined a support group for parents of missing children, some of whom disappeared six years, ten years, fifteen years ago, looking at their dogged campaigns and catching herself thinking, Can't you see they're dead?

She is working her way through Edith's childhood friends, for connections, clues, anything. Pointless, really, but she does it for the sense of contact with Edith, the chance to talk about her, and for the feeling of *doing something*.

'Thought I might contact the EMFs,' she'd said idly to Rollo. 'Though God knows how.'

'That awful bunch,' he replied. And he was right, of course – the EMFs were awful, though Miriam would never have said as much to Edith. The group was given this moniker at school because they read everything by E. M. Forster and discussed it at length in cafés on Finchley Road, drinking lemon tea and smoking cigarettes. When Edith first fell in with them, Ian and Miriam were thrilled (Ian more so) – the intellectual set! Edith was full of literary zeal, so taken by *Howards End* and *A Room with a View*, *Maurice* and *Where Angels Fear to Tread*, that she travelled by train to Firenze and San Gimignano (with Rollo as her rather Forster-ish chaperone, Miriam had insisted), writing furiously in her diary while Rollo listened to pop music through headphones which appeared to be surgically attached to his head. The

EMFs turned out to be very up themselves indeed, pretentious and competitive, especially Electra, whom Miriam had been sure was bulimic and who got a car for her seventeenth birthday.

Miriam preferred Christy from across the road – a few years older than Edith, who liked playing hairdressers and watching TV, and with whom Edith had a sisterly, nonchalant relationship. Last-minute sleepovers welcomed by her delightfully *laissez-faire* Spanish mother, and after-school teas in rumpled uniforms. These days, Christy has two tiny daughters, aged two and four, and a house in Golders Green.

Miriam had gone there a few days back. Christy was kind to her, of course, made her tea (*more tea*), handed her tissues, and apologised to Miriam – she hadn't heard from Edith in years. And then there was the awkward silence when Miriam became tearful. She is growing used to those, too.

'It worked out for you, all this,' Miriam said in a watery voice, sitting at Christy's pock-marked farmhouse table. Her fingers traced the grooves in the wood. 'It could have worked out for Edith, that's what I keep thinking. For Edith and Jonti.'

'Oh, I don't know,' Christy said. 'She was awfully critical of him. Edith's much more ambitious than Jonti.'

The bell rings above Jonti's shop door, which is too minimalist to have a sign, and as it closes behind her, the roar of the buses outside is silenced. They plough up and down this thoroughfare, past frayed gold velvet chaises longues and Fifties Formica tables, tasselled lamp shades, beaten leather club chairs and flaking green-painted dressers – the wares of the antique shops that flank Chamberlayne Road.

Inside, she is greeted by the smell of sawdust and linseed, warmed through the broad shop windows. She runs a hand over one cabinet – oak, she guesses – and admires its slick surface and the triangular joints which lattice together like fingers. Jonti's style is Shaker with something entirely his own. Blocky wooden rectangles with small pegs for knobs like blinking, honest eyes in a quiet face. Dressers without curls or pelmets. Stoic tables. Miriam is astonished at the craftsmanship. He has built all this from nothing. If only Edith could have had more faith.

'Jonti,' she says as he enters from the back, and she is overcome with fondness for him. He has a slight stoop, is wiping his hands on the back pockets of his trousers, and wears a ridiculous beanie hat in grey wool. It is not that he is without affectation (the very location of his shop is an affectation), more that he is without guile. Jonti doesn't have a 'side' – he is as plain as his furniture.

'Mrs . . . Lady Hind,' he says, checking his hands before holding one out to her.

'Miriam, please, Jonti,' and she ignores his hand to hug him about the shoulders.

He had been a resident of her kitchen for long enough, an extra son when he and Edith were eighteen and going about together. When he was around – and he was around a lot – the atmosphere had a good-natured calm to it. He would lean against her kitchen worktop, his hands in the pockets of his mustard cords, and say, 'Anything you want peeling, Mrs H?' Or joke around on the computer with Rollo, waiting for Edith to get ready.

She liked Edith when she was with Jonti; it was as if he planed down her sharper edges. Edith would rush down the stairs in a great pummelling of feet, breathless and lively, saying, 'We're off out, Mum,' dragging Jonti away by the arm, and Miriam would shout after them, 'Have fun, you two.'

Ian, of course, viewed Jonti as a dropout, and it was true he smoked a lot of marijuana (or 'blow' as Edith and Rollo referred to it). He was a couple of years older, was training even then to be a joiner, as if rejecting his private school education, though that had been in the overtly liberal vein: children of singers and artists, no uniforms, and everyone calling the teachers by their first names.

When Edith got pregnant that summer, she'd already had her offer from Cambridge.

It would be quite wrong to suggest Ian made her get rid of it, but his silences over the dinner table forced them all to contemplate how seriously everything was hanging in the balance. Ian had a way of making his face say, 'I am shattered by my disappointment,' which could sting you to the heart. Ian was Edith's raised bar. She strained to please him, and in that striving she did well, Miriam admiring the discipline of their work together because it counterbalanced the elastic feel of her love. Miriam was forever wavering, uncertain of where she should draw the line with the children, while Ian had been made of sterner stuff. 'Never back down when it comes to children,' he would say. 'It's the beginning of the end.' And she thought, what *rot*. They're people – why on earth shouldn't they win sometimes? Have one over on you? Get away with it?

Edith got her four As and her place at Cambridge, and she had gone about with Jonti and got pregnant. Miriam stood silently beside Ian's disapproval, not because she was angry, but because she felt a baby at eighteen was nothing to wish for. Edith's 'death instinct', someone had said – was it Patty, who was doing a course on Freud? Miriam thought it was a more complicated mistake than that – more ambivalent, less destructive.

Miriam and Jonti sit amid the forest of turned wood in two rocking chairs. He has turned the 'closed' sign on the door and made her some green tea, which is foul but she sips it so as not to hurt his feelings.

'I'm so sorry, Mrs H,' he says, and she likes it that he's calling her that again. She had liked being the mother of teenagers – their sweet, ungainly hulks taking up all of her kitchen, like little children in dressing-up bodies.

'Thank you, Jonti. Your work – all this – it's so impressive. How have you done it?'

'Built it up slowly. I was an apprentice for a long time for a nice old chap in Whitechapel. I've only had this place a couple of years. There are still quiet periods where I think it's going to go belly-up, but so far I've had a lot of return business and good word of mouth, so touch wood.' He doesn't have to reach far.

'Well, I'm not surprised. I mean, the craftsmanship is extraordinary. I saw Christy yesterday. She said she was saving for a sideboard. Oh, Jonti, she's got lovely children – two girls.'

His face darkens and she realises she has been insensitive. After the abortion, Edith had become dissatisfied with him. 'No ambition,' she'd told Miriam, and Miriam thought it was Ian talking. She witnessed Edith being cruel – putting Jonti down when they discussed politics or literature during family meals. 'Like *you'd* know,' she'd said to him when he'd once ventured an opinion on Iraq, and Jonti, in his mild way, had sloped off out of their lives, rather bruised but without rancour.

'I'm sorry she was cruel to you,' Miriam says now.

Jonti shrugs. 'It's in the past. I've made peace with it, Mrs H. I hope she's all right, really, I do. I think about her a lot since it was on the news.'

'You've not heard from her?' she asks, though it is pointless.

He shakes his head. 'I'd have told you straight away. Haven't seen her since that summer. That was not a good time. It took me a long time to, y'know, process what happened and then to let it go.' Jonti's mother talking. Miriam remembers how she used to moo on about 'emotional auras', with her frizzy black hair and post-divorce depressed face. She was learning about aromatherapy and healing, and fed him nothing but lentils.

'But you did,' Miriam says sadly. 'More's the pity. I thought you two could have made a go of it.'

'Did you?' he says. 'You never let us know that.'

'No,' she says. 'I didn't, did I?'

Edith has missed out on this gentle man with his big hands and his slow pace and his tolerance. She could have had that sideboard in her lounge, for starters. He would have laid her a lovely floor, put up shelves. There are worse things.

They have fallen into silence and Miriam realises she and Jonti don't have anything to talk about. That period is gone and they can't even reminisce fondly, so sour did it turn. Another thing she has forgotten in the swim of nostalgia: Jonti is humourless. Perhaps it wouldn't have worked out between him and Edith after all – you need a sense of humour to get through marriage.

For a time, she and Jonti sit among the herd of sideboards and chests of drawers, sipping horrid green tea as the buses rumble past outside.

The rain spits into Miriam's face, spattering the shoulders of her beige Burberry mac, too thin a layer for January, and she squints into the wind, up Chamberlayne Road towards Kensal Rise station, relieved to have said goodbye to Jonti and the guilt.

The abortion had changed Edith. Even years later it cast its sad tint, like the spring when Christy was getting married,

184

three or four years ago now. Edith went on and on about how sorry she felt for her friend, with eyes that held Miriam's, pleadingly. 'Far too young. She'll come to regret it. You can't know who you are in your twenties. I'd hate to be settling down right now.'

Miriam descends the steps to the overground station, for the train to Hampstead Heath, remembering times when the sadness lifted and Edith's silly, girlish joy had been allowed to escape like bubbles up the side of a glass – like the time they'd shopped for outfits for the wedding in Fenwick's. Miriam had stared at Edith in the changing rooms as she pranced and giggled, thinking how she loved the very flesh of her. You got used to that with children, love crashing over you like waves. But then Edith had picked out a shockingly expensive dress – £250 – and Miriam balked, not because she didn't have the money but because it seemed inappropriate. She had a sense of obligation – to teach Edith the value of money, that she should not grow up profligate. And, as so often in her brief career as mother, Miriam had spoiled everything. She'd dithered – 'I don't know, Edith, it's an awful lot' – and in her hesitation, Edith read censure, or a limit on love, or some coldness which wasn't there.

No, darling, my dear one, it wasn't that. The train is coming towards her, the tears mingling with the rain on her face. *It was my own stupid inhibition. I'd buy it for you now, Edie, love, a thousand times over.*

Every fond memory is tinged like this, as if Edith can turn the atmosphere, even now. In Fenwick's she had grown sullen, maintaining her dissatisfied stance towards the £80 dress that Miriam bought for her from the Oasis concession, even though she had the figure for it – Edith could carry off the flimsiest high-street fashions.

185

Yes, Miriam was inconsistent – she loved to buy her daughter things, to express love, but no, she couldn't buy her everything all of the time. She frowns as she boards the train, in a silent argument with Edith or some notion of her righteousness. Well, she wasn't going to smother her spontaneity – those times when Edith was little and she'd said, 'Let's go to the toy shop' just because she delighted in delighting a small person, and small people were so easy to delight, so ready to join the ride. But she'd had to say no, too, and face down the hatred. This was her lot, to be so often in the wrong, and so it had been when they went dress shopping and she'd spoiled it all for Edith.

The other passengers stare at her as she presses a tissue against her eyes, trying to stop the tears and failing, knowing that her face must be a torn-up storm of anger, regret, and defensiveness.

Edith has never been quick to forgive. Is this what her disappearance is all about – one huge sulk, like the one in Fenwick's? Oh, she hopes so. She'd be happy to know Edith is alive and to never talk to her again. Anything, but not dead.

The wedding, at the church at the bottom of Church Row, had been so beautiful, Christy vastly pregnant in white, with a ring of flowers around her hair. Miriam and Edith sat together in a pew, and when Miriam looked to her left at Edith's face, the tears were streaming from her daughter's eyes and her mouth was a soundless red twist.

MANON

'So, Taylor Dent,' says DI Sean Haverstock – 'Havers' as he seems to be called by everyone at Kilburn CID. He is bouncing back in his swivel chair. Manon guesses he's about her age: bald, wearing a wedding ring.

'Yes,' she says, 'where are we with his movements in the week before he died?'

'Nowhere, to be honest, without some decent phone work. His was pay-as-you-go, basic, not a smart phone. That's disappeared. Registered activity in the North London area up until Sunday, eleventh of December, but that's as you would expect.'

She nods. 'That ties in with the PM's time of death.'

'Phone was then either lost, switched off, or destroyed.'

'Who's coming up on the call data?'

'You'll be surprised to hear that it was almost entirely PAYG unregistered. Dirty phones. His world—'

'We don't seem to know much about his world,' she says. She wonders if Havers has made any effort at all. Has he sent detectives to interview Taylor Dent's friends and associates?

187

Has he tickled up his Cricklewood contacts – the kinds of guys Dent would have done business with? Has he fuck.

'What about the family?' she says. 'What have they told you?'

'There's a younger brother, Fly Dent, about ten. He was sheltered from the worst of Taylor's activities, it seems. Very much looked after by Taylor: he fed him, washed his clothes, got him to school on time, etcetera. Social workers are onto him now. Mother's a total case. Cheap stuff, y'know: Magners, solvents, methadone. Boy'll be taken into care, I shouldn't wonder.'

'Didn't anyone report Taylor missing? Was there a misper investigation going?'

'Brother came in, yes, on the Monday – think it was the twelfth.' Havers straightens and leafs through some paperwork on his desk. 'It was logged, of course. But a boy like him – if we launched an investigation into every missing young man who was into all sorts, DS Bradshaw . . . He wasn't a minor, don't forget. For all we knew, he was loading up a van with fags in Spain.'

Havers shrugs as if they have an understanding. *A boy like him.* He couldn't care less about the death of a boy like Dent. She can imagine exactly what type of reception his little brother got when he tried to raise the alarm.

A bus flies towards her at such speed she thinks she'll be hit, but it thunders past, its warm air whipping up her hair. The smell of fried eggs and the sound of brakes squealing like trapped pigs; past The Crown and Paddy Power and striped zip bags for the dispossessed outside the pound shop. Every face she passes, every snippet of language in the air, is from another part of the world. The shops are a motley cheek-by-jowl roll-call of immigration, like strata in a rock: McGovern's

188

Free House; Halal kebab;, Bacovia magazin românesc; Serhat Off Licence (Polski sklep); Bosnia & Herzegovina Community Biblioteka charity shop; Milad Persian food; D'Den Exotic African Cuisine; Taste of Lahore; Bestco mini mart, where half the shelves are empty. A rundown, slip-sliding melting pot, and the necessaries blooming like lichen: pawn shop, betting shop, funeral parlour, Western Union Money Transfer.

She keeps walking, and where the shops thin out and the traffic roars louder still is an Ethiopian restaurant, Abyssinia, with red and white cheesecloth curtains in the window, and beside it a grey metal door. 11A. Manon looks up and sees windows blacked by the pollution and grey nets, one pushed back by something – a sack or bag leaning against the glass. It's going to smell in here, she thinks, as her body tenses against it, and she's right, a combination of old frying (congealed fat, the type of smell you get from an unwashed grill pan) and damp. She's been buzzed in and she tramps up the narrow stairwell with her polo-neck over her mouth and nose.

'Yes, yes, come in, come in,' says a woman in a strong Irish accent. She has a ginger fuzz of hair, which is dark grey at the roots, a pale, freckled complexion in among the thread veins, and frightened eyes. She is quick, like a creature burrowing to get away.

'Mrs Dent,' says Manon.

'Dat'll be me.'

'My name is DS Bradshaw from Cambridgeshire Police. I've come to talk to you about Taylor Dent, your son.'

'Taylor's gone, de lord have mercy on his soul,' she says, not looking Manon in the eye. Instead she leads the way in, leaving the door ajar. 'Sorry about de mess . . .'

The smell recedes inside the flat, overtaken by stale cigarettes, which is not unpleasant, almost warming in a way. The light is dim, the carpets dark. The space opens out into a lounge, not much brighter, the nets blocking out the light from outside. The place seems embedded with human cells. A multitude, vibrating, of people long gone, arrested or dead.

Manon and Mrs Dent ('Call me Maur*een*') sit together on the sofa, brown floral chenille. There are open crisp packets on the floor. An overflowing ashtray. An enormous television takes up one half of the room.

'I'll clean dose up. I'll get round to it. I've got to have a camera in me stomach. A camera down in me stomach, see. I don't want it, so I don't. I can show you de letter, you might understand it. I don't understand it, see.'

She gets up again, beetling off in a stooped flurry. She hasn't made eye contact and it's as if she's talking to the air, or to the flat, or to herself. Manon feels curiously invisible, not the first intruder from the state: Kilburn CID, social services, education welfare.

'I don't want it, no,' Maureen says from somewhere in the hallway, and Manon follows her to a filthy galley kitchen with a full sink of dishes and every surface covered with bottles and cans (Magners, red wine, Fanta). Manon's shoes stick to the linoleum. Maureen is pulling on recalcitrant drawers, stuffed with letters and lighters, which she then can't shut. She is distracted by the discovery of a packet of John Player Blues, taking one out and lighting it, squinting at Manon for the first time.

'Where were we?' she says.

'Taylor, your son.'

'He's dead. Taylor's dead, Lord have mercy on 'im. I've had a letter from de doctor, it's here somewhere.' She has gone back to the drawers. 'Dey want to put a camera in me stomach. Oh! I don't want it. Can y'understand it?'

She has pulled out a folded piece of paper and handed it to Manon.

'I don't understand it,' Maureen is saying, beetling back into the lounge.

Manon skim-reads, sees: 'Appointment, twelfth of December 2010, 10 a.m. Gastroscopy, Royal Free Hospital.'

'This appointment was three weeks ago,' says Manon, following Maureen. 'Did you go?'

'Oh, tank God it's over, den. Now who did ye say ye were?'

'DS Bradshaw, Cambridgeshire Police. We found Taylor's body.'

'Oh no! Oh Jaysus, no, Taylor's gone, rest his soul.'

Maureen is contemplating her cigarette. Manon can smell the booze on her, sweated out through her freckled skin.

'Dat's his room back dere,' she says, pointing her cigarette towards the hall.

'Can I have a look?'

'If you like. You're nat de first. Will I make ye a cup of tea?'

'I'm all right, thanks,' Manon says, thinking of the state of the kitchen.

She walks down the hallway, at the end of which are two open doorways side by side. Through one, she sees legs crossed at the ankles. A pair of thin plimsolls, once white, perhaps, the rubber gaping where it meets the canvas. No socks. Even indoors those feet must be freezing in a January like this one. Black skin, shaded blacker at the knuckle.

She puts her head around the door and sees the boy, sitting on the mattress on the floor, his legs outstretched. There's a tiny television on the floor beside the mattress and he's watching it. The mattress – not quite a double but bigger than a single – has two sleeping bags on it. There's a melamine chest of drawers, all the drawers open, at the base of the mattress,

191

so you'd have to crawl to get to it. The boy looks up. His hair is cut close to his head. His eyes, spectacularly dark, are enormous in his oval face. Manon is unable to speak for a moment. It's not that he's beautiful, so much (though he is); it's that he is so intensely sad.

'Hello,' she says.

He looks back at the television.

'What are you watching?'

'*Dance* fucking *Download*. Piece a shit.'

They look at the screen a moment, with its tinny laughter.

'My name's Manon,' she says. 'Funny name, huh?'

He looks up at her. She realises he's too old and too unhappy for games. He wants her to tell it straight.

'I'm from the police. I'm trying to find out what happened to Taylor. Mind if I sit down?'

'*Now* you wanna find out,' he says.

She points at the bit of mattress next to him. He edges away to make room for her and she sinks down, sighing elaborately, the stiff-jointed grown-up. Her knees won't quite bend so she sits like him, with her legs crossed at the ankle.

'What's your name?' she asks, not because she doesn't know, but because the boy deserves some formalities.

'Fly,' he says. 'My name's Fly.'

'Nice to meet you, Fly Dent,' she says, holding out her hand to him and smiling. 'Manon Bradshaw.' He takes it, his palm cold and dry in hers. She looks around her.

'Did you share this room with Taylor?'

He nods.

She notices pirate stickers on the chest of drawers, silver and glittery and curling up at their edges. Skull and crossbones; cutlasses; a pirate ship. Children's stickers, the kind they get free inside magazines. The sleeping bags behind her are entwined.

'I'm very sorry, Fly. You must feel very sad,' she says.

Fly looks at her. His eyes are frightened.

'Did Taylor have a mobile phone?'

Fly nods. 'Course.'

'Do you know where it is?'

He shrugs. 'He always had it – in his pocket. Same as dis one.'

He leans back to reach into his pocket and takes out a phone, rolling it in his hand.

'Can I look?' she asks, as Fly turns back to the television.

'Taylor give it me,' he says, keeping hold of the phone, 'so I could call him. If I need him.'

He presses some buttons and shows her. The word Taylor is on the screen and she presses the green call button. The dead boy's voice says, 'I ain't here, innit! Leave a message and I might call you back, or I might not . . .' followed by shrieks of laughter.

'Is that you laughing with him?' she says, Fly's phone to her ear, smiling as she listens because the laughing is infectious.

Fly nods, smiling too.

She hangs up. He has gone back to looking at the television, so she scrolls about the phone. The only number he has ever dialled is Taylor's. Twenty or thirty times. Trying to find him. Perhaps he plays it as he goes to sleep, listening to his brother's voice and the two of them laughing.

'Are you hungry?' she says.

He nods. 'Taylor brought me KFC. He got the shopping from Bestco. Taylor feeded me.'

'Come with me, then,' Manon says, heaving herself up off the floor in an ungainly fashion.

She walks down the corridor to the lounge. 'Mrs Dent? Maureen?'

Maureen is lolling on the sofa, watching *Cash in the Attic*. She seems only semi-conscious, a tin in her hand.

'I'm just going to take Fly out for something to eat, OK?'

'You're all right lovey, yes,' says Maureen, raising her can, her chin to her chest.

Christ, thinks Manon, I could be anyone.

Fly is big, nearly as tall as her, but still a child. Unmistakably a child, she thinks, as she watches him pull on a thin jacket – the type a tennis player would wear onto court, and about as useless as gauze against the January chill. She knows she shouldn't be taking him out. Interviews with minors (well, it was hardly an interview, was it?) – there was a whole book of protocol, including never to interview them alone. No, she wasn't interviewing him; she was buying him eggs. The boy needed eggs and this, like her taking home a police radio, was outside the bounds of protocol.

They are looking out on an optimistic arrangement of red plastic tables and chairs on the pavement, as if this were Ipanema, not Cricklewood Broadway. Beside them is a wire mesh shelving unit full of Portuguese or Brazilian biscuits and cooking ingredients, mostly starch-based, as far as she can make out (everything on the shelves is yellow). There is a vast flat-screen television bracketed close to the ceiling behind them, booming out a Portuguese game show. The café owner smiles broadly at them, saying, 'Scrambled?', with her pad poised.

'Fried,' says Fly.

'Scrambled,' says Manon, frowning at Fly. 'And extra toast.'

A bus thunders past, slapped with an advert for Wonga. Following it is a plastic bag, bowling along in mid-air, its handles like beseeching arms until it hits a woman in a sari, square in the stomach.

194

'Taylor used to go dere,' says Fly, and Manon follows his gaze to a red awning on the opposite side of the road. Momtaz Shisha Café. 'They all knew 'im in dere.'

'Was he into anything stronger?'

'You mean drugs?' He shakes his head. 'He saw Mum and her boyfriends, all dem losers. Said he'd never touch that shit. Said if I did, he'd kill me.'

In the pit of her stomach Manon feels a resolve hardening. She has to find out what happened to Taylor Dent, what took him from this boy he so evidently loved.

'Tell me about the time leading up to Taylor going missing,' she says. 'When did you last see him?'

'Sunday, it was. We got some shopping from Bestco. He was in a right good mood. We had beans on toast, watched *SpongeBob SquarePants*. He told me to do my homework, get my shit together for school next day. He was on his phone, texting.'

'Who?'

Fly shrugs. 'I din know who he knowed. I mean, he knowed a lot of people – din tell me 'bout them.'

'And was this on his phone, the one you used to reach him?'

Fly shrugs again. 'Sometimes he had more than one. Sometimes not. The phones changed, the ones for his . . . for bidniss.' He looks down sheepishly as if he could still get Taylor into trouble with the police.

'Then what?' asks Manon.

'Then he said he had to go out. Said he be back later. Before he left, he say to me, "Everything about to get a whole lot better, bro." And that was it, that was the last time . . .' The tears fall sudden and fat. This is the first time he's talked about it, she thinks. He looks up at her, his huge eyes liquid with loss. 'He din come back. He never came back. I woke up an' looked beside me.'

She pictures the sleeping bags, one of them empty when Fly woke up on Monday twelfth December. 'Then what?'

'I went to school. I kept callin' him, textin' him. I thought maybe he was workin'. Straight from school I went to the police.'

'What did they tell you?'

'Told me he'd turn up. Told me he not a child, so nuffin' they could do.'

'Can you think of any reason Taylor might have gone to East Anglia?'

'Where dat?' says Fly, looking at the eggs as the plate lowers to the table in front of him.

'It's an area, about two hours from here. Countryside. Very flat. Lots of small rivers.' She can't seem to make it sound much better than that. She thinks about mentioning fog, but stops short. There's a round of applause from the television and the game show host bellows, 'Obrigado! Obrigado!'

'I know it don't look like much,' he says, setting in on the toast, 'but this is a good place. The Persian guys are good guys.' He nods at Momtaz. 'They gives me free tea sometimes. And the guys in Bestco. Broken biscuits, old cakes, innit. They know about Mum. They help us, 'specially Taylor.'

'Did he go to school?'

Fly shakes his head. 'Said someone had to get the money and it wasn't going to be Mum. He was well strict wi' me. Said I was the clever one. I was the one readin' all them books. I wish I didn't now. I wished I got off my butt and helped him.'

'Helped him how?'

'So he could be proper – no sellin' and dealin' and what not.'

'What was the "what not"?'

Fly shrugs. 'This 'n' that.'

'Like what?'

'He din tell me, he din wan me to know.'

'Did Taylor ever mention a girl named Edith Hind?'

'Dat girl on the news? She's famous. She's on telly.' And his eyes light up, as if being dead were as nothing next to the wonder of celebrity.

'Yes, did he know her?'

'Nah.'

'What do you think happened to him, Fly?'

Fly looks at her, and he is all eyes, huge black pupils, wide and vulnerable. He has a way of pushing his lips out when he sniffs that is innocence itself. 'He say he was sorting money for us. He say what was happening now was just, well, our luck about to change. But he din want me to know his bidniss – kept everyfing away from me.' His eyes have filled up again, the wetness un-burst this time. He has the terrified look of someone who is falling off the edge of the world. 'He my brudder.'

'One last question, Fly. Have you ever heard the name Tony Wright?'

He thinks. Sniffs. Shakes his head. 'Did he hurt Taylor?'

'We don't know. But we're going to find out, Fly. We'll find out what happened to Taylor and whoever hurt him will go to prison, I promise you. What's happening now, with you, I mean? Have the social workers told you anything?'

He shakes his head. 'I wanna stay at school, at home wi' Mum. I manage with what the guys at Bestco gimme. I went to a friend's house at Christmas. I'm all right. I don't need no care home 'n' all dat.'

Manon sits back, looking at him. Looking and looking, her mind racing.

'Wait there,' she says.

At the till, the café owner is staring up at the Portuguese game show, agog.

'A word,' says Manon, showing the woman her badge.

She leads Manon to a corridor stacked with food and they stand with the multi-coloured slats of the doorway curtain about their shoulders like plastic hair.

'I want you to keep a tab for that boy over there,' says Manon. 'Give him whatever he wants to eat, whenever he wants it, and send the bill to me. I can give you card details as surety.'

'Is OK, your job. You will pay,' says the woman, smiling. 'He just a boy. I feed him no problem.'

'Right,' Manon says to Fly when she gets back to the table. 'Come on, we're going to buy you a coat.'

'Davy,' she says. She's gasping for breath, leaning against a wall, the phone to her ear. She's looking at the dirty Cricklewood sky, opaque as wool. She cannot seem to get a full lungful. 'Davy,' she gasps.

'Calm down, Sarge. What is it?'

'We've got to help him.'

'Who? Help who?'

'Taylor's brother, Fly. He's in a shithole and his mum's out of it, and no one's feeding him, not now Taylor's gone. Davy, he's going to get taken into care. He's *ten*.' She feels dizzy with the lack of oxygen. A bus roars past and she cannot breathe because she's whipped about by a grey fog of exhaust fumes, unnaturally warm. 'Social workers are onto him. You remember what that woman said from child protection – what was her name?'

'Sheila Berridge,' says Davy. 'Didn't think you were listening.'

'Fine, Davy, fine. I've changed my tune. What can we do?'

'Care's not always bad. Sometimes it's better than where they are.'

'D'you believe that?'

'Course I do. I'm not saying it's lovely. I'm not saying it's mum and dad and roast chicken for Sunday lunch. But people get through it. It's dry, there's food. He might get a decent foster family.'

'Or he might get shoved into a massive care home which is stalked by paedos. I just want someone – a teacher, education welfare, anyone – to keep an eye on him, that's all. Free school meals, I dunno. Taylor fed him and now . . .'

'All right, all right,' says Davy. 'Leave it with me. I'll talk to my mentoring buddy. See if she can't pull a few strings down there. When did you turn so soft?'

MIRIAM

'Iaaaan!' she shouts up the stairs as she makes for the front door, rubbing her hands and thinking she must put the heating on. Their thermostat timer has not been adjusted to all these bodies being home during the daytime.

Miriam opens the front door and there is DS Bradshaw, a rumpled mass of black clothing, a capacious bag dropping off one shoulder. Her curls are pushed back from her forehead. She half-smiles a hello.

'Do come in,' says Miriam, stepping back. 'Gosh, it's freezing. Come on in, yes, that's it, follow the corridor straight down to the kitchen.'

DS Bradshaw walks ahead of her, Miriam following and saying, 'Tea?'

'Lovely, yes, thanks,' says the officer, allowing her bag to slip to the floor beside the kitchen table. 'Glad to see the photographers have gone.'

'Yes, we are no longer of interest, thank God,' says Miriam, filling the kettle at the tap. 'For the time being, at least. The last of them sloped off on New Year's Eve but it was only the stragglers, to be honest.'

DS Bradshaw takes off her coat, laying it gently over the back of the padded banquette and revealing only more black, formless clothing. Perhaps they have to be constantly prepared for death – *harbingers at the ready!*

Ian walks in. 'DS Bradshaw,' he says, offering his hand. His voice these days has no uplift, no spring of humour behind it, which Miriam had always so loved in his greetings.

'Call me Manon, please.'

'Yes, Manon, of course.'

'Tea, darling?' says Miriam.

'Why not?'

'Can you call Rollo down?'

'Yes, of course,' says Ian. 'He's frantically tweeting and Facebook-ing,' he says by way of explanation, and he disappears again to look for their son.

Miriam places a tea in front of Manon, who looks up at her and her face is lit by the window opposite – an angry left eye, swollen, pink-sheened and half shut.

'You'd better treat that, sooner rather than later, by the looks of it. Conjunctivitis,' Miriam says, adopting her GP no-arguing voice. 'Very simple – buy some Chloramphenicol eye drops over the counter. It'll clear up in a day. But make sure you finish the course. There, sermon over.'

'I thought it might clear up by itself.'

'Unlikely.'

'How are you bearing up, Lady Hind?'

'My name's Miriam, my dear,' she says. 'And I'm not bearing up at all. Do you have any news for us?'

'Not about Edith's whereabouts. We have some leads . . .'

'Leads?' says Ian, settling, with Rollo, in the chairs opposite Miriam and Manon.

Manon stretches out her hand. 'Nice to see you again, Rollo. I hear you're running a formidable social media campaign.'

'Much good it's doing. There's a lot of online emoting,' says Rollo, 'often by strangers, which I know I should find comforting but is really quite creepy.'

They smile and sip. In the sad silence of the kitchen, a fly fizzes against the glass of the window. *Tap, fizz, tap.*

'So – leads, you said,' says Ian.

'Well, not exactly leads,' says the sergeant. 'Possible links which need exploring. We found a body.' Then she swiftly adds, 'No, not Edith. A boy – a seventeen-year-old called Taylor Dent.'

'Oh, his poor mother,' says Miriam, her palm across her mouth. *Poor mother, but oh thank God it's not Edith, thank God that wretched mother is not me.* 'What has he to do with Edith?'

'We don't know yet. That's what we're investigating. He is, was, from Cricklewood, not far from here.'

'I think you'll find Cricklewood is very far from here,' mutters Ian.

'Did Edith ever mention the name?' asks Manon.

'Taylor Dent?' says Ian and he searches Miriam's face. They shake their heads at one another.

'I've never heard of him,' says Miriam. 'How did he die?'

'We can't be sure. His body was found on Friday in the river near Ely. Did you know him, Rollo?'

'No, no, I've never heard of him,' Rollo says.

'Did Edith ever try any drugs? Did she buy any marijuana from anyone, for example?'

'No,' say Rollo and Miriam simultaneously.

'She had a boyfriend who smoked a bit – Jonti – but she

202

never wanted it,' says Rollo. 'I know because I was with her when he was smoking.'

'Might she have refused because you were there?'

'I don't think so. It wasn't a big deal – she had no moral problem with it, she just didn't like it, or feel the need for it,' Rollo says.

'We'll need to talk to Jonti,' says Manon.

'I went to see him this morning. He hasn't seen or heard from her. But yes, of course, I'll get you the number,' says Miriam, getting up to fetch her telephone book from the worktop.

The fly is fizzing its death throes again.

Ian gets up and turns to the window, his back to them. He begins to rattle – rather frantically, Miriam feels – at the window lock, trying to lift the metal arm to let the fly out.

She returns to the table, her reading glasses on, and gives Manon the number. Then she looks up irritably. '*Ian*, stop fussing and come and sit down. This is important.'

'Sorry,' he says. 'Is this Dent boy your lead? Do you think he harmed Edith?'

'We're trying to work out whether there's a connection between the two of them first – whether they had ever met, or whether they had friends in common.'

'He was seventeen, you say?' says Rollo.

'A *child*,' says Miriam.

'Which school was he at?' asks Rollo.

'He'd left school. He worked the black market, basically,' says Manon. 'Cigarettes, counterfeit gear, stolen goods, other things, too.'

'I hardly think Edith would know someone like—'

'Oh, Ian, *shut up*,' Miriam snaps, and she is immediately ashamed. 'I'm sorry,' she says to Manon. 'I shouldn't snap.'

'It's all right,' says Manon with a weak smile.

Oh, stop fucking observing us, Miriam thinks. We are like that fly, helplessly bashing ourselves against glass.

'We have the feeling,' says Ian, 'that there is information you are keeping back about the investigation.'

Miriam looks into Manon's face. She can see a decision being made.

'There was another lead, which was a focus of our investigation for a time, but it has proved . . . well, it hasn't gone anywhere.'

'Oh, for God's sake,' says Ian, and Miriam smiles at him gratefully. At least he still has some fight in him.

'Go on,' pleads Miriam.

'We have been looking at someone called Tony Wright. He was released from Whitemoor prison eight months ago, where he'd been serving a sentence for aggravated burglary and sexual assault.'

'*Sexual assault*,' says Miriam. 'I was praying it wouldn't be—'

'It isn't,' blurts Manon. 'He has a cast-iron alibi for the weekend Edith disappeared.'

She has closed the door on Detective Sergeant Bradshaw and the things she shared with them about Tony Wright, the way he held a knife to the throat of his terrified victim.

Miriam and Ian stand in the cold, quiet well inside their front door. He looks at her, then frowns and turns, and in this split second she thinks she can see contempt. For what? For her upset?

He is marching down towards his study and she follows him.

'What was all that rattling about with the window? Can't you sit still for a minute?' she says, spoiling for him to swivel on his heels and give as good as she wants to give him.

204

'Leave me alone,' he says icily. He stands behind his desk, pretending to leaf through some papers.

She walks out of the study and he shouts after her, 'Where are you going – for another lie-down?' and she turns and storms back in, and when she gets there, his face is a jagged mess of fury and accusation. 'Why is your distress the only thing in the room?' he demands.

'It isn't, Ian, but you won't allow me any grief at all. She's my daughter.'

'And she's mine, and you sobbing or lying in a darkened room the whole time doesn't help.'

'What do you want me to *do*?'

He is silent, his head bowed again towards his desk, but she knows he is fizzing and enraged just like her.

'Stop acting like this is my fucking fault,' she says and walks out again.

MANON

She has her feet up on the blue tartan First Capital Connect seats, beside a sign saying *Do Not Put Feet on Seats*. She pulls at her eyelid, peeling it away from the eyeball in an attempt to relieve the scratching. The infection has moved from irritation to pain and yet, when she has passed a chemist – on Hampstead High Street, at King's Cross Station – the urgency of buying the antibiotics has gone from her mind. No chance now – it's 8 p.m. and she has to be in early tomorrow for the *Crimewatch* briefing.

She told the Hinds to brace themselves for renewed press interest – photographers back on their doorstep – when the televised reconstruction of Edith's last journey home with Helena Reed is broadcast on Wednesday evening. Telling them about Tony Wright hadn't been easy, despite his alibi. She recalls the look of terror on Lady Hind's face, which prevented her from describing what had become of his last victim – how he had beaten her about the head with the knife handle so that her face was purple and enlarged. Two weeks after his conviction, she killed herself.

Manon's mobile phone vibrates somewhere deep in her bag. A text, number not recognised.

I am toasty

She smiles. Buying the coat for Fly had brought her myriad unlooked-for pleasures, as if satisfaction were refracted into a fresh rainbow. Picking out a hot-pink sequinned number and saying to him, 'This is a good look for you'; his dry look in response, as if she were the silliest object he had ever come across. Him picking the designer labels, to which she would turn the swinging ticket and say, 'In your dreams.' Most of all, when they had selected together a padded cornflower-blue coat, with white stripes at the chest, she had noticed what pleasure there was in keeping him warm: the thought of the softness of the fleece lining against his skin, the waterproof outer layer sheltering him from rain. It was the best twenty-five pounds she had spent in a long time.

Shouldn't you be in bed? M

No, cos I'm not five.
Anyway, I *am* in bed. I'm wearing it in bed.

She is smiling to herself, up the steps of HQ, into reception, thinking how she must type up her notes, prepare for tomorrow's briefing. Her head is down, unaware of her surroundings, when Bob on the front desk says, 'Sarge, someone to see you.'

Manon looks up, and there he is: his flappy coat, the stoop, horrifying and wonderful – Alan Prenderghast.

'Hello,' he says. 'I didn't expect to see you. I was just dropping this off.'

He holds out a small white paper bag, folded over at the top, with a green chemist sign on it. Manon opens it and takes out an oblong box. The label reads: *Chloramphenicol eye drops, for the treatment of Conjunctivitis.*

'Crikey,' she says.

'I feel a bit like a criminal caught in the act,' he says.

'Gosh – I haven't had time, as you can see.'

'Look,' he says, rather urgently, 'I don't know the form for this. Am I still a witness or something, in the case?'

'No, why?'

'I was wondering if I could take you out. For dinner or something. Or a film, where we sit in the same row. Adjacent seats, even.'

There is a red patch creeping up his neck.

'I don't know, I've got a lot on at the moment.'

They both look down at the white chemist's bag.

'Why don't you think about it?' he says. 'I'll give you my number.'

He puts a hand out to take the chemist bag back off her and pats his pockets for a pen, only to find Bob holding one out to him. 'I enjoyed our coffee after the film,' he says, while writing on the bag against his palm.

'Thanks,' she says, looking down at his writing. The numbers are all bunched up and tight. 'Look, I'd better go – got to prepare for a briefing first thing. Just had a murder come in, plus it's *Crimewatch* this week,' and she lays it there, her job as a police officer, which he must admire, what with his very pedestrian work as a systems analyst.

'Well, OK then,' he says, and she watches him go out of the station doors and down the steps to the car park.

When she turns, Bob is frowning.

'What d'you do that for?' he says.

'What?'

'Turn down a nice chap like him?'

'What would you know about it, Bob?'

'I know it's nice to have someone to come home to.'

TUESDAY

DAVY

'For me,' Kim is saying thoughtfully, 'it would have to be tuna pasta bake with back-to-back *Place in the Sun*.'

Davy is just about to put in his two pennies' worth, which involves crackers and cheese and *Quincy*, but Harriet has shot everyone a look which says: *Shut your fucking gobs, the boss is here.*

DCS Gary Stanton has a collection of important-looking files under one arm and his buttons are straining over his stomach. Time to size up on the shirt front, Davy thinks.

The whole team is gathered around a circular table, which is part of a new stratagem brought back from the States by Stanton, when he went to NYPD on a skills swap residential last autumn. For Davy, things got much more confusing after the residential, because Stanton returned armed with incomprehensible management-speak. Davy's all for a spot of police jargon, which clarifies the lines drawn between good and evil (only last night he watched a DCI on the news outside the Old Bailey telling how they'd 'exposed the villain's web of wicked lies'). But this corporate mumbo jumbo – it didn't clarify; it did the opposite,

210

scribbling over itself in loops and meanderings. It started with just having to 'action' things, instead of do them; then Stanton wanted to 'sunset that line of investigation', which seemed to mean not do it any more. They had moved from 'breaking' an alibi to 'putting it on the radiator to see if it melts'. But then Stanton started talking about 'shifting the paradigm' in order to 'leverage our synergies', and that's where he lost Davy altogether. At one point, Davy had felt quite worried about keeping up in the department, but then he overheard Harriet hissing at Manon, 'What the fuck's he talking about?' and felt better.

Edith Hind has been missing for two weeks and the press have more or less shuffled off. But that's about to change with the *Crimewatch* appeal, especially if what everyone is saying is true. Stanton is about to let the proverbial cat out of the bag (his words), and they'd better all be ready.

'Right,' Stanton says, sounding a bit out of puff. Perhaps he's just walked up the stairs from the press office. '*Crimewatch*. There will obviously be a massive upscaling of media interest and we can expect to be inundated with calls from the public—' Colin groans loudly – 'which we need to take seriously,' says Stanton. 'Lot of powder, so expect some avalanches. We don't know which sighting might be significant at this point, so I want nothing dismissed, please. I don't care how left-field they sound. I will also be raising the issue of Edith's love life in the appeal and the fact that she had male and female lovers. The purpose of this is not to supply fodder for the tabloids, but to flush out Edith's previous lovers, be they secret or in the past.'

Everyone around the table is silent. Everyone is thinking the same thing: it will incense Sir Ian Hind, who will be straight on the phone to Roger Galloway, who will be straight on the phone to Cambridgeshire Commissioner, Sir Brian Peabody, who will be straight on the phone to Gary Stanton.

'I can handle it,' he says mildly, as if reading their thoughts. 'I've got to run this investigation with the same instincts I'd run any other, and that's with the view that she's come to harm and that a lover or sexual liaison of some kind is at the heart of her disappearance.'

'Won't mentioning a female lover make things hysterical?' asks Manon.

'Unavoidable,' says Stanton. 'You pour milk on the step, see who laps it up.'

'Sorry, what?' says Harriet.

'We need people to come forward,' says Stanton. 'And to be honest, we need Edith back in the public mind.'

'Even if it's naked and engaging in some girl-on-girl action,' says Colin, with an inadvertent after-snort.

'Shouldn't we risk-assess Helena Reed then?' says Manon. 'Her world will come crashing down when you go on telly and talk about a female lover. I'd say she wasn't the toughest person to start with.'

'Yes, we certainly need to warn her. Kim, I'd like you to go round there, talk her through the whole thing. Tell her *Crimewatch* is going out on Wednesday night, reassure her we're not naming anyone, but offer her support if she needs it. She can have a liaison officer with her in her flat.'

Kim nods.

'Can we please have an update on the Taylor Dent investigation, Harriet?' says Stanton.

'Right,' says Harriet, with a deep sigh. 'No DNA at Deeping or George Street. No phone contact, as far as we know but, of course, Dent might have had an additional phone or phones we don't currently know about. Met's looking into that one, and of course we're cross-referencing with unknown-515 – the mobile Edith called twice in the week before she disappeared.'

'What about the Dent family?' says Stanton. 'Anything come up?'

'Younger brother, Fly,' Manon says, 'reported Taylor missing on Monday twelfth of December after school, so a week before Edith's disappearance. Taylor hadn't come home the night before. Went out, on some deal or other from the sounds of it. Before he left, he told his brother things were going to change, which indicates that he was going to make some money. Sounded quite pumped about it. Anyway, younger brother woke up on Monday, no Taylor in the bed next to him, got really worried but wanted to wait to see if he showed during the day. Then reported him missing, but the Met basically told him to go away and stop worrying because Taylor was seventeen and old enough to look after himself.'

'In other words, he wasn't worth investigating,' says Davy, thinking of Ryan.

'Kilburn CID have got officers working their way through Dent's associates, but to be honest, they're not that easy to pin down,' Manon says.

'Dent isn't coming up on any rail CCTV out of London. Looks like he must've got here in a car,' says Kim.

'OK,' says Stanton, hands flat on the desk as if steadying himself. 'If there are no firm connections emerging between Dent and Hind, and we can't establish ownership of unknown-515, then I'm going to have to hand the Dent murder investigation on to team two. We just don't have the resources to run the two cases out of one team,' says Stanton.

'But,' Manon blurts, and Davy looks at her. She's shifting in her seat, saying, 'We might find . . . later, I mean . . .' but she trails off.

'Last thing, people,' Stanton is saying. 'Forensic Management Team meeting.' Groans erupt around the room. Money talk

– the FMT meetings balance investigative needs against budget. Tighten your belts, in other words. 'We've been informed that we are overspending on the Hind investigation and that we should rein it in. To that end, Nigel Williams and Nick Briggs are being seconded to team two, to help on the Dent murder, while the scaled-down team continues to work on Hind.'

'Sorry, boss,' says Harriet, 'but you're cutting our team the night before *Crimewatch* goes out and buries us in a steaming pile of false leads?'

'That'd be about the size of it,' he says, up from his seat, the folders back under his arm. 'This is the age of austerity, DI Harper. Haven't you heard?'

'Toast with anchovies,' Colin is saying to Kim, as the room breaks up. ''Cept the oil always drips down your chin, which can greatly mar the enjoyment of *Columbo*.'

MIRIAM

She's awake, bruised by her dream.

If she could, she would avoid sleep altogether, but the nights are so tortured and restless – cups of tea in the kitchen, endless trips to the loo, trying out various beds in the hope a cold pillow might do the trick – that she often succumbs to her exhaustion come late afternoon. In her dreams, Edith appears before her in altered states – wearing strangers' clothes, or with a face transmogrified in some eerie way. A shapeshifter, part gangster's moll, half ghoul.

The police have asked them whether Edith knew Tony Wright or Taylor Dent, and she wonders what web her daughter has got caught in. What does Miriam know about her own child, really? Every detail a fresh assault – the relationship with Helena, the questioning texts to Rollo. What on earth was going on in Edith's life? Any confidence Miriam ever had in herself as a mother has been eroded, and what is that confidence built on anyway, she thinks now – the luck of one's children? The DNA lottery? If they're bright and successful, you congratulate yourself. If they fall by the wayside, the world judges you. These days, she could be told anything at all about Edith and she'd be forced to accommodate it, because she knows nothing. She thought Edith loved her.

Miriam picks up the Mother's Day card, one she has retrieved from her bedside table where she treasures all the missives from her children. In Edith's neat, perfectionist hand:

Dearest Mum,
You are the tops.
I love you, and I know I never tell you that – at least, not enough.
E x

She remembers Ian's mock outrage. 'Why I don't get cards like that?'

'Because her adoration of you is writ so large,' Miriam said at the time. 'She has to express it to me.'

He has been crying in his study. She heard him on her way up the stairs an hour ago, had stopped, one hand on the banister, curious to hear his upset expressed. Man sobs are so uncommon, they were quite interesting. His were strangulated, as if his tears were out to choke him. Hers come unbidden, like a flood, dissolving her outline, and it's as if she has failed to stand up to them. A weakness of tears.

She stood listening, but she didn't go to him. The strain is widening between them, like a jack ratcheting open a notch with every day missing; every detail a fresh violence separating them. Ian's answer to helplessness is criticism, and she is its focus, implied in all his Rushing About Being Important; his interviewing of private investigators (a precaution); his poster printing; calls to their lawyer; and complaints to newspaper editors over intrusion. He never

216

stops, his lined face saying to her: *And what exactly have* you *been doing?*

He never acknowledges the toll on her, in part because she keeps it to herself, like the furtive trip she has taken to Huntingdon where she walked the unsightly route beneath the concrete underpass from the station to George Street. She stopped outside Edith's house, unable to let herself in because its interior, black with fingerprint dust, was too much a crime scene. So instead she went down to the town centre, where she looked into the eyes of every person, and wanted to lift her face to the sky and let out a wail because she didn't know what to *do*. The world is tipping, vertiginous, her organs plummeting away. Fear is so *physical*.

No, she hasn't told him any of this, and every time he looks for her, it seems she's lying on the bed in the dusky half-light of their bedroom, as she is now, the back of one hand resting on her forehead. She notices the wrinkles about her knuckles, pushes at a ring – a huge citrine oval, the colour of honey, in a thick silver setting – with the pad of her thumb, rotating it.

It isn't just her; he's growing increasingly critical of the police, Googling the officers in the investigating team in the hope of tracking their passage through the ranks of the force, the extent of their experience and training. Except all Google brings up are snippets of ancient news stories. She wonders what Ian can extrapolate from DI Harper warning the good motorists of Bedfordshire to lock their cars in 2006. His relief at having Stanton at the helm has been short-lived, Ian's current position on Stanton being that he 'isn't the sharpest knife in the drawer', hence his research into private investigators.

'Why don't you talk to Roger if you're worried?' Miriam said, while they got ready for bed one evening.

217

'I don't want to pull rank on Stanton just yet,' Ian replied. 'It could do more harm than good. Keeping my powder dry for now.'

Rog and Patty had been in touch, of course – an answer machine message and a lovely card with hibiscus on it. *If there's anything we can do . . .*

She presses her hand into the back of her neck to massage it and thinks: these things don't bring you together, they tear you apart. There is no place else to go except towards blame, as if into the arms of a lover. If Ian hadn't pushed Edith so hard. If she, Miriam, wasn't so passive. If Rollo wasn't so *alive*. It was everyone's fault because it was no one's.

Miriam hears the bedroom door handle turn, both longing for and dreading it to be Ian, and soon enough he is sitting on the side of the bed. He strokes her arm – the one laid beside her body – and sighs deeply, but she doesn't look at him.

'I'm so sorry, Miri.'

He starts to cry and she heaves herself up to look at him, curious and moved by him at the same time.

'What are you sorry for?'

'For everything . . . for everything I've done,' he says. He is not looking at her. He is hiding his face from her. 'I haven't been a good husband to you.'

'I feel as if you hate me,' she says.

'Of course I don't hate you. I love you. I love you inordinately.'

He puts his arms around her and she lifts her face to kiss him. He kisses her back, but in a way that has a full stop at the end of it, when she had hoped it would lead on. A consummation. They need to come together and this is how husbands and wives come together, but these things are so often mistimed, their meanings taken the wrong way. How often had they

refused each other out of bitterness or tiredness or standoffish-
ness or a little bit of all three?

'Why don't I take you out for dinner tonight?' he says. 'La
Gaffe, or the new bistro, the French one. Might be our last
chance before the oafs are back on the doorstop tomorrow.'

He is a good husband. He is here and he loves her.
Inordinately.

'It would seem like celebrating,' she says.

'No it wouldn't. Come on. Get up. We don't help Edith by
being prisoners.'

WEDNESDAY

DAVY

'Colonel Bufton Tufton's downstairs, and he's not happy,' says Kim.

'Downstairs? Ian Hind?' says Harriet.

'Downstairs. Pacing like a caged bear.'

'Did we have a meeting I've forgotten about?' Harriet says to Davy, who shrugs, following her at a jog to keep up with her pelt down the stairs, while she says, 'Probably here to bollock me about something.' Then she stops and looks at Davy. 'It'll be the female lover line. I didn't think he knew. Guess the FLO filled him in. Shit, he'll be livid. Typical Stanton, out on a jolly when the shit hits the fan.'

'Is everything all right, Sir Ian?' says Harriet, waiting for Davy to enter, then closing the door to interview room one.

He is pacing up and down, fast, exactly as Kim described, like a bear in a tight space who hasn't been fed.

'Where is Superintendent Stanton?' he says, his navy coat flying as he turns.

'He's not at HQ today,' says Harriet. 'What's the matter, Sir Ian?'

'You are systematically destroying my daughter's reputation.'

'I don't think saying she had a female lover is derogatory, is it?'

'It's prurient,' he says. Davy isn't entirely clear what prurient means. 'It's salacious.' Ah right, thinks Davy, that's what it means. 'It's dirtying her in the mind of the general public, and they don't need much assistance, let me tell you. You are riding roughshod over my family and I—' He is stopped by a catch of emotion in his throat, except he appears to Davy to be too angry for tears.

'Sir Ian, I promise you that is not our intention. We want to find Edith and we want to find her alive. We'll do anything, anything at all, and that includes embarrassing her, and possibly you, though you have no reason to be embarrassed—'

'My wife is crying on the bed, appalled about the things you're saying about Edie, terrified about what your sergeant told us – about Tony Wright. I looked up his offences and they're horrific.'

'We have looked at Tony Wright, just as we look at all known offenders with appropriate previous convictions. It's a line of—'

'A line? You've told us some knife-wielding sexual predator might have had something to do with her disappearance and then you . . . you leave us to it?'

'Wright has an alibi,' Harriet says. 'A very strong alibi. We are just keeping you informed. Look, I know this is upsetting. The reason we assign an FLO is to try to contain these sorts of fears and to answer any questions you might have. Try to calm down, Sir Ian. If you'd like to sit—'

'No, I don't want to sit. Everyone's always telling me to sit or making me drink tea. I don't like our FLO, and anyway, I want to know what you're doing, what the investigation is *doing.* I don't want to be patted by some mooning counsellor who wishes to *contain me.*'

'We are looking at all avenues. Tony Wright is one of our lines of enquiry. Another is the possibility that Edith's personal life – her lovers – is at the heart of what's happened to her. We're hoping the *Crimewatch* appeal will flush out new information.'

'I don't understand,' he says. 'Why, then, is your sergeant also talking to us about a boy – a boy called Dent, I think his name is.'

'That is another line of enquiry.'

'What do you mean "another line"?'

'Taylor Dent's body was found in the river near Ely last week. I think DS Bradshaw informed you of that, didn't she? We are treating it as a murder investigation and we are looking into possible connections with the disappearance of your daughter. The two events had a similar time frame. It would be quite wrong if we didn't look into connections between the two incidents.'

'Forgive me, forgive me, DI Harper,' he says, frowning and shaking his head. 'How can you possibly focus your investigation if you are vaguely looking into everything? If you have multiple lines of enquiry, if you think it might be her love life, or it might be this lowlife, or it might be the boy in the river, then what on earth is your lead? Where is your focus?' He turns, hones in on Harriet with cold, grey eyes in a way which, Davy notices, makes her pretend to read some notes on her clipboard. 'Inspector, is it Tony Wright or Taylor Dent? You don't seem to know. Or is it, in fact, that you're out of your depth being SIO on a case this big, and so you're frantically trying to investigate everything?' He is downright scary-furious, like a headmaster telling her off.

'I . . . we're following up all possible leads,' says Harriet, fingering the corner of a page.

'Which is it?' Sir Ian booms. His knuckles are on the desk and he's hunched over Harriet. It's as if he's about to bang on the table.

'It's hard to say exactly,' says Harriet. 'At this point, multiple avenues—'

'You're supposed to be leading this enquiry, so lead it. Is it Taylor Dent or is it Tony Wright?'

'To be honest, neither of them are holding up that well under scrutiny. But if I, I, I – if I had to, well, I'd say Wright is a stronger lead, but his alibi—'

Sir Ian exhales, straightens, and more gently says, 'Right, so shouldn't you be putting all your resources into Tony Wright then, DI Harper?'

Ian Hind marches out of the room and out of the station, into his Jaguar and back to London, they all hope.

Davy waits with Harriet outside interview room one. She is leaning against the corridor wall, head back, blowing out through pursed lips. 'Fuck,' she whispers. She opens her eyes and looks at Davy, still with her head back. 'That was me at my finest. Watch and learn, Davy Walker.'

'You certainly gave him what for.'

'I did, didn't I?'

'At least he knows who's boss,' says Davy.

Kim is walking towards them, back from visiting Helena Reed.

'How was she?' asks Harriet.

'Yeah, all right. She's a bit out of it. I'm not sure she quite understands what it means in terms of the press an' that.'

'Did you make her aware?'

'Did my best. I told her she might want to lie low, go and

stay with family. Told her officers could sit with her if she wanted. She said she couldn't go to family, was shifty about why, and said she didn't need our support.'

'OK, write it up, will you?' says Harriet.

THURSDAY

MANON

The phones are shrieking, over and above each other, like wailing babies demanding immediate attention. She has 148 unread emails in her inbox. The chorus, persistent and shrill, of keyboards clacking, voices, and mobiles bleeping is drilling into her frontal lobe and transforming itself into piercing pain downwards towards her left eye. The department has gone into overdrive since *Crimewatch* was broadcast last night.

Girl matching Edith's description spotted walking south out of the town; girl matching Edith's description seen walking west out of the town; girl matching Edith's description spotted in Manchester; in Glasgow; in seven separate locations in London. All would have to be followed up. TI. Trace and Interview. Nothing ignored.

The sound has been muted on the television, but there is Stanton, giving more interviews, the red ticker tape running along the bottom of the screen saying – *Det Ch Supt Gary Stanton, Cambridgeshire Police: 'Missing Edith had lesbian relationship. Complex love life at heart of investigation.'*

'Sorry, why have you been put through to this department?'

225

Davy is saying into the phone. 'No, no, I don't want to give you the inside story.' Waits. 'Righto, yes, thank you, putting you through to the press office, caller,' he says, pressing various buttons on his handset and slamming down the receiver with uncharacteristic annoyance. 'Why aren't they putting these calls through to the media team? Why are they coming through to us?'

'Because they lie to switchboard, that's why,' says Harriet.

Colin is in his element, leaping up every five minutes. 'This one says the immigrants are to blame. If we didn't let them flood our borders . . .' He shakes his head, saying, 'Classic.'

Manon is leafing through the pile of newspapers splayed across her desk – across all the desks – every one of them leading on the Hind investigation: *Tragic Edith had female lover*; *Edith's lesbian trysts*; *Missing Edith had secret girlfriend, say police.* Even the broadsheets are carrying it on the front page. *The Telegraph* takes the opportunity to re-run a vast photograph of Edith in her mortar board; something for the brigadiers to gaze at while imagining her disrobed and in a steamy same-sex clinch. The *Guardian* displayed its usual distaste by running it as a basement: *Press frenzy over 'female lover' in Edith investigation.* It got their juices going – girl-on-girl action. Better than that: posh-girl-on-girl action. She prays no one puts two and two together and gets Helena Reed. The Met has had to deploy a protection team to Church Row in Hampstead, where the Hinds are being ferociously doorstepped.

Fergus has walked in. Dark wet patches are leaching through the cotton of his grey shirt at the armpits. His acne outbreak has reddened. He pushes his glasses back onto the bridge of his nose.

'A word, everyone, if you don't mind.'

The department settles, people perching or stood still, but for the phones which keep on crying out.

'We need to be very mindful of attempts to infiltrate this investigation,' he says. 'Most of you will have taken calls from reporters this morning. They are hungry, very hungry indeed – under a lot of pressure for a follow-up to today's revelations. I would strongly advise you not to exchange any details about the case when you are on your mobile phones.'

'Are you saying we're being hacked?' says Stuart.

'I wouldn't rule it out,' says Fergus, and he pushes his glasses up again, the sweat making them slip. 'Just to be on the safe side, don't talk about it on the blower. If you're talking to each other, don't mention names or details, and don't talk to your family and friends about it, OK? Thanks everyone.'

The room breaks up, louder than before. Manon needs to escape the increased decibels, the heightened heat and velocity in the air, the pain shooting across one side of her brain.

'I'm going to the canteen, Davy. D'you want a coffee or anything?'

'This is an almighty mess,' says Davy, and she is startled, not only to hear him express something so despairing but to see the broken expression on his face. 'I mean, what was he thinking? This isn't how we find out what happened to Edith. It's just exploiting her.'

'Normal to shake things up at this point,' she tells him. 'Eighteen days missing, everyone's forgotten about her a bit. We've got fuck-all credible leads. Stanton's just swirling his stick in the sand. Tea? Bacon butty?'

On the way down the stairs she texts Fly.

How is the coat?

Coat is good, but it making me shoes look bad.

She nudges Bryony, who is ahead of her in the canteen queue. 'All right?'

'Oooh, hello,' says Bryony. 'All kicking off round yours.'

'I know. Splitting headache. Phones are ringing off the hook.'

'Any of it sensible?'

'Not so far. You know what it's like.'

'Sit with me?'

'Five minutes, yeah.'

They take a table in the far corner, where Bryony interrogates Manon about her love life.

'So hang on, he came by the station to ask you out, bought you antibiotic eye drops, and you haven't called him?' Bryony is saying, and it's doing nothing for Manon's headache.

The conjunctivitis was gone by Tuesday morning. She'd applied the first drops the minute she got upstairs to the department on the Monday evening, and the next day she was clear and evangelical about antibiotics' supernatural powers. What on earth will the human race do when this medicine stops working? Die in childbirth again. Go blind with conjunctivitis. Kidney failure from cystitis. Commit suicide during a bout of toothache. She thought about it a bit, darkly, and then, on with the day! She'd been briefly full of gratitude, too, towards Alan Prenderghast, but this had evaporated just as fast as the infection so that by Wednesday afternoon, she'd forgotten that she was ever encumbered. She hadn't got round to thanking him, and then she didn't feel like it any more.

It is more than that, she realises now, sitting opposite Bryony and the pressure she exudes. She can't communicate . . . what? Something nuanced and complex about why she doesn't want to get involved with him. The way she stands back from the web of interaction because she can't commit to being inside it.

228

Her sheer ambivalence, which Bryony sees as straightforward but is anything but. Contact is difficult.

'And yet you will put out for whatever hairy sociopath comes your way on the Internet?' Bryony is saying.

Manon shrugs, as if to say, *Search me.*

'There's no helping you. I literally give up.'

'I keep meaning to ring him,' says Manon, and she notices how her voice sounds: slow and dissociated, as if very far away. 'I just don't get round to it. I don't know why.'

'I do. He might actually be nice to you. He might treat you well and give you babies.'

'Come off it,' she says, frowning, and she's angry now at being bulldozed. 'You don't know shit about him, Bri.'

'I know he's already better than the totally awful specimens you normally go out with.'

Manon has stood up abruptly. She's had enough. 'You fucking go out with him then.'

She walks away, hearing Bryony say, 'Manon, come back, I—' before the doors to the canteen shut behind her.

HELENA

Her breathing comes in jolts, stepping down in her solar plexus, then up again, catching in her throat. A ladder of tears. 'They're com-ing to get me,' she says. 'They are com-ing to ge-et me.'

'I think if we can just go back to the dream, we can try to unravel this,' says Dr Young, still voice of calm.

'The-ey are com-ing to ge-et me. The papers . . . It's all ov-er the papers . . . Oh G-o-d, oh God . . .' She places her palms over her face, wet and puffy from the torrent. She wants to hide, for the earth to open and for it to close over her head, welcome grave. Exposure is everywhere, about to happen. She is about to be named. She is filthy.

'The dream,' he says.

In the dream, she was running down suburban streets – Newnham or her parents' street in Bromley, she couldn't tell. Breathless, her clothes torn, pursued by a flock of enormous black crows, with wings flying out behind them like academic cloaks, and angry beaks. Running and running from them as they gained ground, and then she turned a corner and saw her parents' house, the front door of her childhood, and she felt a surge of relief that she would be safe. They would open the door to her and she would get inside and the crows would be barred. She reached the front door and banged with her fists on it and the crows were at the gate. But the door didn't open. Her parents didn't answer, and the horror, the horror, she feels herself collapsing again, folding in on herself. She saw her parents at the window looking at her from the safety of the lounge, leaving her outside to face the crows.

'They wouldn't let me in,' she gasps, her palms wet over her face, the tears seeping to the webbed crooks between her fingers. 'Because I am disgusting.'

'How are you disgusting?'

'Because . . . because . . . the newspapers are saying she had a female lover, but I'm not, I'm not . . . Everyone will think I was her lover, but I wasn't. It wasn't like that, but everyone will think it was dirty, sordid, that I did something to her.'

'Why would anyone make that connection? Is there something about your relationship with Edith, something about that night that you're not being honest about?'

'No, no, you see? You think it. You see "female lover" and you think of me. Her best friend, with her on the night she disappeared. It's all over it – the innuendo.'

Silence.

'But you know what *did* happen,' he says. 'The truth about that night.'

'Yes, I know. No, no I don't mean that. I don't know what happened to Edith, I don't know that. You're trying to trip me up. You're trying to get me to say I was involved.'

Silence, this time of a kind which seems incriminating.

'I wonder,' he says, 'if you feel that I am locking you out – leaving you to the black crows – in the gap between now and our next session on Monday. All this press interest, the feeling

231

you have of exposure . . . Three days is a long time to be on your own with it all.'

She is silent, except for the uneven steps of her breathing.

'We have to leave it there,' he says.

DAVY

'Nice road,' he says. He presses on his key fob and the car answers with its electronic *whup-whep*. The lights flash twice and they walk along a pavement sparkling with frost, their breath smoking and their hands dug into their pockets. It's a relief to be out of the frenetic heat of HQ – a million conflicting sightings of Edith and the deceiving infiltration of reporters who are back on the story.

A ribbon of mist curls through the tops of the trees. He looks into the front gardens: chequerboard tiling and the bare stems of magnolias or lilacs; bicycles chained to black iron railings; bay windows so clean they seem liquid and topped with little proud roof turrets in grey slate.

They have come to the posh part of Cambridge – Newnham – to re-interview Barbara Garfield, wife of Edith's Director of Studies, after she called and told them she had new information to share. Didn't everyone, after *Crimewatch*?

Be nice to live somewhere like this, he thinks – so comfortable with itself. Those front patches are tended by people who listen to *Gardeners' Question Time* and know the names

233

of shrubs. He bets the houses' insides are worn but bookish, not smelly-depressing shabby, like the places they visit for work, pushing their jumpers up over their mouths and noses. No, this is easy-does-it shabby. I-know-who-I-am shabby. Persian-rug shabby.

'Grantchester Street,' he says, checking in his green book.

'Left at the end here,' says Manon.

They walk a little further.

'Did you see,' Davy says, 'Stuart's got a new iPad?'

'That's more Colin's bag than mine,' says Manon.

'Nice one, latest kind, y'know – white one, thin as you like. Says he can't get used to the touch screen. Just wonder how he afforded it, that's all. Didn't think CIs got paid that much—'

He is winded by a body slamming into him from the left. Someone who has hurtled out of the gate from one of the houses they have just passed. 'Woah,' he says, catching her about the shoulders. 'Slow down. Are you all right?'

The girl is stooped over, crying, and when she looks up, Manon says, 'Helena?'

She doesn't speak. Her eyes are red raw, her lips swollen, and she is shaking.

'Helena,' says Manon again. 'What are you doing here? Is everything all right?'

'Everyone will know,' she says, with pleading eyes. 'Why did he say that, about a female lover? Why did he have to say that on telly? Everyone will know. It's all over the papers. They're going to want to know *who*.' And she collapses into Davy's chest.

'Didn't an officer come and warn you about *Crimewatch*? I thought DC Kim Delaney—'

'I didn't realise, I didn't know how huge it would be,' Helena says, her eyes wide with fear. 'The television. It was

234

on the television. I don't know what I thought . . . I didn't take it in.'

'No one knows about you,' says Manon. 'It won't come out, about you and Edith.' She and Davy look at each other over Helena's head. 'No one is going to release your name, Helena. As far as the press knows, you are just the friend she was out with on Saturday night.'

'Look, anyone comes after you, you call me,' says Davy, pushing her away from his chest so he can dig in his pocket for a card with his number printed on it, and so that he can look her in the eye, too. Tell her it's real. They will protect her. 'Now get yourself home and lay low. D'you need a car? I can get someone out here—'

'No, no,' she says. She wipes the wet from her nose with the back of her hand and the movement makes her seem like a little girl. 'I can get home.'

She is looking down at Davy's little white card, with its silver star symbol topped with a royal crown and the words *Cambridgeshire Constabulary* following the blue circle.

'Would you like an officer with you at your flat? We can arrange that,' he says.

'Why are you here?' says Helena abruptly. 'What are you doing on the same street as my, my, my friend . . . I have a friend who lives here.'

'Just routine enquiries,' says Manon, smiling, but this seems only to increase the terror in Helena's eyes.

'Are you sure you're all right?' says Davy. 'I think I should drive you. I've got a car just around the corner.'

'No, no,' and she bridles, shaking Davy's hand off her shoulder. 'I've got somewhere to go right now. I'm not going straight home, you see. I'll be all right.' She sniffs. 'It'll all blow over, right? This storm, it'll pass.'

Manon and Davy watch her as she turns and scurries, hunched and quick-footed, away from them down Grantchester Street.

'Don't like the look of her,' says Davy. 'We should call it in. Tell Harriet she seems vulnerable.'

'Yup, we'll flag it up when we get back to the office after this,' says Manon.

MANON

'Have you finished yet?' asks Manon, smiling at him.

'Not yet, no,' Davy says, sneezing another three times.

'Goodness me,' says Mrs Garfield. 'Are you all right?'

'Do you have a cat?' asks Davy.

'Yes, oh goodness, sorry. Wait a minute, I'll put her out.'

Manon takes a seat at the dining table while Davy blows his nose. They are in a sunken kitchen which gives out onto the back garden. The kitchen floor is a grid of terracotta squares and the cupboards are oak. The room smells of boiling lentils and surfaces just wiped with a faintly mildewed cloth. The dishwasher is going. The round dining table, at the garden end of the room, is covered with a wipeable oilcloth in a pale green William Morris design. On the wall is a picture of Mr and Mrs Garfield in shorts and sunglasses, leaning into one another.

'There, she won't bother you any more,' says Mrs Garfield, coming back into the room and brushing at her skirt. 'Though I can't guarantee her fur won't – it's everywhere, I'm afraid. Now, what can I get you to drink? Tea? Coffee?'

'Glass of water, if you don't mind, Mrs Garfield,' says Davy.

'Sergeant?'

'Nothing for me, thank you.'

Mrs Garfield runs the tap, her finger feeling its temperature, saying, 'I really don't know why I rang. And you must be absolutely inundated after *Crimewatch*. The papers are full of it.'

'Did you remember something that might be important?' asks Manon.

'Silly, really, and you've come out all this way. I mean, sometimes you think something's a thing, and then it isn't a thing. D'you know what I mean?'

'Something about the night Edith went missing, perhaps?' says Manon. 'When your husband came back from The Crown?'

She sets the glass of water in front of Davy, who has his green book out on the dining table. Mrs Garfield doesn't sit down with them. Instead, she returns to the kitchen counter and busies herself, clattering about with various pans and bowls. They wait.

Davy writes something in his book, the date and time probably. Manon looks out to the garden, the wet-grey paving slabs, soil silted and blown about with fallen leaves. It all seems quite dead.

Manon breaks the silence, ever so gently. 'Is there something you're unsure about . . . about Mr Garfield?'

'He wipes his Internet history,' Mrs Garfield says, without looking up, making circular wiping motions on the worktop with a cloth.

'Go on,' says Manon.

'I don't. I don't wipe my Internet history. I'm only ever on the John Lewis website looking at table lamps. Or Amazon. I don't wipe my Internet history – it wouldn't occur to me. So why does he?'

'It occurred to you to look for his Internet history, Mrs Garfield. Why was that?'

'He's always on his computer – lost in this world that I don't know anything about. It's like some secret door he goes through, where he's unreachable, like the screen has stolen him from me.' She shakes her head, then adopts a different tone. 'It's probably nothing – work or football scores. Reading the *New Statesman*. But you don't *know*, do you?' And she laughs, but the texture in the room has darkened.

'Was he with you on the night of the seventeenth of December, after The Crown?'

Mrs Garfield nods. 'As far as I know.'

'As far as you know?'

'I did say at the time, but perhaps I didn't make myself clear. I was falling asleep when I heard his key in the door. I registered that and then I nodded off. I didn't actually *see* him.'

'And your relationship with Mr Garfield,' says Manon. 'How has that been?'

'What do you mean by that?'

'Has everything been normal between the two of you? Has he been behaving normally?'

'As far as I know,' says Mrs Garfield.

Manon waits. If she waits, something more might come. But Mrs Garfield has become more brisk in her clattering and fussing in the kitchen area, her body language saying: *I'm really far too busy for all this.*

'Right, well, thanks very much for your time,' says Manon, rising from her chair. Davy follows her cue to get up, too. 'I'm sure it's nothing to worry about, the computer stuff, but thanks for letting us know. And do call us if anything else comes to mind, Mrs Garfield. We can see ourselves out.'

They pull their car doors shut with a warming *shunk* and

the sounds of outside are cut off. Their coats rustle and they click their seatbelts down into the red slots.

'We going to get Garfield's laptop then?' asks Davy, before he starts the engine.

She already has her phone to her ear, and after a short preamble – 'Mr Garfield, yes, sorry to disturb you, it's Detective Sergeant Bradshaw' – she says, 'We'd like to take a look at your laptop.'

'Why would you want to do that?'

'Just to eliminate you from our inquiries. It'd be best if you gave it to us voluntarily.'

'I'm sorry, I do want to help in any way I can, but all you'll find on my laptop is a series of very dull essays on Tennyson's *Idylls of the King*, that sort of thing.'

'We can have it back to you in a week,' says Manon.

'Really, I'd love to help, but I can't manage without it for a week and anyway, there's nothing on it. Nothing that would be of any interest to you. Look, I'm really sorry, but I've got a study group in five minutes.'

'Mr Garfield?'

'Yes?'

'I'd hate to come and arrest you at the college.'

'Why would you arrest me?'

'Because an arrest gives me automatic powers to search and seize.'

There is silence on the line.

'I'd hate to, you know, create a scene. Uniformed constables at the porter's lodge, asking where you are. Our panda cars with their flashing blue lights outside the college – we love putting our lights on. Officers marching across the quad towards your rooms. All those students standing around watching. You know what Cambridge is like – terrible for

240

gossip. But I'd have to do that in order to get your laptop, you see. But if you handed it over voluntarily, we could keep it all nice and quiet.'

Davy starts the engine as Manon puts her mobile back in her bag. As he pulls out, he says, 'To the college, then?'

'Yep.'

'By the way, I've spoken to my mate – the mentoring buddy. In Brent. Said she's looking out for Taylor's brother, Fly, is it? She had meetings with education welfare and with the school, and they have agreed to work together to keep him at home with his mother.'

'Great. That's great.'

'Actually, she thinks he's amazing.'

I know he's amazing, she thinks. 'How d'you mean?'

'Well, the school said he's gifted. A great little reader. They said you'd expect a child in his situation to fall off the curve, but he's top of his class.'

'Does that somehow make him more worthy of being saved?' she says, in a bid to cover an involuntary flush of pride in Fly Dent. After all, why should she feel pride? It's not as if he's hers.

'Makes him of interest to them,' says Davy, eyes fixed cheerfully on the road. 'My mate'll keep an eye on him. Fly's mum's really sick, you know that, right? Hasn't attended any of her hospital appointments. If she dies, he'll be taken into care. Just to warn you.'

'Yes, yes, I know,' she says, her hands having already dug out her mobile phone, working on a text to Fly.

How is school?

OK, if you like that sort of thing.

241

What did you have at the Portuguese café?

Why d'you care?

Cos I'm paying.

Oh, OK. Toast and jam.

White or brown?

Actually, it was kind of red.

Haha. White or brown toast?

Back off, DS Auntie.

DAVY

It's a short drive to Graham Garfield's college rooms in Corpus, and while Manon runs in to pick up his laptop (just her, nice and quiet, like she promised), Davy sits in his driver seat, checking his BlackBerry. His original request for information from EE about unknown-515 had yielded nothing, but that was before Christmas, so as soon as he was back from his festive break he requested an update, and this has just dropped into his inbox.

Manon is heaving down into the passenger seat, having put Garfield's laptop onto the back seat.

'He wasn't happy,' she says, breathless and rustling in her coat.

Davy is shifting in his seat, making himself more upright. 'Unknown-515,' he says, reading.

'What about it?'

'It's been topped up. Biggleswade, the BP service station. Two weeks ago.'

'That'll have CCTV,' she says. 'Let's head out there.'

'Shouldn't we, y'know, head back to the office, drop off the laptop, give Harriet the heads up on Helena Reed?' asks Davy.

243

'Nah,' says Manon. She's excitable, he's seen that look before. When she gets the bit between her teeth, she doesn't want to stop. 'Come on, Davy, this could be it – this could be the thing that solves it. You and me, and a collar.' She lifts and lowers her eyebrows at him, a bit comedy. 'To Biggleswade!' she says, raising aloft an imaginary sword.

Davy shakes his head and drives.

As they pull into the BP forecourt, Manon is already peering about its low slab of a roof for cameras.

'CCTV for December twenty-third,' she says at the counter, showing her badge to the cashier. 'Have you got it stored somewhere?'

The cashier, a spotty young man of about twenty, is shaking his head. 'Wiped at the start of the year,' he says. 'I only know 'cos I was in that day.'

'Were you on duty on December twenty-third?' asks Davy.

'Nope, don't know who was. I'd have to get my manager but he's not about right now.'

Davy turns round at the squeak of the shop door and sees Manon already leaving. He jogs after her as she strides about the forecourt, scanning the London Road and its wide-spaced bungalows left and right.

'We can speak to the duty manager, get the rota off of him,' Davy suggests to her back.

She is squinting and peering, turning this way and that. 'There!' she says to him, pointing.

'What?' says Davy.

'There, can't you see it? Poking out of the ivy.'

On a brick wall opposite the BP garage, camouflaged by glossy foliage, is a camera – trained on the forecourt. 'Let's see what's in that one.'

MANON

Back in the department, she says, 'There you go, Colin, knock yourself out,' and places Graham Garfield's MacBook Air on Colin's desk.

He lifts its sleek grey lid, saying, 'What's he been up to then, dirty dog?'

'It's his web browser history we're interested in.'

'All leaves a trace,' he mutters, clicking about as if he's owned the laptop all his life. 'Download takes time though, going through all that data.'

The room is quieter than when they left. It seems deflated with collective exhaustion but Manon is fizzing. She wants that film, because whoever Edith was calling the day before she disappeared must hold the key, and Manon is about to get him, about to see his face. It can't be Taylor Dent, unless you can top-up from beyond the grave (the phone companies are probably looking into this possibility) but it could be an associate of his.

Kim is passing round a tray of Thornton's Milk Assortment, so broad and thin it bends, crackling in her hand.

'We bumped into Helena Reed. She looked pretty torn up about the *Crimewatch* stuff. Need to keep an eye on her,' Manon says to Harriet. Kim's mouth is already working on a chocolate – slow, bovine ruminations – but before passing the box on, she takes another.

'Not for me,' says Harriet, taut as ever, perching on a desk, then up again, rounding her shoulders and pulling up her bra strap. 'OK, let's send a liaison officer round this arvo. They can stay with her over the weekend. Make sure you put in the paperwork, all right, Manon? Who gave us those, anyway?' she says, nodding at the chocolates.

'Some old bird handed them in to reception.'

'Christ, it wouldn't be hard to take out the whole of Cambridgeshire nick – you lot'll eat anything.'

'Where's the menu guide thingy,' Colin asks, the box having at last come his way.

'Speed it up, Brierley,' says Stuart.

'I think I'll have . . . No, hang on. Yes, a Nut Caress.' With a full mouth, he says, 'Nothing dirty among his documents so far. Looks like he and Mrs Garfield had a nice time in Broadstairs, mind.'

'When's that CCTV footage coming in?' asks Harriet.

'Any minute now,' says Manon, clicking refresh on her emails. 'Council said they'd have it to me within the hour.'

She creates a new email, types in DI Haverstock, and his address at Kilburn CID fills out automatically. *Just a note,* she types, *to say if anything significant comes in on the Dent enquiry, can you email me? Just keep me up to speed, that's all.* Then she hits 'send'.

She glances at Colin and Stuart – Colin half-clicking around Garfield's laptop, with the odd sideways look at Stuart's new iPad.

'I just can't get to grips with it,' Stuart is saying, swiping at the screen and frowning, to which Colin says (chewing, glasses pushed up onto his bald pate), 'That's normal with a new gadget. You have to hate it for a time. That's how it is.'

'Here we go,' Manon says to the room, opening up the new email which has just appeared in her inbox. It seems an age while the footage downloads, Harriet perching, then up again, pulling at her bra strap. Manon's mind is feeling along the possibilities: an associate of Taylor Dent; a lover they haven't been told about; a drug dealer whose previous convictions will be all over their system. They gather round Manon's screen: Harriet, Davy, Kim and Colin. The grainy grey images flick and turn, one car then the next. 'What was the timing again, Davy?'

'It was topped up at 6.02 p.m.,' Davy says.

Manon jumps along the timeline with her mouse, watching the tiny yellow numbers change in the corner of her screen. 5.59 p.m., and there is a figure in a familiar denim jacket with small round spectacles, hands pushed into his pockets, white hair tied in a ponytail.

FRIDAY

MIRIAM

The perpetual dusk of Central Lobby – its octagon reverberating with self-important shoes. Passes swinging from lapels or hung about necks on ribbons. Miriam sits on a black leather button-back chair while Ian stands nearby, reading the plate at the base of one of the alabaster statues.

Their invitation for Rog and Patty to come to Church Row had been politely declined and she and Ian know why. Ostensibly, it was because of the oafs who had returned to the doorstep – back with a vengeance since the *Crimewatch* appeal was broadcast two nights ago. Miriam could hear them from the bedroom, chatting and laughing, stubbing out their cigarettes on her flagstone step. They hung their cameras on her wrought iron railings as if they owned the place. Their shutters went mad every time Rosa put out the rubbish. Periodically, Ian became incensed and put in a call to someone or other and they retreated to the end of the street, chivvied by some local bobby, but they soon drifted back or lurked in the churchyard close to the house. Ian said the Press Complaints Commission was drafting a letter to editors, asking them to 'respect' the Hind family's privacy at this distressing time', but she'd like to see what good it would do. Everyone knew the PCC was a toothless watchdog.

Anyway, Patty had said, 'We don't want to give them more fodder by rolling up in a government car.' So here she and Ian are, obedient 'strangers', herded through the metal detectors at St Stephen's Gate and waiting now to be fetched.

As they dressed this morning – Miriam rolling up a pair of 10 denier tights as she sat on the edge of the bed, Ian throwing the long tongue of his tie over itself – she said to him, 'Do you think it's because of Edith – because of what they've said about her? Do you think that's why they refused— *Damn!*' The ladder in her tights felt like an injury. She hated the slippery feel of them, and now she had to try another pair.

'That'd be rich, coming from him,' Ian said.

'How do you mean?'

'Nothing.'

'No, come on, Ian, you can't drop a thing like that . . .'

'There was a lot of it at school, that's all.'

If she's honest, she assumed as much, at a school like that. Dropped off at seven years old, no one to cuddle when they fell and scraped their knees, and homesickness considered a disobedience. The school churned out leaders and princes, but they were men forged in the furnace of repression. God help you if you were less than robust; if you missed your mother desperately. When she'd seen pictures of Ian as a boy, she knew that he was one of those sensitive ones: twiggy-legged, with full lips that probably quivered with his tears. He hadn't even raised the notion of Rollo following in his footsteps (apart from some mild comments about the school's excellent facilities for sport). He seemed to know how ferociously Miriam would guard Rollo to keep him safely at home.

249

Anyway, she thinks now, these things are not so clear-cut as everyone might think. Boys experiment, girls too, evidently; their feelings sway one way and another. All part of feeling the way towards adulthood.

Ian told her she was paranoid, but with Rog and Patty she has the sense of rope being let out, as if she and Ian are a boat being allowed to drift. A similar feeling with the Palace, which has remained silent. It seems to Miriam that they have become tainted – the stain of life going wrong, rather like the taint of illness or disability, weight gain, depression, financial difficulty. It has the whiff of not *succeeding* – not staying sufficiently in control.

'Hello, you,' says Patty, and Miriam stands, allowing Patty to clutch her arms and kiss her twice. 'Rog is waiting in his office. Shall I lead the way?'

She clacks ahead of them, saying hello to various suits, down tiled corridors and then up into the realm of endless wood panelling.

Rog is out from behind his desk, crossing the acreage of carpet to where they have entered. 'I thought it'd be more private here than Marsham Street,' he says, reaching out his hand to Ian. 'How are you holding up, both of you?'

Miriam is comforted by Roger's corpulent bonhomie. She thinks of him as a cricketer, the white cable-knit tight over the drum of his belly, jogging towards the batsman, and lobbing the ball over-arm. All Englishness and fair play.

'Not so well, actually,' she says. 'Turns out losing a child is a living torture. They don't tell you that before you have them, do they?'

Ian frowns at her while Roger coughs fulsomely into a fist. Patty has her head cocked like a therapist or an empathising actress.

'Come in anyway,' says Roger. 'It must be ghastly, all of it. Drink?'

Ian and Miriam say, 'Thank you' and 'Please' over each other.

They have been here before, shortly after they won – well, formed the coalition – back in May. The boast tour, Roger called it, laughing. He'd certainly been pleased with himself, and why not.

The room is vast, the carpet swirling away in a luxury of Persian roses, pale with antiquity. Heavy drapes and large lamps. A desk the size of a dining table. Patty is opening a highly polished rosewood cupboard to reveal a deep-set drinks cabinet, cut glasses, decanter and all.

'Goodness,' says Miriam. 'Didn't think they still made those.' For comforting the bereft, she guesses, or firing people. Or those long nights drawing up draconian immigration policy.

'They don't,' says Patty. 'This one's 1930s. Picked it up at Bonhams. I went with Sam – she's got lots more time since she left Smythson.'

Miriam hasn't the energy to deliver what Patty needs. She requires admiration. Ian and Miriam have always been quick to give it but now, standing beside Patty at the stupid Nazi-Reich drinks cabinet while Ian and Rog burble to each other on the other side of the room, and everything stripped away, she and Ian back to the bone, while Rog and Patty are still so pleased with themselves, she wonders what the basis is for any sort of friendship.

'I just don't think they know what they're doing,' Ian is saying, as Patty hands Miriam a bitter lemon in a heavy, textured glass. (Not tea, *thank God.*) She takes Ian a tumbler of whiskey, which is not at all like him, but perhaps more so, recently. 'Saying all that stuff on *Crimewatch*, it just clouds the investigation.'

251

Rog has retreated behind his desk for protection. 'I know you're worried sick, and I can see the telly thing would have been distressing, but best thing you can do is let the police do their job.'

'But there's so much confusion, you see, in the investigation. They keep looking for connections where there aren't any. One minute they say it's this criminal, Tony Wright; then it's her complex love life; next it's this Dent boy. The Edith they describe, it doesn't bear any relation . . .'

Ian's tone has become needy and simultaneously Roger's eyes have grown cold. The trace of the bully in Roger, which is the real seat of his power – a gaze which can flash like steel, the unapologetic way in which he takes up all the air space. Miriam wonders what sort of bully – what sort of punishment he employs, these things rarely being notional, not if they're to have any heft. Perhaps the threat, simply, of being cast out from the circle of influence. The rope gets longer.

'We thought you might be able to get the inside track,' Ian is saying, while looking to Miriam for support.

'I'm sure you understand, I can't meddle in police work. Individual cases – how would it *look* . . .' Roger says.

'Oh, come off it,' Ian says. 'I bet you meddle all the time. I'm sure you're right in there when the *Daily Mail* says you're not taking a hard enough line.'

'Ian,' Miriam says soothingly. 'All we want,' she begins, but wonders what it is they want, really. Rog and Patty can't find Edith for them, which is the only thing that matters. Perhaps they want what anyone wants from the powerful – protection. They want Roger to oil the processes, as they would be oiled for him; to protect them from shoddiness. 'All we want,' she

252

tries again but her tears stop her, and in some way save them all. 'Oh God, I'm sorry,' Miriam snivels as Patty hugs her. 'Can we talk about something else, please? What's your news? How is Calista?'

MANON

'Quiet everyone, please,' says Harriet, and the department falls to a hush. 'As you know, Tony Wright was arrested last night at 5 p.m., he's spent the night in custody, so hopefully he'll be nice and chatty this morning. His flat is now a crime scene. SOCO is still in there looking for anything that could link Wright to either Edith or Taylor Dent. We have,' she looks at her watch, 'six hours remaining in which to charge him with something, otherwise he walks. His brief is going to say the CCTV footage is too grainy for a firm ID and that his alibi for the weekend Edith disappeared still holds tight.'

'Which is true,' says Manon.

'Which is true,' repeats Harriet, nodding. 'So why was Edith calling Tony Wright the week before she disappeared? Twice – once on the Monday, again on the Friday.'

'You don't think she was having an affair with him, do you?' says Davy.

'You'd have to be deaf, dumb, and blind to have an affair with Tony Wright,' says Kim.

'Maybe,' says Colin thoughtfully, as if swilling an exquisite red around his palate, 'she's had enough of all the posh blokes and fancies a bit of rough.'

'Yeah, 'cos it's a tough one, isn't it?' says Kim, holding both hands in the balance. 'On the one hand you've got devastatingly handsome Cambridge graduate Will Carter; and on the other you've got sleazebag burglar Tony Wright. *Who to choose?*'

'There's no accounting for taste,' says Harriet.

'She might find rough men exciting,' ventures Colin.

'There's a lot of hope in your voice, Colin,' says Manon.

'Let's stick to the point,' says Harriet. 'Let's say they were having an affair, preposterous though that seems – it doesn't explain how they knew each other. How on earth did someone like Edith Hind meet someone like Tony Wright? And anyway, he's still here, but she's not, so it's not like they've run off into the sunset together.'

'Maybe he was blackmailing her,' says Manon. 'If it's not sex, it's money. Maybe he knew, I dunno, some dark secret about her and she had to pay him off. Would explain why she was calling him.'

'So we need to look into his finances,' says Harriet. 'Any nice new tellies at his flat. I want the data off all phones and computers from his property. I want forensics from whatever vehicle he's currently using. Let's go downstairs, talk to Wright,' she says to Manon. 'Anything comes in from SOCO, come and get us.'

'Why didn't you tell us you knew Edith Hind?' Harriet says, without preamble.

'Oh aye,' says Wright, and Manon can see he's rankled, he's had enough. 'That girl that's been abducted? She an' I were pals! Ye wan tae cuff me now or wait for the van tae pull up?

Shall we bother wi' a trial or head straight tae Whitemoor, where you can BANG ME UP TILL I DIE?'

Tony Wright has stood up, knocking his chair backwards. His solicitor, a silently composed man in a grey suit with matching waistcoat, casts him a look and he sits back down.

'Tell me about your relationship with Edith Hind.'

'No comment.'

'How did you know her?'

'No comment.'

And so it goes on: every question, so that eventually everyone is going through the motions in a monotone, Wright not even waiting for Harriet to finish her sentences. Until she mentions Taylor Dent. At this, Wright looks genuinely quizzical, frowns, then says, 'No comment' all the same. There is a knock at the door and Harriet stops the recording, and they step out of the room.

'His flat's clean,' says Kim in the corridor. 'I mean, nothing obvious, No items of clothing or anything belonging to Edith,' she says to Harriet. 'No blood on anything. Forensics'll take a bit longer though.'

'Fuck,' says Harriet. She looks at Manon. They both know, unless a miracle happens in the course of the afternoon, they're going to have to let Wright go. 'His brief's going to be all over this,' she says, 'asking what evidence we've got to sustain an arrest.'

'We can't charge him with speaking to her on the blower,' says Manon.

The only way to come down after a week of fifteen-hours shifts is to lose herself in a book or film, so here she is, standing on the cinema steps, head down against the cold, one hand in a pocket and the other texting Fly Dent.

What did you have at the Portuguese café?

Somefin new. She call it Manioc. She says she introducing me to new foods. Not too sure meself.

Was it nice?

Not really. It was yellow. And dry.

Do you think she could introduce you to vegetables?

We met. We didn't get on.

She shuffles forward in the queue for *My Life as a Dog* by Lasse Hallström, reluctant to flip the phone shut, so she is scrolling back through their conversation when a voice says, 'You again.'

Fuck shit bollocks. She tries to think of something before looking up. He is the very last person she wants to see, not because she doesn't like him (she's all at sea over whether she likes him), but because she never thanked him, never called, and she can't bear the awkwardness. Is it too late, she wonders, as she looks up, to cough violently and pretend she's been in bed with flu?

'Alan,' she says. 'How are you?'

'Hurt and rejected,' he says, smiling at her.

'Oh God, I'm really sorry. It was nice of you, the eye drops, and look—' she blinks at him – 'all better!'

'So I see.'

'I kept meaning to call and say thanks. But work – it's just gone mental.'

'Yes, your work,' he says. And he's smiling ironically, as if

257

he sees through her. And she feels annoyed at his presumption, because actually it *has* been mental.

'It affects me. It's important to me,' she says.

'Yes, sir, officer,' he says, smiling again, his hands in his pockets.

'I like you,' she blurts, without realising she's saying it out loud until it's too late. The thought becomes the deed. 'I sometimes show off because I like you.' And as she looks at him, nothing seems honest at all, not even this.

'Swedish season,' he says.

'Yes,' she laughs. 'Swedish season.'

They stand there like that, as if they are an old couple, companionable, except her insides have clenched like an angry fist. Someone pays at the front and they shuffle forward a human width.

'Shall we sit together this time? Would you mind?' he says.

And she smiles. He has forgiven her and she is taken up with the sensation of his proximity – a new feeling, a new smell – and interested in where it might take them.

The boy in the film is called Ingemar. His mother is dying and he keeps saying, 'It could have been worse,' which reminds her of Fly. She feels her phone vibrate and opens it up to see a text from him, containing a photograph of strawberry laces and the words: *One of my five-a-day.*

The cinema screen flickers black and white, colours and daylight. Words are said but she has lost track. His large hand is on the armrest between the two of them and she takes it in hers. Something receptive in her, like a flower opening, sad and vulnerable. He looks at her, then clasps her hand in return, and they both lean in and put their temples together. Her body is shaking on the inside and the vast cinema screen surrounds her with its flickering, meaningless images. She closes her eyes. His hands are big and enclosing, rough on the thumb pads. Foreign hands, new to the touch. He makes tiny stroking movements with his thumb and she can feel the aftershock between her legs. She senses the movement in the air when he blinks. He is seeking out her lips now, soft and dry, very gentle on hers, and her stomach flips over itself. She is dissolving into the dark. Alan the systems analyst, with voluminous corduroys and trainers like ocean liners. Who knew? Something unspoken, like a scent, makes her being reach towards him, and she is ardent, as if all the feelings are hers, far more than his, and she fills up all the more for it being so.

When the lights go up, their heads are still together, though her neck is hurting now and their hands have grown clammy.

'Coffee?' he says, and she nods.

They walk up the cinema stairs to the art deco café, as before. The same table but this time, when he walks towards her carrying their drinks – she's having mint tea to freshen her breath – she notices his elegant hands.

He loops his maroon scarf over the back of the chair, saying, 'I loved the stuff about the dog sent into orbit by the Russians. Think of him and nothing is that bad in comparison.'

Oh, she thinks, you *were* concentrating.

She takes a sip of tea.

He leans forward. 'What now, Sergeant?' he says with an ironic expression, and it's as if he's saying, *Wither the rest of our lives?*

'What now indeed,' she says.

They sip their drinks, each with both hands around their cups and elbows on the table, and she wonders, did anything happen in there? Or did I imagine it all?

*   *   *

259

They lie in her bed. His arm is under her neck and she is holding the weight of his forearm at the wrist. Bouncing it occasionally.

'I think you should know,' she says, looking at the ceiling, 'that my basic position on life is that it's shit.'

'Oh, I'm with you. I only stick around for the food and, frankly, that's often crap as well.'

She laughs. Bounces his wrist in her hand. 'It's like, take Christmas,' she says.

'Brilliant dinner, awful day.'

She laughs again.

'I think part of the appeal is that slight out-of-reach quality,' he says.

'You mean: "Oooh, I'm almost having a good time . . . Oh no, I'm not."'

'Yes, that's it. Well, no, it's more: "I'm going to enjoy it, I'm going to enjoy it, I'm going to enjoy it . . . Oh no, it's rubbish again."'

'It's expectation,' she says. 'That's what kills off enjoyment. Holidays are stressful for the same reason.'

After a time, he says, 'The dog. I've got to go back for Nana – let her out.'

Her insides tighten with the disappointment, but then he says, 'Come with me?'

She opens one eye into the grainy morning light, forgetful for one moment, then sees his crumpled form next to her, burrowed down into the pillow. Blissful January! The cold swirling the room, but oh it is warm in the bed and we are two. *We are two.* She kisses his bare shoulder, smelling his skin, malty and male, like sourdough. Alien male! This is what she needs: a person who is other.

She rolls onto her back and closes her eyes. She feels his weight upon her, his lips soft and dry, his over-sweet breath which he is trying to disguise by keeping his mouth shut, his erection against her leg.

'Well, hello,' she says, laughing.

'Hello,' he mumbles, as if she shouldn't make a joke of it.

His voice is gravelly, his eyes closed like a little rodent, bruised and nocturnal, so she wonders if he's still asleep and wanting her out of his unconscious self, his sleepy, atavistic morning maleness. Oh joy. *Hello, you.*

His head is in her neck as they rock together, sleepily aroused, their faces still closed up, their cells thick with half-remembered dreams.

Over and over, all day in bed, wrapped in his grey linen sheets, her on top, bare-breasted, his face burrowed there; Manon trying to ignore the stoic glances from Nana, who has wandered in like a confused pensioner in a strip joint. In the shower, him insistent behind her, the water pouring down her neck and over the hard stones of her nipples and over his hand between her legs. They cannot stop, or when they stop they seem to start all over again, and each time it is new, each time they are remembering the last time and reinventing it too.

'I'm going to give up my job and just have sex for a living,' says Manon, in a shirt and knickers, her bare feet freezing on the kitchen floor.

'Me too,' he says, leaning against the counter eating toast. How is it that *not* touching, him being a few feet away, is erotic, a kind of come-on? 'Our earnings might take a bit of a hit.'

'Don't care,' she says, sidling up to him, putting a hand down his shorts. And she leads him back to bed.

My heart has made its mind up,
And I'm afraid it's you.

She doesn't want to leave this bubble, the two of them back at
her flat now, exploring each other. She doesn't want the abra-
sive world to shock them awake with its cold obligations. She
looks at the two mobile phones, like black beetles on the side
table – the work BlackBerry and the Samsung Android, which
is for personal use – both switched off because when did she
last have a life? When was the last time work took a back seat
to the rich turbulence of her heart? She has earned this hiatus.
She has earned the right to devote herself to Alan Prender*gasp*
without disturbance, though the phones seem to drag her eyes
to their black heft, and thoughts of whether she should check
in with the office, and in particular with Helena Reed.

No, she will not. Her body is her antenna now and it chooses
him, again and again. And she wonders, surprised, whether
this will be her undoing. How much appetite is a woman
allowed these days? She towers above him on all fours, feeling
like an Alice who's eaten the cake labelled Eat Me and now she
is bigger than the room.

'Come on, how many?'

'Not many,' he says, moving her roving fingers, which have
traced the line of hairs around his nipples until he's laughed
and shouted, 'Geroff!', then entwined them in his, a lock-down,
but playful.

'C'mon, tell me,' she nudges him.

'Um.' He has closed his eyes, lying on his back. 'Only one
serious one.'

'How long was that for?'

'Six months.'

262

She doesn't comment on how slight this is for a man of forty-two. She wants him to ask about her previous lovers, the boy from university she nearly married. How much she'd loved him for seven long years, how sad she was to lose him when it petered out.

But he doesn't ask. All is new, she supposes; all is in the now. This is the new regime! Oh hallowed bed. Who'd have thought that Alan, in all his Alan-ness, would make a right out of all those wrongs – the years alone, the terrible dates. When you meet The One, it all makes sense, it makes the cock-ups seem . . . intentional. And just in fucking time, too.

Hello, you.

SATURDAY

DAVY

Even making the macaroni cheese last night, he hadn't felt right.

Davy thought it would be nice to feed his mother after all she did for him and Chloe on Christmas Day. It'd been a lot of work, his mother had said (quite a few times), especially with no one to help her. He thought a macaroni cheese would be homely and filling for a January Saturday dinner, just him, Mum, and Chloe, who said it was her duty to come along – though he'd begun to have the sense that she was guarding him from his mother, didn't want them to spend time alone together, because there might pass between them a moment to which she was not privy. And then he'd caught himself having a mean thought like that. These were happening to him more and more.

He'd spooned the macaroni cheese into a square white dish and covered it so tightly with cling film that the plastic was an invisible plane. He'd straightened it so the dish was parallel with the splashback, and squared up nicely beside the hob, but it didn't give him any satisfaction.

264

He's all out of sync with himself, he thinks now, as he peels off the cling film and pops the dish into the oven to warm and crisp up on top. He picks up his work phone and dials Helena Reed's number, because she's been preying on his mind – the way she'd slammed into him, her face full of fear. Who was she visiting, all the way in Newnham – and why had she seemed furtive about it? What 'friend' had prompted such a tearful state?

No reply. This time, there is a message telling him her voice-mail is full, so he can't even leave another one. It's the third time he's tried this morning.

'Just me again, Helena, checking in. DC Walker, I mean,' he'd said previously. 'If you get this, just give me a buzz, let me know you're all right.' Still, she has his number if she needs him.

The doorbell goes.

Chloe has straightened her hair so that it hangs in sheets on either side of her face. He's always thought she looks better when she doesn't pull down so hard on the straightening irons – like in the early days when he'd pulled her back into bed after her shower so she hadn't had time for all that gubbins – the fake tan and the heavy black eyelashes which he isn't sure are hers.

Her arms are full of the Saturday papers. 'Thought we could catch up,' she says, breathless.

'Put them in the lounge,' he says, and they pile them on the glass coffee table, the poly-bagged glossy magazines sliding out of the folded sheaves. A tower of innuendo, he thinks, slabs of unsubstantiated hearsay. He can hardly bear to look at them.

'Right,' he says, clapping his hands as the doorbell goes again. 'That'll be Mum.'

They settle, his mum and Chloe, around the kitchen table and Davy says, 'Who's for macaroni cheese?'

He's trying to put the uplift back in his voice but it's not working. It's not been working for days. Manon's rubbing off on him, that's what it'll be. Her gloom, the way she sees things – always the uncomfortable underbelly, never the bright side.

Last night, as they left the office together, he said, 'I just don't think we're going to get to the bottom of this one', and she put her palm across his forehead, saying, 'Are you feeling all right, Davy?'

He frowned, jerked his head away, the crotchety teenager. 'I mean it. It's getting me down this . . . not getting anywhere. We've let Tony Wright go. That boy, in the river, that's going nowhere as well. And all this love life guff. I don't like it.'

'You've got to let it emerge, Davy,' she told him. 'Ride out the confusion, the darkness. Things will become clear, you wait and see. But in the meantime, you've got to allow yourself to be all right with the not knowing.'

And all of a sudden he'd felt completely lost, like a sad hole had opened up beneath him and he was about to fall down into it.

'What's this you've put in it?' says his mother, grimacing and pushing something to the front of her mouth, out between her teeth. She picks it out with finger and thumb and peers at it. 'Nutmeg, is it?' She wipes it on the table. 'Didn't you grate it?'

'I did grate it, Mum. A shard must have fallen in. There's a napkin there.'

The macaroni cheese is so dry he's had to carve it. Even several tablespoons of Branston pickle are doing a poor job of livening it up.

'Everyone at work wants to know the details,' says Chloe.

More animated, warmer in fact, than he's seen her in quite some time. She runs a finger down the line of her hair curtain, pushing it from her eyes without disturbing its plate-like flatness. 'Amazing you're right at the centre of it, what's on the news.'

'Can't talk about it, Chlo,' he says, trying to masticate a rigid piece of macaroni.

'I took some flowers – to George Street,' says his mother. 'Outside the house where the other bunches are.'

'Why?' he asks.

'Well, you want to be part of something, don't you? And it's terrible. But to have it so near – in the same town. I didn't want to miss out. What do *you* think happened to her?'

'He knows everything, but he can't say, isn't that right, Davy?' says Chloe, winking at him.

'Dead then?' says his mother hopefully.

'Male *and* female lovers,' says Chloe. 'Who'd have thought? How many?'

'We don't know.'

'More than one though?'

'We don't know.'

'You do know, you're just not saying,' she says, the proud wife. 'Takes all sorts,' she says to his mother, and they are united at last.

'Did her boyfriend know about it?' asks Chloe.

'I can't talk about it, Chlo.'

'No, course. So have the papers been in touch with you directly?'

'All media enquiries are dealt with by the press office,' he says.

'Still,' says his mother, 'I bet they'd give you a tidy bit of money for extra info.'

267

'I'd lose my job.'

'Not if you were nice and discreet about it.'

'But it's wrong.'

'Gosh, I bet her mother's shocked,' says Chloe. 'Imagine having a daughter carrying on like that.'

'And him a famous surgeon,' says his mother.

Davy is staring ahead, the room's light harsh and blue. He realises this kitchen is about as welcoming as a dental surgery.

'They're people,' he says slowly. 'They're just people.'

He checks his phone again for missed calls or texts from Helena Reed. Perhaps he should pop round there, check she's all right. But then she might have gone to Bromley to stay with her parents – get out of the heat until things calm down a bit.

SUNDAY

HELENA

She can hear them laughing like day-trippers, smoking around the war memorial down below her flat window, though the curtains are drawn. The curtains have been drawn against them since they gathered yesterday.

First there were only a few, but they flew down like birds on crusts, vying with one another around the narrow blue door to the side of Barclays – her front door which has until now seemed invisible. 'Helena Reed!' they called, as if she might open a window and invite them up. When she pulled aside a net to look, they locked onto her, nudging one another, shouting to her and setting their zoom lenses for a grainy shot, so she had quickly retreated. She sat all day yesterday, and all last night, listening to the answer machine click and rewind with each new appeal from strangers luring her with false intimacy – 'Look, this must be a difficult time, we can help' – while she chewed on the skin at the edge of her thumbnail. Wondering who'd released her name.

But then, she's been waiting for this to happen, knowing it would happen, since *Crimewatch*. After slamming into those

269

two detectives outside Dr Young's, she's been a prisoner of her thoughts. Three days, four long nights. Would the police check who she had been visiting in Newnham? Would they find out she was seeing a shrink and assume all manner of mental instability from that? Would they talk to Dr Young and would he mention her terrorised thoughts, and what on earth would the police infer? Would they inform Dr Young that she was Edith's lover, to which he would say, baffled, 'Well, she never told me that,' and to all of them she would appear madder and more inscrutable, a dissembler of the facts about Edith's disappearance?

Thursday afternoon they sent someone round – 'to sit with her', the officer said. A babysitter. Helena had moved round this person in her flat, trying to look natural, but inside she was gnawed at by the sensation of being observed in her own home – they were *watching* her – so she said, 'You go, I'm fine, I don't need looking after. In fact, I'm going to stay with friends.' Helena smiled, her hand on her open front door. The officer/babysitter said, 'If you're sure?' but Helena could see she was glad. She'd received some furtive call about childcare arrangements and she couldn't get away fast enough.

Friday morning, Saturday morning, she ran out early to check the papers, dreading but assuming she would be named, and surprised to find no mention of her apart from in the usual timeline descriptions. So yesterday afternoon, when the crows first gathered at the bottom of her stairs, it was as if the inevitable had taken place.

She stared and stared at the only card she had from the police. DS Manon Bradshaw. The other one – the kindly chap she'd crashed into who'd promised to protect her – his card must've fallen out of her pocket in her rush to get home that day. DS Bradshaw appeared not to be available. Dr Young's practice number clicked through to a machine. She couldn't think what message to leave so she hung up.

This morning, around 10 a.m., there'd been a noticeable quietening outside and she braved a glance through a crack in the curtain. They seemed to have dispersed, perhaps to a greasy spoon for a Sunday fry-up, leaving one or two hapless representatives to keep watch at her front door. She chanced it, out of the need for bread and milk, running down the back staircase – concrete and municipal, the air hung with the smell of stale cigarettes – which brought her via a door with metal push-bar, out by the bins to the rear of Barclays. The cold and rain drove welcome pins into her hands and cheeks as she ran, clasping her hood, to the nearest newsagent, but she was brought up short by the grey box-grid outside and eight images of herself and Edith, flapping in the wind.

Best friend was missing Edith's lover

'Lover' was with Edith on night she vanished

Girls were lovers

It was like looking at images of a very familiar stranger. She noticed how young she looked, though she feels anything but young. She wasn't nearly as fat as she assumed; rather slender, in fact. She tried to see herself as the readers of those rags might see her: unstable, predatory, sexually loose. There was a gap – the outside and the inside, and sometimes it was very wide indeed. Wide enough for you to fall through.

She'd given no thought to how she would get back in and soon she was set upon, enveloped in bodies and voices, the smells of strangers, as she struggled for her key.

271

'Helena, over here!' they shouted as she barged the black mass of jackets, arms, and shoulders, careful never to meet a face. Someone pushed a card in her hand – a blonde woman, she thinks – but she was scrunching her eyes shut, trying to get through them, trying to get her key in the door without dropping the milk. This woman had got up very close and said in her ear, 'We can tell your side of the story. Here's my card.'

Up the stairs, she'd slammed her inner front door and leant her head back against it with her eyes closed. Scheming lesbian Helena Reed. Jealous lover Helena Reed. Murdering Helena Reed. Edith – cloaked in all the innocence of the un-dead, can do no wrong – lured into Helena's crimson bed of joy. Now Helena would always be the vamp, in whatever job interview, PhD viva, applying for research funding, meeting a new man, joining a GP practice. Someone somewhere would look up from their desk and say, 'Helena Reed? From Huntingdon? Weren't you a friend of that missing girl?' And the word 'friend' would drip with all its sly connotations.

It was typical of Edith, blithe Edith, to leave her with all of this, while Helena did all the worrying. It had been like that from day one, the day Helena had knocked on the door across the halls at Corpus Christi. Edith shouted 'Come in!' and there she was, standing on her bed, wearing faded Levi 501s, knocking a nail into the wall to hang up a Modigliani print. On the desk in the window was a vase of anemones, reds and purples and whites, like rich jewels. 'From my mum,' Edith said, breathless, still with her back to Helena. 'Tea?'

Edith was breezy yet determined. She was set on her own course – like the move to Huntingdon – and you could accompany her or you could jog on. Edith, certain; Helena, anxious, following on. She sees how insubstantial she is next to Edith's luminous features, her charisma. And she hates herself for having been their lapdog. All those Saturday nights watching films on their Netflix account, Sunday lunches in their kitchen, Edith lying on the sofa, reading with her head on Helena's lap, Will sat on the floor sipping wine. Helena, the only child in audience to the couple.

She wonders, sat here in her airless lounge while she listens to them laughing and talking on the street below, if she should call her parents. But what if they, too, have crows on the front step, imprisoned together, and she would have to hear it and know she was the cause? When will it end, being trapped like this, with the curtains drawn? And if she ever ventured out into the world, what would she find? She'd called the MIT offices yesterday evening, having no responses again from the sergeant's phone, and she'd got through to a duty person, Constable Monique something, who said she'd 'look into it', but nothing had come of it.

'There's quite a lot of people outside.'

'And what did you say your name was again, madam?'

No point calling today. Sunday was bound to be worse, and what could they do anyway? The story was out now and it couldn't be taken back in. Her own phones – mobile and landline – were filled to the brim with intrusions from people who shouldn't have her number at all, hectoring and bullying her. She couldn't bear to play them back, so she switched them all off.

During the night, by about 1 a.m., the crows had flown off (staying at the George Hotel, probably). Another chance: she pictured herself catching a plane to Rio de Janeiro, then another to Manaus, then a boat to where the Rio Negro meets the Solimões River – the Meeting of Waters, she'd always wanted to see that – and then deep into the tributaries of the Amazon. The world is so big and so beautiful and she'd hardly begun to explore it.

273

She wandered room to room, planning her escape. Where was her passport? What would she wear? Somehow, when she turned around, it was 7 a.m. and the crows were back on her doorstep and she didn't know how she'd get past them, let alone to the Amazon basin. She found herself staring at the back of the bedroom door – and the hook where her dressing gown hangs.

She can't see a way clear. She longs for someone – Edith, if she's honest – to throw a coat over her head and usher her through it all. She stands before the nets in the lounge and the tears flow out of her in a great outpouring. She cries out, though it is silent, her lips cracked. She will never get out, she will never see the Amazon river. She will never be free or happy. And the girl she loves has gone.

MONDAY

MANON

'Lovely top, Kim!'

Kim looks up, surprised.

'Stuart, me ol' mucker!'

Stuart looks at Kim, who shrugs.

'Colin,' Manon says, squeezing Colin's shoulders, and it's like a puff of cigarette smoke plumes out of his jumper. 'What've you got for me today? We're going to find her, I just know we are.'

She hangs her jacket on the back of her chair and reaches into her bag for her purse. She wants to eat and she's thinking: bacon roll, sausages, egg yolk bursting over buttered toast. She is ripe with the eating; her hips seem wider, her breasts fuller. A Manon bursting forth to fruition. She is bovine, sleepy-ravenous, sensual. She wants him to move in, but he's kept his head, his beautiful Alan Prenderghast head. He ducked home last night, saying he had an early start in the morning – 'need to be fresh for Monday' – and he'd kissed her, kissed her again, and they were kissing through the open door of her flat, him with his silly flappy coat on. Her lips hurt and when the door

275

closed, she missed the kiss they had not had. He rang the doorbell and her heart flipped over itself, puppyish and bright. She opened it and grabbed him and he was pulling his coat off and they were at it again, she in an open shirt, astride him on the corduroy sofa.

'Don't leave me,' she said onto his lips.

She begins to text him, bouncing back in her chair – *Hello you, you gorgeous chunk of hunk* – but is stopped by a thud and a billow of air towards her face.

'I take it you've seen these,' says Harriet, hand on the pile of newspapers she's just slapped down on Manon's desk.

Manon straightens. Helena's face stares back at her. The headline says: *Girls were lovers* beneath a red masthead. The blood plummets from Manon's head, leaving it cold, fear tickling up her hair follicles. She looks at Davy, whose colour has drained away.

'Who named her?' Davy asks Harriet.

'We don't know. Could've been anyone. I've sent a couple of uniforms to her flat just now, soon as Fergus showed me these. They're authorised to gain access if she doesn't respond. I've tried her phones but there's no response and all her mail-boxes are full.'

'But we sent a liaison,' Manon says.

'Who she sent away,' Harriet says. 'Told the officer she was going to stay with friends.'

It might be all right, it can still be all right if Helena is found safe and well. She pictures Helena's terrified face looking up at them, tear-streaked. And the phones she turned off, how they lay immobile on the table next to the bed where she writhed, *partaking* of Alan Prenderghast.

Manon closes her eyes slowly, her body churning as shame begins its slow seep, like blood. The one time. The one time . . .

'You warned her, Kim,' Harriet is saying, 'about *Crimewatch*?'

'Yeah, she seemed all right about it, quite calm, but this'll be different,' Kim says, nodding at the newspapers.

'And you put in the risk assessment paperwork on the Thursday?' Harriet says to Manon, who nods.

'If she said she was staying with friends,' says Manon, feeling for an exit, 'she won't be at the flat. When will officers be there? When will we know?'

'Dispatched ten minutes ago. They'll call me,' Harriet says. 'In the meantime, Colin is going to take us through Graham Garfield's hard drive in a mature and innuendo-free manner.'

Colin turns to his desk. 'Lots of drafts of his books on the Victorians, essays on George Eliot, work by his students, some assessment forms from the university, that kind of thing. But—' and he pulls his glasses down from his head, clicking his mouse and the laptop's screen tessellates with web pages, a bright and flickering collage of pornography – 'he was into all sorts. Asian Babes. Big Fatties Who Want It. Frisky Housewives. A man of many interests.' Colin is scrolling and clicking with great fervour. 'Anyway, more significant than all that is *this*,' he says, swivelling around to show everyone the screen. All Manon can see are several lines of web links all beginning 'Facebook'.

'What is it?' Manon says.

'Graham Garfield looked at Edith Hind's Facebook page five times every night the week before she disappeared. And since. Forty visits or thereabouts. Specifically, he has clicked on these pictures – selfies, I believe they're called.'

He brings up several shots of Edith: eyes yearningly intense, looking straight into the lens, one with a jumper falling off her shoulder, one in which she is lying on a bed, holding her phone above her. Just you and her.

'Doesn't prove anything,' says Stuart. 'She put them out there. Why do that if you don't want to be leered at?'

'Proves he had an unhealthy interest in her,' says Harriet.

'What sort of bloke wouldn't go clicking about on those? She's a hottie. What did she expect when she took them?' says Colin.

'Erm, freedom? Autonomy?' says Kim.

'Come off it – lying on the bed like that, all *come and get me*,' Stuart says.

'She might not know any better,' says Kim. 'Everyone's a dick at twenty-four.'

MIRIAM

She opens her eyes and blinks in an effort to adjust to the permanent dusk of the bedroom. She can hear Rosa clattering in the kitchen. Ian will be God-knows-where, rushing about Being Important Yet Again. He's been calling in favours from his friends on the broadsheets, old Bullingdon chums, giving profile interviews to *The Telegraph* and *The Times* – 'turning the tide', he called it. 'Someone has to set the record straight.' They've promised to be sensitive in their probing and give him copy approval before anything is printed.

Even Rollo has a sense of purpose; his father's son. He is at a meeting at the offices of a missing persons charity, discussing a renewed online campaign involving a thousand tweets or some such. She doesn't pretend to understand social media or why anyone would waste their time on it, but she is very glad Rollo has it covered.

She hauls herself up off the bed, her hair damp and flattened, pushes her feet into her sheepskin slippers and walks out to the hall and up a flight of wonky narrow stairs, holding tight to the gentle curve of the banister to Edith's room. On the landing between the children's bedrooms on this uppermost floor, under a mildewed skylight, is a Victorian doll's house in the architecture of their own. A Georgian house within a Georgian house. It was given to Edith when she was small by Ian's mother, Edith Senior. Ian revered the doll's house in the same way he revered his mother, had objected when Edie wanted to fill it with Polly Pockets, as if this somehow diluted its educational purity, when Miriam felt the whole point of playing was to make something your own. She'd have been rather proud if Edith had scrawled across the prim rosebud wallpaper with an indelible pen.

Ian had insisted their baby daughter be named after his mother, when all Miriam's friends were calling theirs Chloe or Jessica. These days, of course, the old dowager names are all the rage; even stalwarts of the Tory party call their children Florence and Alfred with a knowing wink. But back then, Miriam had shrunk from the name – softening it to Edie – yet had borne it, like the doll's house, because she had no choice.

She lies on Edith's bed, in part to muss up the inert neatness of the duvet; gazes at the black violin case on top of the wardrobe, the clip frame leaning against the wall with a collage of photos from that Italian interrailing trip with Rollo, the two of them smiling on the Spanish Steps. Miriam closes her eyes in order to visualise her daughter – to set her mind on her so strongly that she is all that exists and then perhaps it will come to her: a knowledge of where Edith is and what has happened to her, as if by some supernatural telepathic intuiting. She thinks of the relatives of the missing she's seen in the past on the news, who would not give up their dogged searches even in the face of overwhelmingly poor odds. Their final argument was always the same: 'If they were dead, I'd know.' Or its confluence: 'They're alive, I can feel it.' She had

280

always balked at the irrationality of these statements, the way people clung to a lie, yet now it makes perfect sense to her. They cannot cut the cord, not without a body. A body is what they need, otherwise these madnesses spring up like weeds, uncontrollable.

Perhaps, she thinks now, there *is* someone – a psychic or a fortune teller – who could enter this other realm with her and tell her what has happened to her daughter. Someone with telepathic powers, who can speak with spirits or tell her the future. Not the terrible frogmen dredging rivers.

She pads down the stairs towards the sounds of Rosa emptying the dishwasher, through to the front lounge where the curtains are drawn against the rubberneckers, the lamps lit as if it were evening. Their iMac is asleep but she only has to tap a key for it to stir into life. She daren't Google 'Edith Hind'. She knows all manner of salacious rumour is floating about out there, just waiting to be read and wept over; vicious messages from trolls who are actually fourteen-year-olds in affluent bedrooms, their mothers grilling their fish fingers downstairs.

No, instead she types 'psychic NW3' into the search field. There are fifteen serving her area, according to the Yellow Pages, which additionally provides a useful map. She clicks on solveyourmystery.com, a site advertising tarot, palmistry, and compassionate psychic readings. It is probably the word 'compassionate' which secures her business.

MANON

It travels up her spine in a cold bubble: horror, close to excitement.

'This is a fuck-up,' Harriet is saying, pacing. 'A massive fucking fuck-up of the first fucking order.'

'When did she . . . Didn't she call for assistance?' Kim says.

Time has slowed, thickening the air so that Manon can hardly breathe. There is a metallic taste in her mouth like blood.

Davy says, 'I was calling her all weekend but it went straight through to voicemail. I should've gone down there. I don't understand it – she had my number. I told her to call if she needed anything.'

He is sweating, a red patch creeping up his neck.

'Apparently she rang in here late on Saturday night,' Harriet says. 'Call was taken by late-shift auxiliary staff, didn't know who she was, wrote a note in a book, didn't do anything about it. As with any death where there has been police contact, I am self-referring this to the IPCC, which will conduct an investigation alongside Professional Standards. Check if we did right by Helena Reed in our duty of care.'

282

'When?' says Manon, and she is surprised her voice is audible because she feels as if she is under water. 'When did she—?'

'Sometime on Sunday. The PM will tell us more.'

In the silence which has fallen over the department, Harriet tells them how it took a while for the officers to find Helena Reed. Her flat was spotless and deserted, all the cups washed up. It was, they said, how you would leave a property if you were going away, and that's what the officers thought at first.

'She's gone away, that's all, gone to stay with friends, just like she said,' said the uniform.

'Hang on, in here,' said his colleague.

They saw the note first, laid out on a perfectly made bed, and then they found her, hanging from the hook on the back of the bedroom door, using the cord from her dressing gown.

'Oh sweet Jesus,' Manon gasps, a palm over her mouth. It is as if Helena had tidied herself away.

The note said:

That is not what I meant at all;
That is not it, at all.

'Bloody Cambridge students,' says Colin. 'Why can't they leave a proper note like everyone else? You know *You never cared* or *I was all alone.*'

'Someone hung her out to dry,' says Davy, and Manon realises he is staring at Stuart, his fists squeezing open and shut, almost imperceptibly, at his sides.

'We don't know that,' says Stuart, trying to keep it light, but the vein standing up on his neck gives him the frozen look of a chameleon trying to blend with his rock.

'How did they know about Helena Reed and Edith?' Davy demands, and he won't take his eyes off Stuart, approaching

283

him from across the room, and they all seem paralysed, the bystanders. There is so much guilt by association.

'Well, it's not hard to work out, is it? Edith's best friend, with her on the night she disappears. Could've come from anyone; anyone in this building could've spoken to their wives or their girlfriends about it,' Stuart is saying, stepping backwards. 'Or one of the students, like Jason Farrer. He wasn't exactly discreet.'

'Except they don't tend to run with it unless it's come from the police, do they, Stuart?' Davy is saying, and Stuart tries to walk casually behind a desk to put some distance between himself and Davy.

'Still,' Stuart says, 'there's no proof that it came from us.'

'I'll find out,' says Harriet, 'and whoever leaked it will be out on his fucking ear.'

Which isn't true. Manon knows it; everyone in the room knows it, except possibly Stuart. Leaks are impossible to trace and no journalist will ever name their source. The tabloids could have got this titbit from anyone.

'Or she – out on *her* ear,' says Stuart.

'Get him away from me,' says Davy, low and quiet, watching as Stuart makes urgently for the double doors, his mobile phone already at his ear.

'Did she try you, Manon?' Harriet says. 'Did you have your phone on?'

'Course,' says Manon, turning to look out at the car park but seeing nothing of the view. 'I mean, reception's a bit patchy, and I was in and out . . .' Manon's face is prickled with a white heat, like an allergy.

'Hanged,' she murmurs to herself. She's seen lots of victims of hanging, knows exactly what they look like – pale and bloated head to one side of the elongated neck, abrasions from the

284

ligature. Sometimes they have fallen. Sometimes the tips of their toes touch the floor. She's surprised the hook on the back of the door held her, but Helena Reed was not a substantial person.

Manon's mind feels along the territory of the things she could have done: deployed protection to Helena's flat as soon as *Crimewatch* made mention of a female lover; have Davy escort Helena home from Newnham, right then on the Thursday, refusing to take no for an answer; monitored her work phone over the weekend, as she would normally have done, though she wasn't on-call. Four days of neglect, in which Manon did none of these things, for no other reason than she just didn't. Base, looked-for pleasures, and Manon's hunger for them at the expense of every other thought. The shame, the shame of it.

Soon, very soon, it is too much and the lines begin to shift. She tells herself there was nothing she could have done; that she couldn't possibly have known; that she wasn't on duty. Had she been on-call, her phones would have been on. She tells herself defiantly, triumphantly, that her weekend was her own, this job does *not* own her; so she is not lying when she defends herself to Harriet Harper. She is telling a kind of truth.

'Awful,' says Alan, as the colours darken through the double-height windows of his glorious barn. She watches the horizon, a line of fire suppressed by the blue-grey sky.

'Yes,' she says. She approaches his big body, thickened by a woollen navy cardigan with leather buttons, and puts her hands on his hips, her forehead to his chest.

'Poor thing,' he says, kissing the top of her head, and she doesn't know if he means her or Helena Reed.

'Worst thing is, she had nothing to do with it – just got caught up in someone else's mess.'

'Mmm,' he says, his chin resting on top of her head.

'She was ashamed, really ashamed,' she says, and the bubble rises up into her throat and she feels she might cry out. 'She just experimented, that's all, and all of a sudden it was public and the shame of it, the guilt of it—'

'Don't cry,' he says, his hand on her cheek, and she wonders if he means it as solace or whether he is actually asking her not to emote in his presence. She is descending and he is floating up, like the birds beyond his window. The landing and the flying off.

'*I am not Prince Hamlet, nor was meant to be,*' she says.

He looks at her.

'The poem. She was saying she wasn't the lead in her own play.'

On the way over, she'd sat in her car in a traffic jam and she'd looked at all the little heads and shoulders in front of their steering wheels. All these people locked in their own thoughts, enmeshed in complicated lives, each of us believing we're at the centre.

'Wine?' he asks, and she watches him walk away towards his grey, steely kitchen.

'Yes, please.'

She sits in his sagging armchair but there is no view now that the last line of sun has been extinguished. They are together and that's a fact, and she packs her frightened, lonely feelings away. Edith, she thinks. Edith was one of those people who saw herself as the lead. Careless and selfish. Yes, there is corrosive pleasure in blaming Edith Hind. And Helena, the attendant lord, deferential, glad to be of use.

'What does it mean for the case?' he asks, bringing her an oversized goblet of red which fills her hand. Even his *glassware* is nice.

'There'll be an enquiry. Independent Police Complaints Commission. See if we dealt with her properly, which we mostly did. But actually we didn't, of course, because she asked for assistance and the night team didn't respond, or at least not fast enough.' But she stops short of the detail, both to him and to herself. 'We could have stopped her,' is all she whispers into her glass, taking a sip. He has gone back to the kitchen, turning his levers.

'Will you be under investigation?' he asks. 'You personally, I mean.'

She shrugs. 'Each of us on the Hind team will be, as a matter of course. It's standard procedure when someone dies after contact with the police. Won't happen for months, though, not while the Hind investigation is still active.'

He is clattering about in the kitchen. She gets up to join him there, coming up behind him and putting her hands on his hips again.

'I know you have a rule,' she says, 'about week nights and everything, but can I stay? Please? Tonight? I don't want to be on my own.'

'Of course,' he says, and for a moment she is relieved and she hugs his back, and then she is filled with a sense of imbalance; that he is tolerating her.

He shares his steak, rare, and the brown and yellow grains of mustard trail in its wake of blood, the broccoli crisp and dark green. They consume a bottle of red and it makes the threat of Helena Reed come nearer and Alan's unreachable quality, a loneliness too far. Something about him is just beyond her grasp, though she cannot identify it in anything he says precisely. Her movements are clumsy with the wine, and with her sorrow and guilt.

She thinks they might bridge the gap in bed, that this is

where the imbalance might be redressed, but he is even more distant as they come close. It is so nearly there, this almost-love, and every part of her reaches for it excessively. She towers over him, her mouth and her body, the red wine making her woolly and dark, her chest expanding so that nothing is manageable. As they finish and lie back, she bursts into tears – not demure Edwardian tears but incontinent blubbing of the kind that gives rise to rivulets of snot.

He is up on one elbow saying, 'What is it?' in a voice which, though she may be imagining it, seems on the edge of being annoyed.

'Do you feel the same way?' she says, her hand over her eyes. 'Do you?'

He strokes her arm.

'I've been so fucking lonely,' she says in a guttural wail which feels good for about half a second and then feels very, very bad because he says nothing and has lain back on his grey linen pillow, staring up at the ceiling.

TUESDAY

MIRIAM

Twenty-three days missing and she has come so easily to this – to the door of a psychic she has found through solveyourmystery.com. Miriam Hind, née Davenport: once a scientist, always a rationalist, standing at the front door waiting for Julie, the palm reader.

Hers is a 1930s semi in suburban Hendon, its windows so clean they flash what there is of the January brightness. The doorbell a singsongy chime. When Miriam telephoned yesterday, it was in a flush of impulse – she never imagined she'd be booked in the very next day. Julie's diary was evidently not chock-a-block.

The remainder of yesterday, however, and the ensuing night had cooled Miriam's enthusiasm for palmistry; she'd seen how silly she was being. She is here on sufferance, because she has made the arrangement, and arrangements cannot be broken. They must be extricated from politely or adhered to (Englishness again). And yet she hadn't phoned, or texted or sent an email to the 'Contact Me' address on the website. So many ways, these days, of extricating yourself in silence.

I'll explain it's not for me, Miriam tells herself as the door opens.

'Come through,' the woman says, and Miriam steps into a light, mirrored hall with new cream carpet. The heating is on luxuriantly high.

'Should I take my shoes off?' she asks, hoping the answer will be no, because bending is not as easy as it used to be.

'Please,' she says. 'I'll wait for you in the lounge.'

Her manner, the ash-blonde highlights, the taupe cardigan with sequins glinting, has all the suburban fastidiousness of a beauty therapist. Miriam follows her through to a lounge with broad doors giving out to a lawn. It smells of new carpet in here also, and there is a capacious cream leather armchair for Miriam to sink into. Communing with the spirit world is not a bad way to make a living, it would seem, even with an appointments diary as spacious as Julie's.

'So,' she says.

'So,' says Miriam, reserve bristling.

'I'm sensing great sadness, great pain,' Julie says, her head tilted. 'I'm seeing everything out of alignment.'

Miriam nods. It is preposterous that she is here. She must find an appropriate hiatus in which to make her excuses. What would Ian think?

'I'm feeling that you have lost hope, lost your way in this world. The pain is too much. You are confused and unhappy.'

Oh, spare me, Miriam thinks.

'You want to know what lies ahead. How it will all turn out. You want an end to the uncertainty – the miasma, as I like to call it. I can do tarot, palm or aura; which would you prefer?'

'I don't know.'

'A general reading, perhaps. You can pay with a cheque. I don't take cards. Or you could set up a direct debit. I recommend this to my clients – there is a reduction for three visits or more.'

'Shall I?' Miriam asks, reaching for her handbag. 'Now?'

She nods. Miriam writes a cheque, a flat fee of £80 for a one-off reading. No way is she falling for that direct debit baloney.

'May I?' Julie says, taking Miriam's hand slowly in hers, as if it were a priceless ornament, and rotating it palm-up. Miriam notices her burgundy manicure, like blood-dipped talons. 'I am seeing someone you love very deeply. Someone lost to you . . .'

You are reading my age, Miriam thinks. I am of an age for grief.

'A daughter, a beloved daughter, whose safety is in jeopardy.'

You've read the tabloids. You've seen me on the news.

'You want to know what has happened to your daughter,' she says, looking Miriam in the eye, and Miriam's heart begins to race. They both feel her hand quiver.

'Yes,' says Miriam.

'You love your daughter and you are in great pain,' she says. 'You are tormented by thoughts of what might have happened to her. You are in an agony of uncertainty. You cannot grieve, but you dare not hope.'

'Yes,' says Miriam, and it comes out in a gasp, dirty with need. 'Please, I . . .' Miriam is now holding the woman's hand, squeezing it.

'Your daughter is alive,' she says.

Miriam stares at her.

'Your daughter is alive,' she says again in an exhalation, as if she too is in pain, has taken Miriam's pain into herself.

'When will she come back?' Miriam asks. 'Has she been taken?'

Julie closes her eyes, stroking and holding Miriam's hand

291

between the two of hers. She breathes in through her nose, her eyes closed. She shakes her head.

'It's gone,' she says. 'Sometimes it's too powerful. Sometimes it cannot be held.'

'When will you get it back?'

'You will need to come again.'

DAVY

He knows he's got it wrong as he proffers the cup to her and he doesn't care. Manon can suck it up for once. She looks awful, too, perhaps as bad as him – puffy-faced, furtive.

'What's this, Davy? I don't take it black.'

'Have you listened to yourself?' he says. Come on, if you think you're hard enough.

'All right,' she says. 'Jeez, who shat in your handbag?'

He woke at 5.30 a.m., remembering abruptly, as if cut from sleep by the hard steel of his guilt. He looked at Chloe, sleeping next to him. Her hair, sticky with the various products she put on it, lay across her head like a bandage. She's been talking about 'taking things to the next level' and he finds it bewildering, because even a couple of weeks ago he'd have been all for it, but now . . . How little he tells her of the fresh torments in his mind. Yet his distance seems only to fuel her enthusiasm, and he wonders idly if this is the secret about women that other men have known all along and that he's been slow to grasp. Perhaps it's what made a toerag like Stuart Leach such a success with the ladies. Stuart seems to be able

293

to shag Marie from Accounts and then barely acknowledge her in the office.

Davy tries Ryan's social worker, Reeva Dell, again. She always sounds exhausted, a slow monotonous crawl to her voice. But then, social services was full of depressed people.

'His mum moved, I told you – no forwarding address,' says Reeva.

'Right, but she's still under the surname Wade?' he says, thrumming in his mind through the police databases he could try.

'No, no, hang on, she married someone. D'you want the name?'

'Please.'

'Hold on.'

Shuffling papers, clacking on a keyboard. No budget for Vivaldi. Davy wonders what manner of sociopath Ryan's mum's hooked her wagon to this time.

'Right, yes, she's going under the name Jones.'

'Jones? You're kidding me.'

'Why would I be kidding you, DC Walker?'

How am I supposed to trace a Jones? he thinks. And he feels like crying, or pulling the phone from its socket and a chunk of the plaster from the wall, too.

'Has Ryan taken on the Jones name? Has the new local authority been notified that he was on the "at risk" register?'

'Like I said, we don't know where they've gone. It's not like she asked our permission. The boy was returned to her, don't forget.'

'Yeah, but only because . . .' Davy trails off. It's pointless hurling rocks at Reeva Dell.

'I'm sorry I can't help,' she says.

'No, no, it's fine,' he says.

Harriet has come to the desk he and Manon are sharing, resting her knuckles on its surface, her head low.

'Helena Reed's call log,' says Harriet in a murmur so that only Manon and Davy can hear. 'She tried to call you, Manon, three times.'

Davy looks at Manon but she is rummaging in her bag for her phone as if its physical presence will explain this.

'I wasn't on-call,' Manon says, looking up sharply at Harriet. 'I have the right to turn my phone off at the weekend, to have a life. You might want to be married to this job, Harriet, but I don't. Anyway, I told you, the signal can be a bit dodgy in my flat; on and off, y'know?'

'I know you weren't on-call, and this isn't part of any official investigation,' says Harriet. 'I'm just asking you. You know, what the *fuck*, Manon?'

'That's right, it's my fault,' says Manon in a swell of tears, and Davy and Harriet watch her make for the double doors, almost at a run, and slap through them like a swimmer into the surf.

'Graham Garfield,' Harriet says, louder now, so the department can hear. 'What have our background checks given us?'

'One student claims he made unwanted advances, and others say he had a reputation for trying it on,' says Kim. 'Sounds like more of a pest than a predator. Y'know, an opportunist – he tried it on, got knocked back a few times, but every now and then he got lucky.'

'Mrs Garfield know?' says Harriet.

'Doesn't look like it.'

'When we were round there she was wavering about his alibi,' Davy says. 'Having first said she was with him at home after he came back from The Crown, she subsequently told us she only vaguely heard his key in the door as she fell asleep.'

*   *   *

The dank interior of The Lord Protector; wooden floorboards sticky, tinny tunes from fruit machines. Davy rotates his glass at their corner table and tries to tell Chloe what's going on with him.

He's been attempting to explain about work, how much it's a part of how he sees himself. He's trying to describe their duty of care to Helena Reed and how they'd failed her, and how he couldn't get it off his mind. They'd ticked the boxes they were supposed to tick, so why does he feel so bad?

Some part of him is taking umbrage already at the criticism that's heaped on them as officers – always the question of what they could have done better, faster, with immaculate paperwork and utmost sensitivity; what they should learn from what they've got wrong. That person on the night team, DC Monique Moynihan, will probably lose her job, and maybe that's right. But all the while it feels like a war they're fighting, without enough resources. They were only doing their job.

He's trying to form this into words to her; he needs her to understand him at this most crucial time. But when he looks up, he sees that familiar thing Chloe does with her face, allowing all her muscles to go slack in the cheeks so it's like her face is dripping, her eyes stony, like she so often made them – distant and looking over his shoulder.

Instead of chivvying her out of it, he says, 'What's the matter now?'

She shrugs. 'Nothing,' she says. 'I'm fine.'

'No you're not; you're in a huff again. What is it this time?'

She seems wrong-footed by his directness, but she maintains the hangdog slack cheeks. The cheeks of doom, he thinks. Bitter mouth.

'I just think it's weird, you caring so much for a dead girl. A *lesbian* dead girl,' she says.

'Tell me you're not serious,' he says.

Chloe shrugs. 'Your mind's always on other things: *poor Helena Reed, poor Ryan, isn't Manon the genius.* You're never here, in the moment.'

'Christ, Chloe, have you ever wondered why? Have you ever thought what the moment might feel like, for me?' He is rising out of his chair now, surprising himself. 'Being here in the moment with you is like . . . it's like being sucked down into quicksand. It's like drowning.' He feels like ten-year-old Davy, pulling open the bedroom curtains with gusto; his mother in the bed, never getting up, one day to the next. 'You make me suffocate, Chloe,' he says, and he's letting her have it – both barrels. 'You make me suffocate in the misery of it.'

And he finds himself grabbing his coat off the back of the chair and walking out, and even as he's walking, he knows this is one sulk he'll never be able to rectify.

MANON

Is it over so soon, after her stupid outburst in bed? Has she scared him off? He'd communicated with her from the very surface of himself in the morning and she had the feeling he was annoyed that she was cluttering up his daily routine: the showering with an astringent body wash (mint – she tried it and it made her privates sting with unnatural cold), the coffee, the dark neatness of his suit. If only she could undo it – maintain her reserve – she might be transformed in his mind into the perfect lover he almost had. Un-haveable Manon. She aches for Alan Prenderghast.

'Dad?' she says, propping herself up on her pillows, the phone to her ear.

'Hello, lovely,' he whispers. She hears him heaving in the bed, a groan in the background, and Una's voice saying, 'What sort of time d'you call this?'

Manon looks at her watch. It is quarter to eleven.

'Hold on,' he says. 'I'll take it in the study.'

She hears shuffling and the receiver goes down. *Click.* And then he picks up and his voice is expansive at last. 'So, my darling girl, what's the news?'

'She pissed off again?'

'No, Manon, don't do that. Una was just dropping off, that's all. Don't . . . How's things? How's work?'

'Things are all right,' she says sadly.

'Is the case getting you down? I saw on the news, that poor Reed girl. Stanton's taking a lot of heat.'

He is always so very interested, the police his vicarious pleasure. She thinks to tell him the truth about Helena Reed, if only she could grasp where the truth begins and ends, how far her guilt seeps into the corners of it, because he would understand, would believe in her better self. He would tell her it wasn't her fault while acknowledging that some of it perhaps was. They would be silent on the phone, their receivers pressed to their ears, and it would be honest.

'Actually, Dad, I've met someone.'

'Really?' he says, and his voice is genuinely taken aback.

Christ, she thinks, I'm not that bad.

'So, go on,' he says.

'His name's Alan. Alan Prenderghast. He's a systems analyst.'

'A systems analyst?' he says in the same voice he used to say, 'It's a hedgehog, is it?' when she showed him her pictures from primary school. 'What's a systems analyst?'

'I don't really know. He lives just outside Ely.'

She could have added 'drives a Ford' as if she is saying Darcy, yes, Pemberley.

'And you like him?' asks her father, sounding incredulous.

'Not *that* hard to believe, is it?'

'No, no, I'm sure he's very nice,' he says.

Can't he hear the wonder of Alan Prenderghast, her systems analyst from just outside Ely? With the nice glassware? And Nana the dog? Can't he see how huge this is?

They are silent.

299

'When can I meet him then?' he says eventually.

'When you grow some balls and come down to visit,' she says, without malice aforethought, as Davy would have put it.

She pictures her father in his crumpled pyjamas, cupping the phone and casting furtive glances at the study door, surrounded by tartan with stag heads poking out from the walls like surprised intruders, as if he's living some Highland fling as envisaged by Disney, except Una Simmons has the key to this particular hunting lodge. Una Simmons, their very own Macbeth of Moray, who finds ways in which his daughters – well, *this* daughter – cannot fit into their busy schedule, reasons why there isn't room for them to stay at Christmas.

'Spoken to Ellie?' he says at last, a shot back across her bows.

'No, Dad, I haven't spoken to Ellie. Better go now, it's late. You hop back into bed with Mein Führer.' And she puts the phone down.

The feeling in their house had been that Margaret Thatcher was to blame, not just for record unemployment ('fifteen per cent of the workforce,' her father said, shaking his head, always behind a newspaper), but for the miners, of course, and for Murdoch breaking the print unions (a soreness close to her father's heart), and also, in some nebulous way, what had happened in the Bradshaw family. It was all bad, Thatcher and motherlessness. Her father's sadness, in abeyance while her mother's forceful nature lit and burned the house, became their whole microclimate after she died. It was global – despair about themselves and the world. He sighed deeply at the news; he sighed at the *Guardian* and switched to the newly-launched *Independent* ('It is, *are you*?'), but tutted even at that; he sighed at old photographs.

300

Ellie and Manon listened to Kate Bush in their bedroom – well, Peter Gabriel and Kate Bush, to be precise ('Don't Give Up') and cried copiously.

The situation continued for a good five years, during which he said he was 'raising the girls', though he seemed mostly to be behind a newspaper, harrumphing. He switched back to the *Guardian* in a further state of disillusionment and became merely grumpy, muttering about the redesign of its masthead (dual font ITC Garamond Italic next to Helvetica Black! What were they *thinking*?). This seemed an improvement. He went back to writing at the *Fenland Citizen*, where he was editor (the staff having managed quite well during his Grief-Stricken Years) – book and film reviews mostly, or the odd travel piece when it was a one-nighter to Dublin or some such and the girls could be left alone.

Come 1997, their father began taking an interest in himself. He bought his first new items of clothing since the Seventies – a polo shirt and some chinos. He had a haircut, without being told. He began to whistle in the bathroom, to smile, and crack jokes. The root of all this did not emerge for many months and turned out not to be an organic process of healing but a woman called Una Simmons, who worked with him on the paper and wrote a household advice column called *Simmons Solves*. On the night of the general election, they travelled together to the printing presses in High Wycombe, ostensibly to make sure the correct front page went off stone, and the rest, as they say, was a Labour landslide. Things could only get better, so the song went, and they certainly did – for Manon's father at least. And that was more or less when Manon lost him.

She puts the phone on the floor, plumps her pillow and reaches across for the dial on the radio.

Wednesday

Miriam

'No need to clean my study, can you tell Rosa? It's got all my campaign stuff – paperwork, which I don't want shuffled about,' Ian says.

'Yes, of course. Where are you going?' asks Miriam. She is arranging lilies in a vase – great brutes from the Tesco Express around the corner. She doesn't even like them, their dull dark leaves and vulgar blooms, but something about buying them spoke of a reconnect with the land of the living, thanks to Julie from Hendon. Anyway, they brought scent to a winter house.

'For a quick run,' he says. 'You seem brighter.' He is tying the laces on his trainers, toe on the cream upholstered kitchen chair.

'Can you get your foot off that?' she says.

'Yes, sorry.'

She hasn't told him about Julie, of course. Julie would be taken as further evidence of her madness. But with a single visit, Julie has made things bearable.

'I was thinking of going back to the practice, actually,' she says, plumping the stems in a bid to make them fall about naturally in the vase, but they are rigid as scaffolding.

'Good idea. Would do you good to be out and about. Occupy your mind.'

'Stop me thinking about Edith, you mean?'

'Thinking about her doesn't find her.'

'Anyway, I haven't decided yet,' she says.

Her partner at the GP practice, Raj, had called just after Christmas – but only to tell her to take as long as she needed, that he had got in a locum, and that if there was anything to sign (the paperwork when you became a fundholder was beyond belief) he'd drop it round. Twenty-four days missing; three and a half weeks of life suspended, sleepless and confined. Like being under water, it was quiet and engulfing, and there was a strong desire to stay submerged, rather than push up into the brash world where people will ask how she is, how *things* are. Why can't she stay home, arrange the house, remain loyal to Edith in her mind, and reinforced in that connection by Julie? Why wasn't that all right?

'Right,' he says, pushing his keys into a shallow pocket in his joggers and zipping it shut. 'Won't be long.'

An hour later, she has settled at her desk to tackle some neglected household admin: a quote for contents insurance, cheque for the milkman, a meter reading. She realises she needs a stamp and walks through to Ian's study. He keeps a stash in the central desk drawer, among paperclips and envelopes and those plastic label holders which clip onto hanging files. They clatter now under her patting hand. The drawer is sticky and won't pull out fully. She shuffles and lifts at the front but can't see any little books of stamps, so she pats her hand further back, among the elastic bands and stationary dust. Pens, a torch, her finger pricked by a noticeboard pin; then something solid and square, which she can't identify from memory. She brings it out. It is a Nokia. Old and chunky. A world away from the smart phones everyone has nowadays. Grubby about the edges of the screen. On the back are glittery pirate stickers: skull and crossbones, a boat. A child's phone. Why would he—

She runs her thumb over the edges of the stickers and they make a flicking sound, pleasingly stiff against the pad of her thumb. She turns it over in her hand again. It's dead, of course, the battery run down. He must have found it on the ground somewhere.

She returns the phone to the back of the drawer, hearing as she does so, Ian's key in the front door. She pushes at the drawer to close it but it judders and sticks and as she pushes again, he is at the doorway, saying, 'What are you looking for?'

'I just wanted a stamp,' she says, unsure why she feels nervous. 'Doesn't matter.'

He comes between her and the desk and forcibly pushes the central drawer shut, then opens the drawer beside it and offers her a book of stamps.

'Here,' he says.

Six Days Later
Tuesday

MANON

She smiles, closing the front door, and puts her face up to the unseasonal January warmth: sharp, blinding sun, the sky too bright to look at. The air is steely-fresh in her lungs and the river sparkles like diamonds. She wonders how he'll surprise her for Valentine's Day. Flowers? A table at a secluded restaurant? *A trip to Paris?* How quickly being alone vanishes, a country seen from your departing plane – small and far below. Even a short time makes it a distant place, as if the body is quick to relish the enveloping heat in the new territory – *love* – forgetting it is new. One week or one month is enough to make a return unthinkable.

She sinks down into the driver's seat, flipping the visor against the unruly sun, rummages in her handbag for her sunglasses, then starts the car. Has Alan noticed the pounds she must have gained with all their Sunday fry-ups and Friday night curries? Has it put him off, the way contentment is causing her boundaries to blur? The more she expresses, it seems, the less he does, and sometimes she wishes they could return to the cinema steps, when she was demure and he was leaning in. He doesn't like to text or email. Those hearty messages are all from her, sent in a rush of feeling which doesn't need reciprocity, except that when she receives no reply she notices a darkening of her inner world. An image has stored itself in her mind: that skein of birds, landing and flying off on the bank opposite his barn, one touching down as another lifts up, as if they are set in opposition.

She slows at the traffic lights, marvels at the sun's glare off bonnets and wing mirrors, and smiles again, remembering her Sunday: head in his lap; the crinkle of the newspaper; her sleepy satisfaction as she read her book, saying, 'Here's a good word – *agog*.'

'Mmm,' he said, 'so is *bosom*,' giving hers a squeeze, and then they were at it again.

They are two. It'll come. He is private; he has an English reserve which anyone would find charming. He doesn't like to text, is all.

A cloud passes overhead, its dark bulk ominous, and she lifts her sunglasses up onto her head. Still winter after all.

The lights change and she presses her foot down, the car slow to respond. He maintains his Law of Week Nights: a full eight hours, padded silk lavender eye mask on. No sleep-filled rocking, not on a Tuesday. He has got his shit in a pile, his ducks in a row. *Prim Prenderghast for Prime Minister!* He is real and they are together; and yes the birds do fly off, but they land also, and she just needs to give it time.

It was like she said to Bri when forced to help her move furniture around her mother's soon-to-be-rented-out bungalow: 'Loads of people like to take things slow, don't they? It's a normal part of—'

'Over there, by the wall,' Bryony had huffed, with insufficient interest, Manon felt.

'It doesn't mean he's not into it. Hell, I've been in loads of situations where I've felt pressure and it makes you back off, you know? It's just a human reaction.' She was stumbling backwards, the soft pads of her fingers burning under the weight of Bryony's mum's Parker Knoll. 'So the most important thing I can do—'

'Coffee table now,' said Bryony.

'Is stay calm and not put any pressure on him. Y'know, slowly, slowly, catchee monkey.'

It is so nearly there, this almost-love, if she could only stop herself from being too much. Every part of her reaches for him, un-haveable Alan. And as she lands, he flies off.

In the wanting, in the yearning, which is so opposite to all the reluctant dates and ambivalent sex and the not-quite-liking anyone, she feels she has become more fully Manon; an ocean of Manon washing over him. Enough for both of them. She could live in the wanting. What could be more joyful than being certain of your feelings? An end to all those stop-start relationships. She feels sorry, now, for all those poor women out there compromising or fearful of commitment, wondering whether it would work out, or if there might be someone better. She'd been like that for seven long years with the boy from university, and when they'd split up she'd had no idea if it was the right thing, but anyway, all that's behind her now.

All is perfection in the new Alan era, and everything – his big shoes, his flappy coat, his Fungus the Bogeyman head adorned with silk and lavender eye mask, his Weekday Rules – has a rightness to it. What a wonderful father he'll make, train sets scattered across his beautiful barn. He is so *funny*. Sometimes, when he makes a joke, she laughs so hard she does a little wee, although she can't think of a funny thing he's said exactly, not a precise example.

She pulls up, nose of the car pushing at the underside of a bush, turns the key, and all is quiet like a heart stopping. She hauls her bag onto her knees as the car ticks and feels for her phone, the private one, just in case his love has emerged in text form, but the screen is unchanged. So she reaches out to him, as per, setting her fingers typing:

Gawd, only Tues + am already knackered. Roll on takeaway night, angel cakes. Mx

DAVY

He takes a sip of stewed coffee and watches out of the third floor window, a hand in his trouser pocket jangling his keys. He can see Manon slam her car door and then stop, holding her face to the bright sun, basking in it with her eyes closed. As if she is sodding holy.

No more crying in the car park; no more laying her forehead on the steering wheel; no more snatching the lattes from his hand or wiping away smears of mascara. These days, it is Davy who grows impatient with the traffic, as if congestion were further evidence of all that's wrong in the world. His planet's out of alignment. A girl has been missing for more than a month; another is dead. They haven't done their job, thinks Davy, and everything is at odds.

Manon has become . . . breezy. Light. Polite to colleagues, interested in their adorable childrearing anecdotes when she used to make silent vomiting motions behind their backs.

'Aw, what did the twins do on the weekend, Nigel? Run you ragged, did they?'

It annoys Davy beyond measure, the bounce in her step.

309

They've been watching Tony Wright this past week but he hasn't put a foot wrong. The PM on Taylor Dent has come in but tells them nothing: *Whether death occurred before or after the body was immersed into water is impossible to say. Injuries consistent with river damage. Toxicology inconclusive.*

The background checks on Garfield, as well as some uncomfortable questioning of the professor about his Facebook usage, were insufficient grounds for his arrest. No, it was all going nowhere. Garfield had shifted uneasily in interview but not, Davy thought, out of shame, his expression saying: *I am a man. I accept my peccadilloes; why can't you?*

The press have started to itch their beards in longer think pieces, analysing the parameters of the investigation. The police have looked too closely at her immediate circle, is the latest offering from *The Mirror*. Officers have not given sufficient thought to the possibility of a stranger, driving out of the night. A random attack.

How people love to criticise, Davy thinks, shaking his head. It's never a stranger. Well, almost never.

And all the while, Manon is harping on about which new restaurants to try. 'I'm ardent,' she told him yesterday, sitting in the car with brown paper bags on their laps from the fast-food place.

They were on a surveillance job – drugs and prostitution. His lap was warm, his mouth filled with a synthetic coating of trans fats and salt. He murmured, hiding his irritation with a full mouth.

'If there's two people, I'm always the one who's more keen.'

He nodded, biting further into his cheeseburger.

'Except when I'm not,' she said. 'Mostly, I don't like people. And then I'm not ardent at all.'

'Riveting,' muttered Davy, staring ahead.

310

'What I mean is, it takes me ages to find someone I think is really great and then, well, sometimes I knock them over with enthusiasm.'

'Like a St Bernard.'

'Bit like that, yes.'

'Shall we have another cheeseburger?'

She'd nodded, chewing. 'Only 99p.'

'I don't think the price is the issue, is it?' said Davy.

'Get them in.'

He ought to be happy for her but he isn't, and Davy is getting used to his meaner thoughts being in the ascendance. He wonders if he should apply for a transfer – move far away and start over, away from the feelings which are making the minutes and the seconds lugubrious, but he has this new connection with Stanton, like the fragile push of a shoot from a seed, and he can't pretend he hasn't harboured hopes for what it might do for his career.

Time itself has become heavy, the consistency of treacle, and yet he is sure time, for Manon, has sped up in the past fortnight. She talks about Nana as if it's *her* dog. 'Nana's moulting,' she says tolerantly, picking the hairs off her skirt. He pictures that stoic dog, ears like furry sails flapping at the sides of her head, and the image passes smoothly on to Chloe and those plates of straightened hair.

He misses her. He misses her, he misses her, he misses her. Some nights he cries so much his pillow's too damp to lie on. Seven miserable lonely days of missing someone he never should have been with in the first place, yet wanting her back even so. He wonders if he could overlook her lack of human sympathy and generalised air of bitterness, just so he could have the feeling of being together again. Perhaps he misses the chap he was before Helena Reed died, cheerfully intending to marry Chloe, his very own poisoned chalice. Simultaneously, like some sick, celestial seesaw, Manon's personal happiness has supplanted his own, and every day he is faced with a vision of love's smug young dream, written all over her just-had-a-shag face.

He has raked a small but pleasing harvest of earwax under a nail and he rolls it now, between thumb and forefinger, turning from the window. He looks up to see Manon come in through the double doors. She smiles at him across the room and mimes lifting a cup to her lips, mouthing, 'Coffee?' at him.

'Can I have your attention, please?' says Stanton, with his ever-present files under his arm. He smiles at Davy as Davy comes near.

'Everything all right?' he says warmly, to which Davy says, 'Yes, boss.'

'Right, just a quick word, everyone. DI Harriet Harper is taking a leave of absence due to personal circumstances. Any issues arising come to me or DS Manon . . .' He scans the room then finds her. 'Ah, there you are, Bradshaw.'

Elsie must have died, thinks Davy. Poor Harriet. She'll be heartbroken.

'You two can take it from here, can't you?' Stanton says to Davy and Manon, with a hand on Davy's shoulder.

It had begun at Helena Reed's funeral on Friday. Davy stood beneath a black umbrella as the rain streamed in a wall around his personal octagon, all the mourners spattered in silver droplets, the puddles splashing at their patent pumps and polished brogues.

Manon made some excuse as to why she couldn't attend. There was a smattering of students and members of the faculty; Dr Young, looking ashen (Davy recognised him from his police interview). Will Carter attended in an impeccable suit, which flashed through the open flaps of his black raincoat. Davy had come to admire Will Carter. He carried himself with utmost decorum; didn't over-emote at the front of the church but sat with elegant sympathy, paying his respects. He looked even more handsome in mourning clothes, especially the waistcoat element, which Davy never would have thought of himself. And his socks – even his socks, visible when he crossed his legs – were a perfect shade of blue, matching his shirt and tie.

Ian and Miriam Hind attended, which surprised Davy because press innuendo surrounding Helena was still swirling, as if her suicide were part confession.

Edith Hind lover found dead.

Why did Edith's girl end it all?

Lady Hind wore a wide-brimmed hat, which forced her neighbours to duck and swerve while she remained serene. Her neckline sparkled with a collar of black stones. The Hinds cried more than was fitting for a friend of their daughter's, and Davy could see they were in some way enacting a dress rehearsal for their own worst fears. Besides, there was no way of stopping your mind from wandering at a funeral, travelling into all sorts of dark imaginings about your nearest and dearest and how they might die and how you might feel. They were riveting like that.

Helena's own parents were not present, her father having suffered a stroke during the press furore over his daughter's sexuality; her mother was described by the priest as 'incapacitated'. 'Our thoughts are with them,' he said, 'and it falls to us to mourn on their behalf a beloved daughter, friend, and student.'

As the congregation filed out, Davy remained seated in his pew, looking forwards at the large photograph of Helena on an easel next to her coffin. He was staring at his guilt and

313

at his failure to prevent something so wantonly destructive. And as he stared, he felt a body heave down next to him. Stanton's breathing was strained, as if the fat was squeezing the very breath out of him like a fist. They sat together, staring at Helena's image – her expression smiling and innocent of what lay ahead – and there was intimacy in that pew. The constable and the chief superintendent. Then, Stanton said, 'Pint?' and Davy accepted the invitation, in part because, without Chloe, he had nowhere to be on a Friday night. He thought it would be one long arse ache, that pint with the boss, but as they sat at the small round table, he found he was too tired for toadying, so he looked Stanton in the eye and told him how rotten he felt about Helena Reed, and how responsible. Stanton licked the foam off his upper lip and said, 'If you can keep those feelings, Davy lad, – and let me tell you, every minute in the police will chip away at them – but if you can hold onto those human feelings, you might just make a good copper.'

WEDNESDAY

MIRIAM

'Mum?'

It is Rollo's voice calling and she follows it into the lounge, where the curtains are perpetually drawn.

'Look at this,' he says. He stands in front of the television, which is blaring the excessively jaunty theme tune to *This Morning*. The remote in his hand is still lolling at the screen. The television is never on during the day, except the odd black and white afternoon film when Miriam is particularly exhausted.

'Why am I watching this?' she asks.

'Just wait and see.'

The set is a cacophony of exposed brick, floral wallpaper, and primary-coloured soft furnishings, all yelling 'CHEERFUL!' at a bruising volume.

'Here we go,' says Rollo.

The presenters – a blonde woman who resembles Bambi and a white-haired, curiously ageless man – have lowered their voices to denote 'tragedy item'.

'A month ago, twenty-four-year-old Edith Hind went missing from her home in Huntingdon. The police still don't know

315

what's happened to her, but since then a series of lurid revelations have appeared in the press relating to her private life. Indeed, last week, the exposure led to her best friend, Helena Reed, tragically taking her own life. Today, exclusively on *This Morning*, we have Edith's boyfriend here to talk about the girl he loves and to separate the facts from the fiction.'

'That's Holly Willoughbooby,' says Rollo.

'That can't be her real name,' says Miriam.

'Shhhhh,' says Rollo.

Holly's huge doe eyes are looking up from beneath a voluminous sweep of yellow hair. Her voice is laden with condolence, while along the bottom of the screen, Miriam notices, the next item is on flattering trousers, followed by a discussion on toddlers who bite. Something about the lighting on the show makes its world seem thin and breakable.

'You were with Edith for two happy years and presumably you had no inkling of what lay ahead. You must be worried sick about her,' says the ageless man, whose bronzed skin and white hair make him seem like a photographic negative.

Will Carter smiles. He is resplendent in a slate blue open-neck shirt, an exact match for his eyes which, studio lit and in high definition, sparkle on screen.

Ah yes, thinks Miriam, of course.

'I'm worried and I miss her like crazy,' he says, 'but it's also been devastating to see so many lies and innuendoes in the tabloids. It's just compounded all our distress.'

'You mean yours and her parents – Sir Ian and Lady Hind,' says the ageless man.

'That's Phil,' Rollo says to Miriam.

'Has TV reversed the passage of time?' asks Miriam.

'It has for Phillip Schofield,' says Rollo.

'I also need to set the record straight about Helena, who was our dear friend and who never did anything – never *would* have done anything – to hurt anyone. The lies about her have been astounding, with devastating consequences.'

'What a heartthrob,' says Rollo.

'The start of his TV career,' says Miriam. They are standing in front of the television in the pretence they are not stopping, but they both are mesmerised, like babies in front of their first cartoon.

'Actually, I could see him presenting *The One Show*, or one of those nature programmes like *Countryfile*, that sort of thing,' says Rollo.

'Yes, but he's so boring,' says Miriam. 'Look, even Holly's suppressing a yawn – did you see that? Her mouth went all tight.'

Rollo is looking at his mother. 'I thought it was The Tedium That Dare Not Speak Its Name.'

'I can admit it now.'

'Well, I admire him for going out to bat for Edith and Helena.'

'Darling Rollo,' says Miriam, hugging him, then looking at her watch over his broad shoulder. 'Oh gosh, I'm late for Julie.'

'Need your fix,' says Rollo, and she can hear the disapproval in his voice as she leaves the room in search of her handbag.

MANON

She strides the white expanse of King's Cross, dancing a weave through the frowning throng with their bags and newspapers, paper cups of coffee too hot to sip, and every face, almost without exception, fixed downwards on a tiny screen in hand.

Manon takes out her own phone and finds Harriet's number. She will never avoid a person who has been bereaved; never put her own embarrassment before their loss, because she's been on the receiving end; has seen people cross the street to sidestep the conversation when her mother died. And yet she fears Harriet's state of mind.

She strides over the newly laid honey pavements, inset with solar lights, to St Pancras to board the Thameslink to Cricklewood, the phone pressed to her ear.

'Turns out I'm rich,' Harriet says. 'Elsie had twenty grand's worth of granny bonds and she's left it all to me.'

'That's something,' says Manon. 'How are you holding up?'

'Oh, you know.'

'Mmm.'

'Where are you?' asks Harriet.

318

'London. I've come to check on Fly.'

'Good for you.'

'When are you coming back?'

'Oh, I dunno. There's a lot of clearing out to do, y'know – her stuff, things to organise. Monday, probably.'

In body, perhaps, but not in spirit. Manon knows what lies beneath; how people can seem normal and yet grief swirls about like an unseen tide working against the currents of life, the mourner wrong-footed by its undertow. The bereaved should wear signs, she thinks, saying: *Grief in Progress* – for at least a couple of years.

The wind roughs her up on the walk down Cricklewood Lane to the Broadway, making the tops of the trees sway, noisy as high surf. She is meeting Fly at the Brazilian café where she'll settle her bill with the owner, Neuza Lima.

She steps in, relieved to be out of the tumble of the weather, her hair falling at last.

'Hello, Neuza,' she says.

'Sergeant,' she says, kissing Manon on each cheek.

'How's it been with Fly?'

'He is lovely, lovely boy. Gentle boy.'

Fly has pushed the door open, sniffing in that way he has, and Manon smiles broadly at him, though he is reserved – a wan hello and then he embraces Neuza, and Manon is surprised to feel put out.

'Ola,' he says to Neuza.

'*Olá, meu querido,*' says Neuza, hugging him to her broad bosom. '*Bem-vindo,* both of you! Take a seat – nice one in the window. I bring you, what? Coffee? Eggs?'

The window is full of the buses rumbling up and down Cricklewood Broadway and sharp shadows in confusion with the gleam of the glass.

319

'How's things?' asks Manon.

He looks well. Neuza's food has filled out his cheeks and made his eyes shine, yet they are full of sadness still.

'Mum's real sick,' he says. 'Can't get out of bed, can't keep anything down. Doctors say it won't be long.'

'Oh, Fly.'

'She been offered a place in a hospice in Hampstead – Marie Curie place – when the pain gets too much, when I can't . . .'

'Do you know what you'll do when that happens?'

'I'll need to stay with someone. Social worker says it has to be someone good, a good person, a grown-up – otherwise they put me in care.'

He looks into Manon's face, waiting. The room is filled with the sound of sputtering milk and Portuguese TV and Manon turns to look for Neuza, wondering where her coffee has got to.

'Have you got a friend you could stay with – someone from school, maybe?'

'Thought you was my friend,' he says. She is grateful for the approach of her latte and his juice.

'I live in Huntingdon, Fly. It's really important you stay at your school, isn't it?'

'*Obrigado,*' he says to Neuza.

'*O prazer é meu,*' she says, stroking his close-cropped hair.

Manon takes Neuza to one side and asks if she might look in on Maureen Dent, send someone in to clean the flat.

'My niece, she do it. Eight pound for hour.'

'Fine,' says Manon, frowning, wondering how long she can bankroll the Dent family. 'Add it to my bill. Could he stay with you when . . . y'know, at the end?'

Neuza makes a mournful grimace as if she's smelt something

unappetising. 'Is no possible. Is lovely boy but my hasband, he no take in Fly. He not such a good man.'

'OK, right, well, I'll think of something. For now, we'll keep going with the food tab and the cleaning and looking in on them, OK?'

'*Sem problemas*,' she says, and from her warm pat on her shoulder and her competent expression, Manon understands this to mean, 'No problem'.

At home again in the evening, in bed, she listens to the shouts of revellers across the river. A lorry rumbles down some arterial route and its vibrations make the light bulb rattle in its metal shade beside her head like the buzz of an insect. The phone lies on her stomach. She is worrying about Fly. She dials Alan's number.

'Hello,' he says.

'Are you in bed?' she asks.

'I sure am. How was your day?'

'I went to visit Fly Dent in London. He . . . he's only ten. His mum's not got long.'

'Poor boy,' says Alan.

'He wants to stay with me, once she goes into a hospice. He's frightened of being taken into care and I don't blame him. Don't think care would do him any good, to be honest.'

'Doesn't he need to stay near to his school? Thought you said he was doing well.'

'Well, yes, but he needs to be safe.'

In the silence, she realises she wants Alan to persuade her – to do the right thing, to cast practicalities aside and take Fly in, out of goodness, unalloyed. It matters where his compass lies, to which side of hers.

'It's not like I don't have the resources to look after him,' she is saying, without conviction. 'I've got a job, a flat. I've got money.'

'It'd be a lot of disruption, for both of you,' says Alan. 'It's not as if he's your responsibility – not really. This is what the state is for.'

'I s'pose,' she says. 'But don't you have to take people on sometimes? Don't you have to step up?'

'In theory,' he says.

Perhaps, she thinks, grasping for hope, he is protecting their own trajectory – a chance, not to be scuppered by a ten-year-old lodger. Talk about passion killer. He doesn't want to share her (maybe).

'I went out with someone with a son once,' he says. 'Didn't last long.'

'That probably wasn't the son's fault,' she says, before she's had time to think. She wants to divert the conversation away from this dark turn. 'See, that's the good thing about Internet dating – you can specify "no kids".'

'You've done Internet dating?'

'Hasn't everyone?'

'Seems a bit desperate,' he says.

I *am* desperate, she thinks. Or I was. Why lie?

'Didn't you want to meet someone?' she asks him.

'Just rather do it naturally,' he says.

'What's natural? Getting smashed and falling on someone in a bar?'

'No, what's natural is being questioned by the gorgeous Officer Dibble about a dead body,' he says, sounding conciliatory.

She smiles into the warmer silence.

Then he says, 'Did you tell the truth about your age then?'

She sits up. 'What's wrong with my age?'

'Well, thirty-nine – danger zone.'

'I'm sorry?'

'I didn't mean . . . sorry,' he says. 'That was a stupid thing to say.'

'What about your sperm, hobbling about on Zimmer frames?'

'Calm down.'

'Woah! *Calm down?*' she says. 'I want to know. What do you mean by danger zone? Where are we heading? I mean, do we actually want the same things?'

He sighs, as if he's completely exhausted with her. 'I can't do this any more, Manon. I'm sorry.'

She lies there. Stunned. Is that it then? All finished before it even began? What has she done, with her hot head so quick to take offence?

She reaches out to turn on the police radio, hoping Control can take her back to a place of safety. Its low murmurings burble out towards her and she closes her eyes. She turns in the bed, curls into a foetal position, her hands clasped between her knees.

She thinks there will always be a gap. A sad loss of a thing that cannot be had; a will-o'-the-wisp, yearned for but never grasped. A woman who cannot be delayed for long enough. Sudden Death Syndrome, the coroner recorded at her mother's inquest, as if the word 'syndrome' made it comprehensible.

One minute you are loved, and then you are not.

FRIDAY

MANON

She managed a dignified silence for the first twenty-four hours, told herself it was a blip that could come right if she just gave him some space; he would regret what he said, realising what a special thing they were letting go of.

But nothing.

No calls, no texts, and in his silence she has read equanimity. After a bad night, her emotions are as ragged as the Alps. Fitful sleep, wishful dreams, ended by waking to a vision of Helena Reed's body hanging from the back of her bedroom door.

Now, Manon is exhausted, slumped over her desk in MIT, glancing again and again at her phone, her collapsing face resting on the heel of one hand. So far she's sent seven texts, smoked five cigarettes, and pranged the car. And it's not yet 11 a.m.

I'm sorry for what I said the other night. Let's not leave it like this. M

Listen, I know I can be difficult, I do know that. I just want to set things straight. M

Hey Big Al, thinkin' about ya.
(She particularly regrets this one)

Listen, even if you're sure, let's just talk it over, as I believe a song once said.

No wonder you've never had a relationship last more than six months.

It's a fucking relief, to be honest. Cocksucker.

Please don't leave me.

There is Kim at the front of the room, writing on a whiteboard in marker pen, while Manon examines Kim's bottom. It clenches to a point at its base and then joins to two very ample, ocean-going thighs, not even the hint of a gap between them. My bottom's probably as big as that, she thinks. A single person's bottom. I'm about to be forty, I will never have a baby, and I have a bottom the size of— Don't cry. Just don't cry, not in the middle of MIT.

'Dawn's doing baby-led weaning, which is great because they just learn to feed themselves, and they don't grow up with any food issues,' Nigel is saying, as Davy hands Manon a coffee.

'Kill me now,' she mouths at Davy.

She hears the trill of a text message alert and her heart flips over itself just as Kim says, 'Ready, everyone?' and turns to reveal her work on the whiteboard.

DAVY

Now we're getting somewhere, he thinks, reading Kim's looping handwriting. Five weeks missing and we've finally got some detail on Edith Hind's movements in the days running up to her disappearance.

He casts a look at Manon, who is so slumped she's practically laid her head on the table.

'The new information is from Scope – the charity shop on the high street. They've come forward with CCTV footage showing Edith buying a whole heap of stuff on Friday sixteenth of December, the day before she disappeared.'

'Such as?' asks Davy.

'Can't say exactly. Footage is grainy and from the wrong angle to see what's on the counter. We interviewed the old dear on the till but, to use official police parlance, she's quite a few sandwiches short of a picnic.'

'Wouldn't that indicate she's trying to disguise herself?' Davy asks.

'Not really,' says Kim. 'Will Carter says she was fond of

buying clothes at charity shops – fitted with her environmental, y'know, what-not.'

Davy glances at the board.

Saturday 10 Dec: Visits Helena Reed's flat in the early hours. Intercourse with HR.

Sunday 11: Drives out to Deeping in G-Wiz, 3.20 p.m. ANPR return into Hunts at 10.45 p.m.

Monday 12: Pays rent to landlord next door, who says she seemed 'distracted'.

Call to Tony Wright's phone.

Wednesday 14: Visits Helena Reed's flat again. Intercourse with HR.

Friday 16: Second call to Tony Wright's phone. Shops at Scope on high st. Intercourse with Will Carter. He states she was 'highly emotional'.

Saturday 17: Christmas do at The Crown, Cambs. Sexual contact with Jason Farrer. Guided bus back to Huntingdon with HR.

'Well, you know the rest from here,' Kim is saying.

'*Fuck,*' Manon blurts, so the department, Davy included, turns to look at her. Her eyes brim with tears.

'Good to know I had everyone's attention,' says Kim.

327

MANON

Her screen reads *Alan P* – so rare to see his name on her mobile phone – and might this be the volte-face she's been waiting for? Might it be that as she lands, he flies down also, coming to a graceful stop beside her? Might this be the moment he tells her he misses her, that he wants them to be properly together, on week nights and everything?

I'm sorry, Manon. I have enjoyed our time together, but I'm looking for something exceptional.

In her haste to leave the room, all eyes staring at her, she trips over a wastepaper basket and slams into the sharp corner of a desk, wounding her thigh.

'Argh,' she yelps, rubbing her leg and stumbling to gather her phones, her bag, her coat from the back of her swivel chair, knowing only that she must make for the double doors.

Down the stairs, not knowing where she's going or why, she tells herself she definitely won't be responding to that one. There's an end to it. That message, she thinks, lighting a cigarette on the station steps, so characteristically pinched and formal. Her only response must be an arctic silence, laced with disappointment.

Soon, when the cigarette has been sucked down to its orange stump, she's digging into her bag, a frenzy of fingers and thumbs, through furious tears which fall freely all over the little screen.

You'll have a long fucking wait then, dick wipe cock sucking shit for brains.

The buzzer goes and she lifts herself from the bed. The room – the whole flat – is in darkness and she switches on the lights as she makes her way to the handset beside the front door.

'Halloooo!' says Bryony's voice. 'We're here to take you out.'

Manon doesn't reply, but presses the button to let them in. She leaves the door open and sits on the sofa, pulling a blanket around her shoulders as Bryony and Davy clatter in, on a wave of cold air from outside.

'Listen, he's a prick,' says Bryony, 'top totty like you.'

'He might still change his mind,' says Davy, who seems back to his old self.

'Davy,' says Bryony. 'Let's not give the patient false hope.'

'Why do none of my relationships work out?' says Manon.

'None of mine have either,' says Bryony. 'I just happen to have married the latest one.'

'That tosser's left a space for someone better, that's what I think,' says Davy.

'I love you, Davy,' says Manon.

'Come on,' says Bryony. 'You need a drink. To Cromwell's!'

'Urgh, please. Can't we just stay here and watch *Failure to Launch*?'

'Nope, and we are not taking you wrapped in a blanket,' says Bryony, pushing Manon on the shoulder, which fells her to the sofa like a chopped tree. 'Go and get your glad rags on.'

'I'll have a quick tidy-up,' says Davy. 'Where are your Marigolds?'

Bryony puts the Scissor Sisters on the stereo and leads Manon into the bedroom.

'Smells like something died in here,' she says. 'Have you been lying on the bed crying and farting?'

Manon nods.

Bryony makes the bed and opens a window, and they select an outfit – a black tunic dress, tights, and knee-high boots – after which Bryony sits Manon down on a chair to do her makeup. Davy is clattering about in the kitchen, putting away dishes from the sounds of it. Manon has her eyes closed and feels the soft push and tickle of an eyeshadow brush, the sweet scent of Bryony's breath, and her hand on her forehead.

'I don't want to go,' she says.

'Shurrup,' says Bryony.

Three-quarters of an hour later, they're assembled by the front door.

'How does she look?' asks Bryony.

'Million dollars,' says Davy, smiling at her.

'Davy,' says Manon, 'this place looks amazing.'

'Well, there's nothing like a tidy-up to lift your spirits, is there?'

Manon can feel her face crumpling and Bryony notices, saying, 'Hey, hey, come on, don't spoil your makeup.'

The first drink, in the darkness of the bar, is like nectar. Manon begins to feel things loosen and dissipate. Who *cares*? What does it *matter*? Things *pass*!

330

'Fuck it!' she says, raising her glass to Bryony.

'Fuck it, indeed,' says Bryony, raising hers back.

By the second drink, she is grateful to Alan for releasing her from the hell of suburban convention. All that *domesticity*. 'So booorrrrring,' she says to Bryony.

'Bor-ring,' says Bryony.

'He wants to be friends. Texted to tell me. I mean, all of a sudden he's Texts R Us. Friends! What is that *shit*?'

'Dunno,' says Bryony. 'I always thought a good break-up meant never speaking to the person again, except when armed with scissors or in open court.'

'Zactly!'

She surveys the usual suspects: Colin, Stuart, Kim, and Nigel (having a quick half before getting back to 'the lovely Dawn').

'The inspirational Dawn,' whispers Bryony.

'The irrefutable Dawn,' says Manon.

'The seriously fucking knackered Dawn,' says Bryony.

'Twins woke at 4 a.m. this morning,' says Nigel, visibly depressed and gazing into his drink.

Another reason to celebrate, thinks Manon, and orders another double at the bar. Thick and fast they come, bought by others or bought by her. She thinks life is best passed in a blur: imprecise and anaesthetised from the sharper feelings. She is drowning as the gin engulfs her, swaying on the spot, the room spinning, the music pumping in time with the blood in her arteries. She can feel the beat through the soles of her feet.

Stuart is smiling, glittering at her dangerously. They appear to have been talking for some time. Bryony is nowhere to be seen.

'Christ, haven't you been fired yet?' she says, lurching towards him.

'They've got nothing on me. In fact, I'm just bedding in, getting the lie of the land, office hierarchy.'

'You're all about hierarchy, aren't you, Stuart?' she says. She feels as if she can say anything, to anyone's face. 'Like you're obsessed.'

'Who do you rate, then?' he says, his glass raised towards their colleagues nearby. 'Who's a good copper?'

'Me!' she says, close enough to put her cheek on his chest. She's tempted. Any port in a storm.

'What about Harper?' he says, and she sees that look, the same look he'd had when he had complained about the head-mistress 'lording it' at the school where he worked.

'Oh, Harriet's good. Very good. Sexually frustrated, though.' She burps into her fist. 'Scuse me.' She can't feel the bottom half of her legs. Stuart swims in front of her. 'Kim's good. Solid, y'know. Unimaginative.'

'Go on.' This wily fox, his charm a lure into darkness.

The music is so loud, she's had to shout in his ear, to smell him. Foreign male. Exciting and dangerous. She's shouting now, just as before, but her words have a strange echo, as if they have been emitted through a loudhailer.

'Davy'll never be a good copper,' she bellows into the sudden silence. 'Too busy looking on the fucking bright side.'

Her eyes are half-closed, her mind woolly, and she has shouted the words before she registers that the music is off. Someone must've pulled the plug, she thinks, too late.

And she turns, slowly, to see a row of faces staring at her. Kim, Bryony, Nigel, and Colin. Davy at the centre, hurt ears pinned back. She can practically see the follicles standing up on his head.

She starts to burn. She is drunk but also painfully sober. Davy is staring at her and she doesn't know if it's simply what she has said or the fact that she has spilled it into Stuart's malevolent ear. She is so drunk that all her movements are delayed and her eyelids half close again, though there is panic on the inside, as if she can't persuade her body to catch up.

'Davy, I—' she begins, but the music is back on, louder than before, like she's being punched about the head, and he has walked quickly out of the bar.

Before she knows what's happening, Bryony has appeared, carrying her coat and bag.

'Aren't those mine?' she asks, but Bryony has taken her by the elbow, saying, 'Excuse us' to Stuart.

'Oi, I was just—' Manon protests.

'Yes, we all know what you were just doing,' says Bryony.

SATURDAY

MANON

Everything in ruins.

She walks the cold lounge, lighting lamps against the tinkle and spit of rain at the window.

Her pyjamas stink – sweet, fetid alcohol, seeping out through her skin. She sits on the curved corduroy sofa and cries.

If there was only something left: a relationship gone wrong but her work intact; her work compromised but love still offering a future. Instead, it is a desolate landscape, the death of Helena Reed at its centre like a crucifixion, her head to one side. While she was with him, she could tell herself that dereliction of duty had been in aid of something; she hadn't wanted to be married to the job. Now, even the job won't have her.

She sits cross-legged on the sofa, pulls her laptop onto her knees, her phones beside her. She points the remote at the TV, so the news comes on. She needs something, *anything*. She needs an idea.

She Googles Tony Wright. The various reportings of his crimes pop up; a backgrounder after his conviction, in the *Eastern Daily Press*. Whitemoor prison is highlighted in blue, and she clicks idly on the link. The Internet is a journey, down tributaries random and meandering; a journey in which you could lose hours, days, a week, and she's happy to become lost. She reads the Whitemoor Wikipedia page.

In June 2006, an inspection report from Her Majesty's Chief Inspector of Prisons criticised staff at Whitemoor Prison for ignoring prisoners, and not responding to their queries and requests for help promptly enough.

She skims the next part.

A further inspection report stated, in October 2008, that staff at Whitemoor Prison felt fear that Muslim inmates were attempting to radicalise others held at the jail. According to inspectors, officers tended to treat Muslim prisoners as extremists and potential security risks, even though only eight of them had been convicted of terrorist offences. Due to the concerns raised by this inspection, further visits by researchers from the Cambridge Institute of Criminology, commissioned by the Ministry of Justice, were arranged between 2009 and 2010 to interview staff and inmates.

Manon picks up her remote to silence the TV, as something forms, indistinct at present. Cambridge Institute of Criminology. Part of the university. Tony Wright was in Whitemoor when their inspections were taking place. Tony Wright might have been interviewed by the CIC.

She picks up her BlackBerry and finds Wilco Bennett's number, her prison warden contact at Whitemoor.

'Manon,' he says warmly. 'Long time.'

'Everything all right, Wilco?' she says, making a stab at the pleasantries. She has a soft spot for Wilco Bennett: pigeon fancier, holder of socially unacceptable views, which she forgives because he's been incarcerated with sociopaths since 1989. They got to know each other during endless proceedings at Peterborough Crown Court – remand hearings, bail applications, and the attendant delays which often left them sitting on hard benches side by side beneath the courtroom.

'Your Edith Hind girl,' says Wilco. 'Bit of a whopper, isn't it?'

'Mmm,' she says. 'Can I ask a favour, Wilco?'

'Fire away,' he says.

'Tony Wright.'

'Prince Charming, yes.'

'Can you get me his authorised visitor list?'

''S'a while ago now, lovely. He's been out eight months.'

'I know. Are you in the office or is it your weekend off?'

'No, I'm in. I'm not brilliant on the old computers; I think the AV list has to be downloaded onto the whatnot, using a doobrey.' He chuckles at this. 'I can never find the damned thing after that, you know? Downloaded *where*? Still, it's quiet today; I'll see if I can get someone to help me. Any particular span of time, so to speak?'

'I'd like Wright's entire AV list, if you can get it, but I want you to look at 2009 in particular. Call me back?'

'Will do.'

She lies down on the sofa, her laptop at her feet, her hands between her knees. She is cold. She hasn't eaten since sometime late yesterday afternoon, before the Cromwell's debacle. She reaches back, drags a blanket off the back of the sofa to cover herself. She wonders if she should call Davy, but instead turns the sound up on the TV. She lies there, looking up at the ceiling, listening to the burble of the lunchtime news; always the soft stuff – items about the Royal Family or the cost of childcare, for people raising spoons of Heinz tomato soup to their quivering lips. People wrapped in blankets, just like her. She thinks about smoking a cigarette.

'The body of an Afghan man and twenty other refugees have been found in a container at Tilbury Docks,' she hears the newsreader say. 'A man from Ipswich has been arrested on suspicion of conspiring to facilitate illegal immigration into the UK. Abdul-Ghani Khalil, thirty-seven, was arrested alongside three men from Luton in connection with the death.'

She reaches behind her head for a cigarette, which she lights without sitting upright, blowing smoke up into the gathering dusk.

She throws her cigarette butt out of the open third of her car window, then winds it up. Sits, feeling a swell of tears rise in her chest, then lower, plus something else – a kamikaze element. She shouldn't be here alone.

In front of her, the estate road winds away into the shadowy hulk of buildings. A bin, over-full, billows with a white plastic bag stuffed in at the top. At the curve of the road is a group of youths, their hoods up, hunched, stamping foot to foot. She can't see their faces but their bodies are febrile.

She's been on the estate before after nightfall, crouching over the body of a debt collector who'd been sent out here on her own to gather piddling sums for an insurance firm. A mother of three, smartly dressed, pootling into danger in her little maroon Fiat, wearing a white mohair jumper with dainty gold necklace over its roll neck. She should never have been here alone, not at night, and certainly not asking for money. Twelve pounds a week she collected from the man who would eventually stab her to death.

Yet here is Manon, just like the debt collector, alone in the

337

dark. No one to report her missing now, no police colleagues pulling out the stops. No backup.

She slams her car door and makes for Tony Wright's flat.

'To what do I owe this honour?' he says, answering the door.

'Can I come in?' she asks, and he steps back.

She hears him lock the door behind her. 'Cannae be too careful. All sorts round here.'

She steps into the lounge which is dim, except for a lava lamp glowing purple on a shelf, its moving globules like slow marine life. The room smells of incense and smoke.

'Lyn here?' she says, casting about. Her heart is thumping. She feels as if the ground is tipping. What is she doing here, locked inside with Tony Wright?

'No, nobody here, ma wee scone, 'cept you an' me,' says Tony as he walks through to a small kitchen.

He returns carrying a bottle of whiskey and two glasses. He motions to the square table against the wall and she sits at it, a whiskey glass placed before her. She thinks about the two glasses at George Street, one with blood on its shards.

She doesn't say no as he pours; another line she's crossing.

'So,' he says, raising his glass to her and smiling, with that twinkle – Father Christmas and Captain Birdseye.

'So,' she says, and she drinks, hoping it will steel her nerves. The whiskey burns, a tear drop of fire descending her gullet. Her head swims and she feels sick. Perhaps he will tell her what he's done to Edith Hind, how he got away with it, and then he will kill her. Yes, that seems likely now, and she feels calm in the face of it. She doesn't care about herself. She lights a cigarette and so does he. There is so much camaraderie in lighting up together. Another protocol broken.

'Just you and me, Tony,' she says. 'What's the deal? Why was Edith on your AV list?'

338

He looks at her. Blows out smoke. 'She was in the prison doin' some research, interviewin' prisoners. I dinnae remember what for, was a while ago now – 2009. Whitemoor was in a right state at the time. Riots, escapes. Prison wardens were filth, abusin' us. She was askin' loads o' questions about the conditions we were livin' under in the prison. We started talkin'. And we enjoyed talkin'. So I said, if you'd like tae come back, we could talk some more.'

'You were grooming her?'

'Groomin' her for what? I've no' touched her.' He leans forward, jabbing the table top with one finger. 'Ye'll get nothin' on me 'cos I've done nothin' tae that girl. If there's a law says a lowlife like me cannae be pals wi' a classy bird like that, then show me it.'

'What did you talk about, when she visited you?'

'About the prison, life inside. She brought me some books to read. *Jude the Obscure*. Well, I had a lot o' time on ma hands, but even so, I only pretended to read the books she brought me, so that she'd like me all right. I liked talkin' to her, and I liked lookin' at her. No' in a bad way – she's a fine-lookin' girl.'

'So you talked literature, Tony, you and Edith Hind?'

'Ah told ye, I only pretended to read that book just so she'd keep visitin' me. Then ma mother died. I found myself in a very quiet place, ye ken? Inside myself, I mean. Edith came to see me just after. I was in a bad way; *darkness*, ken?' He beats a fist against his heart. 'We started talkin' about deeper things.'

'What did she call you about in the week before she disappeared?'

'This an' that.'

'Ah, come on, Tony.'

'Nothing special: how you doin', Tony, what's happening

339

wi' finding work, seeing your probation officer, whatnot. She's a good person; a really good person. I never had anyone classy like her tek an interest afore. Made me want tae make an effort. Thought maybe I could have . . . I don't know . . .' He trails off.

'Have what, Tony? Have her money? Take her life?'

'Och, there you go again,' and he gets up. Manon gets up too and they square up to each other, making the room feel small. She needs to get out of here if she's going to make it at all, but the front door is locked. Tony is reaching into his pocket slowly. She thinks of the girl, his victim, beaten with the butt end of a knife's handle until she couldn't see.

'Ye see what ye want tae see,' he says, squinting as he lights another cigarette. 'Ye see me, and in your view I'm no' able to change. That's fine. But I'm tellin' ye, Edith Hind has been a good pal in my life, an' even wi' all this *shit*, I'm glad I know her.'

'Know?'

'Know, knew . . . Ah've no idea where she is.'

He has sat down again, his legs effeminately crossed, regarding his cigarette held in a tight hand.

'She's alive, isn't she?'

'I told ye, I don't know what's happened tae the girl. I hope she's alive, aye.'

She has to get out of here, while the going's good. She strides for the door, tries to open it. She pulls at the door, rattling it furiously, until he comes behind her, lays a hand on her shoulder.

'Hey, hey, hey, calm it,' he says, and turns her body towards his. 'There's no need to be jigglin' about like that.' He is so near to her she can smell him – cinnamon and whiskey. Her heart is pounding so furiously she wonders if he can feel it

340

too. 'There ye go,' he says, and he opens the door onto a blast of freezing night.

She is shaking, whether with fear or with cold or with relief to have got out, she cannot tell. She is shaking so much her key will not make it into the lock of her car door. She tries again, holding her wrist with her other hand, trying to steady the aiming of the key's shaft.

Crack.

Sharp hot pain at the top of her skull. Then an ice cold trickle down the back of her neck. Her last sensation: her legs folding beneath her.

The world tips.

SUNDAY

MANON

She is all mouth; impossibly dry, thick as wool. An eye open to a white room. Has she died? It is so white, perhaps this is the afterlife, in which case, it should have a better view. A broad picture window gives out onto leafless trees and the flat roofs of municipal buildings, the sky the colour of porridge. She has a headache which threatens to split her skull.

'Here, you'll need a drink.'

Someone is lifting her neck and she closes her mouth around a straw, the liquid so shocking it sears her temples.

'You're a lucky woman,' he says.

She focuses her dehydrated eyes – first on his white coat, then the stethoscope, then his black stubble. He smells of coal tar soap. His tie is lying on her body. He straightens, places her cup on the bedside unit, and she can see his olive skin and dark eyebrows. Albanian or Middle Eastern, perhaps. She would like to rearrange her hair, wipe the crust from the corners of her mouth.

'That was quite a blow to your head,' he is saying. 'Knocked you out cold. Might have been a punch, or you might've been

342

struck with something. We were concerned the injury might cause a bleed into your brain – that's why we kept you in overnight. How're you feeling?'

'Rough,' she croaks.

He smiles. 'We're going to monitor you a bit longer, run some tests. I'm going to get you some paracetamol. Expect you've got a fierce headache, right?' He is *really* nice-looking, though now she considers it, possibly about fifteen years younger than she is. 'By the way, you've got a visitor.'

The doctor and Harriet dance round each other in the doorway. Manon closes her eyes, her head heavy on the pillow. She feels Harriet's nervous energy lower into the plastic chair beside her bed, her hand coming to rest on Manon's.

'What happened?' Manon whispers.

'From the CCTV, looks like a kid – an addict, probably – was being opportunistic, saw you alone, liked the look of your handbag. What the hell were you doing—'

'Not Tony Wright, then?'

'No, in fact our beloved Tony came to your aid – called 999, saw off whoever'd done it. Anyway, this kid, who we will catch, don't you worry, has seriously assaulted one of my police officers and has now got himself a police BlackBerry.'

'Which is passcode-locked, so don't panic. I'll give a statement to CID. Let them get on with it.'

'Hmm,' Harriet murmurs sceptically. 'Anyway, he'll be going to prison for a *really* long time, which'll sort out his habit one way or the other. What the fuck were you doing there on your own?'

'Edith Hind was on Tony Wright's authorised visitor list in Whitemoor.'

'What the *fuck*?'

Manon nods. 'He reckons they were friends.'

343

They are silent for a moment, contemplating this information.

'Edith was visiting him? Voluntarily?' says Harriet.

'Apparently,' says Manon. 'Wilco Bennett, one of the screws at Whitemoor, is sending me his whole file. That'll give us more.'

'What were those calls about, then, in the week before she disappeared? Did Wright tell you?'

Manon has raised her head from the pillow, 'He says, "Och, this 'n' that. How youse doin?"' She has put on an appalling Scots accent, to which Harriet grimaces and says, 'Where's he from, Bangladesh?'

'Anyway, I don't buy it,' says Manon, head back on the pillow. 'I think something was being set up.'

'Like what – a deal? A meeting?'

'Dunno. I think we've been looking at Wright all wrong. We've been assuming he harmed her when I think—'

The door has opened and there is Davy, his expression reserved.

'I'll have to pull him in – Wright, I mean. Question him about this,' says Harriet. 'Anyway, I'll leave you two to it.'

Davy has sat down on the plastic seat beside her bed. 'Brought you these,' he says, handing her garage forecourt flowers in clear cellophane.

'Chrysanthemums,' she says. She raises the bunch to her nose, sniffs. Frowns. The faint whiff of piss. She hates chrysanthemums and has evidently failed to rearrange her face because Davy says, 'Back to your old self so soon.'

'Sorry,' she says. 'Thank you.'

'S'all right. I bought them because I know you don't like them.'

Her face crumples, dissolving in a sudden well of moisture. She didn't think she had any wetness left in her dehydrated walnut of a head. 'I'm so sorry, Davy. I'd never want to hurt you. You of all people, you're the last person I'd ever . . . I'd ever . . .' Childish judders, up and down. 'You're the best copper I know.'

'I'm not though, am I? Always paddling too hard.'

'Not lately,' she says. 'Lately you've seemed quite shirty.'

'I'm weak,' he says.

'No you're not, you're not weak at all. Look at all the things you do for the kids at the centre, giving up your own time, when I say no to Fly at every opportunity. And the guilt you feel over Helena Reed when I can't even look that in the face.'

Her eyes have filled again and she seeks his face. He looks back at her and smiles, as if her tears are apology enough.

'Slept with Chloe last night,' he says, sheepish.

'Oh no,' she says. 'That'll set you back. Comfort shag?'

He nods.

She rests her head back on the pillow and they sit in contemplative silence.

Eventually she whispers, half to herself, 'I should have *fuckwit* tattooed on my forehead.'

'Wouldn't fit,' says Davy.

'Just *twat* then.'

'That'd fit.'

He leans back in his chair. She closes her eyes. She loves a silence with Davy Walker. Some people give good silence, and he is one of them.

'Being walloped really makes you feel low,' she says.

'You're always low.'

'I know, but more so. I feel . . .' and she starts to cry again, looking at the trees beyond her broad hospital window. She realises they have given her this spacious room to herself because she's a police officer.

'I think you need a dog,' Davy says.

'What?'

'I heard a dog makes unhappy people happy. They're good, y'know, for people who can't form proper relationships.'

'You're a real tonic, Davy.'

She lies there as the light fades through her picture window, waiting for the handsome doctor to discharge her, thinking about Edith, about Tony Wright, the sense that he *knew* she was alive. The hospital radio burbles out the news, still leading on the Tilbury Docks container death. Bryony will be up against it on the Abdul-Ghani Khalil evidence, she thinks as her mind begins its descent, merging with the news report; details of the routes driven by his trucks.

She sleeps.

Monday

Manon

The thrum of her printer is almost keeping time with the aching pulse inside her head. Manon is cross-legged on the floor in pyjamas and thick socks, a blanket around her shoulders. Her back is aching, her knees stiff. The room is crepuscular but for the light from an Anglepoise which she has dragged onto the floor; it is interrogating, with its brash light, the sheaves of paper which surround her.

Paper, upon paper, upon paper, and as the printer spews out more, they flutter down, creating more chaos. *Can't get the AV list off of this,* Wilco Bennett's email said, *so I'm just attaching his entire IIS file – all fifteen years of it. Enjoy!*

The Inmate Information System contained everything about the life of a prisoner: personal details, offence, sentence, possibility of parole, relationships, movements (from that spur on that wing to another), case note information, risk assessments, courses taken, activities, paid and unpaid work, breaches of discipline, offender rehabilitation programmes.

Manon crawls across the white sea, leaving her blanket like a worm cast in sand, to where her phone has vibrated.

347

How's the head? I'd bring you lasagne + Nurofen but my trafficking case has proper kicked off. Bri

She's reminded to take more Nurofen, alternating them two-hourly with paracetamol, though the dull ache remains like a background noise. She pads to the kitchen where the chill curls itself about her neck and ankles. And as she tips her head back, swallowing, she wonders what she hopes she'll find delving into Tony Wright's life inside and – also printing out in reams – the 200-page Ministry of Justice report compiled by the CIC with Edith Hind's assistance. 'Staff–prisoner relations in Whitemoor prison' – a vivid portrait of prison life.

The nice doctor discharged her from Addenbrooke's last night and Harriet has forbidden her from coming into the office. 'Don't be a nutter. Stay home. Recuperate. I don't want to see you in before Tuesday at the earliest,' she said.

Back in her twilit lounge, the pages crinkle under her feet. She crosses one foot over the other and lowers to the floor, pulling the blanket around her shoulders and gathering new sheaves to read.

The first three years of a long sentence are the worst, she has learned. New inmates are put on the induction spur on C-wing and are most prone to existential crises; likely to self-harm. Here are men facing fifteen, twenty, twenty-five years in prison without hope of release. They are desperate for meaning, beset by loss. Tony Wright, then in his early forties, was no exception. He cut his arms with razor blades when he could get hold of them, and blades appear to feature widely in Whitemoor.

She shuffles the papers, then glances at her watch. Four p.m. She began reading at ten this morning, but she must have dozed at intervals right here on the floor, the blanket like a cocoon.

Page 20 of Wright's file: *Emotional outbursts. No reduction in Cat A status.* For years he seemed to suffer the most stringent form of incarceration, every emotion deemed 'risk'. Stints in segregation. One suicide attempt. In conversation with his personal officer following this attempt, Tony Wright said, 'I'm spam. I'm meat in a tin.'

Don't laugh, don't look happy, he wrote in a letter home that was confiscated and kept on file, *cos someone is looking at you on a monitor, deciding you're not suffering enough, and that someone is deciding your sentence review.*

Inmate moved to different cell every 28 days, a note on Wright's file states, including strip searches and 'cell turns', to prevent the formation of gang-style relationships. Or any relationships, Manon thinks.

Paracetamol. Cups of tea. At one point she takes a bath. Perhaps she dozes off once or twice. But she comes back to the floor, the puzzle tessellating in white across her carpet.

The CIC report describes a brutalising regime in Whitemoor towards the back end of Wright's sentence. Staff were distant, distrustful; violence endemic. Where previously high security prisons used to function on a known code – a gentlemanly agreement between the old lags and the screws – the modern, multicultural population of Whitemoor was viewed with intense suspicion by its staff. Prison officers were frightened by the growing Muslim population; while outside, in the run-up to a general election, the press and public were growing less liberal by the day. *Prison should be for punishment, not rehabilitation. Offenders, particularly those convicted under the terrorism act, were having an easy ride.* In response to these hard-line views, the Home Secretary cancelled rafts of arts and education courses inside Whitemoor.

Manon looks up. The printer is growling, turning over against itself. A red light flashes. Paper jam.

She gets up, opens the printer's various drawers and flaps, pulls out an inky drum, fingers blackened, then can't jimmy it back in again. She cannot locate the jammed paper. She slaps the flaps shut again, jabs at the button angrily, turns it off, waits, then on again. She roars in frustration when she sees the red light resume its flashing and thinks she might hurl it against the wall. Then she cries. Alan could've fixed it. Alan probably has a laser jet, which never jams because he checked its reviews on *Which?* And he probably keeps spare cartridges in a drawer. No one can help her with the printer jam. She is alone. And all this time they have misunderstood Tony Wright.

Back sitting cross-legged on the floor, she picks up another page of Wright's IIS report. Tony Wright moved to B-wing, to the spur for prisoners on the enhanced level of the incentives and earned privileges scheme. Things seem to be improving for him. In 2005 he gets a job in the library. A note says he keeps his head down – a 'loner'. *Prisoner 518 focused on serving his sentence and leaving prison at the earliest opportunity.* Wright has learned how to make life better for himself, plus he is nearing the end of his sentence, but in the truly repressive conditions of Whitemoor, he is living in a febrile atmosphere. In another confiscated letter, he writes: *I keep my head down. I don't talk to nobody. My personality's out there somewhere, waiting for me to grasp it when I'm out.*

On the same page is a note: *Prisoner reading* Jude the Obscure *by Thomas Hardy. Material confiscated: violent themes.*

Manon wipes the tears from her cheeks.

Along came Edith Hind: listening to him, trying to understand him. Asking how his day was, how his life was, what his plans might be, and whether she could help him. She must've been the first person to treat him like a human being in fifteen years. Even the words, 'Hello, Tony, how are you?' must've been like a long drink to a man dying of thirst.

She looks at her watch. It is 2 a.m. She pulls the blanket more closely about her shoulders, crawls to the last pages spewed by her now-paralysed printer. Page 258 of Tony Wright's IIS file. Inmate returned to C-wing, Cat A status.

Manon is frowning. What has happened to cause a set-back like this?

Prisoner 518 involved in breach of prison discipline during altercation with prisoner 678 in the gym. Sentence review frozen. In light of prisoner 518's involvement in this violent episode, consideration of parole denied until further risk assessment has been carried out.

Who was prisoner 678? Manon pushes at the papers around her on the floor. They slide over each other like water. She leafs, faster and faster, through the white sea, looking for an explanation for this about-turn after a decade of model behaviour. Then she finds it. IIS file page 259: Prisoner 518 statement, transcribed verbatim from a recording of an interview with prison staff, investigating the gym incident, 21 January 2009.

I was workin' out in the gym by myself, runnin' on the treadmill, when Prisoner 678 came and began working the weights next tae me. Dumb bells an' that. We were nice an' quiet, the two of us, no' talkin'. I seen him about but he wisnae ma pal or nothin'. Anyways, a group of prisoners walked into the gym, white guys wi' tatts. Hated the Brotherhood, these guys. Thought the Muslims had too much power. They surrounded the lad next tae me. I'd like tae use his name, no' his number, if ye dinnae mind, because he's a human bein', ye ken?

So this chap, Khalil – Abdul, I think his first name is – he's carrying on nice an' quiet, lifting his weights, but ye could cut the tension w' a knife. He an' I both knew those guys had come in here fer violence, a 'lesson' it's called in here, 'cos there's no cameras in the gym. All the cuttin' and punchin' in Whitemoor happens in the gym.

'Brother Khalil,' one of 'em said to him. Another of them pulled a blade. They held his arms behind his back and cut his throat. Then they walked out.

I was still runnin' on the treadmill – can ye believe that? – an' ma first thought was: There'll be a lock-down now on the wing. Ah need te get ma stuff 'cos they'll be turnin' all the cells after this. That's what this place turned me into. That's how much o' my humanity's been sucked from me in here. An' maybe there's folk'd say I didnae have any humanity to start with, but I had some. Anyways, I remembered maself at that moment, an' I raised the alarm, an' I tried to stop him bleeding to death until the medic got tae us. He's a person. An' I'm a person, ye ken?

Prisoner's sentence review unfrozen and all privileges restored, says Wright's file, in the light of this statement and supporting statement from Prisoner 678 (A-G Khalil).

Manon looks up, dazed. Tony Wright saved Abdul-Ghani Khalil's life.

TUESDAY

MANON

'That you, Manon?'

Her breath catches in her throat to hear that voice. Can it possibly be? Why now? Perhaps she has a sixth sense for Manon's heartbreak. She did when they were little.

'Hello.'

'I'm . . . I'm sorry to ring out of the blue like this.'

'No, no.'

'Is it a bad time?'

'Um, well, I'm at work, in the toilets, actually. You might hear the echo.'

She pulls at some of the rough oblong towels, jabs at the tears at the rim of her eye and a corner of the towel pokes her eyeball. She bends over double, blinking and rubbing. The phone is heating up her ear as if it's radioactive.

It wasn't just that Ellie's truce with Una had been a treachery too far; their rift was the calcification of years of rivalry, layers of it hardening into silence over time. Small injuries, gathering; some success Ellie had at work, which Manon couldn't swallow; or a fabulous boyfriend; or even just a nice

353

holiday she didn't want to hear about. They stopped calling and then, much sooner than Manon expected, it became too hard to call. Their mother would have banged their heads together: 'I don't care about any awkwardness' and 'Get over yourselves, for God's sake', which would only have made it worse. But their mother is dead, their father all the way in Scotland, which might as well be Canada, Una having subsumed him like some mollusc who crept over the top of him until he disappeared.

'How've you been?' says Ellie.

'Oh, you know . . .'

'No. I don't. It's been three years.'

'And that's my fault, is it?'

Ellie sighs. 'It doesn't matter, does it? I'm ringing to tell you something important. I've had a baby. A boy. He's three months now. Solomon. Well, we call him Solly.'

'A baby? You've had a baby?' The blood drains from Manon's head. She nods distractedly at Kim, who is edging into a toilet cubicle. 'Are you . . . Where are you living?'

'In London. Kilburn.'

'Wow. That's . . . terrific news.'

'Yes. I wanted you to know, Manon. In case you . . . Well, perhaps you'll come up some time. Meet your nephew.'

She pictures herself the prickly pear, lonely visitor to the pink paradise of family life in Kilburn. The park and the swings and Sunday roasts so newly lost to her. Wrinkled aunt.

'Well, it's quite busy in MIT right now.'

'Yes, of course. Must be. You must be a DCI by now.'

'Not quite.'

'I better go. Solly's waking up. We've got Baby Bounce at the library this afternoon.'

Manon is so jealous she cannot speak. Envy is physical, the

sensation of it: difficulty swallowing, a pain around the temples, panic, and wanting to flee the source.

'OK, well, nice to talk to you,' she says. 'Bye.'

She takes more towels from the dispenser, knowing the tears will come again. Oh, but she loves Ellie, loves her so deeply, and now they have come to this – the slights embedding themselves into wounds and no one to knock their heads together except their better selves, which seem always to be in abeyance, held hostage by meaner feelings. On top of her jealousy, in a nauseous wave, comes guilt. My sister with a baby and no mother to help. My sister who I love, my love killed by jealousy. My sister who I hate for having everything I haven't got. It is impossible to be Manon Bradshaw.

Everything is broken and she starts to cry, as Kim emerges from her cubicle to the sounds of a fulsome flush. Did Kim hear the word 'unimaginative' at Cromwell's on Friday? Or is Manon blanching just at the thought?

They nod at each other silently, neither mentioning Manon's tears nor her outburst in the bar.

Back at her desk, she calls Will Carter on the landline.

'When did Edith first toy with the idea of criminology?'

'Summer 2009. After we graduated, none of us – well, practically none of us – knew what to do next. She decided to do a kind of work experience with the CIC – these interviews in Whitemoor – to see if it would be something she'd like to take to postgrad level. I remember she was incredibly excited about that first visit to the prison, full of zeal about reform and education, ideas about teaching a prison course in feminist literature to make rapists explore the female experience.'

'She talk much about Tony Wright?'

'No, she never mentioned anyone by name. I think the

visits ended almost as quickly as they began. I just remember that after a couple of trips to Whitemoor with the CIC, she became really demoralised. Said it was one of the saddest places she'd ever been in. No one treating anyone with a shred of humanity. And all these prisoners without hope and with nothing to do. She said it smelled of cabbage and bleach. She told me there was no interest in rehabilitation in prison. Just overcrowding, lack of money, and the problem of housing this jostling, violent pack of men who the state felt were uncontainable. She went to see Graham Garfield soon after and switched to an English PhD.'

'So you weren't aware of an ongoing relationship with Tony Wright? That Edith was visiting him?'

'No,' he says softly.

'One more question, Will. Abdul-Ghani Khalil – do you know the name?'

'The guy who's just been arrested? The body in the container at Tilbury Docks? Of course, he's all over the news.'

'I wondered if Edith might have mentioned him to you.'

He is laughing.

'Something funny, Mr Carter?'

'You think she was part of a human trafficking ring? Nothing would surprise me about Edith any more.' He sighs. 'Look, I don't know if she knew Abdul-Ghani whatever his name is. But I didn't really know her at all, did I?'

No, you didn't, Manon thinks, but her mind is snagged by the ringing of her replacement BlackBerry, which is scuttling across the desk with each vibration. 'I'm going to have to go, Will, I've got another call coming in. Talk soon.' She puts down the landline, picks up the mobile. 'DS Manon Bradshaw,' she says.

'It's DI Haverstock – remember me? Havers, Kilburn CID.'

'Right, yeah, hi,' she says, her voice a swell of impatience. She wants to interrogate the Wright–Khalil line, see whether it leads to Edith. She doesn't want distractions.

'I've got something on Taylor Dent,' Havers is saying. 'Turns out he had a second phone – for his various business dealings. We arrested one of his associates and he told us about it, gave us the number. Anyway, we've got all the data off it and there's a voicemail you might want to listen to. We haven't got a clue who it is, to be honest, so I'm forwarding it to people who might, even though it's a long shot. Or would you rather I contact team two about this?'

'No, no, I can look at it,' she says, simultaneously typing into the police database. 'Email the audio file over. M_Bradshaw@pcn.co.uk. Thanks.' Then she throws her BlackBerry across the desk.

She pulls up the call data taken off Tony Wright's phone after his arrest, highlights the numbers he called after speaking to Edith Hind – most of them dirty phones, PAYG, unregistered, no records attached.

She tries Bryony's mobile but it goes straight to voicemail.

Need to speak to you urgently. Call me. M

Can't. Massively up against it. Later.

No, Bri. It's urgent. CALL ME.

'What?' says Bri. 'Can't this wait?'
'No, it can't. Are you sitting in front of the Khalil file?'
'I'm *always* sitting in front of the Khalil file. I've started calling my kids Abdul and Ghani.'
'I just want to run these numbers past you. Ready?'

357

'What's this about?'

'Tell you in a sec. Ready? Unknown-638.'

Silence as Bryony types into the HOLMES system.

'Nope.'

'OK, unknown-422.'

'Nope,' says Bryony. 'Oh wait, hang on. Yes. That's one of his. Well, one of his associates, who basically relayed messages to him.'

'Bingo,' says Manon. 'Fucking love you, Bri.'

'What? Tell me. What's this about?'

'Tony Wright made contact with Khalil shortly after speaking to Edith Hind. Khalil and Wright knew each other in Whitemoor. One more thing, Bri. Khalil was trafficking people through ports. Dover, Folkestone, Tilbury Docks.'

'That's right – goods containers and trucks boarding P&O Ferries mainly.'

'And was he taking people the other way?'

'What, you mean *out* of the country? Khalil would take anyone anywhere if the money was right. I *think* – and don't quote me on this – that there's always a drip feed the other way. Y'know, people going back, thinking the Continent might offer a better deal, but border control couldn't care less about that flow so we don't investigate it. Listen, hon, I've really got to go.'

'Just one more thing,' Manon says. 'His drop-offs and pickups – did he operate in Cambridgeshire?'

'Yup,' says Bryony. 'All up and down the eastern coastline – out of Felixstowe, across to the M11, down through Maidstone, and out of Dover. Should we be interrogating Khalil on this, asking if he knows anything about the Hind girl?'

'Not yet,' says Manon. 'Gimme a bit more time.'

'Right, look, I've really got to—'

'Yes, yes, sorry. Thanks, love. Bye.' Manon lays her phone down on the desk.

Her email box says one new message. She puts her head-phones on and listens to the audio file.

After a sprint around MIT, she locates Harriet in Stanton's office, sunken-eyed, clicking about at the computer. Manon is panting so hard, she almost can't get the words out. Harriet looks up.

'What is it?'

Is this a panic attack? Why won't her words come out?

'What, Manon? *Speak.*'

'Audio file,' she gasps. 'Audio file.' She is pointing at the computer.

Harriet opens up the email Manon has forwarded to her inbox and plays the audio file. She and Manon do not take their eyes off each other. The voice – patrician, superior, commanding. *'Meet me at the usual place.'*

'It's him,' says Harriet.

'I know,' says Manon.

'It's fucking him,' Harriet says. 'What date was this recorded?'

'Sunday eleventh of December.'

'Right, I'm authorising an ANPR trace on his plates on Sunday eleventh of December. We need to link this Dent number back to him. I'll bet he wasn't using his normal mobile to make that call, so it'll be a PAYG, paid for in cash. Let's get a date and location for its purchase – Hampstead High Street, I'll put money on it – and let's get our voice experts matching this recording with the recordings of our interviews with him.'

'Shouldn't we run it past Stanton—'

'Fuck Stanton.'

WEDNESDAY

MANON

She and Harriet have been shown into a waiting room that resembles a lounge in a country house hotel. Two leather Chesterfield sofas face each other across a Persian rug. The smell of brewing coffee. On a polished coffee table are arranged copies of *Country Life* magazine and *Homes & Gardens*, and a generous vase of flowers. Around the corners of the room, large lamps are lit.

'Officers,' says Ian Hind, coming out from his room and bringing with him the haste of the busy professional. 'What a surprise. Do you have an update for us? Wouldn't it be best to talk at home with Miriam?'

'Is there somewhere we could speak in private?' asks Harriet.

'Yes, of course. Rosemary,' he says, peering out to where his receptionist sits at a desk in the lobby, 'no interruptions, all right? Do come through.'

He shows them into another stately room where he takes up a seat in a leather chair beside his desk.

Harriet and Manon remain standing.

'Sir Ian,' says Harriet, 'I wonder if you could tell us where you were on the night of Sunday eleventh of December.'

'The eleventh of December? Well, now, that's two months ago. I'd have to consult my diaries, ask Miriam. Off the top of my head, I have absolutely no idea. At home, probably. I usually am on a Sunday night.'

'You see, our cameras have snapshots of your car driving up the M11 towards East Anglia that night, in the direction of March, where your country house is.'

He taps the steeple of his fingers a couple of times, turns his mouth down, looks at them blankly, as if in confusion.

'Yes, yes, that's right – I popped to Deeping. There were maintenance issues to do with the house—'

'Which you forgot to mention.'

'I can barely remember making the trip, to be perfectly honest with you, but now that you mention it . . .' He gives them a condescending smile. Then looks at his watch. 'Is there a significance to this, because I have a patient in ten minutes and I must look over their notes.'

'One more thing, Sir Ian,' says Harriet. 'You have stated that you didn't know Taylor Dent.'

'That's right.'

'And yet you left a voicemail message on his phone saying, "Meet me in the usual place," on the eleventh of December, which was the date on which he was last seen.'

'I'm sorry, what message?'

'Here, I'll play it for you,' Manon says, opening an email on her smart phone and playing the sound file.

'*Meet me. At the usual place.*'

There is silence as the three of them listen, Hind looking at the surface of his desk, Harriet and Manon scrutinising his face. He appears to be making a decision.

'You can't prove that's me,' he says.

'Actually, we have traced the phone. It was purchased by you from Phones 4u on Hampstead High Street on fifteenth of July 2010. We've got a positive ID from the cashier,' says Harriet.

'Look,' he says, 'I want to give the police absolute assistance in finding my daughter, I really do. I was talking to Rog about it only the other day – Roger Galloway, I mean. I was at the Commons and I told Roger how talented I felt the Cambridgeshire team was – you in particular, DI Harper – and that if he was looking at fast-tracking female officers—'

'Ian Hind, I am arresting you on suspicion of the murder of Taylor Dent—'

'Just a minute, detective,' he says, sitting upright. 'Let's not get ahead of ourselves. I'm sure we can come to a mutually beneficial arrangement without all that caution business.'

'You do not have to say anything. But it may harm your defence—'

'One call to Roger and you could move up the ranks very quickly indeed, smart pair like you. He's always saying he wants to see more women in the force.'

'He should stop promoting men, then,' says Manon.

Harriet sighs heavily. 'If you do not mention when questioned something which you later rely on in court. Anything you do say may be given in evidence. Do you understand?'

'I can bury you too, you know.'

'Do you know where Edith is?' asks Harriet.

'God, no, of course not. Look, can we all sit, just for a moment?' he asks.

They nod and sit opposite him on the metal-framed chairs reserved for patients.

'I am not a bad man,' he says. 'It was all sort of an accident. He was blackmailing me, you see.'

362

'We would advise you to have a lawyer present before you go any further,' says Harriet.

'Yes, of course. Can I ask one thing? Don't tell Rosemary outside. There's no need to cuff me or anything, is there?'

'No, we can walk out together.'

In an interview room at Kilburn station, after many hours with an expensive solicitor present, Sir Ian Hind signs a statement.

I met Taylor Dent six months previously, in June 2010. He was working on a building site opposite my home and he would catch my eye as I left the house, smile at me, bare-chested in the heat. I found myself attracted to him. I've been happily married for twenty-five years, but over the years I have had occasional sexual encounters with men. All very transactional – in the showers at the gym, that sort of thing. They were infrequent and never a relationship of any sort. My family are everything to me.

The encounters with Taylor were different. He awakened in me feelings I had last experienced at school. Up to this point, I had managed to compartmentalise my encounters with men from my life as a loving husband and father. But with Taylor, for the first time, something was building. We began meeting on Hampstead Heath. I didn't want Miriam finding out so I bought a pay-as-you-go phone for the sole purposes of contacting him. I told myself it would soon be over – I would give him up, like a bad addiction – and life would return to normal. Yet I couldn't stop. It was more than just the sex, for me at least.

Taylor started asking me for money. It was never explicit, what I was paying for. I would tell him I wanted to help him when we met, give him £50 usually, then it went up to £100 as he became more confident about the relationship. He was asking for money for specific things, trainers for his younger brother, that kind of thing. Then he asked if I had access to drugs at the surgery – he wanted ketamine and barbiturates. I assume he wanted to sell them on the street. I began to supply him with very small amounts, and on one occasion in late September, we took some ketamine together. The drugs made it easier for me to engage in . . . the things we were engaging in . . . the dangerous, illicit things about which I was generally inhibited.

I realised I was slipping into a lifestyle I didn't even recognise, one which threatened everything I had – my work, my family, my marriage. I told him I wanted to stop meeting, that I'd had enough. I wanted my life back, unsullied, but I suppose he'd become dependent on my money and the supply of prescription drugs.

Towards the end of November, he threatened me. He started to tell me details about my family to prove how much he knew. He said he'd tell Edith and Rollo and Miriam what I was – what I'd been doing on the Heath with him. He wanted £10,000 to keep quiet and to go away forever. I agreed to give it to him, that's why I left that message. I agreed to hand over the money on the evening of Sunday eleventh of December. I wanted to pay him off, told myself I was going to resolve this issue once and for all and then we could relax, I could enjoy Christmas with my family.

[Suspect breaks down in tears. Interview suspended.]

I got the money together and I also took some ketamine with me, as I had often done, to the Heath. I want to be clear: my only intention was to give him what he wanted and to start anew. I felt Taylor was a good person, and that what we'd engaged in had affection in it. I know that sounds naive, given that he was blackmailing me, but I felt he would take this money and that would be an end to it.

He was so manic – so bright-eyed, so excited. This was going to change everything for him, he said, this sum of money. He had a younger brother, as I said, and he told me this was going to make his life different. It began to feel as if Taylor was glorying over me, and that he was happy our relationship was at an end.

I told him I had the £10,000 he wanted in the boot of my car and a little something else he might enjoy. I was parked behind Jack Straw's Castle. He came with me to the car, I handed him the bag of money and he took, by way of celebration, quite a powerful shot of ketamine from me. Then he told me that what we had been doing repulsed him – that he was glad it was over. 'Don't have to do that disgusting shit no more,' he said. He looked at me with revulsion and I saw it was all about the money for him.

[Suspect breaks down again. Interview halted for several minutes.]

I saw myself, tiny and humiliated. He never loved me; he never even *liked* me. I revolted him, and all the things we'd done. Something came over me, some powerlessness which transmitted itself into pure rage. I've never felt so white hot with anger before. I pushed him into the open boot of the car and slammed its door down on him. I got in the car and started to drive, no idea where, just anywhere. I found myself travelling the route to Deeping, which is like second nature to me. It was as if the car was driving itself. You know what it's like when a route is embedded in your brain – you can find yourself following it while your mind is entirely elsewhere. Before I knew it, I was on the M11. On that journey I thought: I can drive him out of London and leave him stranded, without the money. Ketamine is a potent analgesic – it causes sedation and amnesia while maintaining cardio-vascular stability. He would be lost. And he would forget.

When I got to Deeping, I opened the boot and he was unconscious but alive, I checked. Ketamine, as I said, is an anaesthetic: it leaves you dissociated, feeling as if you have no control over your legs or any movement at all. I went into the house and put the bag of money into an upstairs bedroom; I don't know why, to put it somewhere safe, out of his reach, I suppose. I thought I would return to get it later.

After putting the bag in the bottom of the wardrobe, I returned to the boot. I felt in his pockets to retrieve his mobile phone. I knew the phone could incriminate me, in terms of contact between myself and the boy – nothing else, you understand, just contact – and I was also taking away his means of getting help. I wanted him to take a long time getting home.

I got back in the car and drove along a dirt track – it was incredibly muddy – which runs across our land and over into the neighbouring farm. I stopped in a wood beside a river and hauled him out of the boot and left him there, semi-conscious, on the ground, about ten feet from the water's edge. I did not put him in a river or drown him or cause his death. He must have come round, groggy, stumbled about and fallen into the river later.

A week after that awful night, we were informed of Edith's disappearance. I was horrified; I still am horrified. I love my family. I would never do anything to hurt them. I know nothing of what's happened to my daughter and I am desperate to get her back.

In my haste to get back to Miriam that night – the night with Taylor Dent – I left the money in the bedroom at Deeping. When officers went to search the house, after Edith disappeared, I was sure they'd find it and ask what I was doing with £10,000 stashed in a plastic bag in the bottom of a wardrobe. I had a plan to tell them (and Miriam) that I was paying cash for some building work to Deeping and that's why the money was there. I waited and waited but no mention of the money ever came. Of course, I couldn't bring it up, or ask what had been found at Deeping; it would have raised too much suspicion.

THURSDAY

MIRIAM

Some people will see it as running away but what do they know of all she's been through? A day can feel like a year. The minutes vibrate like dying wasps. Even the seconds are shuddering, giving up as they fizzle towards a strange, unnatural calm – as if petrifaction is taking place. This might be running away yet it is so much more than that.

She waits at the baggage carousel which is sparsely dotted with business-style cases, the type that resemble a shoe box on wheels. Executive luggage going round and round in La Rochelle arrivals. It's a strange hangar-like space, which in August throngs with pink Britons hauling folded prams off the rubber belt, sweating mothers and fathers carrying toddlers and more weight than they'd like, burgundy passports at the ready. She and Ian had been among them, all those years ago. Rollo in tears over something or other, wanting to ride in the trolley perhaps; Edie perched on the metal edge of the carousel reading, as usual. Ian scanning the belt through the jostling crowd for their motley collection of bags. But this is January, blown about by rough winds and

368

only a smattering of passengers – the odd French businessman, eager to get outside and light a Gauloise.

The sky is filled with voluminous cloud which seem to boil
up over the flat Vendée countryside. She drives under a canopy
of trees, out of Fontenay-le-Comte, the roads smooth and
empty. This is a spacious country. She is relieved to be away
from tight little England and the reporting of Ian's arrest. Soon
there would be the prying do-gooders; friends letting out the
rope. Yes, it is a relief to be in this empty land where no one
knows who she is, much less cares about the depravities of her
husband. Former husband, she should begin to think of him
but can't. She should have known, that's what she returns to
again and again: *she should have known.* When DS Bradshaw
rang on her door last night, Miriam experienced the slowing
of time, like déjà vu. The detective stepping inside the front
door, saying Ian had been arrested on suspicion of murder,
seemed like a repetition of an event which had already
happened, time on a loop, elongated like a stretched rubber
band. She nodded, giving the outward appearance of having
taken in what DS Bradshaw was telling her, but Miriam felt as
if she were below the surface – perhaps of a lake – the sounds
slow and lugubrious. Thoughts not keeping pace, quite.

She went to Ian's study, felt about in the desk drawer for
the Nokia phone, the one with the child's pirate stickers all
over it, which should have rung alarm bells when she first
discovered it but didn't, she supposed, because Miriam had
silenced them. You hear what you want to hear. See what you
want to see. The phone wasn't there, of course. She felt about,
instead, for keys to the safety deposit box they kept behind the
books in the lounge. You could always find the green metal
box behind *Gray's Anatomy.*

'Are you all right?' DS Bradshaw asked, watching her with

a look of intense concern. 'You seem . . . calm. Can I help you with something?' she said, confused as to what Miriam was doing pulling books from the shelves.

At last, she unlocked the box and there it was – the phone, among some foreign currency and a Rolex given to Ian by the Sultan of Brunei. He hadn't tried very hard to hide it.

'I imagine you'll be needing this,' Miriam said, handing the phone to the detective.

'Thank you,' she said.

'Is it the boy's?' Miriam asked.

'I don't know. Possibly.' DS Bradshaw studied Miriam's face, then added, 'There's something else I need to talk to you about.'

The detective told Miriam she thought Edith was alive – 'I don't say that lightly, Lady Hind' – that she may have been smuggled to France by a man called Abdul-Ghani Khalil.

'The Tilbury Docks case, the murder,' Miriam said.

The detective said she thought Edith had been put in contact with Khalil by Tony Wright; that the phone calls between Edith and Wright had been to establish a pick-up point on one of the motorways outside Huntingdon. Wright would have known how to avoid the CCTV cameras; Khalil would have known how to get her across the border without detection.

'But *why*?' Miriam asked.

'People want to disappear all the time. Commonest thing there is. Can you think of somewhere in France she might have gone? To hide?'

Miriam's mind felt about among her memories, like her hand patting in the central desk drawer, as she processed the idea. 'Possibly. I don't know.'

'I need you to give me a list of places she would know – places you've been on holiday where there might be a connection for Edith – so that we can inform Interpol.'

370

'Let me go,' Miriam blurted, and she held the detective's gaze as intensely as she was able. 'Let me go, please.'

'I'm sorry, I—'

'I'm just asking you to delay, that's all. Hold back, give me some time. A day or two, that's all. I have an idea, but I might be wrong. Let me go and see if I can find her, coax her back. Our family's been through enough, don't you see?' She was holding the detective's arms, squeezing them, not letting her look away.

'I can't delay Interpol,' the detective said, 'but they'll be fairly ineffective without strong leads – a place to start, I mean. France is a big country. You'll have a head start if you don't delay, but I should warn you, my DI knows about the Wright–Khalil connection. They'll be interrogating Khalil on this. He might put a pin in the map for them.'

Miriam nodded. 'I understand,' then led the way to the front door and closed it on the sergeant. Then she sank down to the coir matting in a puddle, her cheek on its coarse weave, smelling the boot dust and feeling the freezing winter air roar in under the door's brush strip. She went to bed soon after; her paralysis at war with the urging of the detective to make haste.

Lying in the bedroom, the dancing light playing through a chink in the curtains, she replayed the years of her marriage as if running a cine film in her mind. Did he ever want us? A wife and children? All the holidays – was he trapped, restless in every one? All the times he'd gone away for a conference or to play badminton with Roger. All their tendernesses, their various strains. The arguments and the reparation. She ran them all through a new filter, like a computer program adjusting the figures. She observed, and observed again, as if she might make the oscillation settle.

371

She cried, as the evening melded into night; cried then became still – cataplectic, almost. When she finally drifted off to sleep, the cine film began again, searching for clues in the crackling faded images of family life.

In the morning she heaved a suitcase down the stairs, Rollo's perplexed expression looking up at her.

'I'm sorry to leave you with all this,' she said.

'Where are you going?'

'I can't tell you.'

'Well, can I come with you?'

'No,' she said, her palm to his cheek. 'Darling Rollo. You must stay here. Go and visit him in prison. He needs you.'

The road down into Vouvant winds beneath trees in leaf, past Monsieur Ripaud's riding stables, where Edith had gone on her first hack through the Forêt de Mervent without, Miriam had been horrified to learn from Ian, a helmet.

'Where do you think we get the phrase *laissez-faire* from?' he'd teased, bringing out the smelly cheeses which had filled the fridge of their holiday gîte with a sharp odour. 'She survived, didn't you, Edie?'

'Ew, socks!' Rollo yelled, whenever the fridge door opened and the smell hit him.

It was the summer Edith seemed to discover passion after passion – reading and horses, primarily – subsisting on a diet of French bread (soft white pillows torn from the middle) and peaches, which leaked rivulets of juice down her chin and onto her top. She hadn't wanted Miriam to wash the trousers she rode in because they smelled of Artur, the horse she now ardently loved.

Miriam drives the car up the steep incline to the car park, in the shadow of the medieval Melusine tower. She pulls her coat from the back seat. The wind roars through the trees as she walks to the wall at the edge of the car park, peering over to the distant water below. Gusts stipple its surface into hurrying slicks like scales. She pulls the coat tightly around her and turns towards the bar-tabac, where a carousel of postcards looks as if it might keel over in the wind.

'*Une Anglaise?*' says the man behind the bar. '*Elles sont partout.*'

'*Oui, mais une Anglaise qui habite ici?*' says Miriam. '*Il y a depuis quelques mois?*' She's fumbling about for idioms, like rummaging in an old suitcase. The words are there, but not necessarily in the right order.

'*Bof,*' he says, turning down the corners of his mouth. '*'sais pas.*'

Miriam orders a coffee and surveys the room – a dark space with an enormous television bracketed to the wall, showing some sport or other with periodic cheers. A smattering of people, mostly watching the TV. She decides to take a table outside, despite the cold wind.

She holds down the flapping page of the guide book she has purchased at Stansted for the purposes of finding accommodation, as the barman sets down her cup and saucer. Her leather-gloved hand rests on a page titled: *The Legend of Melusine.*

According to the story, Melusine is said to have murdered her father and, as punishment for this, the lower half of her body was changed to that of a serpent every Saturday evening. Not long after, she met Raymond of Poitou and when he asked to marry her, she agreed on condition that he would never gaze upon her on a Saturday evening. Everything was fine for several years and the couple lived in the château at Vouvant, but one night he broke the promise and saw her in the form of part-woman, part-serpent.

Typical view of female sexuality, Miriam thinks. Serpent indeed. She looks up to see a group of cyclists, just beyond the cluster of outside tables, in full professional gear – Lycra leggings, cycling gloves, streamlined helmets, and wraparound mirrored sunglasses which give them the silvered look of houseflies.

When, during a disagreement, Raymond called Melusine a 'serpent' in front of the court, she assumed the form of a dragon and flew off, never to be seen again.

'*Excusez-moi,*' says a man's voice, and Miriam looks up from her reading. He says he heard her in the bar, asking about a girl – *une Anglaise* – and from his rapid French, she gleans he knows of one.

'*Jeune?*' Miriam asks, squinting up at him, a hand over her brow.

'*Oui, eh bien, dans la vingtaine je suppose,*' he says. *In her twenties.* His directions come in a rush that she tries very hard to follow: '*Tout droit, à gauche, en bas, par la rivière.*'

She is discombobulated. She hadn't quite expected this journey to yield fruit. A flight away from the chaos in England; a pilgrimage into her family's past, yes. But might Edith *actually* be here?

Miriam hastens in the direction in which he has pointed, walking in the shadow of the shops, past the fruit and vegetable shop, and the green-gloss pharmacie, around the corner to the Place de l'Eglise, past the mairie, stuck with a limp French flag, and opposite it, Vouvant's twelfth-century church, broad steps leading up to twin arches.

She can't unravel any of the man's directions from here, and as she turns, examining each possible route, she notices an elderly woman carrying laden bags, who is walking slowly with a rolling gait. The woman is breathless with the exertion as Miriam approaches her.

'*Rivière?*' Miriam asks, pointing down one of the alleys off the Place de l'Eglise.

The woman nods. '*Oui, en bas,*' she says.

EDITH

A day of sharp sun, so beautiful I'm taken with the idea of opening up the tall windows in the bedroom. I spread them wide, setting a cushion on the Juliet balcony, thinking of Lucy Honeychurch opening her shutters at the Pension Bertolini.

The sun cooks my face but the breeze is still fresh, so I'm wrapped in my thickest cardigan. My coatigan. I fetch my copy of *Jane Eyre* but I don't read. I look out instead, calm for the first time in more than five weeks, perhaps because I haven't done my Internet searches today. Head back against the window frame, eyes closed, my eyelids glowing red with the brightness, I hear the patter-pat of shoes in the alley below.

Slowly I straighten, squinting, to see the top of a head beyond the wall. Grey hair. Something familiar about it, then a face upturned and her eyes meet mine, and I am stabbed by familiarity and the shock of love. Beloved face. I drop *Jane Eyre* and it falls from the balcony like a shot bird.

I launch haphazardly into the dark interior of the flat, pummelling down the stairs to open the door to her. What is she doing here? How much will she hate me for what I have done? How much does she know, and how, oh *how on earth* will I tell her? The secrets I have harboured; the secrets that will destroy her. The secrets I have been running from for five long weeks.

I unbolt the door and there is her ashen, accusatory face and she has aged ten years since I last saw her. *My fault.*

'How could you?' she growls.

'Mum, I . . . I can explain. I can, Mum,' I say. 'You don't understand . . .' But my words are stuck. 'I never wanted to hurt you . . .'

'How *could* you?'

'There are so many things you don't know,' I cry. I cannot gather myself, cannot prevent myself crumpling into a child's anguish.

'I thought you were *dead*,' she says. Her eyes red-rimmed, now brimming, her forehead furrowed with disbelief and anger. There is nothing worse than seeing your mother cry and being the cause.

'Come in,' I say, and I pull her towards me, take her in my arms, and she emits a cry of pain, her body heaving into mine. Her shouts, animalistic, are embarrassingly loud, bouncing off the alley walls. 'Come in,' I say. 'I'll make you some tea. I can explain, I can explain why . . .'

She snivels, reaches into her bag for a tissue, and wipes the wetness from her eyes and nose.

I lead her up the dark stairs to my apartment, wondering where I can begin. Explaining my disappearance means telling her things about our family that she shouldn't have to know. I don't know where I can start without hurting her, but I have hurt her already. I bring her into the lounge, take her handbag gently from her and lay it on the sofa, then guide her to a seated position.

'I don't know how to tell you,' I say. I pace. I cannot look at her. She is looking up at me like an expectant child. 'I know things, I saw things—'

'He's been arrested,' she blurts. 'You don't know, do you? Your father was arrested yesterday for the murder of Taylor Dent.'

I stare at her. It doesn't have to come from me, like some malicious lie I've made up; some perverse thing I've imagined to cause her pain. I don't have to be the one to break it and yet I wish he hadn't been caught. I wish she didn't know; that he had got away with it, that they could still be together, and that I could have paid the price instead.

'Taylor Dent? Was that his name?' I whisper. 'I didn't know.'

'You saw,' she says. 'You saw it happen, at Deeping.'

I nod, both of us now in a quiet daze.

'I still don't understand,' she says. 'Why run? Why did you want us to think you were dead?'

'I didn't!' It comes out hysterical, and I am losing myself again. I want to tell the truth but I don't know if I can. 'I didn't, I didn't, I didn't!' I am shouting and pacing. 'I wanted to disappear. I wanted the ground to swallow me up. I couldn't keep his secret and I couldn't turn him in. I couldn't go back to Will and I couldn't face Helena either.'

'Helena—'

'I know,' I wail, fists to my stomach. 'Helena, oh Helena.' It comes out of my belly like fire, my guilt, my sorrow. How much I am responsible for. 'She's dead and it's my fault. You don't have to tell me, Mum. You don't have to show me what I've done, what a mess I've made. I *know*.'

'Edie,' she says gently. 'Edie, calm down. Come sit.'

We light a fire. We gingerly hold cups of fennel tea, as if they might break. They warm our hands and we lean into one another, staring at the flames as they crackle and dance. She is sitting with her knees together, more formal than me. My legs are curled beside me. There has been a lot of silence, the two of us allowing ourselves to exhale.

She is wearing a shirt with a navy William Morris design, swirling leaves and seed pods. My head is leaning on her shoulder. I stare at the pattern on the fabric, the pendant which nestles in the soft wrinkles of her chest. I am moved by her fastidiousness; how smart she looks. Her rings gleam on her fingers, but the skin on her hands is reptilian and her face is dragged downwards with sorrow and exhaustion. My poor mum. My tears fall again, and she kisses the top of my head.

'Can you tell me what happened?' she asks.

'I went to Deeping on a Sunday, early December, it was. In the afternoon. Got there about three – it was still light. I needed somewhere to think, away from Will. I was thinking about splitting up with him.' I look up into her face. 'You knew that, didn't you, Mum? I think you had an inkling that I was going to end it with him. Things had started with Helena, confusing stuff, and I didn't know if they were a symptom of wanting to leave Will, or whether it was the start of something real with her – you know? I was really confused about it all, needed some headspace, away from both of them.

'I'd more or less decided to sleep there. I was lying on your bed – you know how I love it in your bed. It started to get dark and I fell asleep. I woke to clattering sounds downstairs. The house was pitch dark by now and I sleepily thought: "Ah, Mum and Dad are here." But then I snapped awake. I'd spoken to you – remember? – and you told me you were staying home that weekend. Dad had too much work on so you weren't coming to Deeping. I froze, thinking it must be an intruder moving around downstairs. We're so lax about security at

Deeping. I'd locked the front door on arrival – I'm always nervous being in the countryside by myself – but all the same, that key in the porch . . .

'There were footsteps coming up the stairs. My heart was pounding; I was terrified. I slipped off the bed and climbed inside your wardrobe, pulling the door closed and your clothes in front of my face. The intruder came into the room, right up to the wardrobe. I thought I was dead, but he pulled the drawer at the bottom and shoved something into it. I stayed there, cowering, as the footsteps receded. I heard more clattering downstairs, then the front door closed. I crept out of the wardrobe and onto the window seat. The sensor light had come on with his movement and I saw Dad open the boot of his car. I saw a body in the boot – a boy—'

'Taylor Dent,' says Miriam sadly.

'I didn't know his name. I've tried to find out since then – I've Googled missing people and murders in East Anglia – but there's been nothing about a black boy killed in or near March. His death seemed to go unreported.'

'Unlike yours,' said Miriam.

'Yes,' I say, sitting upright. 'In the weeks that followed, I was everywhere, but there was no mention of him.' I slouch back down, against her shoulder. It is easier to tell her my story if I don't look into her face. 'I watched from the upstairs window. I was shaking. I mean, you don't put someone in a boot unless you're doing wrong by them. The boot is where you put animals, not people.'

'Hadn't he seen your car?'

'I parked right at the end of the carport. You know how short the G-Wiz is – he can't have seen it from the drive. My heart was thudding. I knew it was really bad – a boy in the boot. Dad was going through his pockets and the boy's body

380

was rocking, unconscious or dead. He searched until he found something I couldn't see – a phone or a wallet – which he put in his own pocket. My mind was racing, thinking, why does someone go through a boy's pockets – a boy who's unconscious or dead? There was no explanation except the worst explanation.

'Before I could run down to him, demand an explanation, the doors of the car had slammed shut and he had driven away. I went to the drawer at the bottom of the wardrobe to see what he'd stashed there. It was piles and piles of money, bound together with rubber bands in a plastic bag.'

'So you took the cash?' she says. I nod and she smiles wanly, saying, 'At least it stayed in the family.'

'I thought about all the things I could do: return to George Street and Will; pretend I hadn't seen anything; tell the police what I'd seen; tell you; go to Helena. And not one of them seemed possible. I was butting up against each option and it was like being in a dodgem car, hitting the buffers. I thought about flying to Buenos Aires to find Rollo, and then I thought about telling him. The awfulness. Then I wondered if anyone would believe me. I wondered if I would seem mad, the destroyer of our family life. I wondered if in fact I *had* gone mad, and all of it was an apparition, that I should be sectioned. I looked at the money and I thought about disappearing. And it made sense. All I knew, Mum, you have to believe me, was that I wanted to run. My only impulse was to disappear, not to hurt you.'

'But you did hurt me. You hurt me very deeply, Edith.'

'I couldn't bear knowing something that would destroy you, I didn't want to keep his secrets but I didn't want to betray him either. I couldn't go back to Will and I couldn't bear Helena, the confusion of that. I was trapped, d'you see? When

381

I looked at the money he'd left, I knew that was my way of disappearing. Money could make it happen. I could vanish, I knew people who could help me—'

'What people?'

I get up. I can't look at her. 'Another tea?' I say, taking the cup from her hand.

'What people, Edith?' she says.

'Never mind that. You don't need to know what people. That money could make me vanish, as if the ground had opened up, and that's what I wanted.'

I come back into the room with two steaming hot mugs. 'What's happened to him? Where are they keeping him?' I ask.

'He's in Littlehey. Rollo will visit. We've instructed lawyers at Kingsley Napley.'

'Is he all right?'

'I haven't seen him,' she says, and I can see the torment written on her face. 'I will though.' She looks up. 'I will see him. He's still my husband.'

Her look is defiant and I stare at her. 'After everything he's done . . .' I begin.

She frowns. 'I won't explain myself to you, Edith,' she says. 'I won't justify how I feel to *you*.'

We are silent again, but it is not a comfortable silence.

MIRIAM

Saying it to Edith is the first time she has allowed herself to have the thought, and she is surprised by the force of her conviction. He is still her husband. One event cannot wipe away twenty-five years. Yes, she will visit him in Littlehey. It may take her some time, she may feel furious, betrayed, ashamed. But she won't abandon him. Friends may let out the rope, but she will not.

'How did he die?' Edith is asking now. 'Taylor Dent. What did Dad—'

'Drowned,' Miriam says. 'In the river close to Deeping. I don't know what his injuries were. He'd been on drugs – ketamine – which may have been what caused his death when he hit the water. Paralysed, effectively. Anyway, it'll all come out in the trial.'

'So he might have been alive in the boot of the car?' Edith says, and Miriam can see the slow dawning on her face. 'I could have helped him, if I hadn't stayed hidden.'

'A lot of things would have been different if you hadn't stayed hidden,' Miriam says, and she can't keep the censure out of her voice. Relief that her daughter is alive is giving way to hot fury, the kind she remembers from when Edith was little – those times when she lost sight of her in a park or on a beach, and had to search wildly, shouts becoming hysterical and other mothers helping with instinctive urgency. And then when Edith or Rollo were discovered, nonchalantly playing inside a hedge or squatting in the sand, how she would tear a strip off them and make them cry, that they might experience a tiny millisecond of her fear. 'Don't you ever, *ever* do that again.' At the same time holding them very, very tight.

'How *could* you stay away?' she asks now. 'How could you? You must've seen the scale of the manhunt, what the police were doing. You must've known everyone thought you were dead. That we thought you were dead.'

Edith starts to cry. 'Don't you see? It had all gone too far. It had gone too far for me to come back . . .' She is gulping, and Miriam wonders if it is guilt that's catching in her throat. 'It was a thing I couldn't undo, and then Helena died. This whole series of events was set off by me and I didn't even . . . I didn't expect it. The bigger it became – all over the news, the number of police officers involved – the more impossible it was for me to come home.'

'You couldn't send me an email, a postcard, telling me you were all right?' Miriam asks.

Edith turns away. There is something in this question she cannot answer.

'Edith?' Miriam presses.

EDITH

I can feel the gaps in my story, how they must seem to her. I can hear how lame my explanation must sound. And yet, in the quiet of the French countryside, the days went by. The more you don't make contact, the more impossible contact becomes, as if silence can enlarge like a seep of blood. And in the solitude I found space. Freedom. Something heady and illicit. I didn't *want* to return. I can't say that to her. It is a selfishness too far. Her face, the colour of the ash in the grate, would look at me with too much sorrow and disappointment. Well, I've been disappointed too.

'He let me down,' I whisper. 'He wasn't the person I thought he was. He set such high standards for me and all the while—'

'People have inner lives, Edie; you're old enough to know that.'

'But why would he kill a boy?' I say, and in saying it, I've answered the question to myself.

She looks away. I can see she is ashamed.

'Mum?'

385

'They were . . .' she begins. 'They were having a relationship, it seems.'

'A relationship?'

'Yes,' she says.

'Is he . . . ?'

'Is he what?' she says, looking at me sharply. 'Gay? Straight? Are you? Is anyone just one thing?'

'How can you forgive him?'

'Who said anything about forgive?'

'You seem . . .' I begin, but I can't find the right word. Accepting?

'Perhaps I don't set my standards for people quite as high as yours,' she says.

'He has always been the one with impossible standards,' I say. 'The one who set the bar so high when all the while he . . .' I begin to cry: corrosive, satisfying, righteous tears. 'I wasn't even allowed to keep my baby, settle down with Jonti, lead an average life. Oh no, that wasn't good enough, when all the time he was . . .'

She looks up, shocked. 'You could have kept the baby, Edie. We never made you—'

'That's not how it felt,' I say, and I am dealing in half-truths. 'It was made clear to me that it would have been a failure. There were so many expectations.'

'I never knew you felt that way about the baby, darling. We didn't see it as making you get rid of it. We saw it as helping you make a sensible decision – for your life. And maybe we were wrong. I saw Jonti recently, when I was searching for you. And the thought occurred to me that the two of you could have made it work. He's a decent chap. But we honestly thought we were doing right by you, Edie. There's lots of time to have a baby; you don't have to do it at eighteen, when it's so hard.

386

That's not expectation – that's love. We wanted the best for you. I don't mean Cambridge; I mean I didn't want you depressed and alone at eighteen with a screaming infant on your hands.'

She is looking at me now, with the concern I have longed for. She says, 'Oh, I know Ian can be exacting and I can see you might think we wanted you to be perfect. God, maybe there was narcissism in it. I mean, which parent doesn't want to say: "My daughter's gone up to Cambridge"? But that's nothing next to loving you, Edith.'

'How was I supposed to know what I wanted when your expectation was so *huge*,' I say, in a wail. 'When all I ever wanted was to please you? Why is my life defined by pleasing you, when he . . . when he . . . he's done something so immoral!'

It has backfired.

She has stood up and I can see the rage popping at her temples. Her words come out in a low growl, only just suppressing the violence I can see she feels towards me. 'You are the child of a *man*. An ordinary man who has strengths and weaknesses, and who descended into a crisis. Yes, he's done something terrible, for which he will face a very harsh punishment.

'And you are *my* child, Edie, though you show me no love at all. *You* have to decide who you are. You have to decide, Edie. It's not enough to say we made you this, and we made you that, and expectation took away this and pressure demanded that. Stand up and be counted. And if your love ends the moment you find out your parents are people, then my God, there really is no hope for you.'

'But he's fallen so short,' I say quietly. A damp squib.

'So have you, Edith.'

We are silent. Mum has dropped onto the sofa. Her eyes are glazed. She stares into the fire and then says, 'Love is not love, which alters when it alteration finds.' She looks at me. 'He's your father and you should stand by us, as we stand by you.'

ONE YEAR LATER
WEDNESDAY

MANON

'Fly? Fly! C'mon. Homework.'

He groans from somewhere beyond the hall and she waits, looking at the dappled garden, the sun playing through the fingers of the lime trees. Honeyed patio stones radiate with the heat of the day.

'Fly! Come on, stop wasting time.'

He joins her at the kitchen table and hauls his school bag onto his knee with am-dram weariness. His white school shirt has a pen leak at the pocket, a blot of black chequering into the cotton. He smells of sweaty boy. She makes a mental note to buy him some shower gel.

'What treats do your teachers have in store for us this evening?' she asks.

'I have to, like, write a persuasive argument for something, like a party political fingy.'

'Broadcast. Party political broadcast. OK, any ideas?'

'Like why I should be allowed to watch TV after school like them other kids.'

'*Those* other kids, Fly. You're not going to be very persuasive

389

with grammar like that. Go on, then, write it as if you're persuading me.'

'No one can persuade you of nothin', DS Auntie.'

'DI Auntie, to you.'

He splays across the table like a broken umbrella, chewing the end of his pen. He whispers to himself when he starts to write. She gets up to stir the lamb stew, which is bubbling on the hob.

'If you finish that, you can go out for a bit,' she says, her back to him.

'Serious?' he says.

'Serious.'

It gives her pleasure to surprise him with a loosening of his restrictions, even while she knows that same pleasure will tighten to anxiety as she waits for him to come home. She can hardly refuse him these forays: along Mill Lane to the news-agent where he can buy pick-and-mix; to sit on the swings in Sumatra Road; up to Fortune Green where friends from his school congregate in the park and scale the wire fence into the play centre. He is about to turn twelve, is well over five foot, and now walks to school alone.

'No hoodie, though,' she says, thinking of the group of them, how they scare people on the bus. They are so tall and so burgeoning male.

He groans. 'Why?'

'One, because you'll boil in this heat, even if your trousers are right down below your bum, which makes you look completely ridiculous, by the way, but we've had that conver-sation; and two, because I don't want anyone mistaking you for something you're not. You are a lovely, gentle, well-mannered boy, Fly. Don't give anyone any reason to think otherwise.'

'Why should I be stopped from wearing an item of clothing just 'cos of the colour of my skin?'

'Maybe that should be the subject of your persuasive argument,' she says. 'Oh, and Fly? No smoking in the cemetery. And don't come the innocent with me – I know you've done it.'

'Whatevs,' he says in a whisper. His disdain is gossamer light, and she thinks she can detect beneath it his pleasure at the tight boundaries she lays.

'And I want you back by 6 p.m. sharp for supper. Ellie and Sol are coming.'

'OK,' he says. 'Can I feed Solly?'

'I'm sure Ellie would be delighted,' she says, smiling at him. 'What d'you reckon – rice or couscous with the stew?'

'What's couscous?' he says, his eyes down to his books again.

'The grainy one, yellow.'

'Yeah, that one.'

The room is full of pale May light and the smell of cooking meat, and she is struck by how far they've come in their journey to being a family of sorts.

She hadn't thought any of it through. Fly's mother's illness had been swift and brutal. Three months after Ian Hind's arrest and four months after Manon first met Maureen, the stomach cancer killed her, without pause for admission to a hospice. Manon travelled to London without a plan, telling herself whatever happened next would be temporary. She and Fly stayed with Ellie – necessity being the mother of reconciliation – in her little two-bed flat on Fordwych Road, which ran like a vein on the border between Kilburn and West Hampstead. Far from a pink paradise, Ellie had broken up with Solly's feckless father during pregnancy, and was tearfully battling sleep deprivation without respite.

It was cramped. The baby shared Ellie's bedroom, Manon was in the spare room, and Fly was on a put-you-up in the lounge, which he diligently tidied each morning before anyone was up. In this she saw all his worry about the precariousness of his situation.

Those two months living like that – using up all Manon's annual leave and numerous days owing from years of night shifts and weekends on duty – allowed Fly to complete his last term at primary school, where the teachers were invested in him. And it allowed Ellie the odd night off. Ellie and Manon had some understanding of what Fly needed most – the importance of keeping to existing routines after the death of one's mother.

'It's nice – having you around,' Ellie said. 'He brings out good things in you, Fly does.'

But the person who brought out the best in all of them was Solly. How that baby delighted them, Fly especially, who lay next to Solly on the carpet and tickled his toes, blew raspberries on his tummy, and covered his own face with his hands, removing them to say 'Boo!' and Solly's chuckle would ring out, its music like a belly-burst of joy. Squawking, guffawing, high notes like piano keys – it was impossible not to smile when Solly laughed, and he appeared to spend most of his day laughing.

When all her leave was used up, Manon's hand was forced. 'I'll ask Fly to stay with friends,' she told Ellie, 'just while I square things in Huntingdon. I don't expect you—'

'Don't be silly. He has to stay here,' Ellie told her. 'Solly loves him. And anyway, he mustn't be uprooted too much, not after what he's been through. I like the company, to be honest. How long will it take you? When will you be back?' And there was fear in Ellie's eyes that they might be separated again.

392

'Not long,' Manon said, telling herself the changes she was about to make were temporary – a stint in the Met while she sorted out a permanent arrangement for Fly, in a foster family or some such.

Edith Hind returned to the UK with her mother, attending Cambridgeshire Police HQ voluntarily. She wanted to explain, she said. She wore a white shirt buttoned to the top, its pointy collar ever-so prudish, navy cigarette trousers over nerdish brown brogues, and glasses with thick black frames, which Manon thought were probably an affectation. The whole ensemble worked to create the impression of a serious young woman, genuinely troubled by circumstances unforeseen. Despite the demure librarian outfit, she was breathtaking: glossy auburn hair curling beneath her pointed chin; skin like alabaster; slim and graceful. Manon couldn't stop staring, as if she were hungry for more of her, and she wondered if Edith's beauty meant she should face greater censure. Or perhaps less. Did Manon want someone so beautiful to get away with it or did she want to enviously punish her?

She and Harriet sat on the other side of the table to Edith, who was flanked by Miriam and a very expensive lawyer.

'I want to hear this,' said Davy, who stood with his back to the wall. Everyone else, including Gary Stanton, watched the interview in the video room.

'Miss Hind,' Harriet said, with unctuous politesse, 'there were traces of blood in the kitchen of your home in George Street – along a kitchen cabinet and some pooling on the floor, plus some drips of blood in the hallway of your home. Can you explain how they got there?'

'Yes, yes I can,' she said, pushing copper ropes of hair behind one ear. *Adorable.* 'When I got back to the house with Helena,

393

I found I was much drunker than I realised, swaying and stumbling, struggling to stay upright, to be honest.' *Innocent little laugh.* 'In the kitchen I poured myself a glass of wine – this was after Helena had gone – but in picking it up, I knocked it, hard, on the worktop and it literally smashed in my hand, cutting me across the palm. I was shocked by the amount of blood – it literally gushed from my palm. I stared at it for a moment, in that drunken way, as if it belonged to someone else, and in that time it splashed down the kitchen cupboard and onto the floor. I did a rather poor job of cleaning up the broken glass. I put the bloodied shards into the bin and got myself a new wine glass down, which I never used in the end. I stumbled upstairs holding my bleeding hand – which is why there were drips on the hallway floor – and managed to knock half the coats off their hooks as I staggered up to the bathroom for a bandage. I'm sorry,' she said, looking Harriet in the eye, 'if this was misconstrued as an injury following an act of violence. I had no idea it would be.'

'Why did you leave the door to your house open?' Harriet asks.

'What?'

'When Will Carter returned home, he says he found the front door ajar. Why is that?'

'I didn't. I closed it. I thought I did, anyway. Look, I was all over the place that night. I'd had too much to drink. And I was frightened about what I was about to do – I was heading into the unknown. I knew how dangerous the journey could be. I went back and forth, stumbling about. I thought I closed the door but maybe in my haste, in my panic, I didn't pull it firmly enough behind me.'

'So you have stated that you walked out of Huntingdon, out towards Papworth Everard, and on the A428 you waited in an

394

appointed lay-by until a truck pulled up beside you. Appointed by whom?' said Harriet, looking at her notes.

'Abdul-Ghani Khalil.'

'The back of the lorry was opened by a man you didn't recognise and you got in. Inside were several other stowaways of various nationalities. You were driven to what we can only guess was a port – you have stated that you could feel the sensation of the lorry boarding a ferry and driving into the hold. You were let out of the lorry in a lay-by just north of Calais in France.'

'Well, no, it was an aire,' she said, the r rolling in a pointedly French way.

'I'm sorry?' said Harriet.

'I was let out in an aire – a French service station. I was desperately stiff and needed the loo. This was where the transfer took place – to a car, driven again by a man I didn't know. He took me as far as Nantes. I paid him the cash as agreed – four thousand pounds.'

'Agreed by?'

'Abdul-Ghani Khalil,' she said.

'How did you meet Abdul-Ghani Khalil?'

'No comment.'

'Were you introduced to Abdul-Ghani Khalil by Tony Wright?'

'No comment.'

'Did you meet Abdul-Ghani Khalil when you were visiting Tony Wright in Whitemoor prison?'

'No comment.'

'Did you pay Tony Wright to effect an introduction to Abdul-Ghani Khalil?'

'No comment.'

'Did Tony Wright give you instructions for a pick-up which led to you being smuggled across the UK border illegally?'

'No comment.'

'Why did Tony Wright's number appear twice on your phone in the week before you disappeared, once on the day before?'

'We're friends.'

'What sort of friends?'

'Just friends. Have been ever since I visited him in Whitemoor. I was upset about what I'd seen at Deeping involving my father. I wanted to talk to him about it.'

Manon wasn't in Huntingdon for long. Once she returned to North London, there was a work hiatus while she applied for jobs, in which she ate into her savings and the income from letting out her Huntingdon flat (no point selling, given how this was a temporary situation). She took a six-month let on a flat, five doors down from Ellie's, and installed herself and Fly in it. She double-checked with the agent: 'So it's one month's notice on either side, right?'

During this time, she sat her inspector exams and Fly fell apart.

Perhaps it was the move to a separate flat (Manon felt they couldn't keep imposing on Ellie, who wanted to move Solly out of her bedroom). Or the transition to a vast and terrifying secondary school close by. Or just an accumulation of experiences too complex for him to manage. But all of a sudden they were alone together in the face of Fly's rage and sorrow.

'He's started wetting the bed, having night terrors,' she found herself confiding to Miriam, during the hours waiting at the Old Bailey for Ian Hind's various pre-trial hearings, either sitting on the benches outside Court One or nudging a tray along silver tracklines in the canteen. 'I'm so knackered – up five or six times a night, changing sheets. Trying to calm him down.'

'Like having a newborn,' Miriam said.

It was ironic to be leaning on Miriam, who had aged but was also serene with Edith back at home. It hadn't taken that much to persuade Edith to return with her to London, Miriam said. She had a conscience, under all that self-serving narcissism.

'And I say that with great affection,' Miriam said with a smile. 'Told her it was better to go back voluntarily than be dragged back by Interpol. Told her you had made the connection with Abdul-Ghani Khalil and had mobilised French police. It was only a matter of time. She started snivelling, of course – that child is a master of self-pity – but I reassured her we'd hire good lawyers and a PR man to handle the newspapers.'

Everyone at Cambridgeshire wanted to charge the girl with wasting police time, perverting the course of justice, and anything else they could throw at her for sparking a five-week investigation at a cost of around £300k of taxpayers' money. But the Hinds' legal team, numerous and dark-suited, formulated a robust defence stating it could not be proven that she 'intended' the police to infer she had come to harm. The blood, the fallen coats, the door left ajar, were all the accidental detritus of a night of panic and duress. She had merely fled the source of her distress – the crime committed by her father, whom she neither wished to shelter nor betray. The fact that Cambridgeshire Police had upscaled it to a high-risk misper could hardly be laid at young Miss Hind's door. Psychiatric reports stated she had suffered 'mental anguish' in rural France.

'Anguish my arse,' Harriet said.

In the opposite corner were the prosecution arguments: why did she stay away, when she saw, by reading UK press reports online, the scale of the manhunt? How could she justify not

397

telling anyone she was alive and well, even if she didn't wish to return?

A judge looked at the arguments and deemed there was a case to answer, the outcome yet to be determined in court.

At the Old Bailey, as legal wheels turned ever so slowly in proceedings against Ian Hind, Manon sought Miriam's wisdom about Fly, which probably broke some protocol to do with 'sides' but neither woman cared.

'All I know is I can't take much more,' Manon said.

'He's not doing it to spite you,' said Miriam.

'No, I know, but I can't understand what's going on inside him.'

'No, I never knew what was going on in my children either,' said Miriam, and Manon was surprised to be taken as a fellow mother. 'It sounds to me like he needs to know that you'll stick with him, however bad it gets, just like a mother does with a newborn baby.'

She had no idea if Miriam was right but she did stick with him, though not out of nobleness. Out of exhaustion and inertia. This was not a situation she could easily unpick.

She swapped notes with Davy, too, who had seen it all before at the drop-in centre.

'Firm boundaries,' Davy told her. 'It's still love, it just doesn't waver. These kids can't take any flip-flopping. Scares the life out of them.'

He is so wise, now DS Davy Walker under Stanton's kindly wing, and resolutely single, having once more extricated himself from Chloe's clutches following the comfort shag. His life is MIT, bike rides, and his volunteering at the youth centre. 'More than enough,' he told Manon when she'd asked if he was seeing anyone.

Poor Stanton. A standard review of the Hind investigation

by Bedfordshire Police found that: *Detective Chief Superintendent Gary Stanton overreacted in upscaling the disappearance of Edith Hind to a high-risk misper, later a suspected homicide, as there was insufficient prima facie evidence that Miss Hind had come to harm.*

'He can't win,' Davy told Manon, as if he were defending his own father. 'First Lacey Pilkington, where he's told he should have upscaled it sooner, and now this. I don't know how he keeps going.'

'Thinking about his pension, that's how,' Manon said.

She hadn't thought it through, the situation with Fly, though she spent quite a bit of time wondering if she could get out of it. How she might tiptoe away.

Then Fly got ill.

Winter and a fever took such strong hold of him it was medieval, and no amount of paracetamol or Nurofen seemed to bring his temperature down. His heart raced like a mechanism about to spring out of its holdings. Manon couldn't get through to the GP practice – just endless ringing or the engaged signal – so in desperation she rang Miriam, who drove round, parking Ian's incongruous Jaguar next to the skips of Fordwych Road. She checked his vital signs.

'Can eleven-year-olds get meningitis?' Manon asked.

'You've been on the Internet,' Miriam scolded. 'Never look on the Internet for medical advice. You'll diagnose yourself with cancer. Look, you were right to call me – it is a very high temperature and we do need to keep an eye on him.'

They sat together briefly in Manon's lounge on a sofa draped with a cheap cream throw and lit by a tiny lamp on a shelf. Miriam seemed more relaxed than Manon had seen her, though she wouldn't take her coat off.

'How's Ian coping with Belmarsh?' Manon asked.

'Do you know, he's all right,' she said, sounding amused and surprised at the same time. 'He's reading a lot. Teaching an anatomy course to other inmates – ironic, really, as some of them have actually decapitated people. I keep worrying his imperious manner will get him on the wrong side of people – you know, he'll ask for quince jelly with his cheese and someone will punch his lights out. But it hasn't happened yet.'

'The children visit him?'

'Yes,' she said. 'Both of them. We're all doing our time,' she said. Then, rising: 'Look, I'll pop round in the morning on my way to work. Then I can admit Fly if I'm worried.'

Two whole weeks the illness raged through him, though Miriam was satisfied it was only flu; like a tidal wave slapping the pier wall with all its force, his rigid body tensed against it. He shook when he stood to pee. His bedroom smelled over-ripe, as Manon threw open the windows and changed the sheets – a sweetness that was fetid. Eventually he could begin to read and watch TV, but he was hollow-eyed and weak. And then a terrible depression took hold and he cried for his mother and for Taylor. And he blamed Manon, resented her, because she was the nearest target for his distress. His unhappiness was so deep and wide that more than once she wondered if it would ever lift.

The IPCC report into the death of Helena Reed, following contact with Cambridgeshire Police, resulted in a reg 14 misconduct notice for DC Monique Moynihan, who had taken the call from Helena on the night of 7 January 2011. In her witness statement, DC Moynihan stated that staffing levels in MIT that night were herself and two other detective constables. However, one of these detective constables had a period of twenty days' leave owing and this officer had been advised by the division if he did not take the time off it would be lost. DC Moynihan stated that she raised concerns about the staffing levels with DI Kirk Tate but did not file a report on the matter. DI Tate did not recall DC Moynihan raising the issue. DC Moynihan had a number of investigations in progress on the night of Sunday 7 January, which she considered urgent. She said Miss Reed had sounded tentative and shy, but not in great distress when she had rung the department. She noted that Miss Reed had not called 999. Immediately following the call, DC Moynihan and the other detective on duty that night, DC Lee Rayner, were called out to a reported burglary.

The IPCC additionally looked into the duty of care towards Helena Reed by MIT team four investigating the disappearance of Edith Hind. The IPCC noted that the Hind investigation was extremely high profile and required a great deal of police resource. It found that risk assessments of Helena Reed prior to the *Crimewatch* appeal on Wednesday 4 January 2011, undertaken by DC Kim Delaney, and additionally a risk assessment filed by DS Manon Bradshaw, were adequate and adhered to professional standards protocol. However, interviews with Miss Reed's psychoanalyst, Dr Young, revealed that her fragile state was in excess of officers' assessment of her mental health.

The IPCC issued a learning strategy document with a recommendation that all members of MIT team four, which investigated the Hind misper, undertake a duty of care refresher course and complete the two-hour training package on mental health.

Manon hears the vibration of her mobile phone on the kitchen table and walks over to Fly's books, patting among the papers and crumbs until she finds it. A text from DCI Havers of Kilburn CID – her new boss.

Want you on early shift tomorrow, DI Bradshaw.

Her current arse ache, the new job. No Harriet to chat to (now DCI at Cambridgeshire, the rest of the band still together – that rankles) and a twat like Havers lording it over her. And Fly increasingly beset by the Met's stop and search obsession. She's told him to keep the details, to log every single incident, in a notebook in his ever-drooping jeans back pocket, and these she follows up.

'Didn't know he was eleven,' said one Met officer.

'Try asking him,' she replied.

'Sorry, Mrs . . . ?'

'It's DI Bradshaw.'

They didn't like ruffling their own, and she hoped to make it clear Fly was not to be touched, at least to all the officers at Kilburn. A white copper mothering a black boy – didn't that set the cat among the pigeons.

She's worried about some of the lads he's hanging out with at school. Another mental note: to make an appointment with the headmaster. Shower gel, see the headmaster, pick up fruit, bread, and bin bags. When did her lists get so *long*? She casts about for a pad and pen. Buy pad and pen for lists.

When the six-month let expired, she signed for another six, checking again: 'It's one month notice on either side, right?'

Life isn't perfect, she thinks, as the lot of them clatter into her kitchen. It has taken her a while to get on friendly terms with this notion. She had thought perhaps it was perfect for others, just not for her. Or that she could revise and revise and revise life, as if sitting a perpetual Cambridge exam, and it would become perfect. Increasingly, she can find no evidence of perfection in any life. There's always something: illness,

402

divorce, bereavement, or corners of the personality that are devastating to live with. Everyone making the best of it, doing their time, together by accident – like Manon and Fly, because he had no one else and she couldn't back out of it.

'Sit down, everyone,' she says. 'Dinner's ready. Ellie, would you like some wine?'

'Lovely,' says Ellie, and she hands the solid dollop that is Solly to Fly, saying, 'Here you go, do your worst.'

Fly holds Solly about his hip, smiling his hello with a kiss into the little boy's neck while Solly clutches Fly's cheeks with his fat hands and lets out a delighted screech.

Manon and Fly have bought an Ikea highchair for £10 to have in their flat, and a cot for when Solly stays overnight. Fly wedges Solly into his highchair and the baby bangs on the plastic table in excited anticipation of mashed stew. Everyone is seated except Manon, who is being 'mother' with a ladle hovering above the plates.

'Actually,' she says, 'there's something I want to ask Fly, and I wanted all of you to be here.'

Even Solly, who has been waving his arms at the approach of the first of Fly's spoonfuls, stops and looks up with a concerned look on his face, making all of them laugh.

'I want to adopt you,' she says to Fly.

'You what?'

'Ada-boooo!' sings Solly.

'I want to adopt you. I want us to be . . . tied. Make it legal.'

He looks at her for a moment. Then turns back to Solly with a new spoonful. 'So you can nag me forever.'

'So I can nag you forever, that's right.'

She sits down and pushes a piece of lamb about the plate, where it gathers beads of couscous like a wet stone in sand.

'Poon!' says Solly, wrestling Fly for the spoon.

403

'That's right,' Fly says to him. 'Poon.' He moons his face into Solly's, nose to nose, and the boy screeches and clutches at Fly's cheeks again with meaty hands.

'Because I love you,' Manon says.

'Poon!' insists Solly.

'All right, chatty man,' Fly says to him. 'Here comes another one.' He makes the spoon fly and Solly opens his mouth on cue. Then Fly takes a forkful from his own plate. 'This stew is all right,' he says. 'Even though there is veg in there. Is this carrot?'

'No, no,' says Ellie. 'You're imagining it.'

'Can I go round Zach's to play on his PlayStation after?' asks Fly.

'Nope,' says Manon.

Fly has turned to take another forkful of food. He and Manon chew on full mouthfuls, looking at each other.

'Why do you ask when you know what the answer will be?' Manon asks.

He shrugs. 'For a laugh. I figure one day you'll slip up.'

'In your dreams. What do you reckon then, about what I just said? About becoming my son?'

'Yeah. OK.'

ACKNOWLEDGEMENTS

I am indebted to Detective Sergeant Graham McMillan of Cambridgeshire's Major Crime Unit for his help with this book; also to Detective Sergeant Susie Hine of Cambridge CID for advice on the first draft. Inaccuracies are mine, not theirs.

Thank you Superintendent Jon Hutchinson for facilitating my visits to Cambridgeshire's MCU.

For guidance on pathology, thank you Clare Craig, consultant pathologist at Imperial College NHS Trust. For postmortem and coroners detail, thanks to Michael Osborn, consultant histopathologist at Imperial.

For Maureen Dent's Irish vernacular, thanks to Marissa McConville.

For Tony Wright's Scots vernacular, thanks to Eileen MacCallum.

For advice on criminal law, thank you Daniel Burbidge.

The report published by the Cambridge Institute of Criminology in November 2011 into staff–prisoner relations in Whitemoor, on which Edith fictionally assisted as a researcher, is real. It is readily available online and is a riveting and humane read. Find it here: https://www.gov.uk/government/uploads/system/

uploads/attachment_data/file/217381/staff-prisoner-relations-whitemoor.pdf

Thanks Sandra Laville, of the *Guardian*, for advice on hacking and Soham.

Thanks to Sian Rickett, Susannah Waters, Alexandra Shelley, Daniel Burbidge, John Steiner, Deborah Steiner and Zoe Ross for careful reading and good advice. And to Katie Espiner and Andrea Walker for brilliant editing. Thank you Eleanor Jackson, for going out to bat for me Stateside. To Sarah Ballard, thank you for everything, as always. Thank you Tom Happold for being my first and last reader and for all your support. And George and Ben Happold for bundling in from school and filling the house with joyful noise after the silence of the attic.